THRILLER

STORIES TO KEEP YOU UP ALL NIGHT

"Imaginative and impressive…ingenious, supremely readable, fun and often electrifying [these stories] all bear testimony to the art of the thriller/crime story at its powerful best."
Maxim Jakubowski, *Guardian*

"Features some splendid heart-bumpers."
Daily Mail

"Whether you are a crime aficionado or simply want to introduce a novice to the genre…these tantalising tales offer a nifty twist."
Time Out

"…if you like your capers short and sweet, you'll love this collection of thrilling tales."
OK!

THRILLER: STORIES TO KEEP YOU UP ALL NIGHT
edited by James Patterson

**Shortlisted for the Crime Writers' Association
Short Story Dagger Award**

KILLER YEAR: STORIES TO DIE FOR
edited by Lee Child

**Winner of the Crime Writers' Association
Short Story Dagger Award**

EDITED BY
CLIVE CUSSLER

Stories You Just Can't Put Down

MIRA

MIRA is a registered trademark of Harlequin Enterprises Limited, used under licence.

First published in Great Britain 2010.
MIRA Books, Eton House, 18-24 Paradise Road,
Richmond, Surrey, TW9 1SR

ISBN 978 0 7783 0374 9

60-0610

MIRA's policy is to use papers that are natural, renewable and recyclable products and made from wood grown in sustainable forests. The logging and manufacturing processes conform to the legal environmental regulations of the country of origin.

Printed in Great Britain
by Clays Ltd, St Ives plc

COPYRIGHT

For Gayle Lynds and David Morrell
Co-founders
International Thriller Writers, Inc.

CONTENTS

INTRODUCTION

What is a thriller?

It's an interesting question when you consider so many of today's bestsellers fall into that category. Look at the top sellers any given month and you might find novels of suspense, adventure tales, paranormal investigations, or even police procedurals—works by writers who couldn't be more different from each other, and yet their books share a common goal, if not a specific language.

All these books push their readers just a little closer to the edge of their seats. They cost their readers sleep, get carried to the grocery store to be read while standing in line and are held tightly until the last page.

And even though the reader can't wait to see how it's going to end, a book like this gets closed reluctantly, with a feeling of anticipation and longing for the next book that can quicken the pulse and fire the imagination.

As a reader, that's a feeling I know well. I grew up in the heyday of the pulps, devouring stories about globe-spanning adventures, one man facing impossible odds, racing against time to save the world. These were magazines and books that kept you up all night, sometimes reading under your covers with a flashlight.

Adventures that were, simply, *thrilling*.

That's really what I set out to do when I decided to try my hand at writing fiction over thirty years ago. I wanted to write a thrilling story with a modern setting and contemporary characters in the tradition of the great adventure stories that kept me turning the pages when I was a kid. I never imagined that one day my books would be translated into more than forty languages and read by millions of people around the world.

And now, an entire generation later, it seems that tradition lives on, because many of the most successful and finest authors today are writing thrillers. And this book you're holding now brings many of those writers together in a single volume.

This book is called *Thriller 2* because, as you probably suspect or already know, there was another anthology entitled *Thriller* that was edited by my friend James Patterson. The two books share a common source of inspiration, so let me take a moment to explain how this collection came together.

The first *Thriller* was the brainchild of an organization called ITW, which is short for International Thriller

Writers. Barely five years old, ITW's roster reads like a *Who's Who* of thriller writing with 900 members worldwide and over 2,000,000,000 books in print. Headed by current co-presidents Steve Berry and James Rollins, its board of directors has included such notables as Lee Child, Tess Gerritsen, M. J. Rose, Carla Neggers, Douglas Preston, Gayle Lynds, David Morrell and David Hewson. This organization, of which I am a proud member, is dedicated to supporting the readers and writers of thrillers everywhere.

This anthology and its predecessor are collections of short stories written exclusively by ITW members from around the world, not only bestselling authors but also gifted writers you might not have discovered until you read this book.

But the two anthologies also differ slightly. The first *Thriller* included stories featuring well-known or established characters from our writers' novels and series, sometimes seen in a new light but very recognizable to their fans.

Thriller 2, by contrast, consists almost entirely of original stories featuring colorful characters you've never seen before. For the rabid fan, it's a unique chance to discover another side of your favorite author. For someone new to the world of thrillers, this collection is a wonderful opportunity to discover someone who just might become your new favorite writer.

Which brings us back to our question, *what is a thriller?* Or more precisely, what makes a story thrilling?

This collection attempts to answer that timeless question, if not directly than by showcasing over twenty writers who delivered an extraordinary range of thrilling stories. Stories that shock you. Stories that cause your heart to skip a beat. Stories that might make you laugh and flinch at the same time. Stories that you finish and then read again in disbelief, looking for the clues you must have missed the first time around.

There are many ingredients that go into an unforgettable thriller. These stories use them all, but each mixes them together differently, every tale delivering a unique blend of thrills that sets it apart. As a reader I can truly say this is one of the most consistently entertaining and eclectic collections I've ever read.

And as a writer, I'm incredibly proud to have my name on this remarkable book that you're about to read. I hope you find it as thrilling as I do.

Clive Cussler 2009

JEFFERY DEAVER

The stakes are high and time is short in "The Weapon"—
the perfect story to begin the collection. Originally written
for the stage, "The Weapon" demonstrates why Jeff is considered a master of both the modern thriller and the short
story. When it comes time to write a critical scene, Jeff turns
down the lights, shuts his eyes and starts typing. The room
is either heavily shaded or windowless. For some characters in "The Weapon," such a dark room where devious
scenarios are born would still be preferable to the bleak
places they find themselves in. Shaped by today's headlines,
these characters are trapped in an intrigue as topical as it is
thrilling.

Keep your eyes open for this one. Sit in a well-lit room,
with a window. Maybe even go outside and read where
people can see you, and you know it's safe, because Jeff's
stories are anything but.

THE WEAPON

Monday

"A new weapon."

The slim man in a conservative suit eased forward and lowered his voice. "Something terrible. And our sources are certain it will be used this coming Saturday morning. They're certain of that."

"Four days," said retired Colonel James J. Peterson, his voice grave. It was now 5:00 p.m. on Monday.

The two men sat in Peterson's nondescript office, in a nondescript building in the suburban town of Reston, Virginia, about twenty-five miles from Washington, D.C. There's a misconception that national security operations are conducted in high-tech bunkers filled with sweeping steel and structural concrete, video screens ten feet high and attractive boys and babes dressed by Armani.

This place, on the other hand, looked like an insurance agency.

The skinny man, who worked for the government, added, "We don't know if we're talking conventional, nuke or something altogether new. Probably mass destruction, we've heard. It can do quote 'significant' damage.'"

"Who's behind this weapon? Al-Qaeda? The Koreans? Iranians?"

"One of our enemies. That's all we know at this point... So, we need you to find out about it. Money is no object, of course."

"Any leads?"

"Yes, a good one—an Algerian who knows who formulated the weapon. He met with them last week in Tunis. He's a professor and journalist."

"Terrorist?"

"He doesn't seem to be. His writings have been moderate in nature. He's not openly militant. But our local sources are convinced he's had contact with the people who created the weapon and plan to use it."

"You have a picture?"

A photograph appeared as if by magic from the slim man's briefcase and slid across the desk like a lizard.

Colonel Peterson leaned forward.

Tuesday

Chabbi music drifted from a nearby café, lost intermittently in the sounds of trucks and scooters charging frantically along this commercial street of Algiers.

The driver of the white van, a swarthy local, stifled a sour face when the music changed to American rock. Not that he actually preferred the old-fashioned, melodramatic chabbi tunes or thought they were more politically or religiously correct than Western music. He just didn't like Britney Spears.

Then the big man stiffened and tapped the shoulder of the man next to him, an American. Their attention swung immediately out the front window to a curly-haired man in his thirties, wearing a light-colored suit, walking out of the main entrance of the Al-Jazier School for Cultural Thought.

The man in the passenger seat nodded. The driver called "Ready" in English and then repeated the command in Berber-accented Arabic. The two men in the back responded affirmatively.

The van, a battered Ford that sported Arabic letters boasting of the city's best plumbing services, eased forward, trailing the man in the light suit. The driver had no trouble moving slowly without being conspicuous. Such was the nature of traffic here in the old portion of this city, near the harbor.

As they approached a chaotic intersection, the passenger spoke into a cell phone. "Now."

The driver pulled nearly even with the man they followed, just as a second van, dark blue, in the oncoming lane, suddenly leapt the curb and slammed directly into the glass window of an empty storefront, sending a shower of glass onto the sidewalk as bystanders gaped and came running.

By the time the crowds on rue Ahmed Bourzina helped

the driver of the blue van extricate his vehicle from the shattered storefront, the white van was nowhere to be seen.

Neither was the man in the light suit.

Wednesday

Colonel James Peterson was tired after the overnight flight from Dulles to Rome but he was operating on pure energy.

As his driver sped from DaVinci airport to his company's facility south of the city, he read the extensive dossier on the man whose abduction he had just engineered. Jacques Bennabi, the journalist and part-time professor, had indeed been in direct communication with the Tunisian group that had developed the weapon, though Washington still wasn't sure who the group was exactly.

Peterson looked impatiently at his watch. He regretted the day-long trip required to transport Bennabi from Algiers to Gaeta, south of Rome, where he'd been transferred to an ambulance for the drive here. But planes were too closely regulated nowadays. Peterson had told his people they *had* to keep a low profile. His operation here, south of Rome, was apparently a facility that specialized in rehabilitation services for people injured in industrial accidents. The Italian government had no clue that it was a sham, owned ultimately by Peterson's main company in Virginia: Intelligence Analysis Systems.

IAS was like hundreds of small businesses throughout the Washington area that provided everything from copier toner to consulting to computer software to the massive U.S. government.

IAS, though, didn't sell office supplies.

Its only product was information and it managed to provide some of the best in the world. IAS obtained this information not through high-tech surveillance but, Peterson liked to say, the old-fashioned way:

One suspect, one interrogator, one locked room.

It did this very efficiently.

And completely illegally.

IAS ran black sites.

Black site operations are very simple. An individual with knowledge the government wishes to learn is kidnapped and taken to a secret and secure facility outside the jurisdiction of the U.S. The kidnapping is known as extraordinary rendition. Once at a black site the subject is interrogated until the desired information is learned. And then he's returned home—in most cases, that is.

IAS was a private company, with no official government affiliation, though the government was, of course, its biggest client. They operated three sites—one in Bogotá, Colombia, one in Thailand and the one that Peterson's car was now approaching: the largest of the IAS sites, a nondescript beige facility whose front door stated *Funzione Medica di Riabilitazione.*

The gate closed behind him and he hurried inside, to minimize the chance a passerby might see him. Peterson rarely came to the black sites himself. Because he met regularly with government officials it would be disastrous if anyone connected him to an illegal operation like this. Still, the impending threat of the weapon dictated that he personally supervise the interrogation of Jacques Bennabi.

Despite his fatigue, he got right to work and met with the man waiting in the facility's windowless main office upstairs. He was one of several interrogators that IAS used regularly, one of the best in the world, in fact. A slightly built man, with a confident smile on his face.

"Andrew." Peterson nodded in greeting, using the pseudonym the man was known by—no real names were ever used in black sites. Andrew was a U.S. soldier on temporary leave from Afghanistan.

Peterson explained that Bennabi had been carefully searched and scanned. They'd found no GPS chips, listening devices or explosives in his body. The colonel added that sources in North Africa were still trying to find whom Bennabi had met with in Tunis but were having no luck.

"Doesn't matter," Andrew said with a sour smile. "I'll get you everything you need to know soon enough."

Jacques Bennabi looked up at Andrew.

The soldier returned the gaze with no emotion, assessing the subject, noting his level of fear. A fair amount, it seemed. This pleased him. Not because Andrew was a sadist—he wasn't—but because fear is a gauge to a subject's resistance.

He assessed that Bennabi would tell him all he wanted to know about the weapon within four hours.

The room in which they sat was a dim, concrete cube, twenty feet on each side. Bennabi sat in a metal chair with his hands behind him, bound with restraints. His feet were bare, increasing his sense of vulnerability, and his jacket and personal effects were gone—they gave subjects a sense of comfort and orientation. Andrew now pulled a chair close to the subject and sat.

Andrew was not a physically imposing man, but he didn't need to be. The smallest person in the world need not even raise his voice if he has power. And Andrew had all the power in the world over his subject at the moment.

"Now," he said in English, which he knew Bennabi spoke fluently, "as you know, Jacques, you're many miles from your home. None of your family or colleagues know you're here. The authorities in Algeria have learned of your disappearance by now—we're monitoring that—but do you know how much they care?"

No answer. The dark eyes gazed back, emotionless.

"They don't. They don't care at all. We've been following the reports. Another university professor gone missing. So what? You were robbed and shot. Or the Jihad Brothership finally got around to settling the score for something you said in class last year. Or maybe one of your articles upset some Danish journalists…and they kidnapped and killed you." Andrew smiled at his own cleverness. Bennabi gave no reaction. "So. No one is coming to help you. You understand? No midnight raids. No cowboys riding to the rescue."

Silence.

Andrew continued, unfazed, "Now, I want to know about this weapon you were discussing with your Tunisian friends." He was looking carefully at the eyes of the man. Did they flicker with recognition? The interrogator believed they did. It was like a shout of acknowledgment. Good.

"We need to know who developed it, what it is and who it's going to be used against. If you tell me, you'll be back home in twenty-four hours." He let this sink in. "If you don't…things won't go well."

The subject continued to sit passively. And silent.

That was fine with Andrew; he hardly expected an immediate confession. He wouldn't want one, in fact. You couldn't trust subjects who caved in too quickly.

Finally he said, "Jacques, I know the names of all your colleagues at the university and the newspaper where you work."

This was Andrew's talent—he had studied the art of interrogation for years and knew that people could much more easily resist threats to themselves than to their friends and family. Andrew had spent the past two days learning every fact he could about people close to Bennabi. He'd come up with lists of each person's weaknesses and fears. It had been a huge amount of work.

Over the next few hours Andrew never once threatened Bennabi himself; but he was ruthless in threatening his colleagues. Ruining careers, exposing possible affairs, questioning an adoption of a child… Even suggesting that some of his friends could be subject to physical harm.

A dozen specific threats, two dozen, offering specific details: names, addresses, offices, cars they drove, restaurants they enjoyed.

But Jacques Bennabi said not a word.

"You know how easy it was to kidnap you," Andrew muttered. "We plucked you off the street like picking a chicken from a street vendor's cage. You think your friends are any safer? The men who got you are back in Algiers, you know. They're ready to do what I say."

The subject only stared back at him.

Andrew grew angry for a moment. He cleared his raw throat and left the room, had a drink of water, struggled to calm down.

For three more hours he continued the interrogation. Bennabi paid attention to everything Andrew said, it seemed, but he said nothing.

Goddamn, he's good, Andrew thought, struggling not to reveal his own frustration. He glanced at his watch. It had been nearly nine hours. And he hadn't uncovered a single fact about the weapon.

Well, it was time to get serious now.

He scooted the chair even closer.

"Jacques, you're not being helpful. And now, thanks to your lack of cooperation, you've put all your friends at risk. How selfish can you be?" he snapped.

Silence.

Andrew leaned close. "You understand that I've been restrained, don't you? I had hoped you'd be more cooperative. But apparently you're not taking me seriously. I think I have to prove how grave this matter is."

He reached into his pocket. He pulled out a printout of a computer photograph that had been taken yesterday.

It showed Bennabi's wife and children in the front yard of their home outside of Algiers.

Thursday

Colonel Peterson was in his hotel room in the center of Rome. He was awakened at 4:00 a.m. by his secure cell phone.

"Yes?"

"Colonel." The caller was Andrew. His voice was ragged.

"So, what'd he tell you?"

"Nothing."

The colonel muttered, "You just tell me what he said and *I'll* figure out if it's important. That's *my* job." He clicked the light on and fished for a pen.

"No, sir, I mean, didn't say a single word."

"Not a…word?"

"Over sixteen hours. Completely silent. The entire time. Not one goddamn word. Never happened in all my years in this business."

"Was he getting close to breaking, at least?"

"I… No, I don't think so. I even threatened his family. His children. No reaction. I'd need another week. And I'll have to make good on some of the threats."

But Peterson knew they were already on shaky ground by kidnapping somebody who was not a known terrorist. He wouldn't dare kidnap or endanger the professor's colleagues, let alone his family.

"No," the colonel said slowly. "That's all for now. You can get back to your unit. We'll go to phase two."

★ ★ ★

The woman was dressed conservatively, a long-sleeved blouse and tan slacks. Her dark blond hair was pulled back and she wore no jewelry.

Since Bennabi wasn't culturally or religiously conservative, worked with women at the university and had actually written in favor of women's rights, Peterson decided to use Claire for the second interrogator. Bennabi would view her as an enemy, yes, but not as an inferior. And, since it was known that Bennabi had dated and was married, with several children, he was a clearly a man with an appreciation of attractive women.

And Peterson knew that Claire was certainly that.

She was also an army captain, in charge of a prisoner-of-war operation in the Middle East, though at the moment she, too, was on a brief leave of absence to permit her to practice her own skills as an interrogator—skills very different from Andrew's but just as effective in the right circumstances.

Peterson now finished briefing her. "Good luck," he added.

And couldn't help reminding her that it was now Thursday and the weapon would be deployed the day after tomorrow.

In perfect Arabic, Claire said, "I must apologize, Mr. Bennabi, Jacques… May I use your first name?" She was rushing into the cell, a horrified look on her face.

When Bennabi didn't reply, she switched to English. "Your

first name? You don't mind, do you? I'm Claire. And let me offer you my deepest apologies for this terrible mistake."

She walked behind him and took the hand restraints off. There was little risk. She was an expert at aikido and tae kwan do martial arts and could easily have defended herself against the weak, exhausted subject.

But the slim man, eyes dark from lack of sleep, face drawn, simply rubbed his wrists and offered no threatening gestures.

Claire pressed the button on the intercom. "Bring the tray in, please."

A guard wheeled it inside: water, a pot of coffee and a plate of pastries and candy, which she knew from his file Bennabi was partial to. She sampled everything first, to show nothing was spiked with poison or truth serum. He drank some water but when she asked, "Coffee, something to eat?" he gave no response.

Claire sat down, her face distraught. "I'm am so terribly sorry about this. I can't begin to describe how horrified we are… Let me explain. Someone—we don't know who—told us that you'd met with some people who are enemies of our country." She lifted her hands. "We didn't know who you were. All we heard was that you were sympathetic to these enemies and that they had some plans to cause huge destruction. Something terrible was going to happen. Imagine what we felt when we heard you were a famous professor…and an advocate of human rights!

"No, someone gave us misinformation about you. Maybe accidental." She added coyly, "Maybe they had a grudge against you. We don't know. All I can say is we reacted too quickly. Now, first, let me assure you that whatever threats Andrew made, nothing has or will happen to your colleagues or family…. That was barbaric what he suggested. He's been disciplined and relieved of duty."

No response whatsoever.

Silence filled the room and she could hear only her heartbeat, as she tried to remain calm, thinking of the weapon and the hours counting down until it was used.

"Obviously this is a very awkward situation. Certain officials are extremely embarrassed about what's happened and are willing to offer, what we could call, reparation for your inconvenience."

He continued to remain silent but she could tell he was listening to every word.

She scooted the chair closer and sat, leaning forward. "Mr. Bennabi…Jacques, I have been authorized to transfer one hundred thousand euros into an account of your choice—that's tax free money—in exchange for your agreement not to sue us for this terrible error."

Claire knew that he made the equivalent of fifteen thousand euros as a professor and another twenty as a journalist.

"I can order all of this done immediately. Your lawyer can monitor the transaction. All you have to do is sign a release agreeing not to sue."

Silence.

Then she continued with a smile, "And one more small thing…I myself have no doubt that you have been wrongly targeted but…the people who have to authorize the payments, they want just a little more information about the people you met with. The ones in Tunis. They just wish to be reassured that the meeting was innocent. *I* know it was. If I had my way I'd write you a check now. But they control the money." A smile. "Isn't that the way the world works?"

Bennabi said nothing. He stopped rubbing his wrists and sat back.

"They don't need to know anything sensitive. Just a few names, that's all. Just to keep the money men happy."

Is he agreeing? she wondered. Is he disagreeing? Bennabi was different from anybody she'd ever interrogated. Usually by now subjects were already planning how to spend the money and telling her whatever she wanted to know.

When he said nothing she realized: he's negotiating. Of course.

A nod. "You're a smart man…. And I don't blame you one bit for holding out. Just give us a bit of information to verify your story and I can probably go up to a hundred fifty thousand euros."

Still no response.

"I'll tell you what. Why don't you name a figure. Let's put this all behind us." Claire smiled coyly again. "We're on your side, Jacques. We really are."

THRILLER 2

Friday

At 9:00 a.m. Colonel Jim Peterson was in the office of the rehabilitation center, sitting across from a large, dark-complexioned man, who'd just arrived from Darfur.

Akhem asked, "What happened with Claire?"

Peterson shook his head. "Bennabi didn't go for the money. She sweetened the pot to a quarter million euros." The colonel sighed. "Wouldn't take it. In fact, he didn't even say no. He didn't say a word. Just like with Andrew."

Akhem took this information with interest but otherwise unemotionally—as if he were a surgeon called in to handle an emergency operation that was routine for him but that no one else could perform. "Has he slept?"

"Not since yesterday."

"Good."

There was nothing like sleep deprivation to soften people up.

Akhem was of Middle Eastern descent, though he'd been born in America and was a U.S. citizen. Like Peterson he'd retired from the military. He was now a professional security consultant—a euphemism for mercenary soldier. He was here with two associates, both from Africa. One white, one black.

Peterson had used Akhem on a half-dozen occasions, as had other governments. He was responsible for interrogating a Chechen separatist to learn where his colleagues had stashed a busload of Moscow schoolchildren last year.

It took him two hours to learn the exact location of the

bus, the number of soldiers guarding them, their weapons and passcodes.

No one knew exactly how he'd done it. No one wanted to.

Peterson wasn't pleased he'd had to turn to Akhem's approach to interrogation, known as extreme extraction. Indeed, he realized that the Bennabi situation raised the textbook moral question on using torture: you know a terrible event is about to occur and you have in custody a prisoner who knows how to prevent it. Do you torture or not?

There were those who said, no, you don't. That it is better to be morally superior and to suffer the consequences of letting the event occur. By stooping to the enemy's techniques, these people say, we automatically lose the war, even if we militarily prevail.

Other said that it was our enemies who'd changed the rules; if they tortured and killed innocents in the name of their causes we had to fight them on their own terms.

Peterson had now made the second choice. He prayed it was the right one.

Akhem was looking at the video of Bennabi in the cell, slumped in a chair, his head cocked to the side. He wrinkled his nose and said, "Three hours at the most."

He rose and left the office, gesturing his fellow mercenaries after him.

But three hours came and went.

Jacques Bennabi said nothing, despite being subjected to one of the most horrific methods of extreme extraction.

In waterboarding, the subject is inverted on his back and water poured into his nose and mouth, simulating drowning. It's a horrifying experience…and also one of the most popular forms of torture because there's no lasting physical evidence—provided, of course, that the victim doesn't in fact drown, which happens occasionally.

"Tell me!" Akhem raged as the assistants dragged Bennabi to his feet, pulling his head out of the large tub. He choked and spit water from under the cloth mask he wore.

"*Where* is the weapon. *Who* is behind it? Tell me."

Silence, except for the man's coughing and sputtering.

Then to the assistants: "Again."

Back he went onto the board, his feet in the air. And the water began to flow once more.

Four hours passed, then six, then eight.

Drenched himself, physically exhausted, Akhem looked at his watch. It was now early evening. Only five hours until Saturday—when the weapon would be deployed.

And he hadn't learned a single fact about it. He could hardly hide his astonishment. He'd never known anybody to hold out for this long. That was amazing in its own right. But more significant was the fact that Bennabi had not uttered a single word the entire time. He'd groaned, he'd gasped, he'd choked, but not a single word of English or Arabic or Berber had passed his lips.

Subjects *always* begged and cursed and lied or offered partial truths to get the interrogators at least to pause for a time.

But not Bennabi.

"Again," Akhem announced.

Then, at 11:00 p.m., Akhem sat down in a chair in the cell, staring at Bennabi, who lolled, gasping, on the waterboard. The interrogator said to his assistants, "That's enough."

Akhem dried off and looked over the subject. He then walked into the hallway outside the cell and opened his attaché case. He extracted a large scalpel and returned, closing the door behind him.

Bennabi's bleary eyes stared at the weapon as Akhem walked forward.

The subject leaned away.

Akhem nodded. His assistants took Bennabi by the shoulders, one of them gripping his arm hard, rendering it immobile.

Akhem took the subject's fingers and leaned forward with the knife.

"Where is the weapon?" he growled. "You don't have any idea of the pain you'll experience if you don't tell me! Where is it? Who is behind the attack? Tell me!"

Bennabi looked into his eyes. He said nothing.

The interrogator moved the blade closer.

It was then that the door burst open.

"Stop," cried Colonel Peterson. "Come out here into the hallway."

The interrogator paused and stood back. He wiped sweat from his forehead. The three interrogators left the cell and joined the colonel in the hallway.

"I just heard from Washington. They've found out who Bennabi was meeting with in Tunis. They're sending me the information in a few minutes. I want you to hold off until we know more."

Akhem hesitated. Reluctantly, he put the scalpel away. Then the large man stared at the video screen, on which was an image of Bennabi sitting in the chair, breathing heavily, staring back into the camera.

The interrogator shook his head. "Not a word. He didn't say a single word."

Saturday

At 2:00 a.m., on the day the weapon would be deployed, Colonel Jim Peterson was alone in the office on the Rehabilitation Center, awaiting the secure e-mail about the meeting in Tunis. Armed with that information, they would have a much better chance to convince Bennabi to give them information.

Come on, he urged, staring at his computer.

A moment later it complied.

The computer pinged and he opened the encrypted e-mail from the skinny government man he'd met with in his Reston, Virginia, office on Monday.

Colonel: We've identified the people Bennabi met with. But it's not a terrorist cell; it's a human rights group. Humanity Now. We double-checked and our local contacts are sure they're the ones who're behind the weapon. But we've followed the group for years and have no—repeat, no—indication that it's a cover for a terrorist organization. Discontinue all interrogation until we know more.

Peterson frowned. He knew Humanity Now. Everybody believed it to be a legitimate organization.

My God, was this all a misunderstanding? Had Bennabi met with the group about a matter that was completely innocent?

What've we done?

He was about to call Washington and ask for more details when he happened to glance at his computer and saw that he'd received another e-mail—from a major U.S. newspaper. The header: Reporter requesting comment before publication.

He opened the message.

Colonel Peterson. I'm a reporter with the *New York Daily Herald.* I'm filing the attached article in a few hours with my newspaper. It will run there and in syndication in about two hundred other papers around the world. I'm giving you the opportunity to include a comment, if you like. I've also sent copies to the White House, the Central Intelligence Agency and the Pentagon, seeking their comments, too.

Oh, my God. What the hell is this?

With trembling hands the colonel opened the attachment and—to his utter horror—read:

ROME, May 22—A private American company, with ties to the U.S. government, has been running an illegal operation south of the city, for the purpose of kidnapping, interrogating and occasionally torturing citizens of other countries to extract information from them.

The facility, known in military circles as a black site, is owned by a Reston, Virginia, corporation, Intelligence Analysis Systems, whose corporate documents list government security consulting as its main purpose.

Italian business filings state that the purpose of the Roman facility is physical rehabilitation, but no requisite government permits for health care operations have been obtained with respect to it. Further, no licensed rehabilitation professionals are employed by the company, which is owned by a Caribbean subsidiary of IAS. Employees are U.S. and other non-Italian nationals with backgrounds not in medical science but in military and security services.

The operation was conducted without any knowledge on the part of the Italian government and the Italian ambassador to the United States has stated he will demand a full explanation as to why the illegal operation was conducted on Italian soil. Officials from the *Polizia di Stato* and the *Ministero della Giustizia* likewise have promised a full investigation.

There is no direct connection between the U.S. government and the facility outside of Rome. But over the course of the past week, this reporter conducted extensive surveillance of the rehabilitation facility and observed the presence of a man identified as former Colonel James Peterson, the president of IAS. He is regularly seen in the company of high-ranking Pentagon, CIA and White House officials in the Washington, D.C., area.

Peterson's satellite phone began ringing.

He supposed the slim man from Washington was calling.

Or maybe his boss.

Or maybe the White House.

Caller ID does not work on encrypted phones.

His jaw quivering, Peterson ignored the phone. He pressed ahead in the article.

The discovery of the IAS facility in Rome came about on a tip last week from Humanity Now, a human rights group based in North Africa and long opposed to the use of torture and black sites. The group reported that an Algerian journalist was to be kidnapped in Algiers and transported to a black site somewhere in Europe.

At the same time the human rights organization gave this reporter the name of a number of individuals suspected of being black site interrogators. By examining public records and various travel documents, it was determined that several of these specialists—two U.S. military officers and a mercenary soldier based in Africa—traveled to Rome not long after the journalist's abduction in Algiers.

Reporters were able to follow the interrogators to the rehabilitation facility, which was then determined to be owned by IAS.

Slumping in his chair, Peterson ignored the phone. He gave a grim laugh, closing his eyes.

The whole thing, the whole story about terrorists, about the weapon, about Bennabi...it was a setup. Yes, there was an "enemy," but it was merely the human rights group, which had conspired with the professor to expose the black site operation to the press—and the world.

Peterson understood perfectly: Humanity Now had probably been tracking the main interrogators IAS used— Andrew, Claire, Akhem and others—for months, if not years. The group and Bennabi, a human rights activist, had planted the story about the weapon themselves to engineer his kidnapping, then alerted that reporter for the New York newspaper, who leapt after the story of a lifetime.

Bennabi was merely bait...and I went right for it. Of course, he remained silent the whole time. That was his job. To draw as many interrogators here as he could and give the reporter a chance to follow them, discover the facility and find out who was behind it.

Oh, this was bad…this was terrible. It was the kind of scandal that could bring down governments.

It would certainly end his career. And many others'.

It might very likely end the process of black sites altogether, or at least set them back years.

He thought about calling together the staff and telling them to destroy all the incriminating papers and to flee.

But why bother? he reflected. It was too late now.

Peterson decided there was nothing to do but accept his fate. Though he did call the guards and tell them to arrange to have Jacques Bennabi transferred back home. The enemy had won. And, in an odd way, Peterson respected that.

"And make sure he arrives unharmed."

"Yessir."

Peterson sat back, hearing in his thoughts the words of the slim man from Washington.

The weapon… It can do quote "significant" damage….

Except that there was no weapon. It was all a fake.

Yet, with another sour laugh, Peterson decided this wasn't exactly true.

There was indeed a weapon. It wasn't nuclear or chemical or explosive but in the end was far more effective than any of those and would indeed do significant damage.

Reflecting on his prisoner's refusal to speak during his captivity, reflecting, too, on the devastating paragraphs of the reporter's article, the colonel concluded: the weapon was silence.

The weapon was words.

BLAKE CROUCH

Blake started writing stories in elementary school to scare his little brother at bedtime. He has since perfected the craft of creating intense and insulated worlds in which unspeakable evil can exist. A photograph Blake took of a deserted road on the high desert plain in Wyoming was the inspiration for his first book, *Desert Places*. The horrifying villain in that novel is shaped from the terrors Blake thought might be waiting for him in that unforgiving landscape.

Blake's story for this collection, "Remaking," is influenced by landscape in much the same way. Tragic events unfold in a snowy, sleepy Colorado town. From the first scene, in which a man sits alone in the cold, watching a father and son in a diner, you know something is about to go horribly wrong. With a sickening sense of isolation magnified by the blanketing snow, you'll find your fingers getting numb from gripping the pages as you turn them inexorably toward the final scene.

REMAKING

Mitchell stared at the page in the notebook, covered in his messy scrawl, but he wasn't reading. He'd seen them walk into the coffeehouse fifteen minutes prior, the man short, pudgy and smooth-shaven, the boy perhaps five or six and wearing a long-sleeved OshKosh B'Gosh—red with blue stripes.

Now they sat two tables away.

The boy said, "I'm hungry."

"We'll get something in a little while."

"How long is a little while?"

"Until I say."

"When are you gonna—"

"Joel, do you mind?"

The little boy's head dropped and the man stopped typing and looked up from his laptop.

"I'm sorry. Tell you what. Give me five minutes so I can finish this e-mail, and we'll go eat breakfast."

Mitchell sipped his espresso, snow falling beyond the storefront windows into this mountain hamlet of eight hundred souls, Miles Davis squealing through the speakers—one of the low-key numbers off *Kind of Blue*.

Mitchell trailed them down the frosted sidewalk.

One block up, they crossed the street and disappeared into a diner. Having already eaten in that very establishment two hours ago, he installed himself on a bench where he could see the boy and the man sitting at a table by the front window.

Mitchell fished the cell out of his jacket and opened the phone, scrolling through ancient numbers as the snow collected in his hair.

He pressed TALK.

Two rings, then, "Mitch? Oh, my God, where are you?"

He made no answer.

"Look, I'm at the office, getting ready for a big meeting. I can't do this right now, but will you answer if I call you back? Please?"

Mitchell closed the phone and shut his eyes.

They emerged from the diner an hour later.

Mitchell brushed the inch of snow off his pants and stood, shivering. He crossed the street and followed the boy and the man up the sidewalk, passing a candy shop, a grocery, a depressing bar masquerading as an Old West saloon.

They left the sidewalk after another block and walked up

the driveway to the Antlers Motel, disappeared into 113, the middle in a single-story row of nine rooms. The tarp stretched over the small swimming pool sagged with snow. In an alcove between the rooms and the office, vending machines hummed against the hush of the storm.

Ten minutes of brisk walking returned Mitchell to his motel, the Box Canyon Lodge. He checked out, climbed into his burgundy Jetta, cranked the engine.

"Just for tonight?" she asked.

"Yes."

"That'll be $69.78 with tax."

Mitchell handed the woman behind the front desk his credit card.

Behind her, a row of Hummels stood in perfect formation atop a black-and-white television airing *The Price is Right*.

Mitchell signed the receipt. "Could I have 112 or 114?"

The old woman stubbed out her cigarette in a glass ashtray and reached for the key cabinet.

Mitchell pressed his ear to the wood paneling.

A television blared through the thin wall.

His cell phone vibrated—Lisa calling again.

Flipped it open.

"Mitch? You don't have to say anything. Please just listen—"

He powered off the phone and continued writing in the notebook.

★ ★ ★

Afternoon unspooled as the snow piled up in the parking lot of the Antlers Motel. Mitchell parted the blinds and stared through the window as the first intimation of dusk began to blue the sky, the noise of the television next door droning through the walls.

He lay down on top of the covers and stared at the ceiling and whispered the Lord's Prayer.

In the evening, he startled out of sleep to the sound of a door slamming, sat up too fast, the blood rushing to his head in a swarm of black spots. He hadn't intended to sleep.

Mitchell slid off the bed and walked to the window, split the blinds, heard the diminishing sound of footsteps—a single set—squeaking in the snow.

He saw the boy pass through the illumination of a streetlamp and disappear into the alcove that housed the vending machines.

The snowflakes stung Mitchell's cheeks as he crossed the parking lot, his sneakers swallowed up in six inches of fresh powder.

The hum of the vending machines intensified, and he picked out the sound of coins dropping through a slot.

He glanced once over his shoulder at the row of rooms, the doors all closed, windows dark save for slivers of electric blue from television screens sliding through the blinds.

Too dark to tell if the man was watching.

Mitchell stepped into the alcove as the boy pressed his selection on the drink machine.

The can banged into the open compartment, and the boy reached down and claimed the Sprite.

"Hi, Joel."

The boy looked up at him, then lowered his head like a scolded dog, as though he'd been caught vandalizing the drink machine.

"No, it's all right. You haven't done anything wrong."

Mitchell squatted down on the concrete.

"Look at me, son. Who's that man you're with?"

The voice so soft and high: "Daddy."

A voice boomed across the parking lot. "*Joel?* It don't take this long to buy a can of pop! Make a decision and get back here."

The door slammed.

"Joel, do you want to come with me?"

"You're a stranger."

"No, my name's Mitch. I'm a police officer actually. Why don't you come with me."

"No."

"I think you probably should." Mitchell figured he had maybe thirty seconds before the father stormed out.

"Where's your badge?"

"I'm undercover right now. Come on, we don't have much time. You need to come with me."

"I'll get in trouble."

"No, only way you'll get in trouble is by not obeying a police officer when he tells you to do something." Mitchell noticed the boy's hands trembling. His were, too. "Come on, son."

He put his hand on the boy's small shoulder and guided him out of the alcove toward his car, where he opened the front passenger door and motioned for Joel to get in.

Mitchell brushed the snow off the windows and the windshield, and as he climbed in and started the engine, he saw the door to 113 swing open in the rearview mirror.

"You eaten yet?"

"No."

Main Street empty and the newly scraped pavement already frosting again, the reflection of the high beams blinding against the wall of pouring snow.

"Are you hungry?"

"I don't know."

He turned right off Main, drove slow down a snow-packed side street that sloped past little Victorians, inns and motels, Joel buckled into the passenger seat, the can of Sprite still unopened between his legs, tears rolling down his cheeks.

Mitchell unlocked the door and opened it.

"Go on in, Joel."

The boy entered and Mitchell hit the light, closing and locking the door after them, wondering if Joel could reach the brass chain near the top.

It wasn't much of a room—single bed, table, cabinet housing a refrigerator on one side, hangers on the other. He'd lived out of it for the last month and it smelled like stale pizza crust and cardboard and clothes soured with sweat.

Mitchell closed the blinds.

"You wanna watch TV?"

The boy shrugged.

Mitchell picked the remote control off the bedside table and turned it on.

"Come sit on the bed, Joel."

As the boy climbed onto the bed, Mitchell started flipping. "You tell me to stop when you see something you wanna watch."

Mitchell surfed through all thirty stations twice and the boy said nothing. He settled on the Discovery Channel, set the remote control down.

"I want my dad," the boy said, trying not to cry.

"Calm down, Joel."

Mitchell sat on the bed and unlaced his sneakers. His socks were damp and cold. He balled them up and tossed them into the open bathroom, staring now at his pale feet, toes shriveled with moisture.

Joel had settled back into one of the pillows, momentarily entranced by the television program where a man caked in mud wrestled with a crocodile.

Mitchell turned up the volume.

"You like crocodiles?" he asked.

"Yeah."

"You aren't scared of them?"

The boy shook his head. "I got a snake."

"Nuh-uh."

The boy looked up. "Uh-huh."

"What kind?"

"It's black and scaly and it lives in a glass box."

"A terrarium?"

"Yeah. Daddy catches mice for it."

"It eats them?"

"Uh-huh. Slinky's belly gets real big."

Mitchell smiled. "I bet that's something to see."

They sat watching the Discovery Channel for twenty minutes, Joel engrossed now, Mitchell with his head tilted back against the headboard, eyes closed, a half grin where none had been for twelve months.

At 8:24 p.m., the cell vibrated against Mitchell's hip. He opened the case and pulled out the phone.

"Hi, Lisa."

"Mitch."

"Listen, I want you to call me back in five minutes and do exactly what I say."

"Okay."

Mitchell closed the phone and slid off the bed.

The boy looked up, still half watching the program on the world's deadliest spiders.

He said, "I'm hungry."

"I know, sport. I know. Give me just a minute here and I'll order a pizza."

Mitchell crossed the carpet, tracking through dirty clothes he should've taken to the laundry a week ago.

His suitcase lay open in the space between the dresser and the baseboard heater. He knelt down, searching through wrinkled oxfords and blue jeans, khakis that had long since lost their creases.

It was a tiny, wool sweater—ice-blue with a magnified snowflake stitched across the front.

"Hey, Joel," he said, "it's getting cold in here. I want you to put this on." He tossed the sweater onto the bed.

"I'm not cold."

"You do like I tell you now."

As the boy reached for the sweater, Mitchell undid the buttons on his plaid shirt and worked his arms out of the sleeves. He dropped the shirt on the carpet and rifled his suitcase again until he found the badly faded T-shirt he'd bought fifteen years ago at a U2 concert.

On the way back to the bed, he stopped at the television and lifted the videotape from the top of the VCR, pushed it in.

"No, I wanna watch the—"

"We'll turn it back on in a minute."

He climbed under the covers beside the boy and stared at the bedside table, waiting for the phone to buzz.

"Joel, I'm gonna answer the phone. I want you to sit here beside me and watch the television and don't say a word until I tell you."

"I'm hungry."

The phone vibrated itself toward the edge of the bedside table.

"I'll buy you anything you want if you do this right for me."

Mitchell picked up the phone.

Lisa calling.

He closed his eyes, gave himself a moment to engage. He'd written it all down months ago, the script in the bedside table drawer under the Gideon Bible he'd taken to reading every night before bed, but he didn't need it.

"Hi, honey."

"Mitch, I'm so glad you—"

"Stop. Don't say anything. Just hang on a minute." He reached for the remote control and pressed Play. The screen lit up, halfway through the episode of *Seinfeld*. He lowered the volume, said, "Lisa, I want you to say, 'I'm almost asleep.'"

"What are you—"

"Just do it."

A pause, then: "I'm almost asleep."

"Say it like you really are."

Mitchell closed his eyes.

"I'm almost asleep."

"We're sitting here, watching *Seinfeld*." He looked down at the top of Joel's head, his hair brown with gold highlights, just the right shade and length. He kissed the boy's head. "Our little guy's just about asleep."

"Mitch, are you drunk—"

"Lisa, I will close this fucking phone. Ask how our day was. Do it."

"How was your day?"

"You weren't crying that night." He could hear her trying to gather herself.

"How was your day, Mitch?"

He closed his eyes again. "One of those perfect ones. We're in Ouray, Colorado, now. This little town surrounded by huge mountains. It started snowing around midday as we were driving down from Montrose. If they don't plow the roads we may not be able to get out tomorrow."

"Mitch—"

"We had a snowball fight after dinner, and our motel has these Japanese soaking tubs out back, full of hot mineral water from the springs under the town. Say you wish you were here."

"That's not what I said that night, Mitch."

"What did you say?"

"I wish I could be there with you, but part of me's so glad you two have this time together."

"There aren't many days like this, are there?"

"No."

"Now, I just want to hear you breathing over the phone."

He listened. He looked at the television, then the boy's head, then the ice-blue sweater.

Mitchell held the phone to Joel's mouth.

"Say good night to Mom, Alex."

"Good night."

Mitchell brought the phone to his ear. "Thank you, Lisa."

"Mitch, who was that? What have you—"

He powered off the phone and set it on the bedside table.

When the boy was finally asleep, Mitchell turned off the television. He pulled the covers over the both of them and scooted forward until he could feel the hard ridge of the boy's little spine press against his chest.

In the back window, through a crack in the closed blinds, he watched the snow falling through the orange illumination of a streetlamp, and his lips moved in prayer.

The knock finally came a few minutes after 3:00 a.m., and nothing timid about it—the forceful pounding of a fist against the door.

"Mitchell Griggs?"

Mitchell sat up in bed, eyes struggling to adjust in the darkness.

"Mr. Griggs?"

More pounding as his feet touched the carpet.

"Griggs!"

Mitchell made his way across dirty clothes and pizza boxes to the door, which he spoke through.

"Who is it?"

"Dennis James, Ouray County sheriff. Need to speak with you right now."

"Little late, isn't it?" He tried to make his voice sound

light and unperturbed. "Maybe I could come by your office in the—"

"What part of *right now* went past you?"

Mitchell glanced up, saw the chain still locked. "What's this about?" he asked.

"I think you know."

"I'm sorry I don't."

"Six-year-old boy named Joel McIntosh went missing from the Antlers Motel this evening. Clerk saw him getting into a burgundy Jetta just like the one you drive."

"Well, I'm sorry. He's not here."

"Then why don't you open the door, let me confirm that so you can get back to sleep and we can quit wasting precious minutes trying to find this little boy."

Mitchell glanced through the peephole, glimpsed the sheriff standing within a foot of the door under one of the globe lights that lit the second-floor walkway, his black parka dusted with snow, his wide-brimmed cowboy hat capped with a half inch of powder.

Mitchell couldn't nail down the sheriff's age in the poor light—late sixties perhaps, seventy at most. He held the fore end stock of a pump-action shotgun in his right hand.

"I've got two deputies out back on the hill behind your room if you're thinking of—"

"I'm not."

"Just tell me if you have the boy—"

A radio squeaked outside.

The sheriff spoke in low tones, then Mitchell heard the dissipation of footsteps.

A minute limped by before the sheriff's voice passed faintly through the door again.

"You still there, Mitch?"

"Yeah."

"If it's all right with you, I'm gonna sit down. I been walking all over town since seven o'clock."

The sheriff lowered out of sight, and through the peep-hole, Mitchell could only see torrents of snow dumping on the trees and houses and parked cars.

He eased down on the carpet and leaned against the door.

"I was just speaking with your wife. Lisa's concerned for you, Mitch. Knows why you're here."

"She doesn't know any—"

"And so do I. You may not know this, but I helped pull you and your son out of the car. Never forget it. Been what, about a year?"

"To the day."

Drafts of frigid air swept under the door, Mitchell shivering, wishing he'd brought a blanket with him from the bed.

"Mitch, Lisa's been trying to call you. You have your cell with you?"

"It's turned off, on the bedside table."

"Would you talk to her for me?"

"I don't need to talk to her."

"I think it might not be a bad—"

"I had a meeting the next morning in Durango. Had

brought him along, 'cause he'd never seen the Rockies. That storm came in overnight, and you know, I just…I almost waited. Almost decided to stay the day in Ouray, give the plows a chance to scrape the pass."

"I got a boy of my own. He's grown now, but I remember when he was your Alex's age, can't say I'd have survived if something like what happened to your son happened to him. You got a gun in there, Mitch?"

In the back of Mitchell's throat welled a sharp, acidic tang, like tasting the connectors of a nine-volt battery, but all he said was, "Yeah."

"Is the boy all right?"

Mitchell said nothing.

"Look, I know you're hurting, but Joel McIntosh ain't done a thing to deserve getting dragged into this. Boy's probably terrified. You thought about that, or can you not see past your own—"

"Of course I've thought about it."

"Then why don't you send him on out, and you and me can keep talking."

"I can't do that."

"Why not?"

"I just…I can't."

Mitchell heard footsteps outside the door. He got up quickly, glanced through the peephole just in time to see the battering ram swing back.

He stumbled toward the bed as the door exploded off its hinges and slammed to the floor, two men standing in the threshold—the sheriff with the shotgun trained on him, a deputy with a flashlight and a handgun.

Mitchell shielded his eyes—specks of snow blowing in, luminescent where they passed through the LED beam—couldn't see the man behind the light, but the sheriff's eyes were hard and kind. He could tell this even though they lived in the shadow of a Stetson.

The sheriff said, "I don't see the boy, Wade. Mitchell, let me see those hands."

Mitchell took a deep, trembling breath.

"Come on, Mitch, let me see your hands."

Mitchell shook his head.

"Goddamn, son, I won't tell you—"

Mitchell swung his right arm behind his back, his fingers wrapping around the remote control jammed down his boxer shorts, the room fired into blue by the illumination of the television, the laugh track to *Seinfeld* blaring, Wade screaming the sheriff's name as a greater light bloomed beside the lesser.

Sheriff James flicked the light, felt the breath leave him as he blinked through the tears.

He leaned the shotgun against the wall and stepped inside the bathroom.

The cheap fiberglass of the tub had been lined with blankets and pillows, and the little boy was sitting up staring at the sheriff, orange earplugs protruding from his ears.

The sheriff knelt down, smiled at the boy, pulled out the earplugs.

"You okay, Joel?"

The boy said, "A noise woke me up."

"Did he make you sleep in here?"

"Mitchell said if I was a good boy and kept my earplugs in and stayed in here all night, I could see my daddy in the morning."

"He did, huh?"

"Where's my daddy?"

"Down in the parking lot. We'll take you to him, but I need to ask you something first." The sheriff sat down on the cracked linoleum tile. "Did Mitchell hurt you?"

"No."

"He didn't touch you anywhere private or make you touch him?"

"No, we just sat on the bed and watched about spiders and stuff."

"You mean, on the TV?"

"Yeah."

"What's that?" The sheriff pointed to the notebook sitting on a pillow under the faucet.

"Mitchell said to give this to the people who came to get me."

Wade walked into the bathroom, stood behind the sheriff as he lifted the spiral-bound notebook and opened the red cover to a page of handwriting in black ink.

"What is it?" Wade asked.

"It's to his wife."

"What's it say?"

The sheriff closed the notebook. "I believe that's some of her business." He stood, faced his deputy, snow melting off his Stetson. "Get this boy wrapped up in some blankets and bring him down to his dad. I gotta go call Lisa Griggs."

"Will do."

"And, Wade?"

"Yeah?"

"You throw a blanket over Mr. Griggs before you bring Joel out. Don't want so much as a strand of hair visible. Shield the boy's eyes if you have to, maybe even turn the lights out when you carry him through the room."

The deputy shook his head. "What the hell was wrong with this man?"

"You got kids yet, Wade?"

"You know I don't."

"Well, just a heads-up—if you ever do, this is how much they make you love them."

HARRY HUNSICKER

Harry Hunsicker seems to know an awful lot about taking that short step from respectable citizen to flat-out criminal. His award-winning series featuring investigator Lee Henry Oswald is a high-octane tour of the seedier side of Dallas. His story "Iced" has that same feeling of a world turned upside down. The lead characters bear a shocking resemblance to people we might know—even to ourselves— pillars of society crumbling in an avalanche of bad decisions that seemed perfectly rational at the time. All you can do as a reader is hang on and hope, against all odds, someone makes it out alive.

ICED

Bijoux Watson's body slipped underneath the muddy waters of the Brazos River without a sound, a mangled pile of flesh that had once been the biggest purveyor of black tar heroin in all of east Texas.

Chrissie and Tom watched it float downstream, both breathing heavily after dragging the remains to the edge of the water. After a few moments the corpse rounded a bend and disappeared. Chrissie and Tom looked at each other and smiled.

Then they screwed, right there in the mud and gunk, tossing their clothes aside in a tangled heap, their bodies sweaty. Tom felt the crystal meth they'd smoked an hour before course through his limbs like a bolt of sunlight, his groin jonesing for Chrissie and her tight body.

Bijoux was finally dead.

When they finished, they lay side by side on the dirt and listened to the cattle egrets trill overhead and the traffic lumber across the bridge going to Bryan/College Station. The air smelled of water and decaying vegetation and sex.

Chrissie dug a rumpled pack of Virginia Slims from the pocket of her denim skirt. She lit one and blew a plume of smoke skyward.

"I love you." Tom ran his index finger in a circular pattern around one of her breasts.

She sighed and pitched her cigarette in the river. "Daddy always said don't get lovin' confused with screwing."

Tom felt needles cartwheel across his intestines as the last of the meth ricocheted across his battered synapses. He tried to remember what sleep was like.

"But, baby. You said—"

"Bijoux's gone." Chrissie stood and brushed the leaves and dirt from her body. "Things're different now."

Tom tried not to cry as she dressed, an enormous fatigue making his limbs as heavy and stiff as tree trunks. His skin hurt and his vision turned black at the edges.

Chrissie buttoned her skirt and tramped up the muddy slope without a word.

He lay there for a few moments, thinking about Chrissie and the way she contorted her face when she had an orgasm, the sinews and tendons in her neck and how they came to the surface of her silky skin. He thought about doing her again and about the last hit of Ice, the crystalized ampheta-mine, in his briefcase in the car.

Tom scrambled into his clothes and ran after her.

Two minutes later he stepped off the path and onto the asphalt parking lot near the boat landing on the east side of the river. Bijoux Watson's lemon-yellow Jaguar was the only car visible.

Chrissie stood by the front passenger door with her arms crossed, staring intently at the smudged and cracked wind-shield.

Tom walked over and stood next to her.

Explosive residue, blood and liquified body parts coated the inside of the glass.

Bijoux had been in the driver's seat, a two-kilo package of what he thought was Mexican skag sitting between his legs, when Tom pressed the button, detonating the ten blasting caps nestled in the bag of Piggly Wiggly brown sugar. He and Chrissie had been thirty yards away, under-neath a live oak tree with their cigarettes. Bijoux, a loan shark, pimp and dope dealer, was a rabid antismoker.

Tom said, "Guess we didn't think this through."

"No shit, Einstein." Chrissie closed her eyes and pinched the bridge of her nose

Town was ten miles away. They'd ridden here with the dead man to make the transaction, claiming the stuff was hidden by the river.

"What's your plan now?" she said.

Tom opened the front passenger door of the car.

A rank wave of hot air that smelled like blood and feces hit his face, making him gag for a moment.

He took a deep breath and grabbed his briefcase, dislodging what looked like a one of Bijoux's testicles. He plopped his carryall on the hood of the car, opened it and rummaged through the contents until he found the foil-wrapped nugget of methamphetamine. The pipe lay underneath some loan documents due at the title company a week ago, next to the Glock .40-caliber pistol he'd started carrying ever since he'd gotten tangled up with Bijoux Watson.

His fingers fumbled as he jammed the drug into the bowl of the pipe. With the battered Zippo his father had carried in Vietnam, he ignited the crystalized narcotic. Two big lungfuls and all the confidence, power and *cojones* on the planet coursed through his veins, as thick and fast and strong as the muddy waters a few hundred feet away.

Chrissie appeared at his side with a canvas bag she'd evidently found in the trunk. She opened it and pulled out a Ziploc sack full of dirty brown powder.

"Bijoux always traveled with a stash." She licked her lips and produced a needle and a blackened tablespoon from the bottom of the bag.

Tom offered her the pipe.

She grabbed it and inhaled deeply. Then, she set about cooking a dose of heroin.

"Baby, don't do that," Tom said. "Shit's bad for you, dirty needles and all that other stuff."

"Don't knock it until you've tried it." She lowered her

voice. "It makes sex incredible." She pointed the needle at him. "Gimme your arm."

Tom looked at the syringe and then at Chrissie's face. Her eyes were wide with what he assumed to be anticipation. He wanted to say no, but because he had just ingested over a gram of primo Ice and had all the confidence, power and *cojones* in the world, he stuck his arm out.

Chrissie smiled, found a suitable vein and slid the needle in, giving him half the load. She then injected the rest into a blood vessel in her thigh. Together they sat on the grimy asphalt and leaned against the side of Bijoux Watson's bloody Jaguar. Tom felt like there was nothing he couldn't do, no task or challenge he couldn't accomplish. Except for the fact he had no energy, he thought at that moment he could climb Mount Everest.

Chrissie fell against him and said that just as soon as they came down a little, she'd fuck him so hard his toenails would hurt.

Later, it could have been thirty minutes or thirty seconds, Tom heard the crunch of tires.

He opened his eyes as a county squad car pulled up and stopped a few feet from the Jag.

A deputy got out.

Tom recognized him and struggled to remember the man's name. Dean something. Dean, Jr. had been in his wife's Sunday-school class a couple of years ago.

"Tom? Is that you?" Deputy Dean squinted in the afternoon sun and leaned down to get a closer look. "Whole town's looking for you. You ain't been to the bank in three days." The deputy rubbed one hand over his mouth, and his eyes got wide as he looked from Chrissie back to Tom. "You okay? What's wrong with your pupils?"

Tom nodded and pushed himself off the ground, the uppers and downers in his system making everything deliciously hazy and warm and happy.

"Dean, it's damn good to see you." He enunciated each syllable with extreme precision. "The bank. Um, yes, the bank. The bank. They need these very important documents. At the bank. Very soon, Dean. Can you help me with that?"

Tom turned his back to the officer and reached inside the briefcase

"Uh, yeah, sure," the deputy said. "Anything you need."

Tom remembered the man's last name. Chambers. Dean Roy Chambers, his wife and two children lived in a double-wide on nine acres just outside of town. Tom's bank had made the loan.

"Who is she?" the deputy said. "Are you all right, ma'am?"

"She's fine." Tom turned and smiled.

Then he shot Dean Chambers in the cheek, about a quarter inch to the left of his nose, with the .40-caliber Glock.

The bullet was one of those fancy armor-piercing hollow-points the liberal gun-control freaks loved to whine about. It made a big hole exiting the back of the deputy's head.

Chrissie snapped awake as the blast roiled across the empty parking lot.

"What the hell?"

"Took care of the issue, baby." Tom squared his shoulders and sucked his gut in. "Goddamn, that's what I'm talking about."

"You fucking killed a cop." Chrissie stood up, legs wobbly. "That ain't taking care of no issues. That's making new ones."

"He'd seen us together, baby." Tom stuck the gun in his waistband. His heart thumped a disco beat in his rib cage, *whump whump whump.* "Couldn't do anything else. Besides, got us a ride out of here."

"Ah, Tommy. You're the greatest." She staggered toward the cop car.

Tom grabbed his briefcase and ran after her. "I—I love you, baby."

Why does any man begin an affair? Was it the impending fortieth birthday and the loss of vigor and sexual prowess traditionally associated with middle age?

Or was it the utter banality of living with the same woman for the past fifteen years, through the ups and downs of raising three children and a succession of overly precocious golden retrievers. Tom thought it something more profound, the need deep inside every male to experience one thing to the fullest, to nurture a spark into a roaring fire. To throw away the rearview mirror of life and press the accelerator to the floor. To be a man, dammit.

Chrissie sat in the passenger seat of the squad car, knees tucked under her chin, exposing the full length of her tanned legs.

Tom tried to concentrate on the road and not her thighs.

She said, "Where we going?"

"We need to get some more Ice." Tom lit a Marlboro Light with one shaking hand. "Then I figure we get the cash I've been giving Bijoux and head south somewhere. I hear you can live like a king in Costa Rica, with plenty of gringo dollars."

"Do you even know how to speak Mexican?" Chrissie scratched her left breast.

"We're not going to Mexico, baby." Tom pulled around a slow-moving pickup loaded with hay. "We're gonna be the king and queen of Costa Rica. I'll buy us one of those learn-to-speak-Spanish tapes and we'll be fluent in no time."

"Let's just get the Ice and the money first, huh?" Chrissie drummed her fingers on the dash and looked out the rear window. "Then we'll figure it out."

Chrissie had arrived in town one month before, on a one-way bus ticket from Shreveport, vague about her past except it involved a crazy ex with a mean right hook. She'd just gotten a job at the local vet's clinic when Tom had brought the dog in for a bath.

The attraction was instantaneous and electric, beginning with furtive glances and then an accidental brush of their hands when Tom handed over a check. A volley of double entendres ended up with Tom asking her to lunch. To his horror and amazement, she said yes.

He'd persuaded the vet to keep the dog for the remainder of the weekend. He then called his wife and told her an old college friend had gotten thrown in jail in Waco and he was going to bail him out. He'd be home in time for dinner. Probably. It was early Saturday afternoon, and he could tell by her voice she had started on the second bottle of white zinfandel and only really cared about number three.

They went to a barbecue joint one county over and then on to a room at the Shangri-la Motel on Highway Six. The first time they did it, right as he started to come, Chrissie grabbed his balls and gave 'em a good squeeze. Tom had never felt anything as intense and pleasurable and thought he never would again.

That was before they met the next weekend and Chrissie brought a foil package of Ice, the greatest substance known to mankind.

Thirty days later, Tom was in a stolen squad car driving toward a tar-paper juke joint called Jolie's, looking to score enough meth and money to get them to Costa Rica and a new life. Tom took a deep breath and smiled. *This is living, man.*

The squad car slid to a stop in the gravel parking lot of the bar. Midafternoon on a Wednesday and there were only a couple of other vehicles present. A smidgen of the drug remained in the bowl. Chrissie and Tom split it, sucking on the pipestem until their lungs hurt. They hopped out of the auto and pushed their way into the neon gloom of Bijoux Watson's only legitimate business enterprise.

The place was empty except for an old man in overalls at the bar, drinking a sixteen-ounce can of Schlitz Malt Liquor, and the mulatto bartender, an ex-pimp named Teabag Johnson. The jukebox in the corner played Marvin Gaye's "Sexual Healing."

Tom felt the meth track through his body and thought about how appropriate that song was to the situation at hand and how he sure would like to take Chrissie back into Bijoux's office and nail her on the desk, right next to the safe, which reportedly held enough dope to get half of Texas strung out.

Teabag wiped a glass dry and looked at the door behind them as if expecting the owner to arrive.

Tom and Chrissie sat at the bar. Tom ordered two Miller Lites and two shots of Jose Cuervo Gold.

"Where's Bijoux?" The bartender set the drinks down. "Ya'll give him the shit you supposed to?"

"He's been…delayed." Tom downed the tequila in one gulp. "Said for me to get some stuff from his office."

"He told you to get something out a his office?" Teabag frowned and leaned against the bar.

"Yeah." Tom took a sip of beer to cool the fire in his mouth. He nodded toward Chrissie. "Ask her. She was there."

The bartender looked at Chrissie.

"I always thought you were pretty cute, Teabag." She ran her tongue around the rim of the shot glass. "Bet you know how to treat a lady right."

Tom spluttered on a mouthful of beer.

Teabag kept his face impassive.

"I don't truck with no whores no more. The preacher says that's the road to hell." Teabag reached under the bar. "Y'all is way messed up, been smoking too much crack or sumshit."

Tom's vision blurred with anger; the man called his baby a whore. He reached into the waistband of his slacks and pulled out the Glock.

Teabag's hand came out from under the bar with a sawed-off shotgun.

Tom yanked the trigger and missed, from three feet away.

Chrissie threw her beer bottle at Teabag and connected, a solid blow to the forehead.

The bartender raised a hand to his face and pulled the trigger on the shotgun.

The weapon was pointed about a foot to the right of Tom, away from Chrissie, and only a small portion of the quarter-inch-diameter pellets hit their intended target.

The noise was enormous, like a thunderclap in a cave, and Tom felt a chunk of lead tear into his left bicep and another hit the fleshy part of his side, just above the hip.

He jerked the trigger on the Glock as fast as he could. About half the bullets hit Teabag in the chest and head, the remainder colliding with the bottles of liquor on the shelf behind the bar. For one brief, surreal moment the area where Teabag stood was a virtual waterfall of liquid, a mist of blood and booze, eerily illuminated by the neon beer signs on the wall.

The Glock clicked empty.

Teabag coughed once and fell to the floor, dead.

Tom placed his gun on the bar and clamped a hand over the oozing hole in his arm. He felt no pain, only a mild sensation of pressure deep inside the muscle. The old man drinking beer was nowhere to be seen.

"He shot me, baby." Tom grabbed a bar rag and wrapped it around his arm.

"It'll be all right." Chrissie helped him tie the makeshift bandage. "We get in the office, I'll give you dose of medicine, okay?"

Tom grabbed the gun, stuck it in his waistband and picked up the bottle of Cuervo from the bar. Together they headed to the office in the back.

Two weeks after their first encounter at the motel, Bijoux Watson, resplendent in a pink warm-up suit and enough gold chains to outfit an entire rap band, showed up in his office at the bank. He talked his way past the secretary and told Tom he needed five grand or the whole county would know about his little split tail and their love shack over at the Shangri-la.

Tom, on the downside of a two-day bender, put the bank's chairman of the board on hold, in midcomplaint about his president's increasingly erratic behavior, and said, "Who the hell are you?"

Bijoux leaned back and put his Reeboks on top of Tom's desk. "I'm one of those niggas you don't never see, lest we cleaning up your house or serving you a drink at the country club."

Tom hung up on the director.

"I don't know anything about a motel."

"Your gal's name is Chrissie." The man in the garish warm-up suit pulled a piece of gum out of his pocket and stuck it in his mouth. He dropped the wrapper on the floor. "That shit y'all been smokin'. Comes from me."

Tom started to reply but the man held up his hand.

"My place out by the lake. Jolie's." Bijoux stood up. "You be there tomorrow. Noon. With five large in cash."

That had been two weeks and two hundred thousand dollars ago. Money was missing from the bank and people were starting to ask questions. Three days before, they'd hatched a plan to kill Bijoux. Surprisingly, he had fallen for their story, that they had stumbled on some heroin and wanted to use it in lieu of a payment. Tom had said he'd foreclosed on a property and he'd found it when he inspected the place. The rest of it, the blasting caps and the remote-control device…well, it's amazing how resourceful one could be when one had a couple of grams of pharmaceutical-grade meth surfing through one's body.

Now they were in the inner sanctum, Bijoux's office, a place of utter depression for Tom on his five prior visits.

They stood by the door for a moment. There was a battered metal desk in the center. On one wall was a set of book-shelves filled with grimy three-ring binders. Another wall was dominated by a big-screen television set. In the corner sat a large, metallic-gray safe. Tom took a swig of tequila.

The safe had a complicated-looking combination lock. It also had a small key sticking out of the middle of the dial. Tom's brother had a gun safe similar to this one. The key was to hold the handle of the safe in the open or closed position. Not nearly as secure as using the combo but, without using the dial, a lot easier to access the interior. Tom twisted the key, then the spoke handle and tugged.

The door swung open. A tiny light popped on and il-luminated the interior of the safe, exposing stacks and stacks of plastic bags and cash.

"Holy shit." Chrissie's voice was low, respectful.

Tom gulped.

"I bet it's skag." She grabbed a bag at random and slit it with a letter opener from the desk. "Oh, shit. There must be twenty pounds in here, uncut I'll bet."

Tom ignored her and pulled out a similar size pack, but wrapped in darker plastic. The contents crunched as he massaged it. Butterflies bounced across his stomach as he thought about what might be wrapped in the black covering. He grabbed the opener from Chrissie and cut the container, exposing a couple of hundred tightly bound foil packages.

"Baby, it's Ice." His eyes filled with tears. "We got enough to get us through. We're gonna make it."

They laughed and cried and danced together until Chrissie noticed the blood from Tom's wounded side.

"Let me fix that." She pulled up his shirt and examined the damage.

"Uh, yeah. Okay." Tom unwrapped one of the foil packages. "Let's get high first."

They smoked the whole pack, trading hits, until the world was right again and they'd both forgotten about Tom's injuries.

"It's time to split." Chrissie paced the small room.

"See what's out there." Tom piled cash on the desktop and nodded toward a metal door on the back wall of the office.

Chrissie flipped open the dead bolt and peered outside. "There's a truck…and it looks like some kinda road leading into the woods." Tom stopped shoving money into the small duffel he'd found on the floor and joined her at the door.

"It's gonna work, baby." He hugged her, his hand sliding up under her sleeveless shirt to the smooth flesh covering her rib cage. His groin ached and his words spluttered forth, as fast as the bullets from the Glock.

"We'll go to Austin. Then we'll get new IDs. Saw it on a movie on HBO one time, about how people can do that. Then we'll get on the Internet and find us a place to rent in Costa Rica and we'll buy some clothes. A-a-and—"

"That's a real swell plan." Chrissie slipped from his

embrace and faced him in the doorway. "But we need the keys to that truck out there. Unless the folks at banking school taught you how to hot-wire a late model Chevy."

They looked at each other for a moment and then raced back in the office. The Ice made quick work of it. Tom found a cigar box in a file drawer. At the bottom was a GM key and a remote control. He clicked it, and the truck outside chirped.

They smiled at each other and slapped palms across the top of Bijoux Watson's desk.

Chrissie found another duffel and filled it with the speed and heroin while Tom finished loading the money. When they were done, Tom poured them each a shot of Jose Cuervo. They toasted themselves and their cleverness.

"Here's to us on the beach." Chrissie poured another round. "Drinking little fruity drinks with parasols in 'em. Who would 'a thought it?"

Tom downed his fourth tequila of the last half hour and felt it burn all the way to his toes. The Ice kept him alert but not sober. He looked at Chrissie's breasts beneath the thin cotton of her blouse and at her legs, long and shapely underneath the dirty denim skirt. He put his glass down and lurched toward her.

"Baby, let's do it here, before we leave."

"Sure, Tommy." Chrissie held up a hand and smiled. "But first we gotta take care of that hole in your gut."

Tom looked at his left side and saw that it was wet with blood to the middle of his thigh.

"Sit here and I'll patch you up." Chrissie pulled out the chair from behind the desk.

He did as requested.

Chrissie pulled the shirt away and dumped some tequila in the wound. The pain knifed through his side like a sling blade, burning through the last of the heroin in his system.

He struggled not to scream.

Chrissie patted the wound dry with a paper napkin she found on the floor. She fashioned a bandage out of Tom's handkerchief and fastened it over the injury with Scotch tape. The movement and activity were agony and made Tom nauseous.

He burped and tasted alcohol and cigarettes. He wanted to nail Chrissie but it hurt too much.

Finally she was finished. She fixed another hit of Ice and held the pipe to his mouth. He took a couple of puffs and felt the vigor return, though not as strong as last time.

"It hurts," he said.

"I know, baby." Chrissie got out the spoon and dumped a thumbnail portion of heroin in it. After a moment's hesitation, she added a little more. Using Tom's lighter, she heated the drug until it was liquid, then drew it into a syringe.

"Here you go, Tommy. This'll make everything better." She took his arm and injected the full load. He'd never felt anything like it in his life. The alcohol, speed and heroin combined to make him alert but nearly unable to move. Not like he cared to go anywhere. He was warm and comfortable in the padded leather chair, glowing with confidence and power and euphoria.

After a while, he was vaguely aware of Chrissie carrying the duffel bags outside. He kept his eyes open but didn't really see anything until the television set across the room turned on.

Chrissie dropped the remote control on the desktop. The noise startled him.

He blinked and found himself staring at the talking head on the big screen. She was one of the anchors for the station in Waco, the one with the bad permed hair.

The image on the screen shimmered and became the parking lot by the Brazos. A shot of Bijoux Watson's Jaguar and a pair of EMTs loading a body onto an ambulance. That dissolved into a photograph of Tom, his wife and their children. Their Christmas card from last year.

"I—I—I love you, baby." Tom looked at Chrissie, standing in front of the desk with the keys to the Chevy in her hand. His voice was barely above a whisper.

She didn't reply. Her image grew hazy in the dull light of Bijoux Watson's office.

Tom managed to turn his head back to the TV.

The cameras showed his house, the flowers in the front beds he and his oldest son had planted last month. His wife appeared on-screen, mumbling to the reporters, words too indistinct to comprehend. Tom knew he should be sad but wasn't. His breathing became shallow, but it didn't matter. Tom summoned what energy he could and forced his head to make the long slow turn back to where Chrissie stood.

But she was gone.

MARIAH STEWART

Haven't we all dreamed about revenge at one time or another? Getting an abusive boss fired, leaving an unfaithful spouse, or killing a disloyal best friend are all common fantasies—rarely admitted and never discussed. In "Justice Served," bestselling writer Mariah Stewart shows what might happen when a young woman does what the rest of us only think about in our darkest moments. It is a tale of vengeance that takes you to corners of the human heart better left unexplored in real life. And in classic Mariah fashion, the many twists and turns make this story anything but a straightforward tale of justice and revenge.

JUSTICE SERVED

Every time I think back on that night, I can see myself poised at that exact moment in time. I watch the story unfold—it's like watching a movie, you know?—and I wish to God I could relive that instant when I did the unthinkable.

I wait for that split second when I could change what happened, when I could do what I should have done, even if it killed me. Dying that night, possibly as a hero, sure beats the shit out of living with the memory of my cowardice.

It always starts at the same time and place, and try though I might to make it turn out differently, it never does. I see it as it happened, over and over and over.

I am driving Jessie home in my car—not the one I have now, but the one I had that night. The streets are quiet, it's almost two in the morning, and we both have a pretty decent buzz on from all the drinks we'd had that night, Jessie in particular. She'd left her car at the lot rather than drive herself and I offered to drop her off since we lived in the same town, though several blocks apart. We knew each other casually, the way you know someone who works where you work, but who's never worked with you. We'd always been cordial to each other, but never really had all that much to say. Maybe if she'd worked there a little longer, we'd have been a little closer, I don't know. In any event, she was in my car because she'd had more to drink than I had, and the consensus among our coworkers was that her judgment was more impaired than mine.

A lot they knew....

So anyway, in my mind's eye, I see my car drifting slowly through the night, almost like a leaf floating downstream, taking the corners carefully, pulling up in front of her place and putting the car in Park.

"Do you need help?" I ask her. "Want me to come up with you, or wait while you get the door open?"

Jessie looks out the window to the front porch of the three-story Victorian house. There are three mailboxes alongside the front door, one for each apartment. I know that Jessie lives alone on the second floor. I follow her gaze and notice that one of the lights attached to either side of the front door is missing a bulb, but I don't mention it.

"I'm okay. I'll be fine." Jessie holds up her keys and gives them a little shake. "Just peachy. Not to worry…"

She opens the door and swings it wide, unbuckles her seat belt and slides to the edge of the seat.

"Thanks for the ride. 'Preciate it." She pushes herself out of the seat and bends down to face me. "See you tomorrow."

"I can pick you up in the morning if you need a ride," I tell her, but she's already slammed the door and is making her way up the sidewalk, more steady on her feet than I would have expected.

Out of habit, I lock the doors, then reach into the backseat and grab my bag and pull it by the strap and yank it to me, and some of the contents fall onto the floor behind me. Rather than take the time now to scoop them up, I plop the bag onto the passenger seat where Jessie had been sitting. In this brief time, she's made it up the steps of the house and is at the front door. I put the car into Drive, and start to lift my foot from the brake when, out of the corner of my eye, I first notice the shadow moving along a line of trees to the left of the house. I turn my head and there are several more, creeping through the dark toward the porch, and I blink, not sure if I've seen anything at all. But then, there, the shadows draw closer to the house, like wolves stalking in the night.

My hand falls to the door handle and I start to open it, when I realize one of the wolves has remembered that my car still sits in front of the house with the motor running. He turns and eases across the lawn, and through the windows, our eyes meet. His are feral and small, and his nostrils are flared like the animal he reminds me of.

I look back at the house and see that Jessie is now completely surrounded. She's striking out at them and in the dim light of the one bulb that's still lit, I see them laughing at her. The one on the lawn stares me down defiantly, and I am frozen with fear.

And this is the part that I wish I could change. This is where I wish I could go back in time and do what I should have done.

But we know that there are no such second chances, right? What's done is done, you can't change the past—any cliché would fit right about here.

So every time, it's the same as it was: when I finally react, it is with the greatest cowardice imaginable. I hit the gas and drive away, pretending I did not see, leaving Jessie to be plundered by the wolves.

I know what I should do—*I know, I know*—but I am shaking all over. I'm afraid to stop and get out of my car to look for my cell phone in the backseat where it fell when my bag overturned. Besides, if I call 911, they will wonder why I have permitted a friend to be dragged away by beasts without doing something. Screaming. Blowing the horn. Calling the police right then and there.

But my mouth is dust-dry and my brain seems unable to form coherent thoughts. My heart is pounding out of my chest and my skin has gone icy cold. I am sweating and crying as I drive around, wildly, looking for a pay phone— if I call from my cell, they'll know, won't they, that I left her, knowing what was about to happen to her? Finally, in desperation, I drive to a market that's open all night and I find a phone, and with trembling hands, I dial 911. I whisper the words into the receiver anonymously and hang up and slink back to my car.

My face flushed with shame, I start off in the direction of my apartment.

They found her where those animals left her, after they'd done things to her that no one wants to even know about. For some reason known only to God, she was still alive. I went to see her in the hospital, but I never wanted to, never wanted to face her after what I'd done. But driven by guilt and shame, I had to, and I did. If I told you I didn't have nightmares after that, I'd be lying. And if I told you that I did not see the accusation, the burning hatred in her eyes when I came into her room, I'd be lying about that, too.

So I did the only thing I could do. I leaned over and whispered in her ear.

"I'll get them, Jessie. I swear to you on my life, I will get every one of them and I will make them pay."

I know she heard me, but she never reacted. The look in her eyes told me that the very least I should do for her was to bring down the men who'd traumatized her to the extent that she lost her ability to speak.

I spent every week night and every weekend day at a firing range. I shot handguns of every caliber and every weight until I could hit a target dead center with every shot. And even then I practiced until I knew there was no way I'd miss once I aimed and fired. Finally, I felt ready.

It took me three weeks to discover the name of one

of her assailants, but truthfully, one was all I really needed. And I found him in the damnedest place: in our small local paper, where he was identified as a person of interest in the robbery of a convenience store. Daniel Montoya, age twenty-four, had a history of arrests including assault with a deadly weapon and domestic violence. Up until now, his criminal activities had been confined to Shelton, the small factory town ten miles away. What had brought him into our town that night, I could only guess. In my darkest moments, I believed that he was put there to test me, a test I failed miserably. But studying his photograph, I knew his eyes were the ones that had taunted me that night. And just as surely, I knew it was my destiny to hunt him down.

Once I had his name, I had him. His neighborhood wasn't hard to find—and it wasn't anything like mine, that's for damned sure. A few easy bucks on the street bought me everything I needed to know.

Daniel was a pool junkie, played every night at Tommy's Pool and Suds on East Seventeenth Street in Shelton. The bar closed at two, and by two-fifteen he was on his way to his wheels in the parking lot. The last thing he expected was to find a woman leaning against his driver's side door.

Did he think perhaps I was someone he knew, someone whose face was obscured in the dim light of the parking lot? Whatever, whoever he thought I might be, he was smiling as he walked toward me.

"Hello, Daniel," I said in my sexiest voice.

"Hello, you," he replied, never breaking stride as he walked toward me.

"Hey, Montoya," one of his buddies called from across the lot, "Tomorrow, hey?"

"Right, man," Daniel called back, never taking his eyes from mine. "Tomorrow."

We stood staring at each other, listening as the other cars were started and driven from the lot.

"So, pretty lady, what's happening?" he asked.

"You're happening, Daniel."

"Do I know you?"

"You know a friend of mine," I said, my right arm folded across my waist, my hand hidden by the loose jacket I wore.

"Who's your friend?" He stepped closer, sensing an easy score.

"Jessica Fielding." My arm started its slow move from beneath the folds of the jacket.

"Doesn't ring a…"

I could tell the exact moment that bell began to ring. His stare froze, his mouth half opened and his expression went from seductive to panic in the blink of an eye. "Don't think I know her, sorry."

In less than a heartbeat, my trusty little friend was pressed up against his temple.

"Should I describe her to you, Daniel? Should I remind you of the last time you saw her?" I had straightened up and now had him backed up against his front fender.

He was silent, trying frantically, I believe, to find a way

out of this, a way to disarm me. He wanted to grab for the gun, I could see that in his eyes, but he wasn't sure of my strength or my reflexes, so he, like a wolf, was gauging my movements, biding his time when he could move in for the kill. He opened his mouth to speak, thinking to distract me.

"Don't say a word I don't ask you to say," I hissed, jamming the gun into the flesh on the side of his face. "I'm going to ask you a question, and you are going to answer it. No bullshit, understand? One question, one answer, or I will shoot you now, right now."

Sweat beaded on his forehead, and I was certain he understood.

"The name of the others who were with you when Jessie Fielding was raped."

"I don't know…."

"You weren't listening, Daniel. I will repeat this only one more time. I ask a question, you give me an answer, or I do you right now." I was beginning to sweat a bit myself. I wanted this over with. "One last chance, Daniel. Who was with you when Jessie was raped?"

"Some of the guys, I didn't know."

"Then some of them, you did. Give me a name." I began counting backward from ten.

When I got to six, he said, "Antonio. Antonio Jackson."

"Is he from around here?"

Sweating profusely now, he nodded. "He's my cousin."

"Where can I find him?"

"He lives over on Chester Avenue."

"Thank you, Daniel." I smiled, and for a moment, he seemed to relax.

Then I pulled the trigger.

I watched his body jerk, then slide sideways onto the ground. Then, satisfied, I walked into the shadows and through the alley that took me, eventually, to my car parked two blocks away.

I heard the sirens as I started my engine. A few minutes later, I pulled to the side of the road to allow the speeding patrol car to pass me.

That night, I slept straight through until morning for the first time since the night that changed everything.

"One down, Jessie," I whispered in her ear the next night. "Daniel Montoya. One down…"

I left her sitting in her wheelchair, her eyes still trained on something beyond the window that no one else could see. There'd been no change in her expression, but I know she'd heard and understood exactly what I said.

Ten days later, in the parking lot of yet another bar, Antonio Jackson and I came face-to-face. It had been re-markably easy to get his attention. Anytime a tall, well-built blonde beckoned, men like Jackson lost all caution. Even after what had happened to his cousin Daniel, Antonio ap-parently never considered the danger once he saw me perched on the hood of his car, my long bare legs dangling off to one side.

"One name," I told him. "Just give me one name."

He'd hemmed and hawed as I pressed the barrel of the gun to his throat. He stalled and he pleaded and he cried, but in the end, he gave me the one thing I wanted from him.

"Eddie Taylor."

"Thank you, Antonio." I pulled the trigger, and he dropped like a stone.

"Antonio Jackson," I told Jessie the next evening. "Two down."

It took me almost three weeks to find Eddie Taylor because he'd been in the county jail for possession and had only been back on the streets for less than forty-eight hours when we finally met. Like an avenging angel, I stepped out from the alley as he walked in. I knew I had the right guy. I'd spent every one of those twenty days staring at his picture on my computer.

"One name," I'd said, emboldened by my previous success. "That's all I want from you, Eddie. Just give me the name of one of the other guys."

He'd swallowed hard and tears streamed down his face.

"Awwwwww," I mocked him. "Scared, Eddie? Did Jessie cry when she realized what you were going to do to her? Did she cry when you raped her?"

"Listen, let me…"

"One name, Eddie." When he didn't respond, I once again started counting backward from ten. I'd found that to be universally understood.

"Kelvin Anderson."

"Thank you, Eddie." I shot him through the heart.

"Three down," I told Jessie the next night. "Eddie Taylor…"

Obviously, the police were not oblivious to the fact that several young men from the same general neighborhood had been taken out by the same shooter—hello, same gun, which thank God wasn't registered anywhere, I'd been careful in that regard even while I may have seemed careless in others—but they didn't seem overly interested in investigating too deeply. After all, at one time or another, they'd arrested Daniel, Antonio and Eddie. I began to think of myself as performing a public service when I realized that the rap sheets of the three of them would have reached halfway to Pittsburgh. In my own way, I was proud of myself. I was taking the steps necessary to ensure that no one would ever go through what Jessie'd endured. As for my conscience, well, after the night that changed everything, do you seriously think my conscience bothered me over ridding the world of a couple of predators?

A month later I found Kelvin Anderson, and he kindly supplied me with the name of yet another wolf. Frankie Eden and I had a tête-à-tête in the front seat of his car, and later that same night I was able to confirm to Jessie that the count was now four down, and two to go.

Frankie Eden's eyes told me he knew who I was, why I

was there and where his next stop through the cosmos was going to be. He gave up the last two without flinching, and of all of them, I have to say that Frankie was the only one who died like a man.

Bernie Gunther and Dominic Large weren't as easy to track down, but in the end, although it took several months, I'd eliminated every one of them.

After I'd taken out the last of the six—that would have been Bernie—I went back to my apartment and took a long, hot shower. I slept straight through until one the following afternoon, which barely gave me enough time to do what I knew I had to do before evening came. After I'd completed my errands, I took another shower and blew out my hair so that it hung in long soft waves over my shoulders and down my back. I hadn't realized it had gotten so long. I'd been so focused on the task I'd set for myself that I'd barely looked at my reflection in the mirror anymore. I was surprised to see how gaunt I looked, how pale and thin I'd become, which had, I suppose, prompted all those questions at work I'd been brushing off.

"How are you? Are you feeling all right?"

"Have you been ill?"

Yes, I've been ill, I wanted to say. Sick to death of myself, I wanted to say.

"No, I'm fine. Really." I'd smile and make an effort to put a little spring back into my step.

But soon—probably by this time tomorrow, I thought—everyone will know the nature of my malady.

I typed up the letter I'd composed, sealed it and walked the seven blocks to the home of my parents. My father would still be at work; my mother had gone in to the city to have lunch with some friends and would have spent the rest of the afternoon shopping. I owed them the truth—they deserved the truth—but ever the coward, I was grateful to God that I wouldn't be around to hear what any of them would have to say. I could not have borne my mother's look of shock and horror, my father's cold stare of disbelief and disappointment.

I walked back home, feeling just that much lighter that at least in this, I'd done the right thing. I needed to make certain that neither of my parents would think that in anyway, this was their fault, that they'd failed me in some way. I needed them to understand that the guilt, the shame, the failure, was all mine.

I loaded the handgun and tucked it into my bag. I looked around my apartment for the last time, my gaze lingering on those possessions that had once meant so much to me. The antique tables my grandmother had given me, the sofa I'd saved so long to buy, the candlesticks my mom had given me when I moved in. They'd been a wedding gift from an old friend of hers, and she'd never used them. Neither had I.

I sighed and closed the apartment door for the last time. Looking at the lovely millwork that surrounded it, I decided to leave the door unlocked so that when they came to search my place, they wouldn't have to damage anything to get inside.

The drive to the nursing home seemed endless that night. For the first time ever, every light I approached turned red, as if some cosmic something was telling me to stop. But it was far too late for that. I'd done what I had to do, and now I was going to let Jessie do what she needed to do. I passed an old cemetery and thought for the first time about where they'd lay me to rest. Would I be permitted to be buried in the family plot once they learned what I'd done? Again, the only emotion I really felt was gratitude that I would not have to face their horrified eyes when the truth came out.

It was still early evening when I arrived at the nursing home, so I parked my car near the butterfly garden that some local school kids had planted for the residents and turned off the engine. Knowing I would not be needing them again, I left the keys under the driver's seat and sat quietly for a few moments, taking deep breaths and holding them for as long as I could to calm myself. After my nerves steadied, I got out of the car, taking my bag with its special cargo with me. I took the long way to the building, going through the garden and soaking up the scents and the colors. Did one's sensory memories go with them to the afterlife? I wondered.

I went up the handicapped ramp because it took me past the birdbath where, not surprisingly for that hour, no birds were bathing, but the little fountain there still trickled water and I loved the sound. I went through the big double doors in the front of the building in an effort to hold on to the music of the fountain for as long as I could.

Walking past the guard, I smiled and waved. They were all used to seeing me now, and so there were no questions asked while I signed in. Everyone knew me as Jessie's devoted friend. I headed toward the south wing and Jessie's room, trying to conjure up the words to "Don't Fear the Reaper," which, to tell you the truth, I didn't. For me, dying wasn't nearly as bad as living with what I'd done and what I was.

I went into Jessie's room and found her sitting in a chair near the window, her untouched dinner tray on the foot of the bed. I knew how she felt. There were times when the horror of the night that changed everything came back full force and filled me so that the thought of eating made me physically sick.

"Jessie," I said, seating myself on the chair opposite hers, "it's done now. They're all gone. All six."

I opened my bag and felt the butt end of the old handgun, all cool metal hardness. My fingers wrapped around the handle and I drew it out.

"I know you've wanted to do this since the night it happened." I took her hands and placed the gun in them. "It's all right," I told her. "I deserve this. Everyone will know the truth now. No one will blame you. And after it's done, you can come back, Jessie. You can come back into the world, once I'm gone from it."

I sat directly in front of her, my back straight, my vision clear, my conscience for once subdued. I was ready.

Jessie's gaze dropped to the gun in her hand and she stared at it for a long time before looking up at me again. The gun raised slowly, the barrel aimed at nothing in particular. I tapped my chest, right where I felt my heart beating, with my index finger and told her, "Aim here. I'm ready when you are."

I closed my eyes, and waited for the end to come. And waited.

Curious, I opened my eyes just as swiftly, so swiftly, before I could take a breath or utter a sound or reach out to stop her, Jessie's wrists twisted and suddenly the gun was at *her* temple, and the room reverberated with the single shot.

I stared in horror as Jessie slumped forward before falling face-first from the chair onto the floor, red like a fluid carpet flowed around her as if to cushion her fall.

"No!" I screamed as the room filled with people.

Suddenly nurses, orderlies, visitors, residents, everyone who'd been close enough to have heard the shot crowded into the room even before the realization of what she'd done completely sunk in.

"Oh, my God, Jessie," one of the nurses said, "what have you done…?"

What, indeed?

So there I was…obviously I'd brought her the gun with which she'd killed herself, which made me an accessory.

My panicked brain recognized immediately that one, I was not dead, and two, I'd be charged with a crime. But since I was alive, and Jessie was not, at that point, copping to a charge of accessory to murder was definitely more appealing than admitting what I'd really done.

The story I'd tell swirled through my head, bits and pieces tripping over each other as I tried frantically to put one together. And I'd come up with a pretty damned good one, if I do say so myself.

Jessie couldn't face another day living with the memory of what had happened to her. She begged me—*begged* me—to help her to end it. As her friend, as someone who loved her, as the only person to whom she'd speak, how could I deny her that release? Who would doubt that story, knowing what she'd gone through?

I could get off with a light sentence, I knew, once I explained. No one would ever need to know the truth, right?

I was just starting to breathe a little easier when the door opened and my father walked in. He'd seen the story on TV—who in the tristate area had not?—and he'd come down to the station.

But he'd not come to comfort me, or even to ask me why.

His gaze was just as cold as it had been when, as a child, I'd disappointed him in some fashion. I wasn't surprised, frankly, that there'd be no attempt at understanding. There never had been in the past.

In his hands, he held a blue envelope. The same blue envelope I'd left in his mailbox earlier.

"Daddy," I said, ever the coward, holding out my shaking hands, silently pleading for him to give it to me.

But Judge Lucas Bradley—Judge Luke "Hang 'Em High" Bradley—handed the letter over to you. I guess there were other instincts that were stronger in him, other bonds harder to break than the one that existed between father and daughter.

Signed this date: Deanna Jean Bradley

When Detective Mallory Russo finished reading the last page of the statement, she held it up in one hand and said, "You haven't signed it."

"I will." The young woman held out her hand for the pen.

The detective and the once promising assistant district attorney stared at each other from across the table.

"You could have come to me, Dee," Mallory told her. "You could have given me the information and we could have gone after these guys. It didn't have to be this way."

"Yes, it did, Mallory. And may I remind you that none of you were too interested in them even as I was picking them off." The A.D.A. shifted in her seat. "Besides, everything that happened…it was all my fault. It wasn't your fight."

"They're all my fights," Mallory told her. "We've known each other for years, Dee. Why couldn't you have trusted me to take them down?"

Deanna shrugged, her eyes shifting to the two-way window on the opposite side of the room.

"Is he still there, watching? My father?"

"Judge Bradley left an hour ago." Mallory rested her arms on the table.

"You know, he could have burned my letter, he could have kept it and held it over my head for the rest of my life." Deanna Bradley continued to stare at the mirror. "I still can't believe he turned against me."

"Your father has an unswerving sense of justice," Mallory reminded her. "He's always going to follow his conscience."

"So will I, Mal." Deanna sighed. "So will I…."

DAVID HEWSON

David Hewson knows where to find the perfect black rice in Barcelona, the richest coffee in Venice and how to kill a person in a thousand gruesome ways. His wonderful series set in Rome, featuring detective Nic Costa and his stand-alone thrillers share an authentic sense of place, characters with rich lives that began long before you picked up the book and a relentless sense of pacing that pulls you into their world.

"The Circle" is a perfectly symmetrical tale that shatters our comfortable isolation from current events. Through the eyes of a young pregnant woman we see the world from a new perspective as a train carries her from a state of innocence into a state of fear. Hold on tight, because like it or not, every one of us is already along for the ride.

THE CIRCLE

The Tube line ran unseen beneath the bleak, unfeeling city, around and around, day and night, year after year. Under the wealthy mansions of Kensington the snaking track rattled, through cuttings and tunnels, to the bustling mainline stations of Paddington, Euston and King's Cross, where millions came and left London daily, invisible to those below the earth. Then the trains traveled on to the poorer parts in the east, Aldgate, with its tenements and teeming immigrant populations, until the rails turned abruptly, as if they could take the poverty no more, and longed to return to the prosperous west, to civilization and safety, before the perpetual loop began again.

The Circle. Melanie Darma had traveled this way so often she sometimes imagined she was a part of it herself.

Today she felt tired. Her head hurt as she slumped on the worn, grubby seat in the noisy, rattling carriage, watching the station lights flash by, the faces of the travelers come and go. Tower Hill, Monument, Cannon Street, Mansion House… Somewhere to the south ran the thick, murky waters of the Thames. She remembered sitting next to her father as a child, bewildered in a shaking train from Charing Cross to Waterloo, a stretch that ran deep beneath the old, gray river. Joking, he'd persuaded her to press her nose to the grimy windows to look for passing fish, swimming in the blackness flashing by. On another occasion, when he was still as new to the city as she was, in thrall to its excitement and possibilities, they'd both got out at the station called Temple, hoping to see something magical and holy, finding nothing but surly commuters and tangles of angry traffic belching smoke.

This was the city, a thronging, anonymous world of broken promises. People, millions of them, whatever the time of day. Lately, with her new condition, they would watch on the train as she moved heavily, clutching the swelling bundle in her belly. Most would stand aside and give her a seat. A few would smile, mothers mostly, she thought. Some, men in business suits, people from the City, stared away as if the obvious extent of her state, and the apparent nearness of her release from it, amounted to some kind of embarrassment to be avoided. She could almost hear them praying…*if it's to happen please, God, let it not be this instant, when I've a meeting scheduled, a drink planned, an assignation with a lover. Anytime but now.*

She sat the way she had learned over the previous

months: both hands curved protectively around the bump in her fawn summer coat, which was a little heavy for the weather, bought cheaply at a street market to encompass her temporary bulk. Her fingers felt comfortable there nevertheless. It was as if this was what they were made for.

So much of her life seemed to have been passed in these tunnels, going to and fro. She felt she could fix her position on the Circle's endless loop by the smell of the passengers as they entered the carriage: sweet, cloying perfume in the affluent west, the sweat of workmen around King's Cross, the fragrant, sometimes acrid odor of the Indians and Pakistanis from the sprawling, struggling ethic communities of the east. Once she'd visited the museum in Covent Garden to try to understand this hidden jugular that kept the city alive, uncertainly at times, as its age and frailty began to show. Melanie Darma had gazed at the pictures of imperious Victorian men in top hats and women in crinoline dresses, all waiting patiently in neat lines for miniature trains with squat smokestacks and smiling crews. It was the first underground railway ever built, part of a lost and entirely dissimilar age.

When the London bombers struck in 2005 they chose the Circle Line as their principal target, through accident, she thought, not from any conscious attempt to strike at history. Fourteen people died in two separate explosions. The entire system was closed for almost a month, forcing her to take buses, watching those around her nervously, glancing at anyone with dark skin and a backpack, wondering.

She might have been on one of those two carriages had it not been for her father's terminal sickness, a cruel cancerous death eked out on a hard, cheap bed in some cold public ward, one more body to be rudely nursed toward its end by a society that no longer seemed to care. Birth, death, illness, accident... Sudden, fleeting joy, insidious, lasting tragedy... All these things lay in wait on the journey that was life, with ambushes, large and small, waiting hidden in the wings.

Sometimes, as she sat on the train rattling through the black snaking hole in the dank London earth, she imagined herself falling forward in some precipitous, headlong descent toward an unknown, endless abyss. Did the women in billowing crinoline dresses ever feel the same way? She doubted it. This was a modern affliction. It had a modern cure, too. Work, necessity, the daily need to earn sufficient money to pay the rent for another month, praying the agency would find her some other temporary berth once the present ran out.

There were two more stops before Westminster, the station she had come to know so well, set in the shadow of Big Ben and the grandiose, imposing silhouette of the Houses of Parliament. The train crashed into the darkness of the tunnel ahead. The carriage shook so wildly the lights flickered and then disappeared altogether. The movement and the sudden black, gloom conspired to make the weight of her stomach seem so noticeable, such a part of her, she believed she felt a slow, sluggish movement inside, as if something were waking. The fear that thought prompted dispatched a swift, guilty shock of apprehension through her mind. The thought: *this is real and will happen, however much you may wish to avoid it.*

Finally the rolling, careering carriage reconnected with whatever source of energy gave it light. The carriage stabilized, the bulbs flickered back to life.

On the opposite seat sat a young foreign-looking man who wore a dark polyester jacket and cheap jeans, the kind of clothes the people from Aldgate and beyond seemed to like. He had a grubby red webbed rucksack next to him, his hand on the top, a possessive gesture, though there was no one there who could possibly covet the thing.

He stared at her, openly, frankly, with a familiarity she didn't appreciate. His eyes were dark and deep, his face clean-shaven, smiling, attractive.

The train lurched again, the lights flashed off and on as they dashed downward once more.

The young man spoke softly as he gazed at her, and it was difficult to hear over the crash of iron against iron.

Still, she thought she knew what he said, and that was, "They will remember my name."

She tried to focus on the book in her hands. It came from the staff library. The Palace of Westminster didn't pay its workers well, but at least they had access to decent reading.

"Are you scared?" the young traveler opposite asked pleasantly, nodding at the bump beneath her hands.

It was a book on philosophy. She chose it for the image

on the cover: *Ouroboros,* the serpent that devoured itself. If she squinted hard she could imagine the familiar London Transport poster, with its yellow rounded rectangle for the Circle Line, transposed in its place.

"Not at all," she answered immediately without taking her attention off the page.

There was a paragraph from Plato, a description of *Ouroboros* as the very first creature in the universe, the beast from which everything sprang, and to which everything returned.

She felt a little giddy when she realized the words of some ancient Greek, who had been dust when Christ was born, made some sense to her. It was almost as if she could hear his ancient, cracked voice.

The living being had no need of eyes when there was nothing remaining outside him to be seen; nor of ears when there was nothing to be heard; and there was no surrounding atmosphere to be breathed; nor would there have been any use of organs by the help of which he might receive his food or get rid of what he had already digested, since there was nothing which went from him or came into him: for there was nothing beside him.

It was impossible to concentrate. Melanie Darma didn't want to ask, not really. But she had to.

"Who will remember?"

Before he could answer they clattered into Temple. The bright station lights made her blink. The doors opened. A burly, scarlet-faced man in a creased, grubby dark suit entered the carriage, looked at their half, then the other, and sat down in the seats opposite her, as far away from the young man with the rucksack as he could. She could still smell the rank stink of beer, though.

"And why?" she wondered.

The newcomer grunted, pulled out a copy of the *Standard,* thrust his coarse face into it. Then he raised his head and stared hard at both of them, as if they'd broken some kind of rule by speaking to each other across the chasm of a Tube train carriage, strangers conversing beneath the streets of London on a breathless July day.

"I don't know what you mean..." the young man answered quietly.

Perhaps she'd misheard. The train was noisy. She didn't feel well. But now he had his hands curled round the rucksack the way hers fell in place about her stomach, and his eyes wouldn't leave her document bag from work, the green canvas carryall bearing the insignia of the Palace of Westminster, a golden portcullis, crowned, with two chains. It sat in the seat next to her, looking important, though in truth it contained nothing important.

The train lurched into darkness once more, for several seconds this time. She wondered whether someone had moved during that time. But when the lights returned they were both in the same seats, the older man face-deep in his paper, the younger, smiling a little vacantly, glancing in her direction.

She thought of the offices and who would be there, waiting. It was temporary work, six months, no more, until her… "confinement" as one of the older women put it. Temps didn't get maternity pay, even when they were forced to go through interminable interviews and vetting processes, just so they could answer irate e-mails to MPs she never met. The men and women there were, for the most part, kind, in an officious, offhand way. Each day she would nod and smile to the policemen on the door, place her bag on the security machine to be scanned, her ID card against the entry system reader to be checked. Nothing ever changed, nothing ever happened. Behind the imposing, ornate doors of the Palace of Westminster, beyond the gaze of the tourists who snapped and gawped at the great building that sat beneath the tower of Big Ben, lay nothing more than the world writ small: little people doing little jobs, leading insignificant lives, just looking, like her, to pay the bills.

No one ever asked who the father was. She was a temp. There was, of course, no point.

She leaned forward, needing to ask him something.

"I was wondering…" she began.

The man in the creased dark suit glared at her, swore, screwed up his paper and got to his feet.

Her heart leapt in her chest, her hands gripped the shape beneath her fingers more firmly. It was the middle of the day. Violence on the Tube at that hour was rare, but not unknown.

"Don't do anything…" she heard herself murmur.

There was an exchange of intemperate words, and the

thick-set man stomped off to sit in the far end of the carriage. The train burst into Embankment with a deafening clatter. One more stop to go. In her early days working at the Houses of Parliament she had sometimes abandoned the train here and walked the rest of the way, along the Embankment. She enjoyed the view, her left side to the river and the London Eye on the opposite bank, ahead the familiar outline of Westminster Bridge and the great iconic symbol of Big Ben beneath which—and this had long ceased to astonish her—she worked, humbly tapping away at a computer.

There was no possibility that she could walk such a distance anymore. She kept her eyes on the grimy carriage floor and said nothing else. At Westminster Station she got up and left the train without looking at anyone.

The day seemed brighter than when she first went underground. She glimpsed up at the impossibly tall clock tower to her right, blinking at the now-fierce sky.

Then, patiently, as she always did, because that was how she was brought up, she waited at the first pedestrian crossing, until the figure of the green man came and it was safe to walk. It was only a few hundred yards from the mouth of the Tube station to the heavily guarded gate of the Palace of Westminster, close to the foot of the tower, the entrance she had to use. As always, there were police officers everywhere, many carrying unsightly black automatic weapons in their arms, cradling them as if they were precious toys.

No one looked at a pregnant young woman out on the street in London. They were all too busy to notice such a mundane sight. She walked over the final stretch of road when the last pelican crossing allowed, wondering who would be on duty at the security post that day. There was one nice police officer, a friendly sergeant, tall, with close cropped gray hair, perhaps forty, or a fit fifty, it was difficult to tell. She knew his name: Kelly. Everyone else among the staff who scrutinized her bag and her ID card from time to time, asking pointless questions, picking curiously at her belongings, was still a stranger.

Twenty yards from the high iron gates of the security entrance she turned and saw him.

The young man from the train had his rucksack high over his head. He was running and screaming something in a language she didn't understand. He looked both elated and scared. There were policemen beginning to circle him, fumbling at their weapons.

Melanie Darma watched all this as if it were a dream, quite unreal, a spectacle from some TV show that had, perhaps, been granted permission to film in the shadow of Big Ben, though this was, she felt sure, improbable.

She walked on and found herself facing the tower of Big Ben again. Kelly—*Sergeant* Kelly, she corrected herself—was there, yelling at her. He didn't have a weapon. He never carried one. He was too nice for that, she thought, and wondered why at that moment she chose, quite consciously, not to listen to his hoarse, anxious voice.

"Melanie…!"

The bright, angry sky shook, the horizon began to fall sideways. She found herself thrust forcefully to one side, and felt her hands grip the shoulder bag with the golden portcullis close to her, out of habit, not fear, since all it contained was the book on *Ouroboros,* a few bills, a purse containing £20 and a few coins.

Falling, she clutched the canvas to herself, defending the tender swell at her stomach as she tumbled toward the hard London stone.

Two strong arms were attempting to knock her down to the ground. She broke the fall with one knee and felt his chin jab hard against her skull as the jolt took him by surprise. Her stockinged skin grazed against the paving. She felt a familiar, stabbing pain from childhood, loose flesh damaged by grit. Tears pricked at her eyes. She was in someone's arms and she knew, immediately, whose.

She couldn't see him, but he was still on her, tight arm around her throat.

When she looked up three men in black uniforms circled them, weapons to their shoulders, eyes fixed on a target that was, she understood, as much her as it was him.

Half-crouched and gasping for breath, she could see the iron security gates were just a few short steps away: security, a safe, private world, guarded so carefully against violent young men carrying mysterious rucksacks. Someone came into view, face in darkness initially since she was now in the shadow cast by the gigantic clock tower and the day seemed suddenly almost as dark as the mouth of the Tube from which she had so recently emerged.

"Don't shoot me," she said quietly, and realized there were tears in her eyes. "Don't…"

Her hands stayed where they were, on her stomach. Somehow she couldn't say the words she wanted them to hear. *Don't shoot us….*

The grip on her neck relaxed, just a little. She caught the eyes of the man in front of her. Sergeant Kelly—she had never known his second name, and feared now she never would—had his hands out in front, showing they were empty. His face was calm and kind, unflustered, that of a gentle man, she thought, one for whom violence was distasteful.

"It doesn't need to end this way…" he pleaded quietly.

"What way?" the voice behind her demanded.

"Badly," the policeman said, and moved forward so that they could see his eyes. "Let the young lady get to her feet. Can't you see she's hurt?"

Laughter from an unseen mouth, his breath hot against her scalp. She found the courage to look. The old red rucksack was high in the air. From its dirt-stained base ran a slender black cord, dangling down toward the arm that gripped her. Tight in his fingers lay some small object, like a television remote control.

She couldn't count the black shapes gathering behind Sergeant Kelly. They wore heavy bulletproof vests and soft caps. Black, ugly weapons stood in their arms tight to the shoulder, the barrels nodding up and down, like the snouts of beasts sniffing for prey.

"She's pregnant," the sergeant went on. "You see that? *Can't you?*"

The unseen man sighed softly, a note, perhaps, of hesitation. She felt there was some flicker of hope reflected in Sergeant Kelly's eyes.

"Get up…" the foreign voice ordered.

She stumbled to her feet. Her knee hurt. Her entire body seemed racked by some strange, unfamiliar, yet not unwanted pain.

Her captor's young face was now just visible. He was looking toward the tower of Big Ben.

"We're going in there," he insisted, nodding toward the black iron security gates. "If you try to stop me…she's dead." He nodded at the armed officers circling them. "Them or me. What's the difference?"

She wondered how long the men with guns would wait, whether they were already gauging how wide to make the arc of their circle so that they might shoot safely in order to guarantee a kill, yet not be subject to their own deadly fire when the moment came.

*It will be soon…*she thought, and found her hands returning to her belly, as if her fingers might protect what was there against the hot rain of gunfire.

Someone thrust aside the barrel of the closest weapon. It was the sergeant again, swearing furiously, not at her assailant, but at the officers with guns. Harsh words. Harsher than she'd ever heard him speak before.

"There are choices," Sergeant Kelly insisted as he pushed them back.

Hands high, empty, face still calm, determined, he wheeled around to confront the man who held her.

"Choices..." the policeman repeated quietly. "She's pregnant. Isn't there—" he shook his head, struggling to locate the right words "—some rule that says it's wrong to kill an unborn child?" Sergeant Kelly shrugged. "For me there is, and I don't believe in anything much, except what I can see and touch. If you believe—" his right hand swept briefly toward the sky "—something, isn't it the same?"

"You are not my preacher, policeman," the voice behind her spat at him.

"No." Sergeant Kelly was so close that she could feel the warmth of his breath on her face and it smelled of peppermints and stale tobacco. "I'm no one's priest. But tell me this. What will your god say of a man who knowingly takes the life of an unborn child?" He leaned forward, bending his head to one said, as if listening, curiously. "Will he be pleased? Or..."

A stream of angry, foreign words filled the air. The London policeman stood there, his hand out, beckoning.

"She doesn't belong here," he said. "Let her go with me. After that..."

He shrugged.

"You...and *they*..." The way he nodded at the others,

the men with the guns, shocked her. It was as if there was no difference between them and the one who had snatched her, out in the bright, stifling day in Parliament Square. "You can do what the hell you like."

Silence, followed by the distant caterwauling of sirens. This was, she knew, the moment.

"I beg you…" Melanie Darma murmured, not knowing to whom she spoke.

The grip on her neck relaxed. A choking sob rose in her throat. She stumbled forward, out of the young man's grip, still clutching the bag with the portcullis logo close to her stomach.

"Quickly…" the policeman ordered, beckoning.

She lurched forward, slipped. Her knee went to the ground once more. The pain made her shriek, made her eyes turn blurry with tears.

One set of arms released her. Another took their place. She was in the grip of Sergeant Kelly, and the smells of peppermint and tobacco were now secondary to the stink of nervous sweat, hers or his, she didn't know and didn't care.

She fell against him. His arms slipped beneath hers, pulling, dragging, demanding.

They were close to the gate. She found herself falling again, turning her head around. She had to. It was impossible to stop.

The young man from the Tube had his hands in the air. He was shouting, words she couldn't understand, foreign, incomprehensible words, a lilting chant that seemed to veer between anger and fear, imprecation and beseechment.

"Melanie…" the police sergeant muttered, as he pulled her away. "Don't look… Don't…"

It was futile. No one could not watch a scene like this. It was a kind of theater, a staging, a play in real life, performed on a dirty stone stage in the heart of London, for all to see.

Not far away there were men with cameras, people holding cell phones, recording everything. Not running they way they should have been.

That puzzled her.

She fell to one knee again, and felt glad the pain made her wake, made her pay more attention.

The darks shapes with the rifles were around him again, more close this time, screaming obscenities and orders in equal measures. Yet his eyes were on the sky, on something unseen and unseeable.

The rucksack flew from his hand. The ugly black metal creatures burst into life in the arms of their owners and began to leap and squeal. She watched the young man she had spoken to on the Tube twitch and shriek at the impact, dancing to their rhythm as if performing some deadly tarantella.

His bag tumbled through the air, falling to the ground, the wire that linked device to owner flailing powerlessly like a snapped and useless tendon.

That part of the performance was over. It was the dance now, nothing but the dance.

Sergeant Kelly didn't drag her at that moment. Like

Melanie Darma he realized the bomb, or whatever it was, had refused to play its part. Like her, he could only watch in shock and terrified wonder.

She closed her eyes, gripping her stomach firmly, intent on ensuring everything there was normal, as it ought to be. As she half knelt there, feeling the policeman's strong arms on her shoulder, she was aware of two thin lines of tears trickling slowly down her face. And something else…

"Melanie," Sergeant Kelly murmured, looking scared.

She looked at him. There was worry, concern in his face, and it was more personal now, more direct than such a vague and ephemeral threat as explosives in a young man's bag.

Following the line of his gaze she saw what he did. Blood on the pavement. Not that of the man from the Tube. Hers. A line of dark, thick liquid gathering around her grazed knee, pooling as it trickled down her leg.

The wailing of sirens grew louder. Vans and police cars seemed to be descending upon them from every direction. Men were shouting, screaming at one another. A couple were bent down over the broken body leaking onto the ground a few yards away.

Before she could say another thing he bent down, looked in her face, breathed deeply, then scooped her up in his strong, certain arms.

"There's a nurse inside," Sergeant Kelly muttered, a little short of breath, as he carried her through the security gate, past the door and the gawping, wide-eyed officers next to their untended machines, and on into the cool, dusty darkness of the Houses of Parliament.

She knew the medical room, could picture it as he half stumbled, half ran along the narrow corridors. In the very foot of the tower, a clean and windowless cubicle with a single medic in attendance, always. Twice, she'd stopped by, for advice, for support, only to be told to see her own doctor instead of troubling the private resources of the Palace of Westminster.

Except in emergencies.

Sergeant Kelly turned down the final passageway, one that led into the very core of the building. The stonework was so massive here it scared her. Trapped beneath several hundred feet and untold tons of grimy London stone, an insignificant creature, like some tiny insect in the bowels of a towering anthill, she felt herself carried into the brightly lit room, lifted onto a bed there, placed like a specimen to be examined.

It was the same nurse. Thickset, ugly, fierce. The place smelled of drugs and chemicals. The lights were too bright, the walls so thick she couldn't hear a note of the chaos that must have ensued outside.

The nurse took one look at the drying stain on her ankle and asked, "When are you due?"

"Next week."

Her flabby face contorted in a scowl.

"And you're coming to work? Good God… Let's take a look."

She was reaching for a pair of scissors, casually, with no panic, no rush. It was as if life and death cohabited happily in this place, one passing responsibility to the other the way day faded into night.

He was still there as the woman came toward the hem of her dress with the sharp, shiny instrument, staring at the Palace of Westminster bag that she continued to clutch tight against the bump, as if it still needed protection.

"You don't need that anymore," Sergeant Kelly said, half-amused, reaching down for the carryall in her hands.

She let go and released it into his grip. The nurse advanced again with the scissors, aiming at her dress.

"Sergeant…?" Melanie Darma objected, suddenly anxious.

"I'm a London copper, love," he answered, laughing a little. "There's nothing I haven't seen."

"I don't want you to see me," she told him firmly.

The nurse gave him a fierce stare.

Sergeant Kelly sighed, held the bag up for her to see and said, "I'll look after your things outside."

As he opened the door, the faint wail of sirens scuttled inside, then died as he closed it again.

It wasn't like an anthill, she thought. More akin to being in the foundations of a cathedral, feeling the weight of ages, the massive load of centuries of tradition, of a civilization that had, at one time, dominated the known world, bearing down on her remorselessly.

"The doctor might be a man, love," the nurse said as she

cut the fabric of the cheap dress in two, all the way up to the waist.

Then she stepped back, eyes wide with surprise, unable to speak.

It was all there. The plastic bag with the fake blood, and the telltale path it had left down the side of her leg after she burst it with her fingers. And the bulge. The hump. The being she had brought to life, day-by-day, out of stockings and underclothes, napkins and tea towels, until that very morning. *The* morning. When something else took its place.

She knew the wires, every one, because he'd told her about each as he placed them there, around the soft, fat wad of material they'd given him, the night before. There was, she wanted to tell the nurse, no other way to penetrate this old and well-protected inner sanctum of a world she had come to hate. No other means to escape the attention of the electric devices, the sniffers, the security people prying into everything that came and went in this great palace, a place that meant so much to so many.

"I'm sorry," she murmured, reaching for the band of yellow cable, taking the tail to the mouth, as she'd learned and practiced so many times in her small, fusty bedroom of the apartment she could barely afford.

The foreign phrase he taught her wouldn't come. They were, in any case, his words, not hers, codes from a set of beliefs she did not share.

What she did know was the Circle. It seemed to have

been with her forever, since the moment she first set foot in the dark world beneath the ground, hand in hand with her father, as he took the first step on the journey to his bleak, cruel end. By accident she had woken the slumbering beast one cold morning when she first met Ahmed on the stairs, a weak, impressionable creature, defined by nothing but his aimless anger. He was its slave, too, not that he ever knew.

Her mind could not dismiss the image of *Ouroboros* at that moment, the picture of the serpent devouring itself. Or the words of the book that was now in the hands of Sergeant Kelly who was, perhaps, a little way away, outside even, eyeing the shattered body in the street.

The living being had no need of eyes when there was nothing remaining outside him to be seen; nor of ears when there was nothing to be heard; and there was no surrounding atmosphere to be breathed. And all that he did or suffered took place in and by himself.

From nothing to nothing, round and round.

With unwavering hands Melanie Darma held the wires above her belly like a halo, bringing together the ends with a firm and deliberate motion, and as she did so she was filled with the deepest elation that this particular journey was at an end.

R.L. STINE

R. L. Stine's story "Roomful of Witnesses" clearly demonstrates that while truth isn't always stranger than fiction, the strangest fiction always contains a kernel of truth. Based on a real place, this twisted tale could only have been written by R. L. Stine and reveals his wonderfully off-kilter look at the world. Best known for the nearly three hundred million children's books sold, he has an uncanny ability to write pulse-pounding stories that keep you turning the pages without ever losing that childlike obsession with the gory details. Why do so many kids love everything this man writes? Turn the page and find out.

ROOMFUL OF WITNESSES

What happened to Leon is a dirty shame.

I never liked the guy. I'll admit that. I thought he was lower than a squirrel beneath a truck tire.

Bad blood between us? Maybe.

But no one can pin this thing on me. No way. I didn't do it—and I've got a roomful of witnesses.

You heard me right. A roomful of witnesses.

The day didn't start too bad. Yeah, I woke up in the staff bungalow with the same joy, aches and pains in all the usual places, and a wet, hacking cough to remind me I was down to my last pack of smokes.

What else is new?

The sheets on my cot were damp from night sweat. I stood up and stretched. No bones cracking or creaking. Hell, I'm only thirty-eight.

I know my hair is a little thin in front and my cheeks have crisscross lines in them. Charlene says I have old man's eyes. Well, what do you expect? No one ever built a haven for Wayne Mullet.

The top dresser drawer stuck again, and I tugged it so hard, I pulled something in my right shoulder. Groan. The Louisiana humidity doesn't agree with furniture, at least not the cheap, piney stuff they bought for our rooms.

I rubbed the soreness from my shoulder, coughed up something nasty and blew it out the window. Then I pulled on the uniform. Baggy, green cotton pants and lab coat, white rubber-soled shoes. Ha. They make the staff dress like doctors, which always gives me a chuckle.

Wayne, your momma would be so proud.

I crossed the back lawn to the kitchen. A promising day. Morning clouds shielding the sun, although the back of my neck was prickling by the time I reached the big house.

And what were those bugs? So many of them, swirling in such a tight circle, they formed a dark pillar reaching high above my head, and I'm six-three.

Leon Maloney is superstitious as all get-out. I hoped he didn't see this bug thing. He'd probably say it was an omen. Leon is always running on and on about omens. Sometimes I have to show him the back of my hand to make him stop.

He told me his momma had some kind of fortune-teller booth at the back of a saloon in the French Quarter, and she taught him everything you need to know about omens and bad luck. He says she never taught him *anything* about good luck.

Yeah, Leon can be a bitter dude. Why can't he just keep it to himself?

Okay. He's had some real bad luck. I mean last year, for example, one of the old guys pulled out Leon's left eye—and Leon was just trying to serve him some goddamn soup.

I had to slap a few bugs off my face as I pulled open the screen door and stepped into the kitchen. Some kinda swamp flies, I guess. Don't know how they got way out here in the woods.

Think maybe they *flew,* Wayne?

I like to give myself a hard time. Keeps me sharp, you know. But don't *you* try it. Yeah, you might say I'm a little touchy. Momma used to say I'd snap at a gator if I had more teeth.

Hey, I grew up on the bayous and I got swamp water in place of blood, and I saw a lot of things pulled up from the brown water a kid probably shouldn't see.

Well, why get started on that? Speaking of brown water, the coffee smelled good, and they had egg sandwiches this morning on toasted English muffins and the bacon wasn't burned as usual. So how bad could things be?

Leon was already finishing up. He raised his head from his grits bowl and flashed me a good-morning scowl.

Leon has long, wavy blond hair. He's into metal music and I've seen him go nuts on air guitar, making his hair fly around 'til he was red in the face. He says he could be an Allman brother if they'd let him in the family.

Some kinda joke, right? I never know with Leon. It's hard to read a guy with only one eye.

What a loser.

Dr. Nell made him promise to stop blasting his music in the staff dorm because it got the old folks all riled. Leon nodded his head and agreed, but I saw that twitch in his stubbly cheek that meant he was angry.

I wouldn't want to cross Leon. He's quiet and goes about his business taking care of the retired folks here. But once when he had a big knife and was slicing up the fruit salad for lunch, he told me he cut someone once, cut them pretty good, and didn't feel bad about it afterward.

He was holding the knife in front of him and had this weird smile on his face after he told me. And I think he meant it as some kind of warning or threat.

Leon and I had some run-ins back in the day when we were guests ourselves, guests of the Louisiana State prison system. That's when I learned to keep an eye on him. I mean, *two* eyes, ha ha.

Anyway, I finished breakfast, drained the coffee cup and crushed it in my hand. Leon had a stain on the front of his lab coat, but I wasn't gonna be the one to tell him about it. I followed him to the kitchen to start making the breakfast for our guests.

We got two hundred old guys living here, so that meant two hundred fruit smoothies just for starters. Leon and I are slicing and dicing the fruit and jamming it all into the smoothie machine. And I'm filling up glasses. We staff guys get paper cups, but the guests get *glass,* of course.

And Charlene Fowler comes in, all red lipstick and that bleach-blond hair glowing under the fluorescents, green eyes wrinkled into smiles. She's not in uniform. Instead, a magenta midriff top and white short shorts, with enough skin showing to let everyone see her flower tattoos.

She breathes on me and rubs one long, purple fingernail down my cheek, all flirty, or you might say slutty, like the two of us are something, only we're not.

I know she's banged Leon. More than once, I'm sure. But she's always coming on to me, too. Just to cause trouble and make things even more tense between us. I'll give her this. She's a sexy thing, especially for *this* place.

Leon told me to stay away from her once. But he didn't want to fight me. He said it kinda quiet and didn't look me in the eye.

We both know we gotta be careful. Dr. Nell always has her eye on us, and we want to keep these jobs.

Like I said, we both did time in the prison on the other side of the woods from here. Those stone walls poking up from the trees are a close reminder. We know we've got it good here at The Haven.

Charlene stays in my face. Her perfume smells like oranges. Or maybe it's the fruit I'm putting in the smoothies. "Did you forget everyone is leaving this morning?" she says, all breathy, like she's saying something dirty. "You two *boys* are on your own."

I shrug. My shoulder still aches from the dresser drawer. "We can handle it, Charlene."

Leon chuckles. You never know what's gonna strike him funny.

"Dr. Nell says don't forget Ida is still getting the antibiotics," Charlene says. "And no snack bars for Wally. He's put on some pounds. She says to keep your cells on. She'll check in from town."

Charlene gives us this devilish grin. It fits her face fine. "Guess Dr. Nell doesn't trust you *boys*."

Leon raises his eye from the bananas he's slicing. "*You* trust me, don't you, Char?"

"About as far as I can throw you."

"Why don't you stop rubbing your tits against him," Leon says, his voice suddenly as hard as hickory. "Come over here and give *me* some sugar."

Charlene sticks her head out, like she wants to get it chopped off, and the green eyes sparkle. "Why don't you *make* me?"

Leon doesn't give Charlene any warning. He grabs her by the neck, the way you'd choke a chicken, pulls her over to him and pushes his mouth against hers.

Charlene starts to struggle and spit.

And I don't think. I mean, I shoulda just stood there and let 'em work it out. Instead, I lose it. I grab Leon's arm, lower my shoulder and bump him away from her.

That surprised even me. What did that mean? That I wanted Charlene? Or I just wanted an excuse to fight Leon?

No time to think about it. Leon lets out a roar like some kind of swamp creature. He tackles me to the floor and, before I can catch my breath, we're wrestling and rolling around on all the fruit peelings and garbage.

He's sitting on top of me, doing a little jackhammer action with both fists to my ribs. Powerful for a little guy. I'm not surprised. And those bony hands hurt.

Luckily, Charlene is no shrimp. Somehow she manages to pull him off me and step between us. I'm on my back, massaging the ribs. Leon jumps to his feet like a cat ready to spring. But then I see his shoulders sag. He looks away.

And I know he's thinking what I'm thinking. We've gotta back off here and be cool. Our jobs ain't the greatest, but they're all we got.

I stand up and raise both hands. Like truce, man. Leon nods and backs up to the kitchen counter.

I turn and see this grin on Charlene's face, and her eyes are still sparkling, like excited. "Oh, my!" she says in a girlie voice. "Did I cause that?" She even giggles. "Was that really over *me?*"

"Just kidding around," I mutter.

"We were just waking ourselves up," Leon says, stretching.

"Do I have to tell Dr. Nell about this?" Charlene asks, teasing. "I sure hope you boys can be trusted on your own."

She doesn't wait for an answer. She's out the kitchen door. And about a minute later, I hear the staff Jeeps crunching down the gravel drive, which means Leon and I are all alone, in charge of two hundred residents.

We can work together. No biggie.

Most of the old folks here at the home are pretty nice and don't give us much grief. Ida is my favorite. Poor thing's been sick. Usually, she's as flirty as Charlene. The old thing likes to grab me by the ears, pull my head down and smooch me on the lips. But the last few days, she's been lying around moaning, acting pitiful as an old hound dog.

Leon and I brought out the smoothies on a tray and began passing them out around the front room. A couple old dudes were glued to the TV already. They sure love those cartoons, the louder the better.

I handed Frankie his glass. He raised his gnarly hands and signed, "Thank you."

I signed, "Your welcome. How are you today?"

His fingers moved slowly: "I feel a little old."

Leon makes fun of me for talking to the guests. But almost all of them can talk really well, and I don't see any reason not to chat with 'em a bit. They always like it.

Frankie taps my shoulder and signs, "Cookie? Cookie?"

I laugh and sign back, "Later." Frankie is one of the oldest guests and the least trouble. He used to work in some kind of science lab in Texas. His pal Frannie worked in the same lab.

Next up—our *least* favorite dudes. Sweeny and Bo. These two guys were in show business. Big deal, right?

But they act as if they own the place. Try to cross them and—well, that son of a bitch Sweeny bit me twice. Believe it?

They're nasty and bad-tempered and are always getting the other guests all riled. Talk about bad news. The only time their eyes light up is when they're causing trouble.

Leon and I each had one smoothie left on our trays. Sweeny's and Bo's hands shot out. They're grabby as weasels in a chicken shack. I started to hand Sweeny his drink— then pulled it back.

"Hey, Sweeny, watch this, dude," I said. I tilted the glass to my mouth and drank it down. I wiped juice off my mouth with the back of my hand. "Mmmmmm. That was good, man."

Leon laughed. "*We're* in charge today, guys," he said. "No one to give you bad boys a break. Boo hoo." He copied me, gulped Bo's smoothie down in front of the old guy, then licked his lips.

Sweeny and Bo looked at each other like they didn't believe it. Then Bo pointed at us and rubbed his two pointer fingers against each other.

Shame, shame. That's what that means when they rub their pointers back and forth.

"It's not your day," I told them. "Everyone went to town to celebrate a birthday. Know what that means? Leon and I get a little payback time."

Then Leon went too far. As usual.

He gave Bo a little slap across the face. Not a hard slap,

but it seemed to stun him. Leon laughed. "Think you haven't been asking for it?"

Again, I couldn't just stand there. I pulled his arm back. "Careful, Leon. Don't hurt 'em."

He snickered. "What are they gonna do about it?" Leon raised his hand and gave Sweeny a slap. It made a loud *smack,* and the old guy's head snapped back.

This wasn't good. Leon and I have been working here ever since we got out of the can. Six or seven months, taking care of these guys. So far, we'd done okay. I didn't like these dudes any more than Leon did. But why look for trouble now?

Leon gave Sweeny a slap on the cheek. "How's that feel, buddy?"

Sweeny lowered his head sadly and rubbed his fingers together. "Shame, shame."

Leon laughed and raised his hand to give Bo another face slap.

"Leon, you'd better not—" I started.

But I didn't get to finish my sentence cuz Bo grabbed Leon's arm up by the shoulder—and yanked him off his feet. I let out a cry as he whipped Leon over his head and sent him sailing into the wall.

Leon groaned as his body slammed hard into the wall. The whole house seemed to shake, and a stack of DVDs toppled off their shelf onto the floor.

Leon climbed up slowly, looking kind of green. And before he could catch his breath, Sweeny jumped off his bench, shot forward, and head-butted Leon in the gut. Leon went *ooof,* just like in the cartoons, and his face turned from green to blue. Breath knocked out, definitely.

These old chimpanzees weigh about 200 pounds. They're over five feet tall, you know. And adult chimps are several times stronger than humans.

They're big and ugly and dangerous, which is why people send them here to The Haven. They're only cute 'til they're six or so. Then they turn into big, hairy monsters.

I guess it was some lamebrain in Washington who had the idea to open a retirement home for chimpanzees back in the Louisiana woods. When we heard about it in the prison, we laughed at first. Then we started to get angry, thinking about these chimps living in luxury with their DVDs and wide-screen TVs, their playrooms, three meals a day served to them on trays in their puffy armchairs and five acres of woods to play in behind their house.

That made us angry when we looked around at what *we* had.

The ugly, old chimps were living high on the hog, all right. And every day, *we* got the slops.

Did Leon and I have a chip on our shoulders when we started working here? Like I said, we just needed jobs.

But now some bad feelings were out in the open, and we had to tie things up and push 'em all back. Like trying to get toothpaste back in the tube.

Leon was still kinda purple, wheezing and holding his chest. I had to deal with these monkeys.

I stepped forward, thinking hard, trying to look tough. But what looks tough to a monkey?

Bo glared at me, a big, toothy grin on his ugly face, waiting for me to make a move, I guess. Or planning his next one.

Behind us, the other chimps were going nuts. Leaping up and down, screeching and howling, heaving their smoothie glasses at each other. I saw Frankie—good old Frankie—crouch down and take a big dump on the living room floor. Guess he was upset.

Pretty soon, I knew the shit would be flying.

Holding his stomach, Leon pulled himself to a sitting position. He was moaning and groaning. You wouldn't like it either if a 200-pound monkey took a dive into your belly. "Wayne, we gotta get help," he choked out. "Can't let this get…out of control."

We had an agreement with the prison. It was in our rule book. Call 'em up in an emergency, and they'll send the guards running.

But I knew those dudes. Believe me, I knew them too well. They'd come shooting like it was the first day of deer season. I don't know about you, but I always think it's good to avoid a bloodbath before lunch, if you can.

"We can control 'em, Leon," I said. I started to tug him to his feet. He groaned again, rubbing his middle.

I had him standing up, teetering a little, when I saw Bo and Sweeny leap out the open window. One followed the other, and they didn't look back.

No, we don't have bars on the windows. Cuz this isn't a cage, remember? It's a haven. Besides, what chimp in his right mind would ever leave a cushy setup like this?

"Ohmigod! Ohmigod!" Leon kept slapping his forehead and staring at the window. "I'll kill 'em! I'll kill the both of 'em!"

Bad attitude. I was about to tell Leon that his bad attitude got us in this mess to begin with. For a moment, I couldn't decide whether to start packing my suitcase, or go after the two fugitives.

But I'm a hopeful kinda guy, and I really wanted to stick around. So I motioned for Leon to follow me. "We can bring 'em back. They're probably waiting for us in the garden."

Leon glanced all around crazily. I don't know what he was looking for. A weapon? Then he narrowed his eye like he was trying to focus on the situation in hand. And he followed me out the front door.

The screen door slammed behind us. Sounded like a gun going off, and I jumped. I took a breath and told myself to cool out because I had to be the thinking one.

The heat hit us like a tidal wave, and I felt the first trickle of sweat at the back of my neck. The air felt thick and steamy. "They ain't waiting in the garden," Leon said.

"There they go." I pointed just as the two chimps disappeared into a stand of red mangrove trees. Leon and I took off, jogging after them. We ran right through the whirring column of buzzing swamp flies and kept going.

I could hear the two chimps chittering to each other, all excited like. I knew that'd make it easy to follow them. One small break.

"Wait," Leon said, pulling back on my shoulder. "We need something."

"Like what?" I said.

He didn't answer. Ducked into the little, white garden shed. I heard him banging around in there. "Leon—they're getting away!" I shouted. "If we lose their trail…"

Leon came running out carrying a long-handled shovel in front of him, like a spear.

"What's that for?" I asked.

"Convincing them," Leon said.

I sighed. "We *have* to bring 'em back in good shape, Leon. No bruises or nothing. So Dr. Nell and the others can't tell anything went on."

"First, we've gotta bring 'em back," Leon said. He swung the shovel head to part the tall grass, and we stepped into the shade of the trees.

I couldn't see them, but I could hear Sweeny and Bo clucking to each other somewhere up ahead. Leon led the way over the snaky mangrove roots and through the tangles of tree trunks and low limbs.

I decided to try a simple approach. I called to them. "Hey, Sweeny! Bo! Come back here!" That didn't work. I shouted their names some more, but I could just as well have been shouting at the birds in the trees.

I swatted a fat mosquito off my forehead. Leon's face was

red, his blond hair was matted wetly to his head. He carried the shovel on one shoulder now, like a soldier marching to battle. The shovel head kept rattling low tree limbs, but he didn't seem to notice.

"They're heading to the ravine," he said. He spit angrily.

"That's bad," I replied. "They could get caught in the leaf bed." At the bottom of the ravine, the dead leaves from cedar elms are piled five or six feet high. It was just a natural pit, not man-made or anything. Even if it didn't bury them, it would make it almost impossible to pull the two big jerks out.

"Gotta catch 'em before they get stuck in there," I said. I ducked my head under a low vine, pushed between some palmetto palms tilting as if they were windblown, and started to trot faster.

Leon was breathing hard. I could see he was having trouble keeping up. Dude kept groaning and rubbing his sore belly as he tried to run.

We ran into a circle of cedar elms, a small clearing with tall grass in the middle. Three scrawny, brown rabbits high-tailed it over the grass in different directions. I stopped because I realized I didn't hear Sweeny and Bo anymore.

I listened. I could hear tree frogs all around in the high limbs. No chimp sounds. Did they already bury themselves in the ravine? Not too likely. It was still pretty far up ahead.

Leon leaned on the shovel, breathing hard. His shirt was stuck to his body, soaking wet. "Which way?" he muttered, wiping his forehead with his sleeve. He stared into the trees.

"Straight ahead maybe?" I said, pointing. I shook my head. "We came this far. We *can't* lose them. We just can't."

Sure, I sounded desperate, but I didn't care. I was thinking about consequences. Losing our jobs was one thing. But what if the big chimps escaped and got messing with people and hurt somebody or did some real damage? That could be major consequences for *me,* right?

I heard a low growl close behind me. And then a grunt.

I turned and saw two pairs of dark eyes, glowing in the shade of some cedar elms.

Another growl. Like a warning. Two lumbering figures stepped slowly into the clearing.

"It's them," I murmured. "Look, Leon. They made a circle and they're creeping up behind us."

The two chimps stepped forward, hunkered low, tall grass up to their knees. They pointed at us, snarling, pulling back their lips and showing us their big teeth.

I took a step back. Leon raised the shovel. But he took a step back, too.

"Sweeny! Bo! Let's go back!" I shouted.

They kept their teeth bared. They lumbered forward, one step at a time.

I felt a chill run down my spine. "Leon," I said softly, "see what's going down here? They're *stalking* us."

He tightened his grip on the shovel handle. He held it in front of him with both hands. His teeth were gritted. His cheeks were twitching.

I knew what Leon had in mind. Stand our ground and

fight it out with them. But that wasn't my idea. Try to fight two angry, 200-pound beasts? I'd give us better odds at wrestling a cottonmouth.

"Follow me, Leon," I said. "Let 'em chase us. Let 'em chase us right back to the house."

He squinted at me. "Huh?"

"Just keep backing up," I said. "Stay with me. Act like you're afraid. Start backing up. We can lead them right back to where we want them."

It sounds crazy but that's what we did. We backed over the grass and into the trees, retracing our steps. And the growling monkeys stalked us, keeping their distance, but coming slowly and steadily, letting us know this wasn't going to end in a friendly way.

My only question was: when were they going to make their jump at us? If they decided to take it to us before we reached the yard, Leon and I could be chimp meat in seconds.

So, Leon and I backed our way through the trees. I can't speak for Leon, but I'll confess I never was so scared in my life. If you could see the anger boiling off those monkeys' faces, you'd know why. And I can tell you how happy I was to see the house and the front yard come up behind us.

Almost there. "Now what?" Leon demanded. "How do we get 'em in the house?"

"I have an idea," I said. "Can you keep 'em busy?"

He spit on the grass. "You being funny?"

The chimps backed Leon toward the front wall of the house. He raised the shovel, holding it against him like a shield.

Through the window, I could hear the chimps inside, chittering and wailing and screeching and carrying on like holy hell.

Deal with that later, Wayne, I told myself. First get our two runaways safely inside. I thought I knew what might pull Sweeny and Bo in. Breakfast.

I ran down the hall past the front room. I ignored the screams and hollering of the rioting chimps. I knew Leon and me could get 'em soothed once we got in.

Into the kitchen. Still a mess from breakfast, of course. When did Leon and I have time to clean up? I fumbled in the fruit bin 'til I found what I wanted. I pulled two bananas from the bunch and, holding one in each hand, went running back to the front.

I held the bananas out the screen door. The chimps were closing in on Leon, bumping up and down on their haunches like movie chimps, ready to make their attack.

"Leon, get inside," I said. He slid along the wall till he came to the door, then practically dove into the house.

I held open the screen door with my hips and raised the bananas. "Come and get it, dudes. Breakfast. A special breakfast for my favorite buddies."

The chimps stopped hopping and stared at the bananas. Like they were actually thinking about what was the best thing to do.

"Come on…" I urged, waving the bananas at them. "Come on…please…please…"

"Is it working?" Leon called from behind me in the hall.

"Think so," I said.

"I'm gonna beat 'em to death when they get in here," Leon said. He clanged the shovel head on the floor.

"No, you're not," I said softly. "No more talk like that. I mean it, Leon. We're gonna keep our jobs. And we're going to forget this ever happened."

Leon stepped up beside me. "I don't believe in forgetting," he said.

I waved the bananas. The chimps finally took the bait. They stepped toward the door, reaching out their arms. I pulled back a step. The chimps followed. Back a step into the hall. Yes! Sweeny and Bo stepped in through the door. Yes!

Into the front room. The other chimps fell silent, as if stunned to see their pals again. Yes…yes… "Welcome back. Come on, boys. Here are your lovely bananas…."

Sweeny took his banana. He examined it like he'd never seen one before. Then he raised it high over his head—and with a real powerful thrust, jammed it deep into Leon's good eye.

Leon staggered back. His hands shot up to his face. He didn't make a sound at first. Then he began to howl like a swamp dog caught in a gator trap.

He dropped to his knees. He gripped the banana in both hands and pulled—and the eye came out with it.

I guess I froze or something. It was just so sick. I don't know if I could have done anything about it or not. But I didn't.

I just stood there with my mouth hanging open as Bo took the shovel, pulled way back on it and slammed the back of the blade into the side of Leon's head.

I heard a *crack* and saw Leon's neck snap back. Leon made a sound like a hiccup. Then red stuff started to pour out of the side of his face. Like what happens when you squeeze a tomato.

Leon folded up and dropped onto his side on the floor, all bent and twisted, blood puddling under his head. I knelt down beside him, shook him a bit, but it didn't take long to see he was dead.

Was I next?

Struggling to breathe, I jumped to my feet. Before I could back away, Bo handed me the shovel.

Oh, thank God! I thought. But I didn't have much time to feel relieved. Cuz the screen door flew open, and in came Charlene, followed by Dr. Nell and a bunch of other staff workers.

Charlene's eyes went to the floor and she saw Leon and all the blood and his messed-up face. Then she let out a scream that hurt my ears. "Oh, no. Oh, no. I had a *feeling* I shouldn't leave you two on your own!"

I saw what Dr. Nell was staring at. The bloodstained shovel in my hand.

"Now, wait," I said. "I didn't do it. Really. It wasn't me! I got a roomful of witnesses!"

I waved my hand around the room. I gestured to all the chimps that sat there watching the whole thing. "I didn't do it," I said. "I've got a roomful of witnesses."

The chimps stared at me.

"You guys can all talk," I said. "I know you can. Tell Dr. Nell what happened here."

The chimps stared at me. They didn't move. They didn't even blink.

I turned to Bo and Sweeny. "Tell 'em," I said. "Tell 'em the truth. Tell 'em who did this. Come on—*talk!*"

Bo and Sweeny lowered their eyes to the floor, like they were sad. Then they pointed their fingers at me, and began to rub their pointer fingers together, back and forth.

PHILLIP MARGOLIN

"The House on Pine Terrace" shows why every one of Phillip Margolin's books has hit the *New York Times* bestseller list. The story is an intricate puzzle—a crime that leads to a romance that triggers another crime that ends with a mystery, which makes you question every event in the story. Phillip's many interesting jobs over the years—a teacher in the Bronx, Peace Corps volunteer in Liberia, criminal defense attorney—have clearly provided remarkable insight into how ordinary people react to extraordinary circumstances. This is no more evident than in "The House on Pine Terrace," where every character seems to do the unexpected and yet it all makes perfect sense in the end.

THE HOUSE ON PINE TERRACE

There was an intercom attached to the ice-white wall and I used it to call up to the house on Pine Terrace. The voice that answered was the voice on the phone. He sounded just as pleasant now as he had then. Not uptight like I expected a john to be. While we were talking, I heard an electronic hum and the iron gate swung inward. We broke off and I drove my Ford along a winding drive past stands of palm trees. The house was at the end of the drive.

My father left my mother when I was too young to remember him. From a remark here and a remark there, I've figured out that it was no big loss. I do remember that we were always dirt poor. Mama was part of a crew that cleaned houses. You don't get rich doing that, but you do get to see how the other half lives. A few times, when she couldn't get anyone to watch me, she risked getting fired by bringing me with her. The only place she brought me that I remember clearly was the house on Pine Terrace.

When I was little, Mama called me princess. She said someday I would marry a prince and live in a castle and be rich. I've never been married, I'm working on rich and this is the castle I'd live in if I had my way. I dreamed about this house. Fantasized about it when I was alone and feeling lazy. Wished for it when I was younger and really believed I could do anything.

The house was so white the rays of the sun reflected off it. It was long, low, modern and perched on a cliff with a view of the Pacific that was so breathtaking you'd never get tired of it. There was a Rolls-Royce Silver Cloud parked near the front door. Farther down the drive was a sports car so expensive that someone in my tax bracket couldn't even identify it. I looked at my Ford, thought about the small, singles apartment I lived in and suddenly felt like a visitor from another planet.

What I saw when the front door opened confused me. Daniel Emery III was one of the handsomest men I'd ever seen. He was six-one or –two, broad-shouldered and tanned a warm, brown color that made you think of tropical beaches. He wore a yellow cashmere V-necked sweater and tight white jeans. There were no gold chains, diamond pinky rings or the other swinger jewelry turnoffs. He was, in other words, the male equivalent of his dream house and I wondered what in the world a guy like this with a place like this wanted with a call girl.

"You're Tanya?" he asked, using the phony name I'd given when he phoned in response to the ad in *Swinger's Weekly.*

"And you must be Dan," I answered, pitching my voice low and sexy.

He nodded as he gave me the once-over. I was sure he would like what he saw. His smile confirmed my belief.

"You certainly fit your description in the ad."

"You're surprised?"

"A little. I figured there'd be a bit of puffing."

I smiled to show him that I appreciated the compliment.

"Can I get you a drink?" he asked.

"No, thanks," I said, starting to hate what I was going to do. "And we should get the business part out of the way so it won't interfere with your pleasure."

"Sure, the money," Dan said. "One thousand in cash, you said. I've got it here."

He handed me an envelope and I thumbed through the ten crisp hundred-dollar bills inside it.

"One more thing," I said. "What do you expect for this?"

He looked puzzled. "Sex."

"What kind of sex? Do you want straight sex or head? Anything kinky?"

"I thought you said you'd do anything I wanted and would stay the night for a thou."

He was starting to look worried.

"That's right. And you understand there's no rough stuff."

"That's not my style. Now, have we got the business out of the way?"

"Unfortunately, no," I said, flashing my badge. I could hear the trunk of the Ford open as my partner, Jack Gripper, got out. "I'm a policewoman, Mr. Emery, and you're under arrest for prostitution."

What a waste, I remember thinking. I meet the guy of my dreams, who lives in the house of my dreams, and instead of balling him, I bust him. Life can sure be cruel. Then, he phoned.

"Officer Esteban?" he asked, sounding just as pleasant as he'd been during the ride to the station house.

"Yes."

"This is Dan Emery. You arrested me for prostitution three weeks ago."

"Oh, yes. I remember."

"I didn't bother getting a lawyer. You had me dead to rights. I just faced the music and pled guilty about twenty minutes ago."

"Good for you. I hope the judge wasn't too tough."

"The fine wasn't much, but the process was pretty humiliating."

"Hopefully, it won't happen again."

"That's for sure. So, the reason I called. Actually, I wanted to call you before, but I thought I should wait until my case was over. Otherwise, I was afraid it would sound like a bribe."

"What would?"

"My dinner invitation."

Five years as a cop had taught me how to stay cool in the tensest situations but I was completely flummoxed.

"I don't know…" I started.

"Look, you're probably thinking I'm some kind of weirdo, what with answering that kinky ad and all. But, really, I'm not like that. I did it as a lark. Honest. I haven't been with a prostitute since college and I've never had a call girl. I don't even subscribe to that paper. I picked it up at my barber while I was waiting for a haircut. It just seemed like fun. Really, I'm very embarrassed about the whole thing. And I have been punished. You have no idea what it's like for a guy to admit he had to pay for sex in a courtroom packed with giggling people."

I laughed.

"Good," he said, "I've got you laughing. Now, if I can just get you to go out with me I'll be batting a thousand. What do you say?"

I said yes of course, and dinner was everything I'd hoped it would be even if the restaurant was elegant enough to make me feel a little uncomfortable and I didn't recognize half the dishes on the menu. Dan turned out to be a perfect gentleman with a sense of humor and none of that macho bullshit that I'm used to from the cops I've dated. The only thing that bothered me that first night—and I say bothered, only because I needed a word here, not because I really gave it any thought then—was his reluctance to talk about himself. He was an artist at steering the conversation back to me whenever I'd try to find out a little about him. But I was so used to guys who only wanted to talk about themselves that it was actually a bit of a relief.

I didn't sleep with Dan after our first date or our second. I didn't want him thinking I was an easy lay. The third time we dated he invited me to his house instead of going to a restaurant and he cooked a dinner to die for. We ate on the flagstone patio. The air felt like silk, the view was spectacular and not having sex with him seemed downright silly.

The next two months were like a fairy tale. We couldn't keep our hands off each other and I missed him every minute we were apart. Sergeant Groves couldn't figure out why I was being so nice to him. He knew how upset I'd been when he took me out of narcotics and put me into the call-girl sting operation. I'd yelled sex discrimination and he asked me who else he could use as a call girl. The whole thing was supposed to be temporary, anyway.

During those two intense months I learned a little bit more about Dan, and everything I learned made me like him more. Dan was an orphan, whose parents had died in a car crash on vacation in the south of France during his sophomore year at USC. He'd been living in an apartment on his own and continued to stay there until he graduated, even though he'd inherited the house on Pine Terrace. Dan told me that he'd been very close to his parents and the house contained too many memories. It had taken a while before he could stay there without being overcome with sadness.

The family lawyer had provided Dan with advice and an allowance until he turned twenty-one and was allowed to control his inheritance. Even though he was rich enough so he didn't have to work, he was employed as a stockbroker at a small, exclusive brokerage house run by an old college friend. At one point, he confided that he was doing well enough at work to keep up his lifestyle without having to tap into his inheritance.

I didn't go out of my way to tell anyone about Dan but it's hard to keep secrets from your partner.

"The john?" Jack Gripper said, unable to keep the surprise out of his voice.

"Yeah," I answered sheepishly.

"It's the house, isn't it?"

We'd passed the house once on the way to interview a witness and I'd told Jack how I'd been in it as a kid and how it was my dream house. After arresting Dan, he'd asked me if the house was the one I'd told him about and I'd said it was.

"Geez, Jack, why don't you just come right out and call me a gold digger?"

"Hey, I'm not casting any stones."

Gripper really is nonjudgmental. I guess that comes from being a cop for so many years and seeing as much of life as he has. After our brief discussion about Dan and me, he never brought up the subject again, and I didn't, either.

★ ★ ★

We were in bed when Dan first told me he loved me. I hadn't pushed it. Just being with Dan was enough. I've always kept my expectations low. Like I said, I'd grown up poor and I'd fought for everything I had. My apartment was the nicest place I'd ever lived in. Most of the guys I'd dated hadn't lived much better. I was starting to build a nest egg, but I could have done what I was doing for the rest of my life and never put away enough to live like Dan.

I don't want you to think his money was everything, but money is always important if you grow up without it. I want to think I was in love, but I'm not sure I know what love is. I never saw it in my mother's relationship with the occasional man she brought home. Working the streets, I've seen enough women with split lips and enough men with stab wounds to know that love isn't what it's cracked up to be. I've never seen shooting stars or heard bells ring with anyone I dated. Not even with Dan. But, he did feel comfortable and he was sure good in the sack and I guess I felt as close to him as I've ever felt to anyone.

When he said, "There's something we have to talk about," my first thought was he was going to call it off.

"So talk," I said, trying to make it sound like a joke.

The full moon hanging over the ocean made seeing in the dark easy enough. Dan rolled over on his side. He looked troubled.

"We've been together, what? Two months?"

"Sixty-one days, twenty hours, three minutes and one

arrest," I answered, still trying to keep things light. "But who's counting."

Dan smiled, but it was only for a second. Then he looked sad.

"My little flatfoot." He sighed.

"What's wrong?"

"I love you, but I don't know if I can trust you."

That got my attention and I sat up.

"What do you mean, you can't trust me?" I snapped, hurt and a little angry.

"How much of a cop are you, Monica? And how much do I mean to you?"

I thought about that. More the second part of the question, than the first. He'd just told me he loved me. What was he leading up to? I thought about living here, driving the Rolls, wearing clothes like the clothes I saw on movie stars.

"I love you, too, Dan. And I'm not so much of a cop that you can't trust me with anything."

"That's what I hoped you'd say. Look, I'll level with you. Dating a cop was as much a kick at first as dialing a call girl. I'm not sure there wasn't even a little bit of a revenge motive in it. You know, getting you in bed after you'd arrested and embarrassed me."

I started to say something, but he held up his hand.

"No. Let me get this out. It's not easy for me. That's how it started, but that's not the way it is now. When I said I love you I meant it, but I'm not sure you'll want to stay with me when you hear what I have to say.

"You like this house and the cars and my lifestyle, don't you?"

"That's not why I've been seeing you," I answered defensively.

"I didn't say it was. Aren't you curious about how I can afford to keep them up?"

"You told me that you're doing well at work, and about your inheritance. Besides, it's none of my business."

"You really don't have any idea of how much it costs to live like I do, do you?"

"Where is this going?" I asked, suddenly growing a little concerned.

"If you learned something bad about me, that I was doing... That I was dishonest. What would happen?"

"To us?" I answered, confused.

"As a cop. Would you turn me in?"

I looked at him and I thought about us. Like I said, I wasn't sure I loved him, but I liked him enough to know my answer.

"I don't turn in my friends."

"Then I'll say what I have to say and you can decide what you want to do. I haven't been completely honest with you about my financial situation." Dan looked embarrassed, a look I had never seen before. Not even when I'd busted him. "I always thought my parents were loaded, and I assumed I'd inherit what they had, so I never really applied myself in school. I'm pretty bright—I've got a good IQ—but college was one big party and I graduated without many practical skills.

"Soon after my parents died I had a rude awakening. This house, a vacation home, a trust fund and some stocks were all I got. It wasn't peanuts but I learned that they weren't as well-off as I'd thought.

"It never occurred to me that I'd have to pay property taxes, the upkeep on a house like this and all the other expenses parents worry about but don't discuss with their children. The lawyer who probated the estate taught me the financial facts of life. I held out for a while, but eventually I had to sell the vacation home. Then I used up my trust fund and sold off a lot of my stocks to keep up this life-style. Like I said, I have no marketable skills."

"What about the brokerage?" I asked.

"Oh, that's real, and I am doing okay, but what I earn just about covers the property taxes and expenses for a place like this."

"Why don't you sell it?"

Dan looked me in the eye. "Would you? If you had a house like this, wouldn't you do whatever you had to do to keep it?"

I didn't say anything. What could I say? I knew I'd kill to keep this house if it were ever mine. Dan smiled sadly. He reached up and touched my cheek. The heat of his hand felt so good that I missed it when he took it away.

"I knew you'd understand. That's why I love you. We're so different, but we're the same in the ways that count."

"If you don't make enough to afford…everything, and you didn't inherit enough to keep it…?" I asked.

Dan broke eye contact. "There's no way to sugarcoat this, Monica. I've been dealing."

"Narcotics?" I said, stunned. He nodded.

"Cocaine, mostly. No heroin. I wouldn't do that. Some marijuana. I'm careful. I sell to select customers, friends mostly, some of my clients. It's actually the only thing I've ever done well on my own."

I got out of bed and walked to the window. I didn't know what to say.

"Why are you telling me this?" I asked. "Do you have any idea of the spot you've put me in?"

"I do appreciate the moral dilemma I've created for you, but it's not going to be a problem anymore. I love you and I knew I couldn't keep seeing you if I didn't come clean about this. I respect what you do, being a cop. I don't ever want to compromise you."

I turned back toward the bed. "Well, you have. I should bust you after what you've confessed to me."

"You don't have to, Monica. I told you so there wouldn't be any secrets between us, and the reason I'm telling you now is that it's all going to stop. I had to make a choice between you and dealing, and it wasn't even close. But I didn't know how you'd feel about that. If you'd still want to stay with me."

"Why should I object if you stop selling dope?"

"You don't understand. If I stop dealing, *this*," he said, waving his hand around the room, "is all going to end—the house and the cars and the restaurants and…everything."

"What do you mean?"

"What I said. Without the cocaine, I can't afford the life-style and there won't be any more cocaine."

"Because of me?"

"That's the biggest part of it, but there's also a practical reason. If I was religious I'd see the hand of God at work." Dan smiled. "I knew I loved you soon after we met and I knew I'd have to stop dealing if I wanted to keep you, but I didn't know how I was going to get out of the life. The people I worked for are very dangerous. I was afraid of what they'd do if I told them I wasn't going to deal for them anymore and they found out I was dating a cop, and they would have found out. These guys are very connected. I... Well, I worried—really worried—that they might hurt you, or threaten to hurt you if I told them I was going to quit."

"Jesus, Dan," I said, really worried because I knew what he said was true. There are dealers that wouldn't think twice about killing a cop.

"Its okay, Monica. You don't have to worry." He laughed. "Talk about your acts of God." He smiled. "The week before we met, my connection was busted. Then, right after you arrested me, the DEA arrested the head of the cartel he worked for."

"Who was he?"

"Alberto Perez." I'd heard about the bust. Perez was big. "They got him in Miami with millions of dollars worth of coke and they got most of his organization, too. It's *finito.*"

"Your connection didn't sell you out?"

"I worried about that a lot. When we started dating, I was waiting for the other shoe to drop. But it didn't, and I think I know why. I'm small potatoes. The feds aren't going to waste time on someone who deals at my level. You know that. Besides, I'd sold all my product. I was supposed to get some more from the shipment they confiscated. So, I'm clean. There'd be no hard evidence I was a dealer, even if they wanted me. It's been two months now. More since my connection was arrested. So, I'm guessing I'm safe."

I turned back to the ocean but I didn't see it. I was thinking too hard about how much I trusted Dan and what I was willing to do to keep him.

"So, what will you do?" I asked to stall for time.

"I'll have to sell most of what I have. I can get a bundle for the house. The cars will have to go. I sat down with my accountant. I'll be in good shape if I watch my money. But the life you've seen me lead, that's over."

The house! I couldn't bear it. To be this close to living the life I'd dreamed of living for so many years, and then to have it snatched away. Dan was talking but I wasn't listening. I was upset, but there's this thing about me. I can wall off my emotions when I need to make a serious decision. It comes in handy as a cop and it was coming in handy now. I had a good idea of how I could save the house, but I wanted to think before I said anything to Dan. There was too much at stake. So I got back in bed and I wrapped my arms around him and kissed him.

"I love you, Dan," I said. "I want to be with you. You'll

be okay. We'll be okay. We'll be working stiffs. That's not so bad. I've been one all my life. You'll see. We'll be fine."

Dan rested his head on my shoulder. "You don't know what this means to me. I was so worried you'd leave me when you found out how big a phony I am."

"You're not a phony. You just got hooked on this lifestyle the way your customers got hooked on coke. And it's not like you'll have to go cold turkey. We're going to do fine once you sell this stuff.

"And it is only stuff," I said, but I didn't mean that.

I was still working the call-girl sting and busting johns kept me away from Dan for a week. I didn't like the work. To tell the truth, it made me feel sleazy. Most of the poor bastards we arrested had never been in trouble with the law before. They looked so pathetic when I flashed my badge. I guess it was the futility of it all that got me. We were never going to stamp out prostitution. It was the world's oldest profession for a reason.

I felt the same way about drugs. People were always going to want something to make them feel better, even if it was only for a little while, and they were going to buy coke or a hooker even if it was illegal. I thought they should legalize drugs and prostitution and let us concentrate on murderers, con men and armed robbers, but no one in the state legislature cared what I thought, so I spent most of the week after Dan told me about his problem dressed like a high-priced tart.

I spent the other part checking up on Dan. I cared for him, but I'm not naive. He'd lied to me about dealing and I wanted to know if he'd lied about anything else. I used the usual Internet sources to find out what was on the Web. He was quite the socialite and the history he'd given me checked out. Then I ran a check on the house, his cars and everything else he had ever owned. Everything he'd told me checked out there, too. Finally, I used my computer to tap in to federal and state law enforcement files that are only available to cops. All I found was a DUI from his sophomore year in college that was resolved when Dan went into a diversion program. All in all, I was satisfied that Dan was being straight with me, so I set up a meeting with some people I know.

I told Dan my idea after dinner at an inexpensive Mexican restaurant in my neighborhood. Dan joked that I was trying to break him into our new life, but I really liked the place and I liked being able to wear jeans to dinner and not having to worry about not knowing what the dishes on the menu were.

I kept the conversation at dinner about police work, telling Dan war stories about some of the weird things cops encounter on the job, and I waited until we were back at the house on Pine Terrace before I told him what I'd been doing.

"How's everything going?" I asked.

"How's what going?"

"You know, selling the house, the Rolls?"

He looked sad. "I've talked with a few Realtors to get an idea of what it will bring. The Rolls and the Lamborghini will go next week."

"Maybe not," I said.

"What do you mean?"

I felt as if I was standing on a ledge about to jump. I had no idea how Dan would react to what I was going to propose or whether we'd still be together after I had my say.

"There may be a way to save the house and everything else."

"I'm not following you."

"I might be able to put you in touch with someone."

"I'm still not following you."

"You're not the only one with secrets," I said nervously. "I've been doing a few things I shouldn't, too."

Dan stared at me openmouthed. "You don't mean…?"

"I'm not gonna be a cop all my life. I've seen how cops live and what cops make. I want to be someone, Dan. I was working narcotics until we started this call-girl sting. About a year ago I was involved in a big bust. Peter Pride."

"You were in on that?"

I nodded.

"Pride walked."

"Yes, he did. Want to know why?"

Dan didn't say anything.

"Key evidence disappeared and I started a Swiss bank account. Nothing huge, but something for my old age."

"Didn't some cop get busted for that? I thought I read…"

I nodded. "That was the one part I didn't like. Bobby Marino. I had nothing to do with that. Pride hated him and he set him up. It doesn't matter now and there's nothing I can do about it. But, I can fix you up with Pride. What do you say?"

Dan's tongue flicked out and he wet his lips.

"I don't know. These guys I was dealing with… They were bad but Pride's a killer."

"They're all killers, Dan, but Pride's a killer who pays well. I've been tipping him off for a year now. He likes me. You need this," I said, waving my hand at the view, "and I need you. What do you say?"

"Let me think. Pride is a whole new ball game."

Dan called me a week later and we met for lunch. While we waited for the waitress to bring our order he held my hand.

"I've been thinking about Pride and I'll do it."

"Oh, Dan," I said, because it's all I could think to say. He smiled and tightened his grip and I squeezed back. I was that happy.

"One thing, though," he said.

"What's that?"

"From now on, you're out."

I started to protest, but he cut me off.

"I mean it. I didn't like getting arrested, even for a misdemeanor like prostitution. I don't even want to think what would happen if they arrested a cop for what you're doing."

"I'm a big girl, Dan."

"I've never doubted that, but I'm sticking to my guns. From now on, I'm the one taking the risks or the house goes on the market, as planned."

Sergei Kariakin was Russian Mafia, which meant he didn't just kill babies for fun, he ate them, too. The only place he was called Sergei or Kariakin was on his rap sheet where his name was followed by "aka Peter Pride." Sergei loved America, which he called "the land of criminal opportunity," and he had adopted an alias he thought sounded like the name of a movie or rock star. The fact that he was as ugly as his crimes and couldn't carry a tune didn't faze him and no one dared point out these problems.

Normally, there were several firewalls between Peter and the narcotics and sex slaves that were his bread and butter, but he'd made a mistake two years ago and had faced certain conviction until the key evidence in his case disappeared from the police evidence locker. I had a gambling problem back then and someone had told Peter's lawyer about it. One evening, a very polite gentleman who never gave me his name made me a proposition. Within a week, my gambling debt had been retired and Peter's problem had been solved. I stopped gambling cold turkey, but I stayed on Peter's payroll, dropping timely tips about raids and snitches when I could get away with it.

My meeting with Pride took place in the dead of night in a deserted industrial park. Neither of us could afford to be seen socializing with the other. At first, Peter was reluctant to bring Dan into his organization. Even if he hadn't been picked up after Alberto Perez was arrested, Pride worried that Dan was on the DEA's radar screen. I told him I'd poked around and, as far as I could tell, the DEA didn't know Dan existed. I pitched Dan's upper-class clientele and the opportunity it presented to Pride to broaden his market.

A week later, Dan and I met Peter in an abandoned warehouse at three in the morning. The meeting ended with Peter agreeing to front Dan a kilo of cocaine. If everything went well, there was a promise of more to follow. I was so pumped up on the way back to Pine Terrace that I didn't feel the effects of being up for more than twenty-four hours. As soon as we were inside the house I started ripping off Dan's clothing. I don't even remember how we got from the entryway to the bedroom.

The next afternoon, I was so beat I had trouble keeping my eyes open. I staggered into police headquarters and found a note asking me to see Sergeant Groves. Groves was a handsome black man with a trim mustache and a serious demeanor. It was rare for him to lighten up and he looked even more tense than usual when I walked into his office and found him sitting with Jack Gripper and a man and a woman I didn't recognize.

"Shut the door, Monica," Groves ordered. I did and he motioned me into the only available seat.

"You're in deep shit," he said.

There was a DVD player on Groves's desk. He hit the

play button and I heard myself telling Dan how I'd helped Peter Pride beat his case. My heart seized up. The conversation had taken place in the bedroom of the house on Pine Terrace. I wanted to ask how they'd recorded it, but I was too frightened to speak.

"That confession will send you away," Groves said.

My throat was as dry as the Sahara. I knew I shouldn't say anything without a lawyer, but I still asked, "What do you want?"

"Pride," answered the woman.

I was in shock, but part of my brain was running through my alternatives.

"You can't use that tape. You'd have to have bugged the house."

"We can use it if we planted the bug with the permission of the owner," she said, and I felt myself die a little.

Dan had been arrested the day after his connection was busted. Jack Gripper had been in on the arrest and he remembered what I'd told him about the house. Bobby Marino had gone down for stealing the evidence in Pride's case, but I became a suspect when a snitch in Pride's organization told the police that he'd heard a woman took the evidence. One of the tips I'd given Pride had been a setup. Sergeant Groves had given the location and time of the raid only to me. When there was no one at the house that was raided they knew I was guilty, Gripper and I were switched to the call-girl sting and Dan was told to give me a call. Nature took its course after that.

When I found out that Dan had betrayed me I went from shock to anger to bitterness. I saw him once more after my arrest when we were preparing for the setup that eventually put Peter Pride away. He told me he was sorry and really did love me, but he'd had no choice. I don't believe he loved me, but, even if he did, I knew he'd forget about me when the next woman came along; someone who wasn't serving the sentence that would keep me in prison for at least seven years.

There is no view from the cell I share with Sheila Crosby, a 42-year-old embezzler, but I can still see the view from Dan's bedroom when I close my eyes.

Sometimes I imagine that I walk out of prison and Dan is waiting for me in the Rolls. We ride to the house on Pine Terrace and I take a shower to wash away the jailhouse stench. After the shower, we make love. When Dan is asleep, I walk out onto the patio and watch the approach of a storm that's been brewing in the Pacific. It's a magnificent storm, and when it passes, I am as untroubled and serene as the Pacific after that storm. And I am married to my prince, and I am rich, and I live in a castle on Pine Terrace.

MARCUS SAKEY

On his Web site Marcus Sakey gives us a glimpse into his creative mind when he says, "I love traveling, especially if there's a chance of hurting myself. I'm a wicked good cook. I never miss the Golden Gloves. I like bourbon neat, food so spicy the guy sitting next to me catches fire, and the occasional cigar." In very few lines he's given us a clear picture of himself, a skill he applies to his own characters. By the time you've finished reading "The Desert Here and the Desert Far Away," two army buddies, Cooper and Nick, will seem to live and breathe even though you've only known them for a few pages. The characters and their shared history drive this story relentlessly toward an ending that is as surprising as it is inevitable.

THE DESERT HERE AND THE
DESERT FAR AWAY

The Stones are on the stereo and you are wondering what you're doing here, in this dingy Las Vegas bar, with a man you last saw wearing combat BDUs half a world away. Cooper has his head in his hands as he says he can't believe how fucked he is. "A mistake, man. That's all."

You dip a chicken wing in ranch and strip the flesh from it. Cooper makes a hysterical little sound. "Vance is going to kill me. He wants to make an example."

And you laugh, because it sounds funny, something out of a movie, not something people really say to each other. Cooper gets that look, a half sneer, like an older brother about to pound you, only you never had an older brother, just Cooper. "I'm serious."

"Okay," you say, and dump the chicken bone.

"Nick," he says, and puts his palms together like he's praying, and for a second you're back in the front room of a shitty cinder-block apartment, watching Cooper make the same gesture at you over a bloodstained body. "Nick, Nick, Nick, Nickie. I need you, brother."

And you sip your beer and listen to Mick Jagger tell you that ti-iiime is on your side, and think about the best night of your life.

There is the smell of popcorn and nachos, the growl of hundreds of people talking and betting and shouting. The meaty thump of boxers warming up with their trainers, one-two-back, fists quick and feet flickering. A ring girl, five feet nine inches of toned grace in tight jeans and a black bodice chatting up the muscled soldiers at the army booth. This is the Golden Gloves, and tonight is the finals, and you are fighting next.

You stand beside the ring, legs moving like a jogger at an intersection, gloves up, savoring the good looseness of your muscles. There is fear, but you picture a tiny basement room with a bare bulb dangling, and shove your fear in and lock the heavy oak door. From the front row, your girlfriend cheers as you slip between the ropes.

Your opponent has tattoos around both biceps and two inches of extra reach. You saw him last year, and he is good. For a moment your fear bangs on the door, the hinges straining and frame rattling.

You dance the first round. Land a jab, then a hook, then

take one coming out, sudden stars and black spots. The crowd roar is static singing loud as the adrenaline in your blood. When the round is over, you spit water into a bucket, and it comes out pink.

The second goes badly, and a split appears in the center of that door. Your trainer rubs your shoulders, tells you it's not over yet. You just have to believe.

The third and final round, your opponent comes out mean. His eyes look through you. You block one punch, juke out of another. Your shoulders scream and your body has that hot trembly feeling of failing muscles. You throw a jab, but he bats it away and steps forward, winding up a swing that will knock you back to grade school.

But you remember what your trainer said, and you think of her in the front row, and instead of dodging, you step forward with a left hook to the belly that steals his wind. He pauses, just for a moment, but it's enough. You cock your right and let yourself believe.

Then the other guy is on the ground, and though he gets up quick, the ref counts him standing, and stares into his eyes, and then shakes his head. The bell rings and the fight is yours and the crowd goes crazy, and finally you can hear it not as static but as hundreds of voices yelling in joy for you, surrounding you, making you part of something, and a rep from Pipefitters Local 597 hands you a trophy, and the photographer shoots a picture, the flash bright even under the lights, you with one arm up and the trophy in your other hand and your girlfriend in the background, long brown hair flying as she runs to the ring.

You have never felt this good before. It's unbearable to think that this will fade, leave you nothing but a cheap trophy and a job at the Shell station, and so you walk over to the recruiting tent, where the soldiers slap your shoulders and call you a man and say it was a hell of a fight, and that they need men like you, guys who believe and won't quit.

And you sign up.

You PT until you puke. You hurry up and wait. You learn close infantry tactics and Arabic phrases and the name of every component of your weapon. You watch war movies you've already seen a hundred times. But this time is different. You're part of something. A soldier, a lean, mean killing machine ready to kick ass for your country.

A group of you go for tattoos. Crossed rifles and slogans and death's heads. You can't decide, think of backing out. A tall, funny kid named Cooper puts his arm around your shoulders, says, "Come on, buddy. Don't let us down."

You get an American flag on your bicep. Later, looking in the mirror, you flex arms grown thick with muscle, and the flag seems to wave, and you feel a surge in your chest, a soft fluttery feeling like a girl's fingers brushing your skin.

"So how much do you owe this Vance guy?"

Cooper shrugs. "Ten grand."

You blow a breath. "I don't have that much."

"Wouldn't matter if you did." He shakes his head. "I heard through a friend, Vance is sending a guy to waste me. Wants to show that even a soldier isn't exempt."

"Can your buddy help?"

"He's just a friend, not a buddy."

"What about the guy who's coming after you?"

"I've never met him. But he's got a bad reputation."

You lean forward, put your boots on the bar rail. You wear jeans and a T-shirt these days, but the boots are a hard habit to quit. The thing, the army, it gets into you. It's designed to, to teach you to walk and talk and shit the army way, to break you down and make you part of a larger whole. That was what you liked about it.

You say, "Maybe you should get out of town."

Cooper stares at you. "Hey, Nick," he says, softly, "fuck you."

And the heat rises in your cheeks as you remember Cooper behind the M240 Bravo, fingers pulsing in tight clenches that rip the air with explosions. Fighting for his country, shouting and firing as you stand next to him, readying the next ammo belt and trying not to panic. Your first firefight is nothing like you expected, not like the movies you'd watched or video games you'd played. You don't feel like a lean, mean killing machine, not even a little bit. There is a flash, and then a rocket hits the vehicle ahead, knocking it sideways in a wave of flame. You point to where the man had fired, and Cooper swings the machine gun, the bullets tearing chunks from walls and kicking up dust.

When it's over, you walked through the humming distance of things, amidst rubble and trash and thousands of spent shell casings. The forward vehicle survived, but the rocket killed two soldiers immediately, and though the ringing in your ears muffles sound, it's not enough to shut out the screams of a third whose belly was opened.

And the funny thing is that it's in the aftermath that the fear really hits, as you realize that it was just chance that their vehicle was in front; not strategy or fate or a plan, just chance, a matter of which driver had pulled out first. That the difference between life and death was measured in feet and in seconds. Fear burst the door of its basement cage and seized you and didn't let go, not then and not since.

"Sorry," you say, and don't explain what for, and don't have to. The two of you sit in silence. When the door bangs open, you jump, and even though it's been six months, reach for a weapon that isn't there. It only takes a second to come back to the bar, but when you do, you see that Cooper jumped, too.

He gives you a sheepish grin, spreads his hands. "It's funny," he says. "People ask what it was like. And I can't remember. Not really. Too big, too much. After a while, it started to feel like nothing. Beyond computation."

You sip your beer, and nod.

"The guy Vance is sending," Cooper says, "they say he cuts your ears off first." He looks at you, and in the neon light of the bar, you can see fear twist in his eyes like a trash bag in a dark ocean current.

"That's not going to happen," you say.

The M1126 Stryker is twenty-three feet long by nine wide and features an eight-by-eight suspension, tires that can adjust pressure on the fly and roll for miles after being blown, and a 350 HP Caterpillar engine capable of driving the seventeen-ton vehicle at speeds of sixty miles per. It looks like an olive drab duck with too many legs, and the inside smells of the sweat and farts of eleven men.

It is the most beautiful thing you have ever seen.

You are the assistant gunner for the rear weapons team. You wanted to be the primary, even though you're not sure you have what it takes to pull the trigger on a living, breathing person. Still, at the zeroing range you nailed more targets than anybody, figured you had it in the bag. But the sergeant picked Cooper as the primary. You saw the two of them talking, Coop gesturing at you, and he says that he was telling the sarge you should be gunner.

But walking around the Stryker that will be yours, the one you will share with ten other men, the one in which you will serve your country, it doesn't matter. You run your hands gently along the armor.

"Would you look at that?" Cooper stands in the doorway. He nudges the soldier next to him. "I think we got ourselves a true believer." He smiles to let you know he's just busting balls. "Hey, you sure it's your arm got the flag tattooed on it?"

★ ★ ★

After you leave Cooper in the bar, you drive for a while, watching the sun set the sky on fire. It's that hour when the shadows are soft and everything is lit from within. Tourists wander the Strip holding three-foot souvenir glasses. People in business suits talk on cell phones. A cute girl steps out of Whole Foods carrying bags stuffed with free-range macrobiotic whatever. Everyone is happy, on vacation or on their way home.

For a second, you want more than anything to turn the wheel of the Bronco hard and jam on the gas and blast right through the bright front window of the grocery store.

You clench and unclench your fists, take deep breaths. A car behind you honks, and you move along.

From the corner market you get a cheesesteak and a six-pack. You go to the room you rent and turn on the TV and eat dinner sitting at your counter, the news you aren't watching running in the background.

You think about what Cooper said, how life over there had been too big to grasp, to hold. You remember a conversation with a soldier who was re-upping, how when he talked about getting back to Iraq, he slipped and called it home.

You light a cigarette and think about the girl who watched you win at the Golden Gloves. About the way her hair always smelled clean, and a moment a lifetime ago, lying in bed, when she looked up with eyes like June and said she loved you.

★ ★ ★

The body on the floor of the Mosul apartment has half a dozen wounds. He's on his belly, one arm out like he was reaching for something, head cocked sideways and part of his face missing. You recognize him. He's one of the men who frequently hangs around the forward operating base, selling Miami cigarettes. Other things, too, the rumor goes.

Cooper kneels beside him, bent over the body at an awkward angle as though he is going to hug it. The image sticks with you, comes back sometimes months later, along with the abruptness with which Cooper straightens as you come in, and how the first words out of his mouth are "I had to."

You narrow your eyes, say, "What are you doing?"

"Checking for a pulse."

The fear is in you, has been since the firefight. Sometimes you feel your fear wears you like clothing. Today is bad, a dangerous assignment, the squad split up and working the houses separately. Poor procedure, but that was the order, and so when you heard the shots, you were alone in the alley, and came running, jumping piles of trash and discarded water bottles. It occurs to you that the rest of the house is not secure, that there may be others, and the fear spikes again.

Then you notice. "Where's his weapon?"

Cooper winces, and looks at the body, and then back at you. "I told him to get down, but he came at me, and I thought…"

You reach for your radio.

"Wait." Cooper takes a step forward. "Wait." He puts his palms together like he's praying. "If they realize he wasn't armed."

"We have to call on this."

"I know, but…" He rocks his clasped hands back and forth. Stares in your eyes. "I was scared, Nickie."

Everyone is scared but no one says so, and when you see Cooper looking at you that way, something in you shivers. It could have been you alone in here, could have been you who pulled the trigger. You think of basic, him putting an arm around your shoulders and telling you not to let everybody down.

"Did anyone…" Your voice comes out a croak, and you cough, start again. "Did anyone see you come in here?"

"Just you."

You nod. Look again at the body on the ground, the way he is twisted. The blood is thickening on the woven rug. Another dark-skinned man dead in another shitty room. You try to make yourself believe it matters.

Then Cooper says, "Please, Nickie. Please."

In the movies, former soldiers wake up in a sweat, fresh from nightmares of a war that never ends. Not you. You don't dream at all these days. You stretch, make coffee, shower, pull on your boots. Kill a couple of hours at a coffee shop, staring out at nothing.

The Bronco you stored in your parents' garage while

deployed is sun-faded, and the air conditioner doesn't work, but driving it you feel something like your old self. Cooper is waiting on the corner, hands tucked into the front pouch of a hoodie the day is already too warm for. He climbs in, pulls a CD from his pocket, Slayer's *Reign in Blood*. You know it well. Maybe in Vietnam it was Wagner, but in the desert, it was always heavy metal.

You ask, "Where?"

"A parking garage." He gives you the intersection. "I'm supposed to meet him with the money in an hour. Figured we'd get there first, scope it out."

The garage is off the Strip, set amidst warehouses being converted to lofts for whoever lives in lofts. The ramp spirals up through six stories. The top floor is open to the sky. A handful of expensive vehicles are scattered far apart. Car fetishists, terrified of every ding and scratch. You park forty feet from the stairwell, on the far side of the ramp.

The sun is brutal, burning the sky white. The windows are open, and the sweat slicking your chest feels familiar. "It's good."

Cooper nods.

"How many?"

"At least two."

"Armed?"

He nods again. You take a breath, look around. Electricity crackles and snaps between your fingers, the same old feeling you used to get as the squad mounted up. With terrain like this, there's no reason even to discuss the plan. "Okay," you say.

Cooper opens the door, pauses. Turns to look at you. "Nick—"

"Forget it," you say. The two of you share the kind of look that only men who've gone to war together can. Then he slides out of the car and walks over to the stairwell, leans against the wall.

You sit behind the wheel for a moment, listening to the relentless hammer of the heavy metal guitars. Remembering Fritz, the gunner for your Stryker's forward weapons team, a skinny kid with a Missouri twang and a pinch of Skoal perpetually in the pouch of his lip. *Two hundred and ten beats a minute,* he'd said, and smiled. At the time, you'd thought he was talking about his heart.

You turn off the engine and get out. Stand for a moment in the sun, the same sun that lights the other side of the world. You twist the passenger mirror up at an angle, then take a breath, go prone and wriggle underneath the truck.

It isn't long before you hear a car climbing the ramp. The sound gets louder, fainter, then louder again as it winds to the top. You take a deep breath and remember the best night you ever had, how you mastered your fear and let yourself believe.

The problem with the best moment of your life is that every other moment is worse.

The car is a BMW. It cruises up the ramp smooth and soft. You keep your face pointing down, watching out of the corner of your eye, trying to picture a basement room with a dangling bulb and a heavy door. The car parks about twenty feet away, near the stairs, where Cooper stands with his hands in his pocket. Gently, you slide out from under, keeping the truck between you and the men, using the mirror to see.

Two of them, one in a suit, no tie; the other, bigger, in jeans and a muscle shirt. Muscle Shirt gives a casual scan of the parking lot. He doesn't look concerned, lacks the edgy readiness of a man expecting trouble. Still, when he turns his back, you see a pistol tucked into his belt. Cooper raises one hand in greeting, says something you can't hear.

Keeping low, you ease around the back of the Bronco.

Your heart slams in your chest, and you can taste copper. You slide one foot forward, then the other. The distance is only twenty feet. A couple of car lengths. It seems like miles. You feel strangely naked with your hands empty. Step, beat, step.

The man in the business suit says something to Cooper. You screen it out. Fifteen feet. Ten. The sun fires jagged glints off the polished BMW.

You're almost to the man in the muscle shirt when he turns around.

The stars in the desert night were unlike anything you'd ever seen. They flowed across the sky like God had spilled them. Growing up in Chicago, the stars you saw were man-made, skyscrapers turning the night purple. Even when you went camping out in Wisconsin, it was nothing like this.

Sometimes, when things got bad, you closed your eyes and thought of those stars. Imagined yourself on a rise, alone, arms out, a figure cut from the sky. Looking upward. Waiting to be pulled into them.

Hoping.

Muscle Shirt's eyes go wide, and he starts to speak, but you don't hesitate, just take three quick strides and snap off a jab that catches his chin. Your bare knuckles sing. Adrenaline howls in your blood. The fear is gone. You feel better than you have in months. You throw another jab, and he gets his hands up in a clumsy block, and then you crack him hard in the side of the head, near the temple, a wildly illegal blow. His eyes lose focus and his legs wobble, but it's in you now, the rage, the anger that swelled every time a mortar landed on the FOB, every time a man in a terrorist-towel stepped out of an alley leveling an AK, every time the counselor at the VA said that what you were experiencing was typical, that it would pass. You swing again and again. His head snaps back and blood explodes from his nose and he'd fall if only you'd let him.

A loud gasp pulls you from your trance. You forget Muscle Boy. Turn to the man in the suit and start his way, and in a panicky voice he says, "Cooper, what is this—" and then you break his nose. He whimpers and drops to his knees. He looks up with wide, scared eyes, one hand on his nose and the other up to ward you off, like a child menaced by a bully.

The anger and power vanish. You lower your fists. Then Cooper pushes past you, flips Muscle Shirt over. Grabs the pistol from his belt and comes up fast. The man in the suit screams.

You say, "No—" and then there are three explosions and the man stops screaming. Cooper turns to the one on the ground and fires three more times, two bullets in the center of mass and one in the head, just like they taught you in basic.

And you stand there, hands trembling, a shattered body on either side of you as the sun beats down.

"Nick," Cooper says.

You stare.

"I had to. It's done now." He takes off his hoodie and uses it to wipe the sidearm clean. He drops it next to one of the bodies, then starts for the Bronco.

You look at what's left of their heads.

Then Cooper says, "Nick!" His voice sharp. "Come on. Move your feet, soldier." He walks around to the other side of the Bronco and opens the door.

You bend and do something without really thinking about it, and then the sun carves your shadow in concrete as you walk to your truck.

The drive out of Las Vegas is a surreal falling away, first the casinos and bright lights, then the subdivisions that spring up overnight—all those houses, all those people, all the same—and then retail and then diners and then garages and then warehouses and then nothing. Just dirt and sun on either side of US-15.

Cooper is all energy, the window open and fingers tapping, his whole body vibrating like a tuning fork. "Fuck, that was intense," he says, grinning. "I knew you'd boxed, but you beat the *shit* out of those guys."

Your fingers on the wheel are raw and dark with drying blood. He slaps the side of your truck in time with the heavy metal screaming through the tinny speakers. "Where we going, chief?"

You press the power button on the stereo. Cooper looks at you. A long stare. Some of the energy falls away. "I had to."

You say nothing.

"I had to show Vance that coming after me is a bad idea. That it will cost him." He scratches his chin. "Now we can deal. I'll even pay him, when I get the money."

"The guy," you say. Hot dry air roars in the open windows. "He knew your name."

"Who? On the parking deck? So what?"

"You told me you'd never met him. But he said, 'Cooper, what is this?'"

He shrugs. "Vance must have told him."

"It sounded like he knew you."

"He didn't."

Your hands tighten on the steering wheel. You wait. You know Cooper. Silence he can't take.

Finally, he laughs. "Ah, shit, okay, you got me." He turns to you. "I did know him. But the rest of what I said, it was true. And Nickie, thank you. I mean it. I always knew I could count on you."

You nod. It was true. He had always known that. You ride in silence for another couple of moments, then pull off at a lonely gas station. "I'm thirsty."

"Get me something, would you?"

In the minimart you snag a couple of Gatorades and a pack of beef jerky and a can of lighter fluid. The woman behind the counter is as old as death. When she counts out your change, the motion of her lips fractures her cheeks like sunbaked mud. In the Bronco, Cooper has his feet on the dash. As you put the truck into Drive, he opens the jerky, says, "You got a destination in mind, or we just cruising? Because the chicks, man, they're the other direction."

The highway is nearly empty, cars strung out like beads on a necklace. You open the Gatorade and take a long pull. After a few minutes, you take the exit for US-93, a two-lane straight into the cracked brown American desert.

"Seriously, Nick, where we headed?"

"What were you doing when I came in?"

"What?" His eyebrows scrunch. "Came in where?"

"In Mosul. The apartment. When I came in, you were bending over the guy's body. What were you doing?"

He cocks his head. "I was checking for a pulse."

"I've thought about that a lot since I got back. The way you were bent over him. It was strange." You set your drink in the cup holder. "You weren't looking for a pulse, were you? You were going through his pockets."

"That's crazy."

You say nothing, just look at him sideways, put it all in your eyes. For a moment, he keeps it up, the facade, the Cooper Show. Then he says, "Huh," and the mask falls away. "When did you know?"

"I guess I knew then. In Mosul. I just wanted to believe you."

Cooper nods. "See, I knew I could count on you."

"What I want to know is *why*."

He sighs. "I had a sideline going with the guy—weed, meth—but he got unreliable. Always talking about Allah, you know." He shrugged. "And today, well, I really did owe Vance ten grand."

"That why you shot him? He was the one in the suit, right?"

"You don't miss a trick, Nickie."

"Why bring me into it?"

"I couldn't be sure how many guys he'd have."

"No. Why *me?*"

"What do you want me to say?" He shrugs. "Because you buy the whole lie. You win the Golden Gloves and to celebrate, what do you do? Get drunk and nail your girl-friend? Not you. You join the army."

"You used me."

"You let yourself be used."

"I could go to the cops."

"They'd arrest you, too. But you know what?" He shakes his head. "That doesn't matter. You didn't do that in Iraq, and you won't here. *That's* why I came to you. Because you're predictable, Nickie. You never change."

The moment stretches. You remember your trainer saying all you had to do was believe. Remember the feeling of being part of a team, a soldier, and what it got you, a diagnosis of PTSD and a rented room in a city you hate and a raw and formless anger that seems some days more real than any version of you that you once thought might be the real thing.

And then you raise the pistol you took from the parking deck and put it to Cooper's head and show him he's wrong.

Your knuckles hurt and your lips are chapped. There's a line from an old Leonard Cohen song running through your head, something about praying for the grace of God in the desert here and the desert far away. Sometimes you're thinking of Cooper. Sometimes you're not thinking at all.

When the sun slips below the horizon, you get up off the boulder you've been sitting on all day. A quiet corner of searing nowhere at the end of an abandoned two-track, brown rocks and brown dirt and white sky and you.

The Bronco's passenger window is still open.

You reach in your pocket and pull out the can of lighter fluid and pop the top and lean in the window to spray it all over your friend and the front seat and the floorboards, the smell rising fast. You squeeze until nothing else comes. You think you might be crying, but you're not sure.

The butane catches with a soft *whoomp* and a trail of blue-yellow flame leaps around the inside of the truck you once loved. The upholstery catches quickly, and Cooper's clothing. Within a minute, greasy black smoke pours out the windows, and a fierce crackling rises.

You stand on the ridge of the desert and watch. Another truck engulfed in flame beneath another burning sky, and you still standing, still watching.

And then you turn and start walking alone.

CARLA NEGGERS

Throughout her extensive career, Carla Neggers has excelled not only at creating vivid characters, but also at placing them in circumstances where Mother Nature is as much of a threat as the killers they face. Whether in the lush Irish ruins of *The Angel,* the frozen mountain range of *Cold Pursuit,* or the salty Maine air of *The Harbor,* the protagonists in Carla's stories must confront not only the harsh realities of their situation, but also the brutal conditions of their environment.

In this sense "On the Run" is both a classic adventure story and vintage Carla Neggers. On an isolated trailhead in the unforgiving mountains of New Hampshire, Gus Winter and the fugitive holding him at gunpoint will grapple in a life-and-death struggle. The temperature is dropping and both men are feeling the cold's embrace when this story begins.

ON THE RUN

"This is where they died?"

Gus Winter shook his head. "No. Another half hour, at least."

The fugitive shivered in the cold drizzle that had been falling all day. "Ironic that you'll die up here, too," he said.

"If I die, then you'll die. Help won't arrive in time to save you. Just like it didn't arrive in time to save them."

Them.

Gus kept his expression neutral. They'd stopped in the middle of the rough, narrow trail for the fugitive to catch his breath. He was compact, thickly built and at least twenty years younger than Gus, but his jeans and cotton sweater weren't appropriate for the conditions on the ridge. His socks were undoubtedly cotton, too. He didn't wear a hat or gloves. He carried a hip pack, but he'd already consumed his small bag of trail mix and quart of water.

Three hours ago, he'd jumped from behind a giant boulder just above a seldom-used trailhead up Cold Ridge, stuck a gun in Gus's face and ordered him to get moving. Now they were on an open stretch of bald rock at three thousand feet in the White Mountains of New Hampshire on an unsettled October afternoon.

The weather would get worse. Soon.

Gus looked out at the mist, fog and drizzle. The hardwoods with their brightly colored autumn leaves had given way to more and more evergreens. At just over four thousand feet, he and the fugitive would be above the tree line.

Gus said, "Most hypothermia deaths occur on days just like today."

"That right?"

"It doesn't have to be below zero to die of the cold."

The fugitive hunched his shoulders as if to combat his shivering. He had a stubbly growth of beard, which made sense given the story he'd told Gus about escaping from a federal prison in Rhode Island two days ago. His dark eyes showed none of the discomfort he had to be feeling.

Gus wasn't winded, and he was warm enough in his layers of moisture-wicking fabrics and his lined, waterproof jacket. He wore a wool hat, wind-resistant gloves, wool socks and waterproof hiking boots. His backpack was loaded with basic supplies, but he couldn't reach back for anything, take it off, unzip a compartment.

If he did, the fugitive had said he'd shoot him.

The fugitive coughed, still breathing hard. Sweat trickled

down his temples into his three-day stubble. "I'm not dying of the cold."

"Try not to sweat," Gus said. "Sweating is a cooling mechanism. The water evaporates on your skin and promotes heat loss. You don't want that."

"You want me to freeze to death."

"No. I want you to give yourself up. Walk back down the mountain with me."

The fugitive stepped back behind Gus and waved his gun, a .38-caliber Smith & Wesson that he must have picked up somewhere between prison and New Hampshire. "Get moving."

"It's a good idea to keep moving, but not so hard and fast that you sweat. It's easier to stay warm than to get warm."

"Shut up."

Gus started back along the trail and heard the crunch of small stones as the fugitive fell in behind him. The trail dropped off sharply to their left, and in the valley below, the bright orange leaves of hardwoods managed to penetrate the gray. Every autumn, leaf-peepers flocked to northern New England to see the stunning foliage. Today, in the rain and fog, they would be gathered in front of fires at cozy inns and restaurants, or headed home.

Gus realized it wasn't his bad luck that the one person in the White Mountains with a gun had found him. The fugitive had targeted him. Watched for him.

Why?

Before long, the valley would disappear in the fog and

low cloud cover, and dusk came early this time of year. Even with the flashlight he had in his pack, Gus knew it would be increasingly difficult, perhaps impossible, to see from one trail marker to the next. The fugitive wouldn't find his way on his own. He didn't know Cold Ridge. Gus did. He'd lived in its shadows, hiked its trails his entire life—not counting his two years in the army. He'd come home at twenty expecting to get married, have a couple of kids.

Things had worked out differently.

Because of the ridge and its dangers.

"There's a shoot-to-kill order out on me," the fugitive said, matter-of-fact.

"No such thing."

"Liar."

Gus stepped over a smooth, slippery rock. "The purpose of deadly force isn't to kill. Its purpose is to stop you—someone—from killing or seriously injuring someone else. It's about public safety. It's not about killing."

The fugitive snorted. "Why not shoot me in the knee?"

"Shoot you in the knee, and you can still fire off a round or stab someone. Apply deadly force, and you can't. But if you live—then you live. The purpose was to stop you, not to kill you."

"You'd shoot to kill me if you had the chance."

"Toss your gun off the ridge." Although he wasn't known for his patience, Gus kept his tone reasonable, persuasive. "Let's walk back down the trail together. Keeping your gun pointed at me puts you at risk of getting shot yourself. If the police see you—"

"It's just you and me up here. And the ghosts. Don't try to fool me. I know we're almost there."

Yes, Gus thought as he led the fugitive around a familiar bend in the trail. They were almost there.

He slowed his pace, mindful of the slippery rock, and the fugitive moved in closer. "You're picturing yourself firing your Glock into my chest, aren't you?"

Gus didn't own a Glock. "I'm picturing you wrapped up in a blanket in front of a nice fire in a woodstove. Safe. No worries about tripping and falling up here. No worries about hypothermia. No worries about getting yourself shot."

"A .40-caliber Glock." The fugitive's teeth chattered, but derision had crept into his voice. "Isn't that what you carry, Mr. Senior Deputy U.S. Marshal Winter?"

Gus maintained his steady pace. He saw now what had happened three hours ago.

The fugitive believed he'd snatched a federal agent.

Specifically, Gus's nephew, Nate Winter, a senior deputy U.S. marshal visiting from Washington. He and Gus had similar builds and were just thirteen years apart in age. Wearing a hat, carrying a pack, Gus could understand how someone could think he was Nate.

He didn't correct the fugitive's mistake.

The trail became steeper, and the drizzle turned to light rain. Behind him, Gus could hear the fugitive shuddering and shivering, cursing at the cold. "You're in first-stage hypothermia," Gus said. "Shivering is your body's way of trying to get warm. Your core temperature is already below normal. You're still conscious and alert, but you won't stay that way."

"I'm fine. Keep walking."

"As your core temperature drops below ninety, your co-ordination will become more and more impaired. You'll become weaker. Lethargic. Confused."

"You'd like that, wouldn't you?"

"You'll stop shivering." Gus had explained the stages of hypothermia to countless hikers over the past thirty years. "You'll be at an increased risk of cardiac arrest."

"It won't happen—"

"It *is* happening. It's happening to you right now."

"I'll take your gear and leave you. You'll freeze long before I do."

"You need me to get you off this mountain alive," Gus said calmly.

"All I have to do is go downhill."

"It's not that simple. You're in a wilderness area. The main trails are to the south. Even if you managed to avoid falling off a cliff—even if you didn't run out of potable water—and you made it off the mountain, you'd still be miles from the nearest help."

The fugitive was breathing hard now. "More lies."

"I'm just telling you how it is," Gus said. "And no matter what you do—leave me, take me with you—you'll still be wet and cold. It'll be dark soon. Do you know how to protect yourself from the cold overnight?"

"Stop talking."

Gus pretended to stumble slightly on the trail and deliberately ran into a half-dead spruce tree. A sharp sticklike lower branch dug into his cheek and drew blood. He gave an exaggerated yelp of pain and let a few drops of the blood drip onto the gray granite at his feet.

"Hold up." The fugitive shoved his gun into Gus's back and sniffled, but he didn't stop shivering. "The blood. Clean it up. Use your glove. Do a good job."

Squatting down on one knee, Gus used the thumb of his black, windproof glove to wipe up the blood, which was already mixing with the rain water.

The fugitive stood over him. "Think I'm stupid? I know what you're doing. You're leaving a trail for your marshal friends." He squinted down at the cleaned-up blood spot. "Back on your feet. Don't try that again."

Gus shrugged as he rose up straight. "No one would notice a few drops of blood in this wilderness."

"A search dog would."

Gus pressed a gloved finger to the cut on his cheek, as if he didn't dare let more blood fall onto the trail, but as he started back up the trail, he noted the snapped branch on the spruce with satisfaction. A search-and-rescue team wouldn't miss it. Just as they wouldn't miss the other clues he'd left during the past three hours.

His bread-crumb trail.

He'd participated in enough mountain rescues over the years to know how they operated. By now, Nate and his wife and his two sisters and their husbands—all gathered in Cold Ridge for a long weekend—would have realized Gus's quick walk up the trail had gone bad. They'd do a fast-and-easy search for him before notifying the authorities, who'd launch an official search.

Were they thinking, even now, that he'd simply gone off trail and fallen? Or were they aware that an armed-and-dangerous fugitive was in the area?

Did they know his name, what he wanted?

The fugitive coughed, his shivering constant now. "All right, stop," he said abruptly. "Take off your pack and set it on that rock there. Nice and slow."

Gus complied, aware of the Smith & Wesson pointed at him. The fugitive's hands had to be stiff from the cold, his fingers wet and slippery. If he just dropped the gun, fine. But Gus didn't want him accidentally firing off a round.

"Unzip the main compartment and dump out the contents," the fugitive said. "Again, nice and slow. Don't do anything stupid. I want to see what you've got in there."

Gus did as instructed, shaking out three energy bars, a water bottle, an emergency whistle, waterproof matches, dry clothes, a compass, trash bags that could be used as an emergency shelter.

The fugitive toed a trash bag with his wet sneaker. "That's a lot to carry for a day hike, isn't it?"

Gus shook his head. "I always pack more than I think I'll need. If I use everything, I know I didn't pack enough."

"Where's your gun?"

"Not here."

"You're a federal agent. You go armed 24/7. You're supposed to have a gun."

Gus didn't know if that was true or not. He and Nate had never discussed those kinds of details. The fugitive had frisked him for weapons in the first minutes after he'd jumped out from behind the boulder, but Gus hadn't realized it was, at least in part, due to mistaken identity. "Why didn't you check my pack for a gun sooner?" he asked.

"I didn't need to. Touch it, and you were dead, anyway. Let you carry the extra weight of a gun."

His logic made sense. "Do you want to change into dry socks at least?"

"No. Give me your water."

Before Gus could comply, the fugitive reached down with his free hand and grabbed the plastic bottle from among the dumped-out contents. He used his teeth to open the flip-top and drank deeply, even with his chattering teeth.

He shoved the bottle at Gus. "Close it. Don't drink any."

Once again, Gus did as requested.

"You're older than I thought you'd be," the fugitive said. "What's with the white hair?"

"Hard life."

"I hate marshals."

Gus said nothing.

"How much farther now?" the fugitive asked.

"To—"

"To where your mummy and daddy froze to death."

Gus pushed back a surge of anger and gazed down toward the village nestled in the valley below Cold Ridge, lost now in the gray clouds and fog. He could see his nephew and nieces on that cold, awful night thirty years ago.

Nate, seven. Antonia, five. Carine, three.

Waiting.

"They got caught in an unexpected ice storm. It was all over the papers." The fugitive sounded amused now. "Can you imagine? A young couple with three little kids, freezing to death up here."

Gus rose up straight. He'd been twenty and newly home from war. He'd looked at the faces of his young nephew and nieces and wished he could have died up on the ridge in the place of his brother and his wife. Instead, he'd become the guardian to their three orphans.

They were all married now. Antonia and Carine had little ones of their own. Nate and his wife, Sarah, were expecting their first child in a few weeks. A boy.

If he died up here today, Gus thought, the little ones— like grandchildren to him—wouldn't remember him. They weren't old enough.

There was some consolation in that.

The wind picked up and swirled the gray horizon, creating a wavelike effect that had a tendency to disorient, even nauseate, novice hikers. As an outfitter and guide, Gus had encountered hikers of all descriptions in the mountains. Most were eager and well-meaning, determined to enjoy their experience while taking proper precautions.

The fugitive poked his gun into Gus's back. "Well? Answer me. How much farther?"

"Fifty yards. Maybe a little more. We need to be careful in the fog. We don't want to walk off the edge of a cliff." He glanced back, slowing his pace. "You don't need your gun. I'll take you wherever you want to go. I won't run or mislead you. I don't want you to hurt anyone else."

"I want your coat," the fugitive said suddenly. "Get it off."

Gus paused and shrugged off his pack and coat. The fugitive took it with one hand and put it on over his wet sweater, taking care to keep his gun at the ready.

He zipped up the coat and gave a shudder of obvious relief. "I don't know why I waited this long."

"Because you underestimated how cold you'd get. It happens all the time." Gus noticed raindrops already collecting on his navy sweater, but its thick wool was a better insulator when wet than the fugitive's cotton. "What's your name?"

"Fred."

It wasn't his name. "What are you looking for up here, Fred?"

The fugitive didn't answer. His shivering had lessened, but it wasn't necessarily a good sign. He motioned with his gun, still clenched in his half-frozen hand, and Gus started back along the trail.

The fog wasn't going to lift. The wind wasn't going to let up.

The rain wasn't going to stop.

"Let's get to where you want to go," he said wearily.

They came to the spot where his brother and sister-in-law had died. He'd been a firefighter. She'd been a biology teacher. These days, weather reports were more accurate, but even so, people died on Cold Ridge.

"There's a rock formation just past where your folks died. It looks like a toaster."

The fugitive's words were slightly slurred, but he continued. "Do you know it?"

"I do."

Gus stared into the shifting fog and clouds. He could walk right past the toaster-shaped rock formation, and the fugitive would probably never know it. Then what? Shoot Gus in the back? Drop dead from the cold? But as he continued along the trail, his legs heavier now, the pack grinding into the small of his back, Gus knew he wouldn't mislead his captor. He'd just take him where he wanted to go.

The wind was steady, at least fifty miles per hour with higher gusts. He had hiked up all forty-eight peaks in the White Mountains over four thousand feet, and he'd experienced hurricane-force winds. But nothing had prepared him for the jumble of emotions he felt at being here—on the ground where his brother and the woman he'd loved had died.

His brother had taken him up this same trail before Gus had left for basic training.

"Be safe, Gus. I'll be here when you come home."

He pushed back the memory and nodded to a rock outcropping just ahead, barely visible through the shifting gray. "There. That's it. It looks just like a toaster."

The fugitive stepped up next to Gus and pulled the coat's hood over his head. It would help break the wind but otherwise wouldn't do much good. His hair was wet.

He wasn't shivering at all anymore.

"Pal," Gus said, "listen to me. You need to get warm. Let me help you. You don't want to die up here, do you?"

He waved the gun, still clenched tight in his right hand. "Behind the rocks. Go."

Gus sighed and made his way off the trail, the wind going through his layers, the rain soaking his layers. He pushed through scrubby balsams clinging to the thin soil and climbed over a tumble of boulders to the granite formation. It jutted ten feet out of the ground below a rounded knoll.

The fugitive panted, stumbling on the boulders as he followed Gus behind the outcropping. They were out of the wind now, at least.

"I knew I'd make it back here," the fugitive said.

Gus could hear the wind whipping through the valley,

up onto the open ridge. He shivered. He preferred to keep moving.

But he followed the fugitive's gaze to a mound of dirt and rock between the base of the rock formation and the knoll.

A shallow grave.

"Who's buried there?" Gus asked.

"Smuggler. He tried to cheat the wrong man."

"Meaning you."

The fugitive didn't answer, his eyes gleaming with excitement as, with a burst of fresh energy, he got onto his knees. The rain let up now, too, and he set the Smith & Wesson next to his right knee and started moving baseball-size rocks with his red, frozen hands.

"You've stopped shivering, but it's not because you're warm," Gus said. "Your core temperature has dropped to the point that your body is focused just on keeping your vital organs working."

"I know what I'm doing."

"Do you? You're slurring your words. As hypothermia worsens, you get more and more confused. Your mental state—"

"Shut up." The fugitive glared up at Gus. "I'm digging for gold."

Was he digging for gold, or was he hallucinating? Despite his slurred speech, he sounded perfectly lucid. He continued to grab rocks and toss them aside, keeping his gun close by as he worked.

Gus stood back. He became aware of another presence

up on the knoll in the wind and gray. His teeth were chattering now. His hands were shaking. He wasn't sure if he could trust his senses. Was he so far gone with hypothermia himself that he was imagining things?

"My coat's not enough. You're wet," he said. "I've rescued a lot of people off the ridge who were in better shape than you are now."

The fugitive looked up at him. His eyes were still, focused, even as he struggled to speak. "You're not the marshal."

Gus shrugged. "Never said I was."

He kicked the fugitive's pile of wet rocks, creating a distraction, and a man swooped down from the knoll.

Nate.

He leveled a gun at the fugitive.

"Hands in the air. Now."

"Do it," Gus told the fugitive. "Don't make him use deadly force."

The fugitive raised his hands, and Gus grabbed the Smith & Wesson.

He thought he saw a flicker of fear in the fugitive's eyes and shook his head. "I'm not going to shoot you," he said, handing the gun to his nephew. "The situation doesn't call for deadly force. Not anymore."

Two more men appeared behind the rock outcropping. Antonia's husband, a U.S. senator and former rescue helicopter pilot, and Carine's husband, an airforce para-rescueman. They, too, were armed.

Then came Antonia, a physician, and Carine, a nature

photographer who knew the White Mountains at least as well as Gus did. Maybe better.

He hadn't imagined them.

"We weren't going back down the mountain without you," Nate said, his voice catching. "I wasn't losing you before my baby boy gets to know you."

Gus sank against the wet rock wall. "I'm worn-out," he said, "and I'm cold."

Nate nodded to the fugitive. "What did he want?"

"Gold."

"And a dead marshal. You didn't tell him he had the wrong guy?"

"You weren't the right guy, either."

A search-and-rescue team arrived with stretchers and made Gus get on one, but he climbed off after a hundred yards and walked the rest of the way down off the ridge.

It was dark and cold, the sky clear, when Gus and his nephew and nieces and their spouses and little ones gathered at the Cold Ridge lakeside home of a federal judge. Her name was Bernadette Peacham, and Gus had known her since kindergarten. She hardly spoke as he helped her get a pile of blankets from the shed and spread them out on a tarp laid on the wet ground in front of her big outdoor stone fireplace. A fire was roaring. There were marshmallows and hot cocoa.

Beanie, as Gus had called Bernadette for decades, dried off an old Adirondack chair. "You could have died up there," she said as she plopped down. "If Nate hadn't spotted your trail… I don't want to think about it."

"All's well that ends well."

The fugitive's name was Frank Leonard. Two years ago, Nate had recognized him at a hardware store in the village of Cold Ridge. His mug shot was on the USMS Web site, and Nate had a good memory for faces. Leonard was wanted for failing to appear in court on a federal drug charge, and running in to Nate was especially bad timing for him—he'd just killed a fellow smuggler up on the ridge. They'd met there to divide the gold bars they'd received as payment for smuggling drugs and arms over the Canadian border.

Picking the toaster-looking rock formation near the spot where Nate's parents had died had been Leonard's idea. On the way down the ridge, restrained in his stretcher, he'd told Gus that even then he didn't like marshals. "They'd been after me for weeks. They never let up. I thought it was funny, picking that spot."

Funny.

He and his partner in smuggling argued, and Leonard killed him and buried him as best he could, then hiked back down the ridge to clean up loose ends. The gold bars were heavy and awkward, and he wanted to get his ducks in a row before he went back on the ridge, fetched the gold and disappeared, a rich man.

Only Nate had discovered him first.

When he escaped from prison two days ago, he headed

straight to Cold Ridge, but he couldn't remember how to get back to the spot where he'd buried his colleague and the gold.

And he wanted revenge against the marshal who'd recognized him. He couldn't believe his luck when he spotted Gus on the trail and mistook him for Nate.

Bernadette picked up a long, sharp-ended stick as Gus settled into the chair next to her. For a while, he'd wondered if he'd ever get warm again. But he was downright hot now, the flames licking up in the black sky.

"Why did you go off on your own this morning?" Bernadette asked.

"I had something on my mind. Beanie, these guys…" He motioned toward Nate, Antonia, Carine, their spouses, their children. "They're my world."

"I know, Gus. You've been there for them all these years. It was good that they could be there for you today."

"I'd have nailed that bastard one way or the other, but I was pretty cold. And that's not what I'm talking about right now." Gus turned to her, the flames flickering in her eyes. "Beanie, we've known each other a long time, you and I, and I haven't had a romantic thought about you, ever."

She gave a shocked little cough. "Thanks a lot."

"Until lately. Now I can't stop thinking about you."

"So you went up that trail this morning to get me out of your mind?"

"No. To figure out how to ask you to marry me."

"Ah." She picked up a stick and stabbed a fat marshmallow onto the end of it. "You asked me to marry you when we were in the first grade. Remember?"

Actually, he didn't. "What did you say?"

"I told you to go soak your head." She smiled and handed him her stick with the marshmallow. "You're my hero, Gus. You always have been. It's just taken us a few decades to figure out we belong together."

"I'm taking that as a yes."

Bernadette laughed, and Gus leaned forward and dipped the marshmallow in the flames. He was warm in front of the fire with his family and the woman he loved, and life was good.

ROBERT FERRIGNO

Robert Ferrigno has a background that would give him instant credibility with the type of intelligent but questionable characters who populate his books. Armed with a degree in philosophy and a masters in creative writing, Robert left the academic trail to spend five years as a full-time gambler living in dangerous places with dangerous people. Then he became a journalist, but instead of sitting behind a desk typing, he landed a job that had him flying with the Blue Angels, test-driving Ferraris and learning about desert survival with gun enthusiasts. Now a bestselling thriller author, his experiences have clearly given Robert a unique perspective and an unforgettable voice.

"Can You Help Me Out Here?" showcases an ability to mix humor with suspense and a knack for creating villains that make us smile even as they send chills down our spine. No doubt Robert has met people like this somewhere in his travels. The rest of us will be happy to meet them through his words.

CAN YOU HELP ME OUT HERE?

"How much farther?" said Briggs.

The accountant tripped over a tree root, almost fell. Sweat rolled down his face, his hands duct-taped together behind his back. "Soon."

Briggs grabbed the accountant by the hair and gave his head a shake. "*How* soon?" He jammed the barrel of the .357 Magnum against the man's nasal septum. "You may like tramping around in the great outdoors, but me, I just want to shoot you and get into some air-conditioning."

"I…I appreciate your discomfort," said the accountant, blood trickling from his nose, "but Junior wants my ledger detailing his financial transactions for the last eight years, so…" He dripped blood onto his gray suit, a soft, pale man with calm eyes. "So you better treat me nice, and keep your part of the bargain."

"Nice?" Briggs glowered at him, a beefy, middle-aged thug in a red tracksuit. "Maybe I fuck nice and just start blowing off body parts until you come up with it?"

"That would be a mistake on your part." The accountant held his head high. "I have a…refined and delicate nature. I'm already experiencing heart palpitations from your rough treatment. You torture me…you could send me into shock. I might die before I give up the journal." He sniffed back blood. "What do you think Junior will do to you then?"

"You didn't tell me…" Briggs swatted at the mosquitoes hovering around him with the revolver. "You didn't tell me we were going to be slogging through a swamp."

"That's where I hid it," said the accountant. "And it's not a swamp. It's a wetlands."

"Swamp, wetlands, who cares? It smells like an old outhouse," said the other killer, Sean, a tall beach-bum with bad acne and a Save the Salmon, Eat More Pussy T-shirt. "What matters, mister, is that we're going to keep our part of the bargain. You lead us to the journal, you get a double-tap to the back of the head, no muss, no fuss."

"I abhor pain," said the accountant.

"Trust me," said Sean, "you won't feel a thing."

The accountant glanced at Briggs, then back at Sean. "Do I have your word on that?"

Sean gave him a thumbs-up. "Scout's honor."

"That's not the goddamned Scout's sign." Briggs raised the index and middle finger of his right hand in a V. "*This* is Scout's honor, dumb-ass."

"That's the peace sign," said Sean, "and don't call me dumb-ass."

"It's the peace sign *and* the sign for Scout's honor," said the accountant.

"What's this then?" said Sean, giving the thumbs-up.

"Keep walking," Briggs ordered the accountant, "and stay out of the poison ivy."

The accountant started back down the narrow path, brush on all sides, trees overhanging the trail.

"Fine," said Sean, hurrying to catch up to them, "*don't* answer me."

Five minutes later, the accountant turned to Briggs. "Are you saving your money?"

"What's that supposed to mean?" said Briggs.

"A simple interrogatory," said the accountant, his yellow necktie crusted with blood. "I wanted to know if you saved a portion of your money or lived paycheck to paycheck."

Briggs swatted at the mosquitoes darting around him. "I do okay."

"I could give you some suggestions," said the accountant. "Something that would allow you to defer taxes and put your money to work for you—"

"Taxes?" Briggs laughed.

"You don't pay taxes?" said the accountant.

Sean shook his head. "Me, neither."

"Big mistake," said the accountant. "You don't want to fool with the IRS."

"How much farther?" demanded Briggs.

"I kind of like the idea of my money working for me," Sean said quietly. "Like having a maid. Or a slave." He made a motion like he was cracking a whip.

"Good for you, Sean." The accountant tried to scratch his nose with his shoulder. "Now you're thinking. I can give you some tips—"

"You think this is a fucking *seminar?*" said Briggs. "Move!"

"Is that how you got this place?" Sean said to the accountant. "Making your money work for you?"

"Absolutely," said the accountant. "I've got forty-five acres here, owned free and clear. Practically surrounded by national forest. I enjoy privacy…up until now."

"We should listen to this guy before we pop him, Briggs," said Sean. "Maybe take some notes."

Briggs slapped a mosquito that had landed on his cheek, his face flushed and as red as the tracksuit now.

The accountant stopped.

"This it?" said Briggs. "Are we there?"

"Can you help me out here?" said the accountant. "I…I have to urinate."

"You're only going to have to hold it for a little while more," said Briggs.

"I *have* been holding it," said the accountant.

"What do you expect us to do about it?" said Briggs.

"I expect you to cut my hands loose," said the accountant.

"I got nothing to cut the tape with and not sure I would if I could," said Briggs. "We might not be able to find you if you take off running—this is your home turf."

"I have no intention, Mr. Briggs, of wetting my pants," said the accountant.

"If it puts your mind at ease, sir," said Sean, "you're going to piss yourself anyway when I give you the double-tap. It's a natural reaction…loss of control, you know? A real mess, too. I seen it plenty times."

"Yes, Sean, but I'll be *dead* then, so it won't matter to me," said the accountant. "Now, being presently alive, it *does* matter."

"Oh." Sean nodded. "I get it."

The accountant wiggled his fingers behind his back. "Do you mind?"

Sean bent over the accountant's hands, tearing at the tape, while the accountant shifted from one foot to the other.

"Please hurry, Sean," said the accountant.

"Tapes all tangled up," said Sean. "I…I can't do it."

"Told you, dumb-ass," said Briggs. "That's why I use that kind of tape, 'cause you can't get it off."

"Then one of you is going to have to unzip my trousers and hold my penis while I urinate," said the accountant.

Both Sean and Briggs burst out laughing.

"I'm quite serious, gentlemen," said the accountant.

"Pal, if you want someone to hold your joint, you're out of luck," said Briggs, still laughing. "Now, I had a partner ten years ago…*he* might have accommodated you."

"If you force me to wet myself, Mr. Briggs, I can promise you with absolute certainty, that I will not lead you to the ledger, no matter what you do to me," said the accountant.

Briggs punched the accountant in the side of the head, knocked him onto the ground. "You sure about that?" He kicked the man in the chest, then grabbed the accountant's bound hands, jerked him to his feet, bones popping. "You *sure?*"

The accountant didn't say a word.

Briggs lifted the accountant's hands higher and higher, the man bent forward, silent, tears rolling from his eyes onto the dirt. Still silent. Briggs finally released him, out of breath.

"Damn, Briggs," said Sean. "I believe him."

"Yeah," panted Briggs. "So do I." He wiped sweat off his forehead with the back of his hand. "So grab his joint and help him take a piss."

"*Me?*" said Sean.

Briggs shrugged. "I cleaned up after the two software geeks. They must have had the combo platter at El Jaliscos but you never heard me complain. While you were 'oohing' and 'aahing' over their fancy laptops, I was mopping out the car."

"I'm not doing it," said Sean.

"You were the one who forgot the handcuffs," said Briggs. "That's why I had to use the tape."

"I don't care," said Sean."

"Gentlemen," said the accountant. *"Decide."*

"Did I share on the last job?" said Briggs. "I didn't have to, but I did." He glanced at the accountant. "Last job we found...I found a half-kilo of smack in Mr. Unlucky's dresser. I didn't have to share it with you, but I did."

"The smack was stepped on, and we probably should have turned it over to Junior anyway," said Sean.

"Gentlemen?"

Sean stared at Briggs.

"You know it's fair," said Briggs.

Sean jabbed a finger at the accountant. "I ain't touching it with my bare hands." He walked around until he found a tree with wide leaves, tore a couple off and strode back to the accountant. "Don't say a fucking word." He unzipped the accountant's trousers, fumbled out the man's penis holding the leaf around it, then pointed it into the brush. "Hurry up."

The accountant closed his eyes.

"Come on," said Sean, giving the accountant's penis a slight shake.

"I'm trying," said the accountant.

"You're the one who had to go so bad," said Sean.

"Oh, *Sean,*" drawled Briggs, "I cain't quit you."

"That ain't funny." Sean looked at the accountant. "I'm going to be hearing that for the next week."

The accountant sighed. "I...I can't do it. It's just...I can't."

"Fine." Sean stuffed the accountant's penis back into his trousers, didn't even bother zipping him up, the leaf sticking out of his fly. "Just take us to the damn ledger so I can blow your brains out and forget this ever happened."

"I'm sorry," said the accountant. "It's not easy, you know."

Sean wiped his hand on his pants.

"If it helps," said the accountant, "we're almost there."

"About time." Briggs looked down at the patches of standing water all around them. "Getting really muddy."

"Lot of rain lately," said the accountant, walking ahead, the ground sucking at his shoes. "It's really beautiful here after a storm, all kinds of flowers popping up." He walked slightly off the trail, splashed through a puddle. "See that tree up ahead?" He pointed with his chin. "The one with the split trunk? The journal's in a waterproof container under a large flat rock—"

Briggs pushed him aside, stalked across a mossy clearing toward the tree, right through the water. He was in past his ankles trying to high-step free before he stopped and looked back. By then it was too late. He was up to his knees and sinking fast.

"Don't move!" said the accountant.

"Get me out of here!" shouted Briggs.

Sean pointed a pistol at the accountant. "You did this."

"There's underground springs all over this part of the woods," the accountant said to Sean, ignoring the pistol. "Nobody knows where they'll pop up next."

"Hey!" called Briggs, the muddy slurry almost to his waist now.

"Quit struggling, Briggs, you'll only sink faster," said the accountant, stepping slowly into the clearing. "Stay calm."

"How about we trade places and *you* stay calm, mother-fucker?" said Briggs, perfectly still now.

"Sean, go find a long tree branch," the accountant said gently. *"Hurry."*

Sean crashed into the underbrush.

"I'm…I'm still sinking," said Briggs, a cloud of mosqui-toes floating around his head.

The accountant watched him stuck there, the late-after-noon light seeping through the trees.

Sean rushed back, dragging a long, dry branch. "Is this okay?"

"Perfect," said the accountant. "Hold it out in front of you…but be careful where you step."

"I'm scared," said Sean.

"Fucking *do* it, Sean!" cried Briggs.

Sean edged carefully into the clearing, one foot in front of the other, testing the ground under the water to make sure it was solid. He waved the dry branch at Briggs.

"You'll have to get closer," said the accountant.

Sean took another few steps, started to sink, the watery muck level with his high-tops. He reached out with the branch.

Briggs lunged for the branch, missed it by at least three

feet. His movements drove him deeper into the slurry, chest-high now. "Closer!"

"It's okay, Sean," said the accountant. "Just a little farther. Lean forward with the branch."

Sean hesitated, took another step toward Briggs, bent over, the branch extended as far as he could.

The accountant put his foot against Sean's ass, and *pushed*. Sent him sprawling.

Sean screamed, facedown, spitting out muck as he fought to get out, but only got sucked in deeper and deeper. He grasped at the tree branch. It snapped.

The accountant watched them struggle. Sean weeping, frantic, mud in his mouth, sinking fast. Briggs moved slowly, trying to work his way toward the edge of the clearing.

"There really is a natural spring under there," said the accountant, hands still taped behind his back. "Been that way since I was a boy. *Deep,* too. No matter what you throw in, it just gets swallowed up. I tossed a neighbor's new bicycle down there one time. Shiny red Schwinn with streamers on the handlebars and a chrome fenders. Never did like that kid."

Briggs reached for a tuft of grass, but it came apart in his hands. He tilted back, the slurry past his chest now.

Sean made a final choking sound, and slipped under the surface.

"If you can hold your breath long enough, Briggs, maybe you can find that bike on the bottom," said the accountant. "See if you can ring the bell."

Briggs reached down, fumbled for something, the movement pushing him deeper. His head was under the surface when his hand broke free, just his hand, holding the .357. He blindly got off three shots with the revolver before his hand disappeared along with the rest of him.

One of the shots had been close enough that the accountant heard it zing past his ear, but he hadn't flinched. Just smiled. You take your chances...

He stepped back from the quicksand, deftly slipped his bound hands under his feet and in front of him. He worked at the duct tape with his teeth. Took him ten minutes. The clearing was still by then.

The accountant rubbed his wrists, bringing back the circulation. He adjusted his necktie, then pulled out his cell and called Junior.

"It's done," said the accountant.

"It go down like you wanted?" said Junior.

A breeze stirred the grass around the edges of the quicksand. "Pretty much."

"Nothing's going to come back at us?"

"No." The accountant watched a muddy bubble pop. "Not a thing."

"I can't abide thieves," said Junior. "I need to be able to trust the people work for me."

The accountant studied a couple of iridescent green dragonflies hovering over the surface of the water.

"Never understood why you don't just do things the *easy* way," said Junior.

The accountant pulled the leaf Sean had used out of his fly, zipped up his pants.

"Where's the fun in that?" He snapped the phone shut and started back toward his house.

JOE HARTLAUB

When he's not practicing law, Joe Hartlaub is a highly respected book reviewer, so he's no stranger to what makes a good thriller come to life. "Crossed Double" shows how sharp dialogue can make you feel like you're not just reading a story but also eavesdropping on the two people at the table next to you in a restaurant.

The characters in "Crossed Double" might be made of questionable moral fiber but they are not without their own code of honor, as a father tries to explain to his wayward son. You could say that this story is a parent lecturing a child about right and wrong, but this is a thriller, so make that *wrong* and wrong.

CROSSED DOUBLE

C.T. is unhappy.

He shouldn't be. He has time on his hands, money in the bank and pussy on the side. He has breakfast—coffee, cream, fried egg sandwich, cheese and sausage on a toasted bagel, crunchy but not dark, if you would be so kind—sitting in front of him at Lisa's, his favorite diner in Columbus. His son, Andy, is sitting across from him, and it's still like looking in a mirror, even though a quarter-century separates them. All should be well, except for the story that Andy is telling him. C.T. has to keep his hands on the table to keep from smacking the stupid out of the kid, which, C.T. thinks, would take about three weeks once he started. Eight years out of high school and still fucking up like a three-year-old.

Andy is telling C.T. that he borrowed money from Kozee, who is a whack-job. Everyone knows it. He's a

DLR—Doesn't Look Right—and only a wet brain or someone fresh off of a Greyhound bus would ever do business with him. Even the girls who troll the Ohio State North Campus bars, with their tramp-stamps and thongs showing and who shave once a week whether they need to or not, find Kozee a little too outside of the box for what they have in mind.

Kozee fills a doorway wide and high, all muscle, bald head, cold blue eyes, veins running up and down his arms like one of those transparency pictures in a medical school textbook. He looks like he's waiting to catch a ride from one of the Four Horsemen of the Apocalypse. Any one will do. He gives off a primal odor of trouble, of danger, of death, a long and slow one devised especially for you. The Greenbrier Project boys, who cruise the Washington Beach grid with impunity and occasionally venture into the Glen Echo maze, step off when they see him shamble 'round the way. There are a hundred stories about Kozee, told in alleys that run behind no-name bars on East Fifth, on street corners in Hawaiian Point, in doorways of shabby apartments in those sections of the Short North where the gentrification begun twenty years ago hasn't quite reached.

And Andy borrowed money from this guy, even after hearing how Kozee had gotten into the unsecured loan business. A Mex named Jeffe had been running the corner action on Fourth and Eleventh. Kozee had started hanging around and Jeffe, having missed the memo about Kozee, got into his face about it being bad for business, having a crazy-looking, fucked-up white boy hanging around, scaring business away. Kozee hadn't said a word, just head-butted the silly beaner, breaking his nose, and then biting it off like it was a Tootsie Roll or something, spitting it back on him more or less in place. One of Jeffe's crew tried to help him up, but Kozee said to stay away from him, just let him roll around screaming in the parking lot, let Jeffe figure out if that was good or bad for business. Kozee was back on the corner the next day, not saying it but everybody knew: it was his corner now. Wasn't anyone there that was gonna argue with him, least of all Jeffe.

So nobody is fucking with Kozee. He is, as they say, shitting behind the tall cotton. Kozee is like a mutual fund; he's involved in enough different enterprises so that if one dries up another usually picks up. Kozee took up a loan-sharking operation a few weeks ago when the mayor of Columbus, a high yellow with movie-star looks and the requisite ability to look competent without having a clue, declared a hapless war on drugs. So Kozee drops drugs and starts lending money at an interest rate that makes Chase Visa look like a benevolent enterprise. You don't want to be late with Kozee. He doesn't hire some bitch to call you every day and inquire about your payment. He breaks your door down and beats your ass. And this is the guy Andy goes to for a loan.

Andy's thing with Kozee, however, is only part of the elephant pissing on C.T.'s morning. Andy's stupidity isn't limited to a business transaction with a psycho; no, Andy's wires are crossed worse than that, as becomes evident when Andy starts talking about Rakkim.

C.T. knows Rakkim, a big guy, an underachiever in his midthirties who for seven years has been delivering pizza for Midnight Crisis, a twenty-four-hour North Campus pizza joint. Midnight Crisis has been described as "employing the unemployable since 1993," and "unemployable" certainly applies to Rakkim, who up until a couple of months ago was a quiet guy who walked around oblivious, as if listening to an iPod through headphones or something, except that he doesn't own an iPod. The only time that C.T. had seen him at all animated was in the Midnight Crisis party room at Rakkim's thirtieth birthday party, which featured cake, liquor and a red-headed hooker from a High Street strip club, who gave Rakkim a lap dance and a blow job while those assembled, including the woman's husband, howled in beery approval.

According to Andy, however, Rakkim has been acting like a little bitch for the last few months. Some third-string Ohio State tailback had given Rakkim shit about paying for a large pepperoni and slapped him across the face. Rakkim, totally out of character, had jacked the guy's jaw, breaking it. All of a sudden, Rakkim becomes a legend in his own mind, acting out. Among other things—and this, according to Andy, is the cause of his instant problem—Rakkim hasn't paid for a nickel bag that Jeff had fronted for him the month before.

C.T. remembers Jeff from when Andy was in high

school, a quiet kid who wouldn't say shit if he had a mouthful. According to Andy, Rakkim has no complaints with Jeff about the quality of the bag or shorting on the weight; Andy solemnly assures C.T. that Jeff would never do such a thing. Andy is pretending to be oblivious to the eye fuck that C.T. is giving him across the table at him. C.T. wondering, *how do you know this?* Now, Andy says, Rakkim just won't pay Jeff, or return his phone calls, he's just ignoring Jeff, blowing him off.

Jeff, according to Andy, is not a big-time dealer. Like a lot of the Washington Beach guys who deal small and local, he sells only to his friends with just enough markup for his own stash and to make his rent and lights. It's a fragile street economics model that collapses if someone in the chain doesn't come through. And Rakkim didn't come through.

What has C.T. ready to play Whack-A-Mole with his son's head in Lisa's is that Andy has interjected himself into this mess. A couple of months ago Jeff, for whom budgeting is a science on the order of quantum physics, had been short for his rent. Andy, being a bro, and not wanting Jeff to interrupt his dealing, had slid a few Benjamins to Jeff. Now Jeff is telling Andy that since Rakkim had stiffed Jeff, Jeff had to stiff Andy. The result was that Andy was short, so...

"I went up to see Kozee," Andy says. C.T. is looking at Andy across the dining table as if he was a turd floating in C.T.'s coffee. Lisa's Café is quiet, only the two of them as customers, C.T. listening to this utter bullshit and torn between fatherly love and disgust. He begins mentally ticking off the various problems here—the borrowing of money, the drug involvement, the total fucking stupidity he is hearing come out of his son's mouth—and shakes his head as he looks out of the front window.

Traffic on Indianola is quiet this early in the morning, and the sun is out, promising the first decent day after months of a bitterly cold and depressingly gray winter. C.T. had his breakfast sandwich cut into neat little squares and it's now gone, though he cannot remember having eaten any of it. He is, as is his custom, dressed all in black, mock turtleneck and pants, shoes and socks, hat and leather coat. He sticks out at Lisa's like a stiff prick at a county fair. He can tell that the owner of the restaurant, a gray-haired hippie who hasn't changed his spectacles or his jeans since George McGovern ran for president, isn't sure whether he likes C.T. and Andy coming here or not, their hood ambience not fitting in with the "peace, love and brother-hood" vibe of the place. They sit and mind their own business and never raise their voices, so fuck him, and besides, what is the guy going to say, don't come here anymore, you're scaring away my Nader For President traffic? For just a minute, C.T. wishes he was somewhere else, on a hotel balcony overlooking the Atlantic Ocean, lying on a chaise lounge and reading a novel while two twentysomethings in bikinis flip a coin to see who will give him warm head first.

C.T. shakes his head and looks at his son. "You remember

Brando's first line in *The Godfather,* Andy?" C.T. says, looking at him over the top of his coffee cup. Andy shakes his head, says no. C.T. widens his cheeks by grimacing, then does a more than passable Don Corleone, asking Andy, "Why didn't you come to me first, instead of going to a stranger?"

Andy laughs, still amazed, at twenty-five, at his dad's talent for mimicry. It's an uncomfortable question, however, and C.T. is serious. Andy shakes his head again. "I wanted to get this one done on my own. I can't keep coming to you all of the time."

"I understand," C.T. says. It takes an effort for him to keep his voice level. "But the last guy you want to have anything to do with is Kozee. You know how when you step in dogshit when you're wearing cross-trainers, and it stays in the cracks forever, and you need a knife to dig it out but there's always some left? That's what dealing with Kozee is like." He takes another sip of coffee. "But I don't get why this was your problem. It was Jeff's problem. And Jeff is now *your* problem. He borrowed the money from you. But he's got money now, and you don't. He still has money for dope, he hasn't been evicted or anything, he's not an orphan, and I saw him last night in the Surly Girl, trying to pick up what I think was a woman, who, regardless, was out of his league. So he's got money. Your money."

C.T. watches Andy sip on his soft drink—how can anyone drink that shit at 7:00 a.m., it's beyond him—and waits for what's next. Andy hasn't changed since he was ten years old.

When he gets caught in the juices of his own lies, he'll slough deeper into the stew until he's neck-high in his own bullshit.

Andy surprises him, though, coming at it from another direction. "How do you know?" he asks. Andy should know better, having heard enough stories about his dad— hell, he saw enough of them happening while he was growing up—that he's aware that little happens on the north and east sides of town that his dad doesn't know about. But he has to ask.

"How do you know?" he asks again.

C.T. ignores the question long enough to take a last sip of coffee, wondering how anyone—even an old hippie— outside of a police precinct house can fuck up a cup of Folgers. He motions for the check.

"How about," he says, as he pulls a twenty out of his pocket to pay the bill, "I'll show you."

Jeff opens his eyes and he is looking up a big tube. The tube is hard metal, because when he starts to jump up he hits his forehead on it, and, considering all of the alcohol he drank the night before at the Surly Girl, his head doesn't need any more aggravation. Aggravation is what he has, though. He's got two guys in his bedroom, locked door notwithstanding, both of them wearing ski masks. Jeff starts to jump out of bed but his forward progress is impeded by the barrel of the gun that is now pressed up against his left eye. "Good morning, Starshine," says the guy holding a gun, the guy nearest his bed, the guy wearing a gray ski mask and a blue peacoat. Jeff opens his mouth to scream but only a strangled little rasp comes out before the gun barrel is jammed between his teeth and down his throat. The guy with the gun says, "Wudda wudda" in a singsong voice and wags his finger from side to side, which for some reason scares Jeff more than the gun. "The only thing I want to hear out of you is information, my friend. Where are your Benjamins? No screams, no bullshit, no excuses, just where they are and we'll be down the road." Jeff feels the gun barrel ease out of his mouth so he can talk, but it's still pointed at him, pressed directly against his forehead, hard. His eyes are crossing trying to look at it. He feels his bladder let loose under the covers, first it's warm and then almost immediately cold, and he's embarrassed, though the two guys don't seem to notice. Jeff tries to scream, but his throat constricts and he can't manage much more than a hysterical whisper. "The back of the closet! On the floor! There's a suitcase full of dirty underwear! It's in there!"

Gray keeps his eyes on Jeff but jerks his head at the other guy, the one wearing a black ski mask, and nods toward the closet. Black steps over to the walk-in and begins digging through the mess on the floor and finds the suitcase. He opens it up and hesitates for a second. He doesn't want to stick his hand into the underwear, which is so filthy that it's almost twitching, but he does anyway and after rooting through it for a couple of seconds he pulls out a thick wad of bills, folded over with a rubber band around it. He doesn't say anything, just takes it over and holds it in front of Gray's line of vision. Gray sticks his chin out and nods, and Black peels off ten bills, making sure that they're not going to walk out of there with a Michigan roll.

Jeff is terrified. He looks like Linda Blair in *The Exorcist,* sweating and his eyes all wild. His head is pinned to the bed by the gun but his body is twitching uncontrollably. That money is promised to some nasty folks, and if it turns up missing Jeff will be better off being shot. The situation puts him next door to stupid, and that's why, almost before he knows that he's doing it, he grabs for the gun, trying to shove it away as he sits up, thinking that somehow the two guys will be distracted enough that he can get away. He hears a shout and then for just an instant the pain in his head gets a thousand times worse and then it all goes black.

"Fuck me," C.T. says, leaning back in the driver's seat of his car, Andy next to him. They're parked out toward the street in a medical building parking lot off of Cleveland Avenue in Westerville, just a couple of guys who look like they're waiting for a wife or a girlfriend getting an MRI or Pap smear or some fucking thing. Two ski masks—one gray, one black—are sitting on the console between them. "Fuck me. Who would have figured Jeff for Captain America?"

"Yeah, well Captain America died last year, and Jeff is still alive," Andy says. "You think he's awake yet?"

"I dunno. When he does wake up, he needs to go down to University Hospital and treat himself to a neurological."

C.T. shakes his head. "I smacked him pretty hard. Stupid asshole. Good thing the gun wasn't loaded. They'd be finding little pieces of Jeff all over Washington Beach for the next year." C.T. takes his pistol out of its pocket holster and begins reloading the 9-mm hollow points back into the clip, keeping an eye on the parking lot so as not to give anyone walking by a heart attack.

"Aren't you glad it wasn't loaded, though?" Andy asks.

"Not really." C.T. slips the clip home and ratchets a round into the chamber. "If he had come out from under the covers with a derringer or something we'd both be laid out on a cooling board down at Schoedinger's right now, instead of taking in the local ambience." C.T. wipes his hand across his face, inhaling deeply, watching a middle-aged and grossly overweight couple walking in their general direction, looking like a pair of twin dirigibles that have come untethered at a Macy's Thanksgiving Day parade. "Now," C.T. said, gesturing, "let's see what our involuntary benefactor has bestowed upon us."

Andy hands the wad of bills to his dad. It is, indeed, not a Michigan roll at all, it's just the opposite, in fact, a roll of fifties on the outside and the rest Benjamins. "How much did you loan Jeff?" C.T. asks.

"Three hundred."

"You dumb-shit." C.T. starts pulling bills off the roll. "Would you like that in fifties or hundreds, sirrah?"

"Fifties." C.T. looks at him. "Please," Andy says.

C.T. counts off six bills. "Next time remember the First

National Bank of Dad. You'll deal with a higher class of lender." He begins counting the rest of the roll while doing an eerily on-target impression of a stoned-out Jeff. "Gee, Andy, I don't have any money—five hundred—ya see, dude, Rakkim really fucked me over, man, I don't have any money—seven hundred—I'm sorry, Andy, but it's Rakkim's fault, and my rent is due, and I don't have any money—nine hundred fifty—maybe you can stall Kozee for a few days, but I'm tapped out, I don't have any money—one thousand, three hundred, fifty." C.T. exaggerates shuffling the wad into a neat pile and tapping it, imitating Oliver Hardy. "I should drive back there and shoot that little cunt myself for being a lying sack of shit and causing my heartbeat to race."

"What are we going to do with the rest of the money?" Andy asks.

"We're going to donate it to the Sisters of the Poor Claires." Andy is staring at C.T., incredulously. "What do you think we're going to do with it? We're keeping it. Interest on your loan, collection fees…why, by the time we total everything up, Jeff may still owe us some money." C.T. puts the rest of the money in his pocket and says, "Now look, you need to keep bugging Jeff about what he owes you. If you stop asking him, it'll look strange, and he'll wonder about your sudden largesse. But what's the lesson here?"

Andy shrugs, but answers, "I should have come to you?"

C.T. shakes his head. "That, too. But remember what I said about your problem being Jeff? He's not your friend.

He hung your ass out to dry." C.T. shakes his head again. "Shit. Hippies. Drug dealers. Fucking Kozee. What are you doing with these people anyway? I taught you better than that."

Andy doesn't say anything. He has no answer, not one that will make C.T. happy, anyway. He does have a question, though. "What about Kozee?"

C.T. stares out the windshield for a minute, then starts the car up. "I'll take care of that freak," he says.

Kozee is laughing.

C.T. doesn't think he's said anything funny, but Kozee is mightily amused. He throws his head back now, really into it, laughing his ass off.

For being a whack-job, Kozee has taken really good care of his teeth, C.T. thinks, a few fillings here and there but otherwise everything is straight and white and sparkling. C.T. can see all the way back to Kozee's second fucking molars, the guy has his mouth open so wide.

Kozee and C.T. are sitting in what used to be a 7–Eleven. It's a blind pig now, not even officially a store, but there are some chips and loosies on the counter and beer in the cooler, the forty-ouncers that the mulies love and that are sold with impunity 24/7. The candy on the counter appears to get dusted once a year whether it needs it or not. There's an occasional rustle in the dark corners of the store and in the aisles, and C.T. thinks that at some point a year or two ago Orkin should have been called in.

He and Kozee are behind the counter at a small table, the only people in the store. The rest of Kozee's crew is outside, because, after all, C.T. is older and soft-looking, and if Kozee had muscle in the room with him, it would look like he couldn't handle things, right?

Kozee, at the tail end of a laugh, leans forward. "Y'know, everyone says you're straight up, but you're out of your mind. Your son—Andy, right?—owes me five, three on the loan and two on the vig. And I'm gonna lend him money again and again and again."

C.T. is trying to keep it calm. It's been a long day, and it's not even half over. Worse, he is in danger of missing that all-important one-o'clock feeding. He is thinking of how easy it would be for him to kill this goon; it would cause more problems than it would solve, but he is within a minute or two of past caring. He says, "I don't like repeating my-self—"

Kozee half rises out of his chair, and leans over into C.T.'s face. C.T. can see that it registers with Kozee, just with an eye blink, but still it registers with Kozee that C.T. doesn't lean back or give ground. "Listen, you old fuck, you don't tell me what I do. I didn't get all this—" He pauses for a second, because C.T. is looking around at the half-empty shelves while Kozee is talking to him, looking at the paper on the floor that seems to move on its own, the dust every-where, and his eyebrows slightly raised, like he's thinking whoopee-shit, disrespecting him. This pisses Kozee off. He pokes his finger toward C.T.'s chest to get his attention back.

At least he tries to.

Kozee suddenly can't move his finger. C.T. has grabbed Kozee's finger in midpoke. He thumps it down on the table that's between them, and he comes up with some sort of little knife out of nowhere, it looks like one of those guillotine blades and he's wearing it like a ring. The blade is pressed against Kozee's pointer finger, right where the finger meets his right hand.

"I don't like being interrupted, either," C.T. says softly. "Now sit down, slowly, and I'll talk, you listen. I'll walk out of here with a promise from you, and you'll still have your hand in the same shape it was when I walked in, so you won't have to explain to your crew of little pussies how the head pussy got his finger cut off by an old man."

Kozee slowly sits down. This old fuck, he's pulled a knife out of nowhere, caught his finger and had it down on the table so fast it would take longer to tell about it, like that fat old blind guy on the reruns of *Kung Fu*. Kozee, for the first time since he was ten years old, before he started hitting his growth spurt, is actually scared.

"Now listen to me," C.T. says, slowly, like he's talking to a cat. "You're not to lend money to my son anymore. His credit is no good here. You give him no reasons, no hassles, you just tell him no. In return, you get to keep your finger. And as a show of good faith, I keep quiet about that strap-on hooker you visit. The one in the second-floor walk-up on Hudson and McGuffey. With the lifesize naked dummy she keeps in the window to tell her clientele that she 'be open for bidness.'"

Kozee's eyes at this point are wide-open. Nobody is supposed to know about that shit. He can't believe the shit that this old fuck knows, how he talks, how he acts, not even breaking a sweat and the guy is serious, he *will* take Kozee's finger. Kozee wants to kill this clown, but the guy is reading his mind again.

"Yeah, I can read your mind," C.T. says, "and it's the shortest book in the library. If I'm struck by lightning or a car or something, the MPEG of you and your whatever winds up on muchosucko-dot-com and a half-dozen other Web sites before my body's even cold. And I'll take more than just your finger if you come after me. Are we solid?"

Kozee nods. He is furious and scared and is thinking that he will kill this old guy if he ever gets the chance but at the same time he knows he'll never get the chance.

"Oh," C.T. says, "one other thing. Don't even look at my son. You'll pray for St. Joseph to give you a quick and happy death." He runs the edge of the blade softly, almost gently, across Kozee's finger before he releases his grip and then he snaps his finger and the blade disappears, like he's a sideshow magician or something. Kozee looks down and sees a thin line of blood at the joint, and for just a second he's afraid to lift his hand off of the table, for fear his finger will still be lying there. C.T. gets up and throws three bills on the table— one, two and three—and looks around again, a contemptuous look on his face. He walks through the door without looking back, and gets into and starts up his car like he's just left church or something and he has nothing else to do for the day. Kozee is furious, he's trembling so badly he doesn't think he'll ever stop. One of his boys comes in to use the bathroom, and as he walks by the table he is staring at Kozee's hand.

The finger, Kozee sees, is still bleeding.

Three days later Andy calls C.T. at 6:00 a.m. in the morning. "Guess who wants to talk to you?"

"Jeff," C.T. says.

There's a long silence on the line. "Did he call you, too?" Andy asks.

"No. Did he say what he wanted?"

"He wants—" Andy pauses and tries to contain himself, but he can't help laughing "—for you to help him with a problem."

"That's what I do," C.T. says. "Have him call me."

The following Tuesday C.T. and Jeff are sitting in Lisa's. Jeff has a circular bruise in the middle of his forehead from where C.T., while wearing his ski mask, had pressed his .38 special, and another lump along the right side of his head where C.T. had pistol-whipped him. C.T. has been listening to Jeff lay everything out, from Rakkim ripping him off to borrowing money from Andy to getting robbed by a couple of heavy-duty mokes who are now, apparently, in the wind.

When he's done, C.T. doesn't say anything for a minute, just sits and sips his coffee, then asks the waitress for a refill before he starts in on Jeff.

"First of all. You tried to pull a game on Andy." Jeff starts to protest, but stops when C.T. raises his hand like a traffic cop. "Don't ever do that again. When we're done here, you're gonna pay Andy back his three hundred, and another hundred for his troubles." Jeff doesn't look happy, but nods his head. C.T. says, "I can't fucking hear your brains rattle. Is that a yes or a no?"

"Yes, yes, sir, I'm sorry," Jeff says. C.T. waves it away.

"Okay. We understand each other." C.T. takes a sip of coffee, and looks at the waitress for a moment, bending over a table across the room. The woman is new at Lisa's, maybe her midthirties, probably too young for him, but she looks good in a pair of jeans, bent over a table, taking an order. She is the type of slum goddess that the Clintonville neighborhood has attracted by the busload for decades. He imagines her for a moment on a hotel balcony, kneeling in front of him, then turns back to Jeff.

"Now, your problem isn't these mokes who ripped you off. Your problem is Rakkim. He owes you money. You get it from him. What he owes you and then some. For your trouble."

"How I am supposed to do that?" Jeff says.

C.T. takes another sip of coffee, and stares at Jeff over the rim of the cup. The coffee, he thinks, is really good this morning. The old hippie who owns the place is home where he belongs so he can't fuck it up. C.T. looks at the waitress again and she smiles over her shoulder at him.

C.T. smiles back at her, then smiles at Jeff.

"How about," he says, "I'll show you."

LAWRENCE LIGHT

Lawrence Light is no stranger to the world of financial skullduggery that his character Karen Glick tackles in *Too Rich To Live* and *Fear and Greed*. As an award-winning reporter covering Wall Street, Larry writes about the world Glick investigates. His real-life experience has given him insider information on the corrupting force of greed. And has given him his own share of enemies along the way.

"The Lamented" takes a slightly different turn as it examines the toll greed can take on the human conscience, even in characters who seem to lack one of their own. When their past pays them a visit, some unsavory individuals discover how easily the line between reality and imagination is blurred. But when all is said and done, payback is as unavoidable as it is deadly.

THE LAMENTED

When the man he'd killed a year ago walked into the bar, Joe Dogan was surprised. So surprised that he fell off his stool.

Dogan lay on his back on the sticky floor, his eyes as rounded as the moon, and mouthed words silently. His glass rolled away from him, trailing bourbon.

Brad Acton, dead a year now, smiled, showing his fine teeth. Brad's well-cut suit fit just right on his trim, tall body, and his well-cut blond hair flopped just right down his noble forehead. Brad seemed delighted to be here, even though this had to be the seediest bar in Camden, New Jersey, arguably the nation's seediest city. When he was alive, he had been perpetually delighted, and everyone was delighted by him.

With a smile as bright as the day outside, Brad took a step toward where Dogan lay sprawled.

Dogan managed to make a sound: "Noooooooooooo." He closed his eyes and shook his head. It must be the booze. A few times before, after tipping too many wet ones, he'd had hallucinations.

Slowly, warily, Dogan opened his eyes. The bar was empty again. The light from the revolving beer sign was the brightest thing in this dark place. It twinkled off the treasury of neatly shelved booze bottles. The afternoon shined beneath the door. The bartender—

Wobbling, Dogan climbed to his feet. He steadied himself with a good, strong grip on the edge of the bar. "I need a drink," he bellowed.

Where the hell was the bartender? The little weenie had diligently poured his drinks without complaint, even when Dogan drove the two other customers out, threatening to kill them if they didn't stop yapping about politics.

His .45 lay on the bar. Dogan hefted the gun and admired it in the light from the revolving beer sign. Nice, powerful weapon.

Oh, yeah. The bartender left after Dogan had waved the .45 in his face. Dogan remembered now. Couldn't the jackass tell that Dogan was only kidding around?

"That's the gun you killed me with."

Dogan gulped painfully, as if he were swallowing an entire lemon down his suddenly parched throat. He turned around with elaborate, jaw-clenched care.

"It's in better shape than you are," Brad said, pleasantly enough. He stood a mere two feet from Joe. The breezy, confident way Brad acted—this could have been another election campaign stop for him.

Dogan tried to say, "You can't be here." Instead, it came out as: "Yaaaacunbur."

"Why not?" Brad said. "It was a year ago tonight."

Dogan was breathing at a marathoner's tempo. He could hear his heart slamming wildly inside his rib cage, as though it wanted to escape.

"Joe, Joe, Joe. What am I going to do with you? That no-show county job that Robert Stagg arranged for you isn't doing wonders for your character. Drinking in the middle of the day? Your job is supposed to be on the roads. Hard work, but honest work."

"I—I—I—I—I—I—I—I—I—I…"

Brad's smile grew still more incandescent. "Robert and you and I really must get together. Tonight makes sense. How's tonight for you?"

He reached out to shake Joe's hand. Like any masterful politician, Brad was a skillful and eager shaker of hands.

Dogan screamed and backpedaled in panic. He knocked over several barstools and fell hard on his butt. He lost his hold on the gun. It went spinning off on the floor. Making wounded animal noises, Dogan crawled away from the bar. With hands and knees scurrying, he did not dare look back at Brad.

"Robert Stagg only paid you ten thousand to kill me," Brad said. "I'm worth a lot more than that. Ten thousand? Chicken feed. Too bad the Justice Department is going to bag him. And on a corruption charge, not for my murder. How is that justice?"

Dogan stopped crawling when his head hit the jukebox. Fortunately for him, drink dulled the pain. The collision jolted the juke to life. It played an old Michael Jackson tune, the one with Vincent Price. He slumped against the machine, staring at the fading tattoo that decorated his thick forearm: a heart pierced with an arrow.

Fearfully, Dogan raised his gaze. He brought his fingers, sticky from the filthy floor, to his stubbly cheeks.

Skanky's Tavern was empty once more.

Dogan clasped the jukebox to get up. He moved unsteadily, whether from the shock or from the bourbon, to the bar. En route, he successfully stooped to collect his .45 from the floor. He knew he had to leave before Brad appeared again. But first—

Dogan trudged behind the bar and hoisted the bourbon bottle. He glugged down torrents of the blessed stuff, burning his gullet and soothing his nerves. The bottle emptied, Dogan threw it against the wall. It shattered satisfyingly.

Checking around for Brad, Dogan stalked—actually weaved—out of Skanky's. He shoved the .45 into the pocket of his ratty jacket. The early spring sun assaulted his retinas. He stumbled as the pink, purple and green circles swirled. Then they disappeared, and he could see again. With his head tilted back, the first thing he saw was the soaring mass of the Benjamin Franklin Bridge over the wrecked rooftops.

His chin fell to his chest. Two small kids, maybe around nine or ten, were messing with his motorcycle. One had the stones to sit on it, his pipe-stem arms extending to the handlebars. "Vroom, vroom," he cried with joy as he twisted the throttle in imaginary acceleration.

Dogan pulled out the keys to his Harley, but dropped them on the stained sidewalk. "Get off my damn bike, you little bastards," he roared at them. Then he slowly reached down for the keys, taking care not to fall over.

"You drunk as a monkey," shouted the one sitting on the bike. Both kids tittered.

The keys retrieved, Dogan drew himself upright. He didn't like kids. He didn't like blacks. The truth was he didn't like anybody. And he double-disliked anybody messing with his bike. Even Christ himself had no business messing with Joe's bike. And Christ hadn't been to Camden in a long while.

Dogan struggled the gun out of his jacket pocket. The sight was caught in some fabric. He ripped it free.

"White man's packing," the kid on the bike cried out and he jumped off agilely. Laughing, the two of them ran away.

Stewed as he was, Dogan realized he shouldn't be brandishing his weapon on the street. Not for fear of cops, who were as scarce as a brontosaurus in the fossilized ruins of Camden. This neighborhood, Dogan knew, was Mister Man's turf, called H Town, for heroin. To the north was Dope City and to the south was Crackville. But in this swath of Camden, Mister Man was the absolute ruler, his power akin to Kim Jong-Il's. In H Town, no one pulled out a piece unless Mister Man okayed it. Mister Man had the monopoly on firepower here. Dogan stuffed his .45 back into his pocket and jerkily mounted his bike.

He kick-started the Harley Night Rod into life. In a flash of chrome, he sped his 7,000 r.p.m. screamer through the rutted roads of H Town, past the unending series of boarded-up, graffiti-marred row houses and stores, past the dry fire hydrants, past the dead streetlamps. He headed for Wilson Boulevard, where he could open her up. If a cop stopped him, he had the juice to skip away free. Robert Stagg would ensure that.

What Joe Dogan needed was wind through his hair. What he needed was to wipe out the daytime nightmare of Brad Acton, dead a year now.

The memorial ceremony for Brad Acton droned on ad nauseam. The marbled, colonnaded lobby of the county courthouse overflowed with worshippers, recalling how their beloved Brad had been snatched from them a year ago today. The courthouse sat on Market Street, a drab strip of bail-bond offices and pawnbroker shops. It was the largest employer in Camden; make that the largest legitimate employer. A concrete, Depression-era monument to the futility of government to bring about a civil society in Camden, the courthouse was festooned with too many blown-up photos of the late, great Brad.

Robert Stagg, a high-level county official, sat in the

front row and suffered through the sentimental twaddle about the "historic Acton legacy." Both New Jersey U.S. senators and the governor were on hand. Up at the podium was that moron Denny Shaughnessy, blathering about how Brad was "the best freeholder this county has ever seen." A few seats down from Stagg was Denny's wife, crying bitterly. Brad had been screwing her for years.

"Brad would've been our next congressman from the First District," Denny was saying. "Then a year ago, at midnight, some son of a bitch gunned him down. On his own doorstep. In Haddonfield, for God's sake." Denny, a fellow freeholder from the suburbs, was offended that a crime would occur in wealthy Haddonfield. Violence was too gauche to be permitted there. It was as if Haddonfield had become Camden.

To Stagg's right was Brad's widow, who still looked great if you didn't look closely. She wore a Donna Karan suit that needed dry cleaning. Her knees were spread like a schoolgirl's. She chewed her brunette hair.

Everyone had been dismayed that Stagg had married Diana Acton, so soon after Brad's death. But since Brad's murder had devastated her, they got used to the idea.

"Take me home, Robert," Diana said in that little-girl's voice she had adopted lately. "This is all stupid."

"If they ever find the coward who murdered Brad," Denny ranted, "I want him to swing from the highest tree."

"This will be over in a moment," Stagg whispered to his wife, containing his exasperation at her, at Denny, at the whole idiotic ceremony. He wanted it to be over, too.

"There's no need for it," Diana went on. Stagg shushed her gently. He had always treated her gently, even when he shouldn't.

"I played football at Haddonfield High with Brad, and thanks to him, we won the state championship two years in a row," Denny said, calming down some.

With rancor, Stagg recalled his service as team manager, when he waited on Brad like a servant, when he was the target of the team's jokes and pranks, when even Brad called him "Stagg the Bag" for his shapeless body.

"Once Brad became a freeholder, he started to turn around our county seat," Denny said. "If he'd lived, Camden would be cleaned up. Brad always kept a promise."

The county's white, bucolic suburbs surrounding Camden pretended to be impressed by that pledge, Stagg remembered ruefully. The truth was the wealthy sub-urbanites didn't care about blighted inner-city Camden, the county's shameful dark heart, a drug-ridden, gang-run hell. When Brad agreed to back Stagg for the Board of Free-holders, the county's governing body, Stagg bravely said he'd campaign on resurrecting the city of Camden, too. Brad told him not to bother; he had that covered.

So Denny Shaughnessy nattered away, Sheila Shaugh-nessy sobbed and Diana Acton—she insisted on keeping the name from her first marriage—twiddled her thumbs in her lap. Robert Stagg wished she had taken a bigger dose of Halcion.

His attention wandered around the lobby, transformed

nauseatingly into the Saint Brad Cathedral. He knew almost everyone in the crowd. And he liked that they gazed at him with respect, much as they had with Brad. He had been asked to speak, of course, yet had demurred out of concern for Diana. He needed to be at her side constantly.

Stagg's eyes bugged out.

There. In the crowd, by the elevators. Standing tall. The blond hair over his forehead. Smiling as if every day was his birthday. Staring at Stagg.

Stagg whimpered involuntarily.

"What's wrong, Freeholder Stagg?" asked Jimmy Sparacino, the Democratic Party's county chairman, who sat to Stagg's left.

"Nothing, nothing, nothing." The vision of Brad had vanished in the throng.

"I wish you'd spoken today," Sparacino whispered. "You were Brad's best friend. I understand about poor Diana, but…"

Sparacino liked to refer to Brad's widow as "poor Diana." Luckily for her new husband, Diana was far from poor. She had inherited a load from her rich family, and Brad's fortune had passed to her, also. Now it was Stagg's.

Stagg thanked the chairman for his concern. "This is a rough day for her," he said in a low voice she couldn't hear. "All the memories rushing back—it's hard to handle."

When Brad chose Stagg to run, Sparacino had objected, saying, "Stagg's fat, he's bald, he's ugly. The only reason to vote for him is he's your gofer." Since Brad's death, Sparacino had changed his mind and come to value Stagg's brains. As he should, having none himself.

At long, painful last, the ceremony ended. The dignitaries stood up to greet, gab and guffaw. Smiling is to politics what dribbling is to basketball. But Stagg wasn't in the mood to play the game today. He took Diana's arm and led her out.

He passed the U.S. Attorney, Javers, who was flanked by his young Dobermans in their Brooks Brothers suits. They regarded Stagg hungrily. "We'll see you tomorrow morning at nine, Freeholder Stagg," Javers said from somewhere above his bow tie. "Sharp."

Stagg couldn't meet the man's eyes and instead looked to the side, toward the crowd. "Talk to my lawyer, Mr. Javers, not me."

As they reached the crowded door, Diana said, in her nursery school cadences, "What did that mean-looking man in the bow tie want?"

"Some nonsense Justice Department fishing expedition about the widening of Salem Turnpike in Lindenwold. I pushed it through the board." Stagg didn't mention to her that the road project benefited a monster shopping mall that went in a year later. Or let on who owned the mall.

Diana walked like her old regal self. Perfect posture, proud stride. Too bad she didn't talk like her old self. "The ceremony was stupid. Stupid, stupid, stupid."

"Whatever you say, Diana." In fact, this was Diana's

only sensible utterance in a long time. "I know this was difficult for you."

"It's stupid because Brad is alive."

"Alive?"

Her laugh was one he'd never heard before, almost like a crow's cawing. "He was here today. I talked to him. Why have a memorial ceremony when he's alive?"

Stagg grimaced. "You're mistaken, Diana. I myself saw someone in the crowd who looked a lot like Brad. But Brad is dead. We're all on edge today."

As they reached Stagg's Volvo, parked in his designated spot, his cell phone rang. The display read Homey the Clown. He groaned and flipped it open. "Freeholder Stagg," he said, full of entitlement and self-assurance.

"Brad's come back for me," Diana said, getting into the car.

A Barry White–deep voice came on the line. "Hello, neighbor." The gangster got a kick out of his recent move to a Haddonfield mansion from his old Camden row house. "Are we good for tomorrow? Or are we bad?"

The confidence in Stagg's voice faltered. "The U.S. Attorney has nothing to link you and me and Salem Turnpike. This is a crock. Javers can't—"

"Enough, neighbor," Mister Man said. "I be checking, is all."

"While you're at it, check where my money is. My banker in Luxembourg says not one red cent has arrived this month from you."

Like Brad, Mister Man was ruffled by nothing and no one. "Always with you and the money. Brad Acton never mentioned the money. He had class up the ass. Neighbor, you not just a freeholder. You a freeloader."

"Well said. Brad the classy guy. What an original viewpoint. Now if that will be all, I need to take my wife…"

"I got me another reason to call. We got us a problem."

"Where's Brad?" Diana called from the passenger seat.

Stagg sagged. "Oh, no. Now what?"

"That crazy-mother white-trash boy of yours, the one with the no-show job on the county road crew." The drug lord sounded angry. "That drunken hunk of human garbage named Joe Dogan. He be in one of my bars in H Town today, Skanky's, pointing his piece at my peeps like he the Frito Bandito. Customers and bartender went running. Then he aimed the gun at two little kids. Can you believe that?"

"Oh, Lord. Not Dogan." Stagg shook his head. "Fine. I'll give him hell. Again."

"I know Dogan took care of our problem with Brad Acton, neighbor. But I am sick of his presence on this earth. I'm not gonna give him hell, I'm gonna send him to hell. I mean, little kids?"

"Do what you want with him. I'm tired of Dogan, too."

When Stagg settled his copious behind into the driver's seat, he saw that Diana was smiling and humming.

"I'm glad you're back in a good mood, Diana."

"He said he'd come to the house tonight." Diana's strange grin widened. "He looks wonderful. Brad is back. I am very, very happy."

* * *

The moon was a tight, white fist overhead. By nightfall, Joe Dogan was getting very frustrated, not to mention very drunk. He sat on a bench in a deserted park by the Cooper River. A full six-pack of beer was beside him, sweating, still cold. The other six-pack was almost gone. Only one can remained in its plastic yoke.

Cursing, he fished his phone out of his pocket, and for the umpteenth time, stabbed redial. He got Stagg's cell-phone voice mail, as usual. "Call me back, you fat sack of crap," Dogan snarled. He'd left the identical message the time before, and the time before that.

Stagg had told Dogan never to contact him unless there was an emergency, like the cops asking about Brad Acton's death, or if Dogan got into a jam that would interest the law. And Dogan was never to go to where Stagg lived. A year ago, that had been in a garden apartment in Cherry Hill. Now, Dogan knew from the scuttlebutt, Stagg lived in Acton's palatial house and was married to the widow. What a babe like Diana Acton saw in a piglet like Robert Stagg was beyond Dogan.

"Must have a wart on the end of it," Dogan muttered as he popped open the last brewski in his first six-pack.

Wait. In his wallet. He had a scrap of paper with Brad Acton's home phone number. It was unlisted. Stagg had given him the number a year ago, so he could call and be sure Acton was home.

★ ★ ★

Dinner was a horror show. The latest cook refused to set a place for Brad. When Diana screamed at her—for not whipping up Brad's favorite dessert, peach cobbler—the woman stormed out.

Stagg tried to settle Diana down in front of the TV in the cinema-large entertainment center. A Discovery Channel show on hunting was playing; a deer fled through the woods with baying hounds in pursuit. But she wouldn't stop chattering about Brad's miraculous return to life.

Stagg tried to watch the show. But her comments grew more and more irritating. "Brad was the loveliest man" and "you have no money, really."

"I make plenty of money."

"How? All you ever did was puppy-dog behind Brad." She gave a brittle laugh. "Oh, I know. You are taking bribes. From that gangster who moved to Haddonfield. That's why the mean man in the bow tie wants to put you in prison."

Slumping even deeper into the huge, overstuffed chair, Stagg said, "Diana, maybe you should go to bed. Have you taken your meds?"

This behavior was new. She'd been mostly lethargic in recent months. The doctor said to be careful if she became delusional. The risk of suicide was small, but couldn't be shrugged off. Stagg kept the kitchen knives locked up. Ditto the German Luger, which Brad's father had brought back from World War II.

"Since Brad is back, we should get our marriage annulled. I can't be married to you. You aren't Brad. I only married you because I needed someone to take care of me. But you are nothing."

"How thoughtful of you to say. I'm going outside."

"Brad will take care of me again."

Stagg fetched a large sweater and poured himself a modest measure of Chivas. It was a bit chilly on the patio, but better than listening to her insanity.

He sloshed scotch around in his tumbler, standing next to the empty pool with its dead-leaf-coated bottom. The plastic rope with the floats, which divided the deep end from the shallow, lay coiled on the greening lawn like a dead snake.

Stagg's memory fell back to high school days. Brad always had a pool party here for the football team. Stagg, as team manager, was also invited. Senior year, to everyone's delight, Brad and Denny swung little Stagg by his ankles and wrists, and tossed him into the pool. Stagg couldn't swim. That was even funnier.

The night after that party, Stagg stayed hidden among the trees and spied on Brad and Diana, the virgin queen of Haddonfield High. It was the apex of his life up to then, seeing Brad deflower lovely, naked Diana, poolside.

Another big, world-beating memory: how, tending to the stunned Diana in the wake of Brad's death, he brought her groceries in on a night as starkly moonlit as this one. How Diana rose from the swimming pool, water glistening on her bare skin, her forty-year-old body as taut as a teenager's.

How under that hunters' moon, she had smiled at him. Diana, naked for him. That night was the true apex.

Diana's shrill cry broke the reverie. She stood in the French doors to the study. "You have a phone call."

Stagg trundled inside. The landline phone display read Joe Dogan. Wonderful. That dirtbag must have kept the unlisted number from a year ago. "What do you want?"

Diana was climbing the stairs. "I'm tired. Wake me up when Brad comes."

Dogan had ingested his usual royal portion of spirits. "You gotta help me out."

Had Dogan heard that he was on Mister Man's priority boarding list for evacuation from the planet? "I'm getting sick of this, you idiot."

"You think you're smarter than everyone," Dogan slurred. "Well, I'm not the idiot. You're the idiot."

"Brilliant comeback," Stagg said. "Repartee worthy of Dorothy Parker."

"Never met the bitch," Dogan said. "We got a problem,"

"*We* do, huh? Let me guess. You got another drunk-driving arrest on that stupid motorcycle, and I have to fix things with the cops. No, your supervisor on the county road crew called, and you told him you'd kill his children if he didn't back off. No, you were drunk and groping women at T.G.I. Friday's happy hour, and one called the cops. I've bailed you out so many times for so much asinine behavior that I'm losing track."

With a moan, Dogan said, "Have you seen him?"

"Who?"

"Brad Acton came to me in a bar in H Town this afternoon. He said he wanted to see us. Both. Tonight."

Stagg sighed. "My wife had the same hallucination. Her, high on meds. You, high on booze. Astute observers, the two of you."

"He was real, man. I mean, not like a ghost. I couldn't, like, see through him."

"I can see through you. You are a serious alcoholic. Go get dried out."

"He knew how much you paid me to do him. Plus, the no-show job on the county roads. How could he know that?"

"Because it is in your drink-addled head. Today is the anniversary. It brings back the trauma, makes you imagine things. You don't have to be Freud to understand that."

"He knew you are gonna get a barbed-wire enema from the feds. Mister Man pays you off, Stagg. Everybody knows it."

"You know nothing," Stagg snarled. "Brad was ten times as dirty as me. He came from family money, but wanted more. He introduced me to Mister Man. Then when Javers came sniffing around, Brad wanted me to be the fall guy. He wanted me to take Mister Man down, too."

"I remember every minute from a year ago."

"Meantime, King Brad stays simon-pure. Well, ha-ha, Brad. For the first time in your pampered life, you lost."

Dogan didn't seem to be listening anymore. "I tell you,

he seemed like flesh and blood. Like you and me. I bet I could put another bullet in him, and that'd be that."

"Check yourself into rehab, you cretin."

"I don't want to face him alone tonight, man."

Stagg slammed the phone down.

A wind came up and blew about the budding branches of the ghostly trees. Winter and summer warred in the sudden draft off the river, and Dogan shivered. What was he doing sitting here like a frozen pond toad?

Dogan got on his bike and blasted away from the riverfront park. In a jiffy, his Harley's loud engine was invading the smooth, quiet roads of Haddonfield, Brad Acton's hometown. In Haddonfield, trees flower first, and their perfume seeped down from the elegant mosaic of branches that covered the old lanes.

The Harley brayed down King's Highway, the town's main street, where subtly lit colonial storefronts displayed chic clothing and leather goods. Tomorrow, the slender, blond women of the marvelous men of Haddonfield would float past those storefronts, browsing, blasé.

A year had gone by and beer had fuzzed his thinking, hence Dogan took a while to find Brad Acton's house. He clattered through the lovely streets until he saw the right landmarks. Left at the three-century-old church, right at the giant white-board mansion, left onto Cypress Avenue.

Front yard carriage lamps shed soft glows on the brick and flagstone walkways flowing from the smooth road to the fine wood doors that guarded the aristocratic stone houses. Through the latticed windows of those handsome homes came the lamplight of the Haddonfield elite, who ran the world.

Acton's house, though, lay in darkness. Girded by vigilant firs, watched over by towering oaks, it seemed almost un-inhabited. Then Dogan saw the two cars parked to the side: Stagg's Volvo and Diana Acton's Jaguar. He killed the bike's motor and dismounted.

It had been a year ago, around midnight. About now, his watch said.

He couldn't stand there forever, hypnotized by the house, the night, the clock. Dogan walked cautiously up the sloping, well-barbered lawn, bathed in intense moonglow. The wind, a devilish mix of warm and cold, made small gasps among the trees' flowers.

A shadow shimmered among the tree trunks. Dogan gave a start and yelped. He yanked his .45 out of his coat pocket, tearing more fabric. "Killed you once, I'll kill you twice, bastard," he said through bared teeth.

His gun moved in small semicircles, pointed at where the movement had been, as he marched up the lawn. With his attention fixed on the trees, he missed seeing the ankle-high miniwall bisecting the lawn in front of him. Dogan went down hard, swearing.

Hell, last year, making this same approach, he'd tripped on the miniwall. He had been drunker then, but this couldn't be a coincidence.

The wind came again, colder now, and enveloped him with a harsh sense of dread. Was he reliving the same night from a year ago?

The castlelike front door loomed in front of him. Dogan punched the doorbell button, and heard sweet chimes inside. As he had a year ago.

He hit the button again. As he had a year ago.

Somehow, he smelled burnt gunpowder. As he had a year ago.

Stagg had clumped wearily up the stairs, left his clothes on the floor of his dressing room and climbed into his pajamas. He heaved into the broad bed, where Diana lay, asleep. Good. No more nonsense from her. He had barely slipped into sleep's welcome oblivion when the doorbell chimes rang. Repeatedly.

Diana was screaming. "Don't go down there, Brad. Don't go."

He was fully awake. "I'm Robert, dammit."

Finally, Dogan heard footsteps beyond the door. A muffled voice asked him who he was and what he wanted. Just like a year ago.

He replied the same. "It's me. Joe Dogan. Robert's guy. It's about Mister Man."

An inside light went on. The bolt slid open. The door swung inward. A man was in the threshold.

Brad Acton stood there, in his nice suit, with his nice hair, smiling. No one could smile like Brad.

Dogan raised the gun and pulled the trigger. The first shot splattered that handsome head. He pumped bullet after bullet into the body, as it lay on the Persian rug.

He stumbled down the lawn. He needed a drink. Was he out of beer?

A Mercedes slid to the curb, beside the parked Harley. A large black man, in a white suit and fedora, climbed out. He glanced at the motorcycle, then spotted Joe Dogan weaving toward him. Joe carried a gun. In the moonlight, Mister Man could see the slide was back and the weapon was empty.

"I'm on my way home and I see that this human garbage has blown into Haddonfield. They don't allow your punk-ass kind here."

"I killed Brad again," Dogan said.

"Do tell. A lotta killing going around."

Mister Man pulled his Glock out of its shoulder holster and blew a large hole in worthless Joe Dogan's chest. The fool fell backward onto Brad Acton's fine lawn and began to bleed on it.

Mister Man turned to his car, then stopped when he glimpsed the silhouette of a man up in the Acton house. A tall man standing in an upstairs window, taking in all that had happened on the moon-bright lawn. A witness.

Was it Stagg? Mister Man had better find out the state of play, before the neighbors called the cops. Of course, the lots here were far apart and the refined folk nearby may not have heard the gunfire. Or if they did hear, they wouldn't know what it was. This was Haddonfield, not H Town. He had a little time, he figured.

Mister Man loped up the lawn, Glock at the ready. The tall fellow in the window waved. He was blond, well-dressed and familiar. Then he stepped out of sight.

The front door gaped open. Mister Man stepped gingerly inside.

"Oh, sweet Jesus."

A pajama-clad Robert Stagg lay on the fine carpet, in a lake of blood. His bald head was a mass of goo. Bullet holes riddled his globular body. He was as dead as Camden's hopes.

"You can't come in here. This is Brad Acton's house."

A woman's voice. Mister Man looked up.

Diana Acton, lovely in a diaphanous nightgown, stood in the hall. She held a Luger in a two-handed grip. It was pointed at Mister Man.

He held out a conciliatory hand and advanced toward her, speaking low. "Let's be cool. I was in business with your husband. Both of them."

Diana opened fire. Mister Man keeled over and landed on Stagg's body. The gangster twitched a few times. The blood stained his white suit. Whether it was Stagg's blood or Mister Man's own blood was hard to tell. She dropped the gun.

Robert Stagg, Joe Dogan and Mister Man were all dead. Diana was pleased. Brad always kept a promise.

Diana turned. She had heard a voice say her name. "I'm coming, Brad, darling," she called with a radiant smile. "I'm coming to bed."

She ran up the stairs.

LISA JACKSON

Lisa Jackson is known for her legion of fans and for her fascination with the motives of her characters. Her stories explore the puzzle of complex relationships and the clues that can only be found in the rich personal histories of her protagonists. In a way that makes her novels as moving as they are thrilling, she confronts the fear faced by her victims and doesn't shy away from the harsh truth that terror and madness touch far too many lives in the real world.

Nowhere is that skill more evident than in "Vintage Death." Here we have a story that is classic Lisa Jackson—a perfect blend of romantic suspense and danger that creates empathy and suspicion for the characters in equal parts. She shows us the complexity of family relationships and how important—and dangerous—families can be.

VINTAGE DEATH

"Don't go."

The words rang through the vestibule, an anxious plea, but then that was my mother, always the worrier, forever on the verge of a breakdown. That her voice trembled was no big deal. The original drama queen, that was Mom.

"I have to go, okay?" I yelled my response through the closed bathroom door in the upper hallway. I wasn't going to put up with her overhyped paranoia. Not that she didn't have a reason to be frightened, terrified even, but, hey, someone had to get the job done and that someone had to be me. No one else was volunteering.

"You should call the police. There was that nice detective…what was his name? Kent something? I can't remember."

Noah Kent, I thought, *Noah way. Noah police. Not this time.* "Forget it, Mom."

"He's still on the force."

Of course he was. Noah Kent was a lifer—married to his job. Even after the accident that nearly cost him his badge. Just ask his ex-wife.

"Then call Lucas. You've got to still have his number?"

I stopped dead in my tracks.

Lucas Parker.

Ace detective.

Handsome as sin.

And a major prick.

Of course I still had his number.

Oh, yeah, that's what I'd do. Give Parker a call. "I'll handle this on my own." I wasn't about to be budged. I put on my bra, which, gently padded, added two cup sizes to my breasts, giving my slim frame a little bit of a curve…like hers.

Then I slipped on a sleek black dress, one with a nipped-in waist and wide neck. A little on the sexy side for my taste, but tonight it would do nicely, I thought, critically eyeing my reflection in the vanity mirror. And besides, the invitation had indicated everyone was to wear black. Just as there were those "all white" parties, Silvio D'Amato had gone with a black theme. All the better.

After pulling my hair away from my face and securing it, I donned a dark auburn wig, which curled softly under my chin and brushed my shoulders. Spidery eyelashes much longer than my own highlighted my eyes, which were now a deep shade of brown, compliments of tinted contact lenses. A little padding tucked into in my cheeks helped with the transformation. My teeth were a little off—nothing I could do about that but keep my mouth closed. I added a tiny spot of color under my cheekbones and blended it with my foundation, making my complexion appear seamless. Carefully, I brushed on a touch of smoky eye shadow.

The effect was amazing.

I was barely recognizable.

No one at the party would suspect my true identity. Which was perfect.

I stepped out of the bathroom, made my way down the hall in three-inch heels, then discarded them for a pair with a shorter heels that didn't pinch my feet so much. Besides, they were easier to walk in. Considering the fact that I'd be holding a glass of champagne while mingling with the other guests on uneven flagstones, the second pair just made more sense.

Especially if I needed to run.

And, of course, I snagged a pair of leather gloves that I tucked into my purse.

Once in the hallway again, I paused for a second at the open door to Ian's room. A cold sense of déjà vu settled over me like a shroud. Everything was as it had been. A set of Transformers action figures displayed upon a bookcase with a few Legos, picture books, his twin bed, perfectly made, the dinosaur motif evident in the curtains of the wide window… Oh, God, the window…

My throat tightened as I stared at it, the innocent-looking panes overlooking the garden and farther away, over the tops of other houses on the hill, the bay with its blue waters turning dusky as night approached.

I closed my eyes.

Leaned against the doorjamb.

Thought of him. Ian…only five…poor, poor baby.

"Are you all right?" Mother's voice floated up the staircase from the floor below. I had to pull myself together. No matter how much pain blackened my soul, tonight, I had to act as if I were carefree, as if I truly was the woman I was pretending to be.

I took a deep breath before clearing the thickness from my throat. "I'm fine, Mom," I lied, sounding cheery. "Be down in a second."

Now, just do this!

At the top of the second-floor landing, I stared down the curved steps and faced Dear Old Mom who, on her scooter, gasped as she saw me. "Oh…my…God… I…I can't believe it."

I forced myself down the long flight. "Think I'll be able to pull this off?" I asked, making my voice breathy and low and twirling at the top of the landing.

"I…I…"

"You're in shock." That was encouraging. *Very* encouraging. "I'll take that as a 'yes.'" I hurried down the stairs where my mother sat dumbstruck in the marble foyer, soft light from the chandelier bathing her in its kind illumination. At "somewhere north of seventy" she still looked great, her hair a shimmering platinum shade, only a few slight wrinkles visible, her petite body, if not as svelte as it once had been, damned close.

If it hadn't been for the scooter, she would seem a decade younger than her age.

"You can't do this," she said desperately, gnawing at her lower lip. "You won't get away with it."

"Just watch me."

"Seriously."

"Look, Mom, no one will recognize me. And *she'll* be there."

"That's why you can't go." Mom was in a near panic. Good Lord, the woman was high-strung.

"Don't worry. If anything goes wrong, I'll call and you can dial 911 to your heart's content."

"No reason to be snide," she sniffed.

"Then let it go." In the front hall closet I found a long black coat and a scarf, both of which I donned as Mom fiddled with the cross dangling from a chain around her neck. No doubt she was whispering a dozen Hail Marys to save my wretched, vindictive soul.

Little did she know that my own heart was beating as wildly as a timpani being pounded by a frantic heavy metal drummer. My hands were clammy and adrenaline spurted crazily through my veins.

"Just…be careful."

"I will," I promised. I reached for the doorknob but

stopped and faced my poor mother once more. "You know I have to do this. She killed Ian."

"You can't be certain."

"I know she did it. I was there! I found him! In the garden—" I pointed frantically to the side of the house, the area I'd loved as a child with its dark foliage, creeping vines and gravel paths leading to secret, private hiding places where squirrels nested and owls roosted. I hated that place now. I fought the urge to break down completely. "I saw her in the window. Looking down. But she tried to blame me," I said. "And you."

Mom nodded slightly, unable to meet my eyes as the ancient grandfather clock near the door ticked off the remaining seconds of our lives.

"He was just a child," I reminded her gently. "Your only grandson."

Mom's eyes closed. She swallowed back tears and rubbed the gold cross for all it was worth. "This isn't the way. It's not right." Her lower lip quivered.

"An eye for an eye, Mom. It's in the Bible."

"Wait…" She was confused. "'An eye for an eye'? But I thought you were just going to talk to her…."

Damn. "Just an expression." Anger burned through my blood again, the same quiet rage that overtook me every time I thought of my baby's senseless death. My outrage and pain hadn't always been silent. I'd wailed and screamed, shouted oaths and sworn vengeance. When I'd found my son's body, broken from a horrible push through his bedroom window, I'd come apart at the seams, had been forced into seclusion, drugged and analyzed and then, of course, accused of being out of my mind. I'd actually had to suffer accusations that I had shoved my son through the window to his death on the garden path below.

It made me sick to think about it. Even now I swallowed back the bile that rose in my throat and shuddered at the image scored in my memory. Ian's tiny broken body lying upon the cold stones of the manor.

Black rage poured through my soul.

"I think…I think you— We should let it go," Mom said, blinking to stave off tears. "It's been five years."

"And she got away with murder. Your grandson's murder."

"Oh, please, don't do this."

"Too late, Mom. I just want to talk to her. Let her know that I'm on to her. Give her a good jolt."

"Why would she confide in you?"

"Because they always do. Murderers want to crow. To brag about their accomplishments, or…if it truly was an accident, I'll see her guilt, her remorse. She won't be able to hide her emotions."

"You think." Clearly Mom was skeptical. From the hallway near the den came Mom's little dog, Peppy, a brown-and-white terrier-Chihuahua mix, toenails clicking on the polished marble. The beast gave me its usual response—a nasty little snarl. "Peppy, stop that!"

The dog jumped into Mom's lap and continued to growl as it regarded me with dark, suspicious eyes.

Time to leave.

"Don't worry. I'll be back soon!" I brushed a kiss over her brow, leaving a lipstick mark and rubbing it out before Peppy had the chance to lunge. Then I dashed out the door, my heels clicking on the brick walkway that curved to the front gates. Ferns and rhododendron shivered in the breath of wind and rising mist.

Mom really pissed me off. I love her to death, but she has never been one to take action. Ever. While Dad was alive she let him push her around, just so she could live in this grandiose house. Perched high on the hill, the "Old Dickens Estate" with its four floors, brick facade and glittering beveled glass windows had an incredible view of San Francisco Bay, the angular rooftops of Victorian mansions and the Golden Gate Bridge.

Nice house. But was it worth the verbal and physical abuse she'd had to endure until Dad finally decided to end it all by hanging himself in his private den?

I didn't think so.

In the garage I found my old, nearly forgotten BMW and climbed behind the wheel, then saw her Mercedes, barely used, parked in another bay. Wouldn't the Benz be a better choice? Arrive in a shiny luxury car and have it valet parked, rather than screeching up in the old three series with the dent in one side? Of course it would. Mom kept her keys in a crystal dish on a small Louis XVI table near the front door.

And the gun.

The damned pistol.

I'd forgotten to pack it in my purse. It was up in my bedroom where I'd left it earlier, but I'd have to make some excuse to run back upstairs. Luckily Mom couldn't get that decrepit old elevator to move fast enough to chase me down, even if she wanted to.

I checked my watch.

No doubt I'd be late.

Even with the valet parking.

But so be it.

I hurried back inside, bolstering myself to go one more round with Lorna and her insipid dog.

Security detail.

What a laugh.

Lucas Parker walked through a two-hundred-year-old breeze-way that was part of this aging monastery. The monks were long gone, the archdiocese having sold off the stucco and stone buildings and rolling acres to Ernesto D'Amato over a century before. Nowadays the vines they'd so carefully cultivated produced some of the best grapes for Syrah in the country, making D'Amato Winery world-renowned. Thus Silvio D'Amato Junior was currently the "King of Syrah," if you believed his overblown press.

Parker didn't.

In fact, he didn't give a rat's ass about any kind of wine.

Not that it mattered. He was just the hired help tonight. An ex-cop from the local police force here to ensure that the snobs and wanna-be snobs sipping the famed wine and nibbling on overpriced cheese and razor-thin crackers were safe.

And why wouldn't they be? Located in the hills surrounding the quaint tourist town of Sonoma in the Valley of the Moon, D'Amato Monastery Estates had never, to date, had a break-in. Not one bottle of their prize-winning Syrah had been reported stolen, never even a trespasser discovered, not so much as one grape missing.

Parker thought hiring security was overkill.

Yet, here he was, wearing a tux with a collar that was far too tight, his shoulder-holster properly hidden, feeling useless. He'd retired from the force a couple of years back. Early retirement, thanks to a stakeout gone wrong and a stray bullet that had lodged in the lumbar region of his spine.

The bullet had been surgically removed and Parker had learned to walk again, but active duty was out. His partner, Noah Kent, still felt like shit that he wasn't able to stop the bullet that had nearly severed Parker's spine. Like so many cops, Kent thought he was Superman. "Your name isn't *Clark* Kent," Parker still told him. Kent was still on the job and Parker was a P.I., one with a very slight limp and sometimes a lot of pain.

And he'd known he should never have taken this job.

Unfortunately he'd been chosen for this detail by Silvio D'Amato Junior himself. Silvio just happened to be Parker's brother-in-law. Well, technically *ex*-brother-in-law, as Resa, a few years back, had decided that living with a cop just wasn't her style.

Trouble was, Parker had known it wouldn't work a long time before she'd come to terms with the truth. They'd married over Silvio Senior's objections, then divorced over his shame. No one in Silvio D'Amato's lineage had ever been divorced. Parker could still hear the old man ranting, that fake Italian accent rumbling as he called Theresa, "Resa, my *bambina* Resa. How could she do this to me? I am blessed with six children and my youngest brings shame to the family. It breaks my heart."

There was plenty of that going around, Parker thought as he shot a look toward Silvio Senior, who had passed the family business to the hands of his namesake a couple years ago. Silvio Senior's dark eyes were huge behind his spectacles as he pressed a plump, manicured hand onto Junior's shoulder, whispering, always whispering in his ear.

When Parker had married Resa, he'd had no clue how enmeshed a family could be, each member tied into another, torn and tortured, loyal and yet longing to escape. From Silvio Junior's need to please and outdo his father right down to the seething jealousies of Mario and Antonio that they had not been the chosen ones, the family was rotten with dysfunction. Anna, now collecting appetizers, would no doubt head to the restroom to purge soon. Julianna, who was greeting guests at the door, had gone under the knife so many times that Parker was convinced her eyes wouldn't close at night. Only Theresa, his Resa, had survived the family unscathed.

Or so he'd once thought.

Add to that the sick rivalry between Silvio Senior and his brother, Alberto D'Amato, bad relations that didn't even die with Alberto awhile back. Parker had learned, the hard way, that the D'Amato *familia* was one sick clan. In the end he'd found it ironic that Resa's old man had bulked so much over their divorce while the rest of the family was quietly going to hell.

According to family lore, the divorce had nearly caused Resa's ailing mother, Octavia, to die of mortification. However, Octavia had survived and was now holding court in the garden, a bejeweled cane at her side and a blanket on her lap. She was attended by one of her sons, Antonio, the happily married father of four who couldn't keep it in his pants. Octavia didn't notice Parker as she sipped from a glass that didn't so much as quiver in her elegant long fingers. The matriarch forever. Diamonds dripped from her ears and encircled her throat, wrists and fingers. Not one to hide her wealth was Octavia D'Amato.

All six of her children were in attendance. Parker caught sight of Mario and Anna, two of Resa's siblings, schmoozing up clients near the flowering vines that had overtaken a wall of the old cloister. He told himself he was prepared in case Resa showed.

He tried not to think about her, about how hard he'd fallen or how fast. It had been unlike him. Until Theresa D'Amato he hadn't believed in love at first sight, or being obsessed with a woman, or even settling down. But Resa with her smoky brown eyes and naughty, knowing smile had caught his attention. She was coy and smart, and when she threw her head back and laughed that throaty little chuckle, he was doomed. Dark coppery hair, long legs, a tight butt and firm breasts that filled his hands—you get the picture.

Getting her into bed hadn't been difficult; she'd been as hot for him as he'd been for her and their lovemaking had been nothing short of mercurial.

Until it had gone cold.

Stone cold.

On the heels of Ian's death.

Oh, hell.

His heart twisted and he forced his mind to the present. To the D'Amato winery and the party where he was supposed to be sharp and steady, the "heat" even though he was no longer a cop.

What the hell was he doing here? Why had Silvio asked for him by name?

But Parker knew.

Parker's duty was not so much to keep out terrorists, thugs or would-be thieves, but more to ensure that the riffraff, specifically anyone connected to Silvio Senior's brother, Alberto, did not make an appearance. Years ago Silvio Senior had scammed half the family fortune from the significantly less clever Alberto, his younger brother. Alberto had died a few years back, but his progeny had survived, and they all had long memories, fueled by acrimony.

Parker walked through an arbor wrapped in grape vines and about a billion sparkling lights. The evening was cool, bordering chilly, but the party was in full swing. Knots of guests clustered outside on the flagstone patio, an open garden area that had once connected the cellarium, a storage area for the monastery, and the chapter house, where the monks had met to mete out chores and discuss their sins. Rumor had it that some monks had been buried beneath the flooring, though Parker thought that sounded like something D'Amato had made up to give the place more mystique.

Along one wall, inside the alcove surrounding the garden, a string quartet was playing classical pieces that Parker vaguely recognized. Silvio's attempt at culture.

D'Amato's garage was open, his array of vintage cars from the 30s, 40s and 50s, all parked on a gleaming tile floor, their glossy exteriors polished to a high, almost liquid gloss. Past the courtyard and through the main house, a waterfall cascaded into an infinity pool that shimmered turquoise amid mosaic tiles and thick, fragrant shrubs. Everywhere, liveried waiters passed out stemmed glasses of the most famous of the D'Amato vintages.

On the far end of the courtyard was a raised dais, complete with arbor, lights and microphone. Silvio Junior was slated to speak to the group, a hand-picked assortment of bigwigs invited to sample his latest vintage.

A bunch of crap, Parker thought, and checked his watch.

A big black guy with a shaved head stood with his back to one aged pillar. Oscar, Silvio's personal bodyguard and leader of his security team, looked even more uncomfortable than Parker felt. His collar pinched tight around the thick muscles of his neck and he was three hundred pounds if he was fifty. "The man's going to be speakin' in a few. Everyone's got to have their cell phone turned off."

He glanced at the open door where a thin blond woman in five-inch heels and shimmery silk dress paced the foyer, cell phone pressed against one ear, an unlit cigarette in her free hand.

"Everyone, here, in the courtyard," Parker clarified.

Oscar shook his head. "Everyone period. Including you."

"No way."

"That's what he said, I'm just passin' it on. I'll be behind the stage, you take the front, okay."

Parker wasn't going to let the phone thing drop. "Security needs phones."

"We have walkie-talkies," he reminded him.

"Ancient technology."

"Silvio…he's not exactly high-tech, now."

"I can carry a loaded sidearm in here but no phone?"

Oscar rolled his palms up to the starlit sky. "I just follow the rules, I don't make 'em." And then he spied the blonde in the foyer and took off on a mission.

Parker watched him go. No way in hell was he turning off his phone. He switched it to Vibrate, left it in his pocket and decided that was good enough. Silvio would have to deal with it. The way Parker figured it, Silvio D'Amato was lucky Parker was here at all.

At that moment Silvio Junior appeared on the dais. All eyes turned toward the robust man with the shock of silver hair and thick black eyebrows. Though barely five-eight, Silvio had a presence about him that was only enhanced by his Armani suit and Italian leather shoes. He appeared strong and confident, a man to be reckoned with, rightful heir to all fortunes D'Amato.

Planting his back to a brick column, Parker scanned the old monastery grounds with a critical, suspicious eye. Old, rambling structures like this could be a nightmare to secure. Though the walls and adjacent structures had a fortresslike appearance, they were filled with dark nooks and deep crannies, unseen hiding spots. There were shadowy caverns cut into the hillside to house the wine barrels, as well as a maze of underground tunnels that could easily become routes of escape should anyone want to take a shot at the top runner for the wine country's "vintner of the year." There was access through the grape receiving platform and shipping dock. A bell tower loomed high above the tasting room, which had once been the church. The tower itself was dark now, the staircase leading upward secured. And yet...

He glanced up at the highest point of the turret, focusing on the belfry, that dark open space under the roof. For a second he thought he saw movement. Weird. He'd checked the lock himself, so he knew it was secure. Probably a bat, as it was a little past twilight, when bats and owls and insects stirred.

Squinting, he saw no dark shape hunched near the railing. No assassin setting up a high-powered rifle aimed at the stage and Silvio D'Amato's cold heart.

But really, who would want to harm Silvio or this, his pride and joy?

A question he'd asked Silvio when his ex-brother-in-law had strong-armed him into this gig. "We all have enemies, Parker, you know that. Just as we all have secrets." His brown eyes had darkened and he'd taken a sip from his glass of Pinot.

Secrets…anyone entangled with the D'Amato family got the crash course on family skeletons.

"Should I be watching for someone from Uncle Alberto's side of the family, or have things been quiet on that front?" Parker had asked Silvio Junior.

Although Silvio let the question drop, the vein pulsing in his forehead had provided all the answer Parker needed. "Just do the job I'm paying you for," Silvio had snapped.

But it wasn't money that drew Parker here tonight. Though he was loath to admit it, Parker couldn't stay away. He hoped to see Resa again. Call it idle curiosity or something deeper, but he'd never been able to resist a chance to be near her.

Resa…

He was on alert for her as he walked the perimeter and observed the guests all talking, laughing and sipping ruby-red wine. He recognized more than a few faces—relatives or business partners he'd met at family to-dos when he'd been married to Resa.

A lifetime ago.

After a brisk stroll past the chapter house and the former dormitory he did a perimeter check of the garden area, but found nothing that warranted a second glance. The cellars seemed secure, the kitchen and dining room were occupied by a frenzied staff that had been screened and cleared before the event.

And then he saw her.

At least a glimpse.

Resa.

His heart clutched. He'd known there was a chance she'd show up, but had thought that if Silvio had mentioned that he'd be there, she might have passed. Apparently not so. He caught a glimpse of her walking down a long hallway lit by candles, her dark hair sweeping her shoulders.

Or maybe he'd been mistaken.

That woman didn't seem to move with the same grace he remembered of Resa, or was that his imagination? Had he made her more of a sensual enigma with the passage of time? Just as wives who died suddenly were often elevated to sainthood in the surviving husband's mind, maybe his perception of Resa was imbued with sexual mystery.

Get it straight. Remember how it played out, he reminded himself. Yes, she'd set her sights on him. Yes, she'd come on to him, lured him. Yes, she'd used him to rebel against her family and yes, she'd tossed him aside when the going got rough. But had he created an image of a woman who had never really existed?

The woman with auburn hair joined a group, and he realized it couldn't be her. With Resa, there was always that tug in his gut, that chemistry.

He couldn't let himself be distracted. Whether Resa was at the event or not, he had to pay attention. Silvio was taking the stage, smiling, welcoming people to the D'Amato Monastery Estates and the crowd seemed rapt, all eyes turned toward the dais. So far so good.

He turned away from the dais and saw her again…this time closer to the old chapter house doorway. Instinctively, he eased toward her, moving around the edge of the crowd and along the passageways of the cloister.

Remembering.

How they'd come together; how they'd been ripped apart.

Though she didn't look over her shoulder, she slipped through the doorway to the old library. Behind him Silvio's voice boomed through the speakers.

"…our unique blend…oaky, with just a hint of pear…"

Parker barely noticed. He told himself that he wasn't following his ex-wife just to talk to her, but that there was something secretive and restless about her. Something that required soothing.

As if Resa is going to do anything desperate. Come on, Parker, you know better. Get back to your job. Forget her.

But he followed her through the library to the dormitory and the night stairs, which were originally used by the monks in the evening to get from their rooms to the church.

But they'd been locked. Right? Hadn't Oscar said they'd all been secured?

Hell.

She was ahead of him, walking swiftly, stirring the flames of candles flickering in wall sconces, all part of the ambiance of the party. Into the stairwell she went, and he held back the urge to shout or startle her.

At the stairs to the church she stopped, turned and sent him a sizzling glare that melted his bones. "What the hell are you doing here?" she demanded.

He approached, smelled the scent of gardenias, a perfume he'd always equate with her and those incredible nights of twisted sheets, sweaty muscles and pure heaven.

"I was hired. What about you?"

"Invited. I'm family. Remember? You're not. Not anymore."

He ignored the barb. "So why aren't you out celebrating and lifting your glass to your brother?"

Her smile twisted wickedly. "Being part of this family is a dubious honor at best. Listening to Silvio—" She rolled her expressive eyes and turned a slim palm toward the heavens. "Come *on!* Talk about boring."

"Then why show?"

"Free drinks," she said, then laughed at her own joke.

He was caught again. Quick as lightning he was trapped in that invisible but steely hold she had over him, and she knew it. He saw it in the warm liquid brown of her eyes, the curve of her mouth.

"It's good to see you." The words slipped out before he could catch himself.

"I don't know why." Her brown eyes met his, and he felt locked in her gaze, lost in her scent, a mixture of gardenias and fresh rain. "Nothing has changed, Lucas. We can't fix what's shattered."

He wanted to tell her that it didn't matter; he was willing to settle for the things that remained whole…a pair of brown eyes so warm they could ward off a winter night, a hint of gardenia and spring rain. But before he could find the words, the moment had passed. The window closed.

Lifting an eyebrow, she said, "If you'll excuse me, I'm on my way to the ladies' room." She turned on a heel, then looked over her shoulder. "And you're definitely *not* invited."

A reference, no doubt, to the times he'd sat on the rim of the tub while she'd bathed in mounds of scented bubbles and allowed his hands to wander under the piles of foam and through the deep water to touch her in the most intimate of places. There had been candles surrounding the tub and they'd sipped wine, D'Amato Chardonnay, and she'd moaned in pleasure until he'd lost control and joined her.

Water and bubbles had sloshed onto the floor, the candles had flickered and some had sizzled out, but they'd made love in the claw-foot tub filled with warm soapy water, their bodies slick and hot and wanting.

Even now, he remembered that passion. How exciting, sensual and fierce it had been.

Before it had died so suddenly.

Killed by a lie.

Damn.

Caught in the memory, he watched her go as his cell phone vibrated against his leg. He pulled the phone from his pocket, saw that his old partner, Noah Kent, was calling. Not unusual. It was Friday night and sometimes, after a few drinks at the local watering hole, Kent would phone. He could wait. Parker slid the phone into his pocket again, then looked up to spy Resa walking through the library, then turning left at the far doorway. Wait… The restrooms were to the right. She should have known that. To the left was a dead end. The locked stairwell led up to the bell tower and down to the catacombs where barrels were stored in the hillside.

Behind him, Silvio's voice droned on about the hints of vanilla from French oak barrels in his latest creation. The speech was background to the pulse beating hard in Parker's ears as he pursued her.

Did she go up or down?

Should he follow?

No. Go back to the party. Do your job, then get the hell out. Who cares what she's doing? It's obviously some sort of cat-and-mouse game, the kind you know is dangerous and she knows you can't resist?

But he heard something above. The scrape of a shoe? Hell. He tried the door and it was unlocked. He found his walkie-talkie, tried to raise Oscar but got only loud, static-laden feedback. So much for stealth. Switching it off, he entered the staircase and considered taking his gun out of its holster.

Why? It's Resa. You saw her come into the stairwell, and she's not a threat.

Not to anyone but you.

Setting his jaw, he waited. Ears straining.

Did she go up…or down?

Toward heaven, or hell?

He turned toward the lower stairs as another footfall scraped overhead. Slowly he began the climb up the spiral staircase, the only sound the thudding of his own heart.

Why the hell was Resa luring him up here?

Surely she'd known he'd follow.

Up, up, up.

Nerves tightening with each step.

Something about this wasn't right, not right at all. He reached into his shoulder holster, pulled out his Glock, released the safety and set his jaw.

No way would he fire at Resa…or…?

The narrow opening was just over his head. He squinted upward, weapon drawn, ascending slowly, knowing he was an easy target.

She was there, leaning over the railing, standing alone in the darkness. He relaxed for a second. "What're you doing up here?" he asked, lowering his pistol.

She turned then, her face in shadow and in a breathy voice whispered, "I'm waiting for…" Her voice trailed off and she stiffened.

Something wasn't right. He felt it.

"I've been waiting for five years." The voice was different now. Low. Dangerous.

In a heart-stopping instant, he knew his mistake, saw the gun.

He swung his weapon up.

Bam! Light flashed from the muzzle of the gun pointed straight at his heart.

Parker hit the deck as he pulled the trigger, firing wildly. Too late.

Hot agony seared through his gut. He stumbled, still firing crazily as he fell backward on the steep stairs, beginning to tumble. He caught the smallest glimpse of his assailant's face, the wild fury of ringed brown eyes haunted by the pale light of the moon. His gun clattered out of his hand, falling into the gaping hole where the ropes hung.

Clunk! His head smashed a wooden riser. Hard. Pain exploded behind his eyes as he slid and rolled, gravity pulling him downward, each wooden step catching his body, bruising him. He heard something crack—a rib? And all the while the lifeblood oozed out of him…hot, sticky. It smeared the dusty wooden steps. He threw out a hand, grabbed the railing, stopping his crazy descent on the small landing before the stairs turned again.

There were noises.

People screaming.

The rush of footsteps.

He tried to stay awake, to remain conscious, but the

blackness pulled him under. The last thing he saw, in the periphery of his vision, was his attacker jumping down into the center of the tower.

Bong! Bong! Bong!

His brain was nearly crushed with the thunderous peal of bells clamoring so loudly the stairs shook.

"Resa," he called weakly. "Resa…" And then he slipped under the veil of darkness.

Parker? Lucas Parker had shown up? Of all the rotten, dumb luck!

I was furious! Seething as I slid down the bell ropes, I tried to think clearly. *She* was supposed to have followed me up into the tower. I was sure she'd spot me and be intrigued enough to climb the stairs, then fall to her death, just as poor Ian had fallen.

It would have been such a fitting, ironic end. Perfect in every detail.

But Lucas had spoiled it all.

I couldn't think about that now. I dropped the .22 pistol, letting it fall to the floor below. My only consolation was that I was free to end this all another time, as long as I escaped. Which wouldn't be too difficult in the ensuing chaos. Already there was a near-riot going on, people screaming and running, panic sizzling like an electric current through the hallowed walls of the winery.

The gloves frayed as I zipped downward, the friction from the old ropes heating my palms and fingers, just as it had when I'd been a child and first discovered I could slide quickly from the top of the belfry to the floor.

As soon as my feet hit the ancient stones, I took off down three flights of stairs to the lowest level of winery, the cellar that had once been my playground. Alone, very much alone. I knew these old caverns and tunnels better than anyone and, of course, I still had the keys, squired away from when I was a kid. The locks hadn't changed. Silvio, my skinflint cousin, was too damned cheap.

But there was pandemonium above. Scurrying footsteps. Shouts. Horrified screams.

Don't think about them. Or her. Just keep running!

I moved by instinct, but my brain was pounding. Why the hell had that son of a bitch shown up? He'd been divorced from Resa, airbrushed out of family portraits. And what the hell had happened to *her?* Just two minutes ago I saw her enter the library.

I'd planned everything so perfectly, spent the last five years in *that* place, plotting the perfect moment for my revenge, and then Lucas Parker had to show up?

I'd caught a glimpse of him earlier and couldn't believe it, the former cop stalking the perimeter of the monastery walls.

My feet moved soundlessly through the dimly lit corridors, my breathing regulated from years of running. I clutched an aura of calm, despite my fury that my plans had been ruined.

Down a long, shadowed corridor illuminated by a single

string of lights, past barrels stacked high, around the far corner and up an old flight of stairs to a door I'd already unlocked, I raced. The door opened to the old infirmary where sick monks had once been treated. Now the small rooms were filled with supplies for the winery.

The muted sounds of chaos within the winery walls mixed with the scream of sirens from outside. Someone had called the police. That part I'd planned. I tore off my wig, dress and padded bra, kicked off the stupid-ass shoes, cleaned my face with some of those sanitized wipes, peeled off the eyelashes and pulled the stuffing out of my cheeks.

Then I opened the bag I'd left here earlier, grabbed my jeans and shirt, and yanked them on along with a pair of beat-up running shoes and a dark jacket. The kayak was waiting on a bank beneath a eucalyptus tree and the nearby river flowed rapidly away from the winery to a small town where I could catch a train into the city. I planned to take my "Resa" clothes and dump them into the bay. I would fling them from atop the Golden Gate. With a little luck, I'd escape once again.

And disappear.

For a while…

Three days later, Parker woke up mad as hell in a hospital bed. A stern nurse told him he'd been out for three days. An IV dripped some kind of painkillers into his arm, but it wasn't working. On a scale of one to ten—with the nurse's stupid chart of little happy and frowny faces indicating pain level—he was at eight, maybe nine, where the red face was frowning but no longer shouting expletives.

But he didn't give a damn.

The surgery had been a success, the bullet removed, his intestine repaired, his dislocated shoulder snapped back into place, his ribs only bruised. The concussion had been slight.

He'd been lucky, the doctor had said.

Lucky, my ass!

He closed his eyes for a second, trying to figure out how to get out of here. Pronto. In his experience, hospitals were dangerous places, full of the sick and dying.

"Lucas."

Her voice came to him in a dream. Soft and breathy, but this time, no sound of laughter or lightness.

Disbelieving, he opened an eye and saw her in the doorway. She looked frail and frightened, unlike the woman who'd turned his life upside down. There were dark smudges beneath her eyes and her lips trembled slightly. He blinked, thinking she might be a vision, a figment of his imagination, even a hallucination from the drugs, but no, she was there.

He tried a smile and failed, but she saw he was awake.

"How…how do you feel?"

"Worse than I look."

From her guarded response he suspected he looked pretty damned bad. His mouth tasted foul and as he shifted on the hospital bed his entire body screamed in pain. He winced, but she didn't seem to notice.

"They're going to arrest me," she said, and swallowed hard. Fear gripped her, casting dark rings around her brown eyes. "The police have been following me, but…but I was able to lose them and sneak in here."

"How?" he asked, before he thought twice. Resa was nothing if not quick. And clever.

She ignored the question. "The police, they think I tried to kill you. They've been putting together a case. A few people claim that they saw me in the belfry right before the shots were fired."

He tried to lift his head but the ache sucked his strength. Hadn't he seen her there, in the bell tower?

"And there's more. They think I killed Aunt Lorna that night, too, but…but I think they're having more trouble proving that."

"Aunt Lorna?" he repeated. "Alberto's wife?"

The cobwebs in his mind stretched thin, fading.

"They…they found her in her house. I heard on the news that she fell…off her scooter and down the stairs. But the police think she might have been pushed. Oh, God, Lucas, I didn't do it. You have to believe me." Resa's face was drained of color and a small tic had developed at her temple.

"Slow down. Start over."

"I don't have an alibi. I was home alone about the time Aunt Lorna died. I was getting ready for the party. I knew you'd be there and I was…I was excited. Anyway, I went to the party, hung out for while, then I saw you. Do you remember our conversation in the library?"

"I remember." That much was clear.

"You went up, I went down to the wine cellar, thinking you'd follow, then I heard gunshots and ran up the stairs but you were already...already..." She looked at him and shook her head.

"Jesus."

She stepped forward, touched his hand and all the warmth and passion that they'd once shared came back to him. It clouded his mind like a drug. No...he couldn't go there now.

He reminded himself of the many times Resa had deceived him, the way she'd masked the truth to protect her family, to cover up the transgressions committed behind those sacred walls.

Gritting his teeth, he drew his hand away.

"You have to help me, Lucas," she said, pleading. "I can't be put away for a murder I didn't commit."

And there it was between them.

The lie.

The one they both knew existed.

From the hallway came the sounds of the hospital: whispers, softly rattling carts and gurneys, the ding of a bell announcing that an elevator car was about to arrive.

"Do they have any other evidence?" he asked.

"The gun, the one they found in the belfry. It was mine, Lucas. It was the .22 you gave me."

He hardly dared breathe. "Your pistol."

"It must have been stolen," she said, looking over her shoulder. "I didn't shoot you, I swear it."

"I know." His voice was faint, but the image was solidifying in his head. Mad, dark eyes in the moonlight. A square jaw braced in fury. And a complexion nubby from the scrape of a razor.

The face of a man.

"It wasn't you," he said, weak with relief. "I know it wasn't."

"Tell the police that, will you, please?"

"It's going to be okay, Resa. Please, I'll take care of you. I can protect you."

"No." She stepped back as if stung by his suggestion. "There is no protection in this world. I learned that with Ian. You can't protect me, Lucas, and you can't change what's happened. No one can escape the past." Fighting tears, she backed toward the door.

"Resa, wait…"

He shifted in bed and, fighting the pain, levered himself up onto his elbows, but she was already gone.

"You look like hell," Noah Kent said cordially.

"Don't try to cheer me up."

It had been less than three hours since Resa had left. Parker had tried and failed to get Dr. Woods to release him from the hospital. Still, Kent was a welcome sight, dressed in pressed slacks, a blazer and shirt and tie, as if he were on his way to court.

"They letting you out of this place?"

"Nah, but I'm going anyway."

"Not a smart move."

"One of many," Parker said, wincing against the pain in his belly.

Kent cut to the chase. "She came to see you, didn't she? She was here, earlier."

"Who?"

"Don't mess with me, okay? Theresa D'Amato was caught on camera in the parking lot. Hospital security has been on alert for her since you checked in." When Parker didn't respond, Kent went on. "Okay, two guns, both registered to you were found at the scene. One, the Glock, has your prints on it, the other, a .22, has Theresa's."

"I gave it to her years ago, but she wasn't in the belfry that night," Parker said.

"Who was?"

He frowned. "I—I'm not sure."

"Think real hard."

He'd been picturing that face all morning. He could see the shooter turning to him, a face so like Resa's, but so different. "It's a little blurry."

Kent eyed him critically. "No more bullshit, Parker. I know you lied when the kid died. And I know you're lying now. So stop yanking my chain and give it to me straight. Was Theresa D'Amato in the bell tower?"

"Not in the belfry, no."

"Then who? Who shot you?"

"I…I think it was someone who was trying to look like her. I only saw the face for an instant and it was dark, but…" He swiped a hand over his forehead, a bead of sweat there. "I think it was Frankie D'Amato."

"Her cousin."

Parker knew it sounded nuts. "But he's in a mental hospital."

"Not anymore." Something shifted in the hospital room— the tiniest drop in temperature. In that heartbeat, with his partner hesitating, Parker sensed what was coming and it scared the hell out of him. "I tried to call you about that," Kent said.

"It *was* him?" Parker gaped. "Frankie D'Amato."

Kent leaned forward in his chair. "Frankie D'Amato walked away from the hospital Friday sometime. No one knows exactly how it happened, but they think he slipped into scrubs, then pilfered some poor nurse's locker. Probably walked out of there decked to the nines."

Parker felt his entire life beginning to unravel. Frankie D'Amato, Theresa's cousin, had been institutionalized in a mental facility for five years…ever since Ian's death.

"And on the day of the escape, what happens? Frankie's mother, Lorna, is found dead at the base of the stairs, a convenient accident, if you ask me. Then you're shot in the belfry of the D'Amato Monastery Estates at a gala hosted by Frankie's uncle. Coincidence?" Kent shook his head, clasped a hand over one knee. "I don't think so."

"You're serious?"

"Dead." And he was. Gone was any twinkle in his eyes. "Someone worked real hard to make it look like Theresa was in the tower. Octavia and a few other guests swear they saw Resa in the belfry. Then there's a pistol registered to you that was found on the floor, as if someone had dropped it."

"Not Resa."

"Well, her prints are on it."

"I gave her that gun a long time ago."

Kent nodded. "I knew you'd defend her. Lucky for you, we've got some evidence that leads in another direction. We found hairs at the scene—synthetic."

"A wig."

"And pieces of leather in the bell rope, the escape route the attacker used."

"Gloves," Parker whispered, remembering his assailant sliding past him on the ropes.

"That's right. So if the assailant was wearing gloves, there'd be no new prints on the gun."

"It was Frankie," Parker said.

"I think so. Shoe prints are larger than Theresa's, and a silver Mercedes registered to Lorna D'Amato was left with the valet, who remembers the woman who dropped it off. Someone who looked a lot like Resa, but, the valet thought, a little larger. Even though Frankie's small for a man—five-six—it would be tough to look as petite as Theresa."

"What about Resa's car?" Parker asked. "Didn't the valet see her, too?"

"She parked in the family's private lot, didn't want to get stuck in all the hoopla."

"It wasn't Resa," Parker insisted.

"We're looking at all possibilities, but right now Frankie D'Amato is our prime suspect. The guy's got lights on upstairs but nobody's home. He knows the winery well, was raised there before Alberto was pushed out. Then there's the matter of Alberto's suicide. Was it? And Lorna's death down the stairs?"

Parker sensed what was coming.

"Then there's Ian D'Amato."

"Let's not go there."

"Why? Because you lied in your deposition? Lied to protect Resa?"

Parker ground his teeth together at the notion. At the time he'd thought he was protecting the woman he loved, but the lie had actually only fanned the fires of hell that were the D'Amato code of secrecy.

"Frankie swore Theresa pushed the kid to his death, that he witnessed the whole thing."

"She was with me."

"I know you alibied her, Parker, but that never really hung together for me."

A dull roar, like the sound of the sea in a cavern began in Parker's head. "You would believe a mental patient over me?"

"I'm not saying I believed Frankie. I don't think I ever heard the true story on that incident. Which had to have affected Resa deeply. She was the kid's mother."

"Yes," Parker hissed. Everyone knew this much.

"And yet she let her aunt Lorna raise him. That's kind of odd, don't you think?"

"She was young. Unmarried."

"Even so," Kent continued, "Theresa allowed her child to be raised by an aunt and uncle who were at odds with her side of the family."

"They offered."

"And why was that?"

Parker closed his eyes, wishing for escape. "It happened before my time."

"We know that. You didn't meet Theresa until a year after the kid was born and married her a year after that. Then three years later, when the boy was five, he dies and you get a divorce soon after."

"I don't see what this has to do with—"

"Sure you do, Parker. No more bullshit."

The roar was getting louder, the surf pounding through his brain. "Theresa didn't kill Ian."

"Then who did?"

Parker didn't answer.

"So this is the way I think it went down. Theresa goes to her aunt's house to take the kid away. The nanny is out, probably with Alberto, and the kid is supposed to be in his room. Theresa sneaks up the back stairs and goes into Ian's room, but he's not alone, is he?"

Parker waited. Knew what was coming.

"Frankie's there with the kid, and she freaks. Apparently no one told her about how Frankie got kicked out of three prep schools for deviant behavior. All a family secret. So back in the kid's room a fight ensues and somehow the boy falls out the window. Frankie always insisted Theresa pushed him. You and Theresa testify that he was playing too close to the edge. So the death is ruled an accident and Frankie snaps."

It smacks Parker for the second time that day—the lie. "It was a terrible tragedy," Parker says quietly.

Noah Kent stared at his ex-partner as if Parker were a moron. "You're sticking to that story."

"It's what happened."

"And so Frankie gets sent away and he spends the next five years plotting his revenge. Maybe he knew you would be there at the winery, maybe not, but somehow he's going to set Theresa up to take the fall, so she'll have to be locked away and suffer as he has since the kid's death."

"Sounds like you've got this one sewn up."

Kent folded his arms. "Hey, after all these years I ought to be good at this. If you'll excuse me, I got a perp to track down." He started for the door, then stopped. "Just one more thing. Who was Ian's father?"

The question iced over Parker's aching head. "Theresa never said."

"Yeah, right…and the kid was cremated, right? Convenient. It would be nice if there was some chance of running his DNA."

Parker's heart nearly stopped.

"The way I figure it," Kent said, "Frankie D'Amato

might just have been the kid's father. That's why the boy was being raised by Alberto and his wife. They were Ian's grandparents. Just like Silvio Senior and his wife, Octavia."

Parker didn't agree, though his partner had it right. Kent had obviously spent some time puzzling it all out.

"Who knows how it played out? My guess is that Frankie raped Theresa, and the family kept it hush-hush. On the day Ian died, Frankie probably found her there in the room with the kid and freaked out."

Close, buddy. Kent was so close to the truth….

He had insisted in accompanying Theresa that day when she went to take the child away from the D'Amato's San Francisco mansion. Ian had begun to turn inward, and Resa suspected abuse. She's seen no alternative but to remove her son until she was sure the environment was safe. But upon entering the child's room Resa came upon a horrific scene, the abuse obvious.

Frankie had snapped, turning his wrath on Resa, and in the ensuing struggle Ian had climbed to the windowsill and pressed himself into the corner, edging away from Frankie.

That was the scene Parker came upon when he rushed up the stairs, responding to the sound of frantic voices. Parker's sole mission was to get the boy away from the window and out of harm's way.

"Stay right there," he had told the boy gently, moving stealthily so as not to startle him. "Don't be afraid. No one's going to hurt you."

But Frankie had snarled, swinging at Parker, then lunging

toward Ian, who gasped in fright. Galvanized by fear, the boy scooted back, hunkered at the edge of the window for a second, then quietly slipped out.

"There was a family history of abuse. Alberto D'Amato, Frankie's father, had trouble keeping his hands to himself, too. So for Frankie to pass it on…" Kent shrugged. "Like father, like son. That sound about right?"

Parker looked away. "If I knew then what I know now…"

"Hell, Lucas, we've all got regrets. But sooner or later, if you don't let some of it go, it's going to eat you up." Kent shoved his hands in his pockets, looked down at the floor thoughtfully. "That whole family is bad news, man. Real bad."

Parker couldn't argue.

He'd heard it all before from his own damned conscience. He should have intervened earlier. He should have saved Resa's kid from Frankie's abuse. He should have wrung Frankie's skinny neck, the slimy predator. He should have known what was going on, but he didn't. Too little, too late.

Resa could not forgive herself.

Frankie blamed her for everything that went wrong; she had been his victim since childhood.

"Do you have any idea where Frankie D'Amato is?" Parker asked. The Frankie he knew would not drop his vendetta, which meant Resa was not safe. He had to protect her.

Kent shook his head. "But we'll find him." He sent

Parker a cutting glance. "Especially now. He went after one of our own."

"Retired," Parker muttered.

"Same thing."

Parker groaned. "I got to get the hell out of here. Sign me out, will you?"

Kent rested one fist on the doorframe. "Promise me you'll stay out of bell towers for a while?"

"That's an easy one." Parker rubbed the back of his neck, but it didn't ease the ache in his head. Resa was right about not being able to escape the past. There was no escaping it, but maybe it was enough to survive it. Survive the past and damn well try to get a handle on the future.

He swung his legs to one side of the bed and took the first step. One painful step at a time.

TIM MALEENY

Mel Brooks once said, "Tragedy is what happens to me. Comedy is what happens to you." This couldn't be better illustrated than in "Suspension of Disbelief." Tim is an award-winning author who knows that even in the darkest moments humor can be found.

This story takes a sideways glance at the complex relationship between a bestselling writer and his editor. Fortunately most authors' experiences with editors have not been quite as unusual as those of the fictional mega-author featured in this story, but the familiar tension between art and commerce was clearly the inspiration for this fantastic tale. Tim takes the conventions of a classic thriller and twists them hard, until we are left with a punch line that is simultaneously funny and disturbing.

SUSPENSION OF DISBELIEF

"Give us the manuscript or we'll kill your wife."

Jim Masterson stared at the narrow man threatening him, trying to remember when they'd first met. A long time ago, before Jim was married. At least a year before he was published. A lifetime.

"All we want is the book, Jim."

"It's not finished."

"That's why I'm here."

Jim watched his editor of more than ten years help himself to one of the overstuffed chairs in front of the desk, carefully setting his briefcase on the hardwood floor. Carl Ransom had always dressed immaculately, even in the old days. Today it was a gray suit and cream silk shirt, the half-Windsor tight enough to squeeze any last vestige of humanity from his narrow frame.

Carl leaned forward to slide a computer out of his brief-case, a sleek titanium notebook that opened like a thinly veiled threat.

"Where did we first meet, Carl?"

The question threw the editor for a moment. He blinked a few times before the corners of his mouth turned. "The Four Seasons, breakfast. I was a junior editor at the time and you—"

"Just got my first publishing contract."

Carl nodded as he busied himself with the laptop. "Feeling nostalgic, Jim?" He unceremoniously pushed a row of pencils to one side. "Jesus, after all these years, I still can't believe you write with those things."

"My readers haven't complained." Jim scooped the pencils up protectively and arranged them closer to his side of the desk. Ten number two's, each sharpened to a perfect point, arrayed next to ten red Bic pens. Jim evenly spaced the pens and set them next to the neatly stacked pile of manuscript paper.

Carl reached into the briefcase again, then slid a small plastic card into a slot in the laptop. *Tap, tap, tap.* "They have these things called computers now."

"The Internet's distracting."

Carl snorted. "Listen to you. For your next book remind me to get you a walker, maybe a hearing aid."

Jim ignored him, listening to the susurrus of traffic three stories below. His office door was closed, as was his habit when writing. Normally his only company was the classical music from his stereo and the view, but today he'd made a mistake. He'd let someone inside his sanctuary.

"Voilà!" Carl spun the laptop around and slid it forward. "What do you see?"

Jim squinted at the monitor, where a rectangular window on the screen showed a video of a woman in a dress walking across a Manhattan street. He looked closer. The view was from several stories up, maybe four or five.

The woman carried a briefcase in her left hand. The brief-case didn't have a shoulder strap and looked heavy, as if it were overstuffed with anything and everything a busy woman might need over the course of a day. It looked all too familiar.

Jim felt a knot tighten in his gut as his heart stopped. "That's Emily."

"Bravo." Carl brought his hands together with a languid *clap, clap.* He leaned forward. His right index finger was poised over Return on the laptop's keyboard. "And for bonus points, what do you see *now?*" The skin under his nail turned white as he mashed the key.

A red circle with two lines intersecting it appeared over the image of the walking woman as she made her way through a throng of pedestrians. Even as she dodged a man with a stack of boxes on a handcart, the animated crosshairs stayed on her.

"A team of snipers is tracking her progress for the next forty-five minutes." Carl rubbed his hands together. "We know her routines, her regular appointments." He made a theatrical turn of his wrist. "So unless we get the final pages in…*forty-four minutes,* Emily will be shot in the head."

"How—" A trickle of sweat started down Jim's spine as he looked at his editor's ascetic face, searching for a smirk, some sign that a punch line was on its way. But Jim had never known Carl to have a taste for practical jokes. As utterly mad as it seemed, he knew this was real.

"Amazing what they can do with computers nowadays, isn't it? The tech department pulled this together—you should see what they're doing with our Web site. Virtual chats with authors, interactive short stories. You really need to embrace technology, Jimbo."

Jim started to rise from his chair.

"Not so fast, cowboy." Carl tapped more keys and three additional windows appeared on the screen, each with a different view of lower Manhattan, a shifting crosshair at the center of every one. Emily moved through the upper left screen, oblivious, a duck in a pond.

"Covering the upper left is Bob, my assistant editor. He's an ex-marine, which comes in handy. Upper right is a buddy of his, I forget his name, but we've used him before. An expert marksman. This one here is Steve—he normally handles the romance writers. And this—" Carl's finger circled the crosshairs in the lower right quadrant. "That's the summer intern."

"You're full of shit."

"*Am I?*" Carl slammed the top of the laptop down. "You have any idea how many books we sold last year with your name on them?"

"I didn't write most of those books."

Spittle almost oozed from the corners of Carl's mouth. "Take a guess."

Jim shrugged. "Millions."

"You're off by a factor of ten." Carl took a deep breath and forced a smile, pried open the laptop. "And you're correct, you only write one book a year, per your contract. But we put your name on those other books, in much bigger type than your cowriters. Want to know why?"

"Because I'm a writer who's sold a lot of books."

"Because you're a *brand*." Carl blew out his cheeks. "You like being rich?"

Jim looked around the spacious office, visualized the rest of his three-story town house, one of several he owned in cities around the world. He knew it was a rhetorical question.

"Let me put it in perspective." Carl pulled a sheet of paper from his briefcase and glanced at a row of numbers. "You are the face of a franchise that generated *hundreds* of millions of dollars over the past decade."

"So?"

"So people get killed for a helluva lot less. This isn't some corner crack deal we're talking about here. You think I'm happy about this?"

Jim tried to remember the last time he'd seen Carl happy. An image flashed across his mind of a young editor sitting across from him at breakfast, just two guys talking about writing and books until their eggs got cold.

"What the hell happened to you?"

"I moved on." Carl worked the muscles in his jaw. "I became the caretaker of the house that Jim built, while you…you stayed behind that damn desk."

"You're insane."

"Jim, pick up a pencil and start writing." Again the flourish with the watch. "We've pissed away seven minutes."

"I can't finish the book in half an hour."

"Bullshit. Two months ago you showed me a rough draft, with only one chapter to go. I know how fast you write, you could bang out the ending with your eyes closed."

Jim selected one of the pencils and rolled it back and forth, trying not to look at the computer screen. "I don't know how the story is going to end. Call it writer's block if you—"

"Writers get blocked, brands don't." Carl steepled his hands together. "Besides, we know how it's going to end. We already discussed it."

"It doesn't feel right." Jim stole a glance at the screen. Emily had moved into the upper right quadrant. Her long brown hair was loose around her shoulders as she hefted the briefcase. "The characters wouldn't—"

"Don't start with that writer crap about the characters telling you what to do." Carl looked as if all the acid reflux in the world was holding a convention somewhere deep in his esophagus. "The characters aren't alive, but your wife is—for now."

"This book will have my name on it," Jim said deliberately. "No one else's."

"This is a thriller." Carl's nostrils flared. "Hero saves the day. The guy gets the girl, or the girl gets the guy, whatever. Oh, and the bad guy gets his comeuppance."

"That doesn't seem very thrilling."

"You give the people what they want. That's your fucking job."

"Maybe they want something different. Something unexpected."

"You've become a fantasy writer now? What world do you live in?"

"You write the damn ending."

"Believe me, I would." Carl pushed his wire-frame glasses up on his nose. "But like you said, this book will have your name on it. The *one book a year* that gets scrutiny from the critics, the one that sets the standard for all the books to come. And that book, my friend, that book needs your *voice*." Carl said the last word as if it tasted bad, his own voice bitter around the edges. "Those jarring juxtapositions, those evocative metaphors that you're known for."

Jim felt sweat on his upper lip and looked at the computer screen. Emily was in quadrant three. As she walked, she brought her hands up and pulled her hair back away from her face, so Jim could clearly see her profile. He forced himself to breathe.

Carl sighed. "I'm not a writer, we both know that. I handle continuity, eliminate redundant phrases. Clean up the mess you leave on the page."

Jim watched Emily step off a curb into traffic, her heels

just visible beneath her slacks. He always wondered how women could walk in those things. He took a deep breath and turned his gaze back to Carl.

"I need a week."

Carl shook his head. "We're on deadline. And this time the emphasis is on the first half of that word." He picked up a pencil and held it between his thumb and forefinger. "Finish the damn book."

"It'll feel forced."

"Every month this book is delayed costs us—" Carl waved his arm around the room, a gesture that encompassed the known universe. "You, me, the publishing house, the chain stores. You think I'm ruthless, try negotiating with the chains. What's the value of a human life when you're operating on that scale? Every month costs us millions, Jim."

"Millions."

"This is the entertainment business, partner. Timing is everything."

Jim kept his eyes on Carl's fighting the urge to track Emily's progress.

"You're bluffing."

"Excuse me." Carl spun the computer around and tapped a few keys, then turned it back toward Jim. The four live screens had been replaced with an article from one of the daily newspapers, lifted off their Web site.

Despite himself, Jim began to read the headline out loud. "'Local author kills himself after murdering—'"

"'—his family.'" Carl shook his head. "Tragic. He was one of ours. Paranormal, gothic romance. We made a fortune during the vampire years."

"Kill me—or Emily—and there's no more books."

"Actually, there's one more." Carl hit another key and an image of a book cover popped onto the screen. "I had the boys in the art department work this up. Whattaya think?"

Jim blinked at his own face, a publicity photo from last year. An easy smile next to lurid type, his name across the top in bloodred letters.

"It's true crime, of course." Carl shrugged. "Not as big a market, but it'll cover our investment. After that, we turn someone else into a franchise."

"Franchise."

"You think you're the only thriller writer in the world?" Carl tapped another key and the book cover disappeared. "Give 'em the shelf space, plenty of guys could sell a ton of books."

Jim almost started laughing but the sweat on his palms made him stop. "How long have you been planning this?"

"Remember a few months ago, when we sent you with two other writers to that police firing range?"

"Research for the next book."

"Exactly. How many rifles did you fire that day? Wasn't there a hunting rifle with a scope, a sniper rifle, a couple of others. How many?"

Jim looked at the quadrants on the computer screen and felt his blood congeal.

"Four."

"With your fingerprints all over them."

"It'll never hold up."

Carl smiled, an expression that looked like it hurt. "Famous author of serial-killer novels. Writer known for gruesome torture scenes. Don't you think a jury would agree that you fit the profile?"

"I'll tell them the truth."

"We're talking about the law, here. The truth is irrelevant. Face it, Jim, you're fucked. Finish the book, live happily ever after. You can't seriously be thinking that if we don't pull the trigger today, there won't be tomorrow? Or the next day."

"Have you read the book lately, Carl?"

The question momentarily disarmed the editor. "What do you mean?"

"The ending we talked about, it just won't work. People will see it coming."

"You haven't changed in over ten years. People *want* to see it coming."

"It won't be believable."

"Since when does that matter? Suspension of disbelief is the cornerstone of a thriller, buddy. You should know that better than anyone. You think James Bond can really survive all those explosions without messing up his tuxedo?"

"But this character—he's different. He doesn't always do the right thing."

"Your books have a moral compass," said Carl. "That's what we're selling. Reassurance. Faith in the outcome. So have a little faith and start writing, or we'll kill your fucking wife."

"Okay." Jim lifted the manuscript and removed the bottom page, glancing nervously at the clock. "But I don't think I can finish in time."

"Show me something and I'll go away. Just get a few words on the page and maybe I can buy you some time. We can always kill your wife—or someone else close to you—another day."

"Let me show you what I'm talking about." Jim turned the page around so it was facing his editor. He carefully selected one of his red pens and took the cap off, circled a paragraph near the top of the page. "Read that."

Carl slid the laptop to one side, just as the image of Emily jumped to the lower right quadrant. Jim took a deep breath and held it, wondering if he loved his wife more than his characters. Thinking about all the things that had changed since he first sat down in his chair behind this scarred desk and started writing so many years ago.

He thought about continuity and the suspension of disbelief, and he wondered whether any of that mattered in the end as long as you told a good story.

"So what's your point?" Carl adjusted his glasses as he looked up from the page. "I read it, it's great. So what happens next?"

"This."

The pen shattered the lens before puncturing the right eye. Jim shoved it forward with an underhand motion, rising out of his seat as he forced it deeper into Carl's brain. The overstuffed chair flipped backward and Carl's head hit the wood floor like an overcooked egg. His legs kicked once, twice, and then he was dead.

Jim came around the desk and knelt next to his editor. There was surprisingly little blood, and he made a mental note to get that right the next time he wrote a murder scene.

He stood and ran his hands through his hair, willing his heart to slow down. Took a deep breath, then another, opened the door to his study and prayed he hadn't written himself into a corner.

The town house was quiet. But there, almost beyond hearing, tiny voices from downstairs. Jim felt a surge of adrenaline and bounded down the stairs two at a time.

Emily was sitting on the couch, watching television. She smiled when he cleared the threshold and Jim felt his heart explode. Before she could say anything he was across the room with his arms around her. He kissed her and let it linger until she gave him a squeeze and stepped back to look at him.

"It's nice to see you, too."

"I didn't hear you come in."

"I knew you were writing, silly. I never disturb you when your door is closed."

"You look nice." Jim let his eyes wander across his wife

from head to toe, her simple cream blouse and brown skirt a nice complement to her hair. He thought about how she'd been wearing a dress in the upper left quadrant on the computer and then slacks in the third one. How she'd been lugging a heavy briefcase in one frame and then running her hands through her hair in the next. They must have shot the video on different days, or perhaps it was some other technical wizardry.

Amazing what they can do with computers nowadays.

Continuity and attention to detail did matter, but not as much as knowing your characters. He'd known his editor for a long time and could tell when he was lying. When to suspend disbelief.

Emily never came into his study. He'd wait until she went to sleep, then move the body into the garage. A cop he'd interviewed for a story last year told him about a pier on the west side where the mob guys liked to dump bodies. Something about the currents pulled the body under, then took it out to sea.

He'd keep Carl's cell phone and make random calls to restaurants and airlines over the next couple of days, make it seem like Carl was still alive, then break the phone into pieces and throw them in the trash.

"Did you cut yourself?"

Jim glanced down at the red smear across his right hand. He forced a smile and wiped it across his jeans. "Just ink."

"You and your pens." Emily stepped over to an end table where an answering machine sat, its light blinking. "Your editor called and said he might be coming over. Want me to play the message?"

"No, thanks. I already talked to him."

"What did he want?"

"The usual. Deadlines."

"You finally get that ending figured out?"

Jim rubbed his fingers together, where after years of writing, ink the color of blood had left its mark.

"Yeah," he said. "I think I'm happy with how the story is going to end."

SEAN CHERCOVER

This former P.I. has the experience to infuse his writing with a heavy dose of authenticity. His realistic portrayals of both cops and the down-and-outers of the world have garnered Sean high praise and well-deserved awards. His first novel, *Big City, Bad Blood,* even gets praised on the FBI's Web site for its accurate depiction of law enforcement. His writing has been compared to Steve Hamilton, Lawrence Block and Dennis Lehane, but as his readers know, Sean has a powerful voice all his own.

Sean's intense love of scuba diving is sometimes reflected in his fiction, so it's fitting that his experience in the waters of the Caribbean can be felt in "A Calculated Risk." Tom Bailey, the main character, uses his deep passion and understanding of the water and boats to make a living. He's brushed up against the wrong side of the law many times before but this job takes him firmly over the edge. The real question is—will he be able to come back?

A CALCULATED RISK

Tom Bailey turned the wheel over to starboard and guided his forty-two-foot power catamaran, *Zombie Jamboree,* just inside the coral reef, relying on the lower helm's depth finder and night-vision monitor. He stole a glance at the luminous hands of his Submariner: forty minutes until dawn. Perfect timing.

The man who called himself Diego said, "How's our timing?"

"Perfect."

"Better be."

A threat? Or just a common expression. The man's tone was even, carried no particular menace. It was hard to tell. And because they were running dark, Bailey couldn't read anything in the man's face.

But he was tempted to say, *Or what?*

He said, "Dude, you came to me, I didn't come to you." He checked their GPS coordinates, cut the engines. The tide would take them in quiet from here. "Twelve minutes and we'll be right on Labadee Beach."

Labadee was a private beach within a walled compound on the north shore of Haiti. Royal Caribbean Cruise Lines owned the beach and the compound. The whole place would be empty until the next cruise ship arrived on Thursday. This was Tuesday. The *Zombie Jamboree* drifted in on the tide and the men didn't speak until they arrived at Labadee.

Right on time.

"Can we get close enough?"

"She's a cat, she draws three feet," said Bailey.

About thirty feet from shore, Bailey said, "You jump in now, you're about up to your nipples. Tide's behind you. You can wade in from here." They walked out to the aft deck, Bailey carrying a flashlight with a red lens to deaden the light, the other man carrying a black Pelican case. About the size and shape of a thick briefcase, but made of injection-molded plastic, with O-rings and strong latches and a one-way purge valve.

Watertight.

The man who called himself Diego stopped on the swim step, looked up at Bailey. He said, "You remember what I told you."

Bailey smiled. "Don't worry about me."

Even in the dim light, the man's eyes shone with

contempt. "I have to worry about you," he said. "You are the one part of the plan I can't control. I know *I* won't fuck up. I plan everything, down to the minute, and then I execute with precision. I leave nothing to chance. The only chance of failure is if *you* fuck up."

"Bad logic," said Bailey. "If I fuck up, then you fucked up by hiring me, dude." Bailey didn't usually say *dude* this often. But he could tell that it bothered his client, and he didn't like his client.

The man looked to the deserted shore, back at Bailey, and launched into it again. For the seventh time. "You head straight for Dominican waters. You stay there. Go fishing. Go diving. Work on your tan. Whatever. You don't go ashore. You don't get drunk. You don't smoke grass. You put down anchor at the end of the day, like you're settling in for the night. You go dark. You stay dark. You return here at eleven-thirty tonight. Right here. Yes?"

"Yes, Diego." Bailey waved the flashlight toward shore. "And I signal with three flashes, at three-minute intervals."

"All right." The man let go of the railing, sunk until his feet hit the sandy bottom. He was about up to his nipples. He started walking toward shore, the black Pelican case floating out in front of him on the calm water, its handle in his left hand.

Starlight glittered silver off the black water, creating a gossamer wake behind the man as he waded in. There was the gentle hiss of the tide kissing the sand, and the ever-present tree-frog music, floating on the sweet island breeze. And that was all.

Not a soul on the beach to witness the arrival of the man who called himself Diego.

Bailey jabbed at the purge valve of his regulator, then stuck the regulator in his mouth. He put his right hand over his face, applying pressure to both mask and regulator. Left hand, holding the spear gun, pressed against his chest. Rolled back, plunged into the Caribbean Sea.

Like falling into a warm bath. Beneath the surface was where he felt truly at home. At peace. He needed the time down here, and tried to get a dive in every day.

He kicked his fins, got some depth, pinched his nose through the silicone mask and cleared his ears, kicked again in the direction of the anchor line.

The top of the coral reef was forty-two feet from the surface, and Bailey added a little air to his BC as he arrived. He floated along the top of the reef, pulled the rubber tubing back to ready his spear gun.

Tried to concentrate.

But his mind was busy, replaying the initial meeting with his client.

"Your monkey cannot come along," said the man, and gestured to the vervet monkey that sat on the starboard bench devouring a mango. The monkey mistook the man's gesture, let out a piercing shriek and scooted back a foot, clutching the mangled mango to her chest.

"Relax, I don't want your fucking mango," said the man. Then, to Bailey, "See? He's loud."

The wake of a passing yacht caused the *Zombie Jamboree* to rock ever so slightly, and the man overcompensated with his leg muscles like a subway virgin, almost stumbled, but corrected in time. The man was clearly not possessed of sea legs, and Bailey didn't relish the idea of a seasick passenger. He decided to charge extra.

Bailey took his feet off the gunwale and planted them on the deck, stubbed out the joint he was smoking.

"She."

"What?"

"She," Bailey repeated. "*She's* loud. Her name is Miss Judy." He took a swig of Dos Equis, then rubbed the cold bottle against his bare chest. "Anyway, she doesn't live aboard. She's just a friend, she's not my monkey. She's not anybody's monkey." He hit the man with a goofy smile.

The man waved Bailey's words away impatiently. "I don't give a shit. Boy monkey, girl monkey. Your monkey, not your monkey. The monkey is not to come with us on this trip. Understand?"

"Sure. No monkey."

Bailey didn't like this man, but then again, he didn't like a lot of his clients. Liking your clients was not part of the people-smuggling business.

Most of Bailey's clients were rich Americans sneaking into the Bahamas to engage in some extramarital recreation, or to drop some cash at the local casinos. The smarter ones came to stash money in offshore accounts. Bailey didn't smuggle *things,* just people. There was too much risk when you started moving unknown cargo across international borders. You might get boarded and find yourself holding fifty keys of coke. Or guns. Or anything. It wasn't worth it if you got caught, and even if you didn't, there were moral considerations. Where were the guns going? Would they be used to liberate people, or enslave them? Were the drugs going to middle-class suburbanites, or would they contribute to the rot of the inner cities? So Bailey saved himself the headache. People were easy. Easy to move, easy to hide. And people-smuggling had always seemed morally uncomplicated.

Free people moving about freely. The idea held great philosophical appeal. At least, it used to. Things changed after 9/11, but Bailey was a good judge of people and he knew he'd never smuggled a terrorist. Not yet. Lately, he had started to consider the merits of retirement. Of going legit.

He could continue to run the *Zombie Jamboree* as a fishing charter, simply knock off the undeclared, cash-only side business. But if he were going legit, it wouldn't be as a fishing charter. Too much stink, and all his time spent on the surface, and too many asshole customers who blame the captain when the fish don't bite.

No, the plan for going legit went like this: move to an island where he wasn't known—an island with a good economy and stable political climate. Barbados was perfect. Buy a small dive shop there, and hire a couple of young guys to help run the place. Maybe even move ashore and charter the cat for pleasure cruising. Or hire a local captain to babysit the fishing tourists.

That was the plan. But it was a plan with a significant price tag, especially on an island like Barbados. If he stayed with the people-smuggling sideline, he might make the nut in a couple years. But if he went legit as a fishing charter, what with the cost of fuel these days, it could take another decade.

So a couple more years of people-smuggling, and out. He'd still be a few years on the right side of forty when he reinvented himself yet again, this time as a law-abiding dive-shop operator. He might even meet a nice woman, fall in love…have a kid.

Or maybe he was kidding himself. But what the hell. He'd come a long way on this ongoing journey of personal transformation; might as well buy in to the whole dream. Stranger things have happened.

The man who called himself Diego was no terrorist, but neither was he simply a playboy looking for a good time or a tax dodge. Whatever he was, he was a hard guy. Dangerous. Not weightlifter hard—those body-proud posers were only dangerous to themselves. Like Bailey, this guy had a lean and flexible musculature. His hardness was a mental hardness. Hence, dangerous.

Whatever this guy was, he was a *bad dude.* He knew it, and he knew that you knew it, and he never made any effort to convince you of it. That's the way it is with truly dangerous men. They never try to convince anybody. They just *are.* If you're an even halfway bad dude, you'll recognize it. If you don't, you're not worth worrying about.

Bailey recognized it. He'd been a bad dude himself, in a former life. But that was before the first reinvention. These days he was known, to those who thought they knew him, as a friendly expat American who liked rum and reefer, diving and women, in approximately that order.

Among the Caribbean's expat, live-aboard set, there were two distinct groups. There were those, like Bailey, who never talked about their former lives, and there were those who never shut the hell up about their former lives. All you had to do is pull up a stool next to them at the beach bar and you'd hear all about it, in excruciating detail.

Dot-com millionaires who struck gold with an IPO and then dumped out just ahead of the bust; stock-market day-traders who'd had the discipline to quit while they were ahead; software developers; venture capitalists; real estate speculators; doctors and dentists who'd diligently saved their money and retired while still young enough to live the rest of their lives chasing after Jimmy Buffett's bliss. The stories were all different, and all the same.

And of course there were the trust-fund babies. Their former lives consisted mostly of homogenous boarding schools and ski trips in the Alps and absent parents and kindly nannies. Bailey preferred the second-generation trust-fund babies; they seemed to have accepted their lot with a little more grace than their furiously idle parents.

Bailey's group—those who didn't talk about their former

lives—consisted of retired arms dealers, drug runners, mercenaries, white-collar embezzlers and blue-collar thugs. A
growing number of Russian "businessmen." Also scattered
around the Caribbean were former civil servants, mostly of
the U.S. and U.K., some of France, and a few Israelis. Civil
servants, true, but not the kind that ever saw the inside of
a cubicle. Bailey had worked for Uncle Sam, in his former
life.

The man who called himself Diego didn't seem to fit any
of these categories. He used the name Diego and spoke with
a slight accent, but Bailey guessed that the accent was no
more authentic than the name. He lacked the olive complexion, and while he had a good tan, it looked like it had
been recently acquired in a salon. Bailey guessed the man
for an American, but he couldn't be positive.

Bailey's initial dislike of the man only intensified while
they talked. Although the man made no effort to act tough,
ego asserted itself in a pronounced attitude of superiority. An
attitude that says, *I'm smarter than you and everyone else on this
island, and I resent having to deal with men of lesser competence.*

Still, there was no concrete reason to turn the man down.
The gig was easy enough—pick the guy up at the Flying
Fish Marina in Clarence Town, get him to Haiti, drop him
off before sunrise, pick him up the same night, deliver him
back to the marina the next day. The first pickup and final
drop-off would happen in full view, and Bailey would have
the boat set up like a regular fishing charter. Fighting chair
in place, rods prominently displayed.

And the money was good. Ten thousand American dollars, plus fuel expenses. Cash. Always in cash.

Bailey returned to Labadee Beach at exactly eleven-thirty that night. He cut the throttle down to idle and scanned the shoreline through night-vision binoculars.

Nothing. He grabbed the big flashlight with the red lens, pointed it toward land, flicked the switch on and off three times. Glanced at his watch.

Three minutes later, he did it again. Still nothing.

Another three minutes, and then the flashlight dance again.

Where the hell was this guy?

After the fourth flashlight signal went unanswered, Bailey moved to the aft deck's portside throttle controls and eased the cat closer to shore. He checked his watch again. Fifteen minutes. Something was very wrong.

I plan everything, down to the minute, and then I execute with precision. I leave nothing to chance.

And now the guy was late.

Bailey reached for the flashlight again, but before he hit the switch, there was a rustling of bushes at the top of the beach. The man who called himself Diego burst into view, ran down the beach and splashed into the water, the Pelican case in his left hand.

Bailey swung the boat around as the man waded out in a jog. He cut the throttle and moved to the swim step, keeping his eye on shore.

The beach was empty. Nobody giving chase.

The man clambered aboard. There was blood on the front of his shirt. A lot of blood.

"I'll get the first-aid kit."

"Stop."

Bailey stopped, turned back. He looked the man over. No evidence of injury.

The man stared him down, said, "I had a nosebleed."

"Right."

"Just get us out of here, fast."

"Fast or quiet," said Bailey. "You can't have both."

"Fast."

"You got it." Bailey climbed up the ladder to the fly-bridge helm. "Hang on." He jammed the throttles forward and the twin diesels roared up from idle. His blood-splattered passenger grabbed the ladder for support, but stayed down on the aft deck.

As they came around the reef, automatic weapons fire rang out from shore.

Pap-pap-pap-pap-pap-pap.

The man who called himself Diego flattened against the deck, but the gunfire sounded more like protest than attack, and it died rapidly. At this distance, with only dim starlight and no moon, with the boat running dark at thirty knots, the men on shore must've known they couldn't hit anything. They'd be aiming at the sound of the engines and their bullets would be well off the stern. Still, Bailey felt adrenaline leak into his bloodstream, and blew out a long breath.

Haiti had a meager Coast Guard and Bailey didn't think they'd be able to scramble a boat out in time, but he stayed up on the flybridge where he could spot any unwelcome company, just in case.

No boat appeared.

Outside the protection of the reef, the sea rose up and the swells grew to about seven feet. No challenge to the stability of the cat, but Bailey wondered if an unexpected storm was in their future. He'd checked the marine forecast earlier in the day, but conditions change quickly in these parts.

He switched on the radio. No storm on the way. Small consolation.

No moon. *I leave nothing to chance.* Damn. Bailey had noticed that it would be a moonless night when he'd checked the tide calendar. It should've raised a red flag, but he'd been too busy thinking about the ten thousand dollars. Too busy chasing his dream.

And now everything had gone to dog shit.

Bailey told himself to take it easy: cut out the self-flagellation and focus on the present situation. Yes, his client was wearing someone else's blood, and yes, there'd been men with automatic weapons on the beach. But automatic weapons were relatively easy to come by in Haiti; the men on the beach could've been gangsters as easy as cops.

And then the radio rendered Bailey's rationalizations impotent.

The Caribbean News Agency was reporting that

Dominic Martel—the leader of Haiti's pro-democracy movement—had been shot to death that evening as he dined with his family in a restaurant in the town of Cap Haitien. Cap Haitien was only six miles southeast of Labadee Beach.

Shit. Bailey felt his stomach turn over. His client was an assassin.

Still no boat appeared, and he realized that there would be none. They'd gotten away clean. But now he had bigger things to worry about. Now he had to worry about his client. It was time to start being active, instead of reactive. Time to put the old skills to work.

There was no boat giving chase, but down on the aft deck, the man who called himself Diego could not see over the swells. Bailey set the autopilot, grabbed the flashlight and moved to the ladder, as if in a hurry.

"We got company," he called down to the man. "Get inside." He came down the ladder at speed and ushered his client into the pilothouse. The man didn't argue.

Bailey opened a trapdoor in the cabin floor and climbed down a steep set of metal stairs into the port hull, just ahead of the engine room. It was hot and loud down there. He flipped a switch and fluorescent lights flickered to life in the ceiling.

"Come on, come on," he said, waving at the man. He pressed on a false wall and it opened, revealing a small padded closet just large enough for one person. There was a built-in seat, also padded.

The man came down the stairs, clutching his case. He looked dubiously at the custom-built people-hider.

Bailey said, "It's safe. It has its own ventilation. If we get boarded, they won't find you."

The man stepped inside, but he didn't look happy about it.

Bailey pushed the false wall back into place. He climbed up the stairs, got a water bottle and a box of extrastrength Gravol from the galley, returned and pressed on the wall.

"Here," he said, and handed the bottle to the man. He held the box of Gravol up for the man to see, then popped a couple of pills free of their blister pack. "Take these." The man did not reach for them. "Listen," Bailey said, "I'm gonna have to cut across the swells to lose these guys and it's gonna get rough down here. You don't take these, you're gonna be puking all over yourself in about ten minutes. I can't afford to have you choking on your vomit while I'm up top."

The man swallowed the pills. Bailey shut the secret door.

At the lower helm station, Bailey shut off the autopilot and switched on the running lights. He turned the wheel and pointed the boat so that the swells hit sideways instead of head-on. The boat rocked side to side.

Then he reached forward and flipped a toggle switch, shutting off the ventilation to the people-hider.

He thought things through. The man who called himself

Diego had taken a brief nap after Bailey had picked him up at the marina, but had not slept on the overnight journey from Long Island to Haiti, and Bailey doubted that sleep had been on his agenda during his time ashore. So he'd been awake at least thirty hours.

Shutting off the ventilation wouldn't kill the man, but the oxygen level in the people-hider would deplete. Between that and the extrastrength Gravol, Bailey figured the man would be unconscious within the hour.

Bailey pressed on the secret door and eased it open. He was greeted by a beautiful sound. Snoring. The man who called himself Diego was asleep, reclined on the seat, his head resting against the padded wall. The Pelican case had slipped from his grasp and lay on the floor.

Bailey took the case, and gently closed the door.

Up in the lounge, Bailey flipped the latches and opened the case. He withdrew a map that showed a section of Haiti's north shore, from Labadee to the town of Cap Haitien. Beneath the map was a semiautomatic pistol. He lifted the pistol from the case, smelled it. Cordite. He put the recently fired pistol aside. There was money in the case. American money, about $30,000. Bailey fished around under the cash, found a passport. A U.S. passport. He took it out of the case and opened it.

His blood ran cold. Staring back at him was the standard passport photo of the man who called himself Diego. But the name on the passport was Tom Bailey.

I leave nothing to chance. So the man who called himself Diego wasn't done killing.

Or thought he wasn't. Bailey could take care of this threat without breaking a sweat. The man was asleep and Bailey had his gun. Easiest thing in the world, to walk downstairs and put a bullet in the man's head with his own gun. End of threat. He could weigh down the body with an anchor and some line. Dump the body at sea, along with the gun. Done. Finished. Pretend it never happened.

But then Bailey thought about it from the other man's perspective. A change of identity would mean relocating. It was an expensive proposition. It would mean a significant sum of money waiting for him in his new destination. Had to. But there was nothing else in the case to say where.

And that led Bailey on a new train of thought. Was this a crazy idea? A reckless bet? No, he decided. It was time to go legit—now—and this could set him on his new path. The man had an ego problem; he would play on that.

This was a calculated risk.

He would have to put the case back the way he found it—passport under the money, gun on top and the map covering the gun. Then return the case to the people-hider with the man and switch the ventilation back on.

Sunrise was breaking over a calm sea when the man emerged from below. The case was in his left hand. The butt of the pistol peeked out from his waistband.

"Good morning," said Bailey. Cheerful.

"Where the hell are we?"

"Almost home. We made it." Bailey gestured out the windows, to a speck of land on the horizon.

"That's Long Island?"

"Yup. I'll have you back on dry land in half an hour."

"You got an extra shirt I can have?"

"No problem." Bailey got a T-shirt from the stateroom in the starboard hull. When he returned, the man was pointing the gun at him. He tried to look surprised. "Take it easy, Diego," he said. "If you don't like the shirt, I'll get you another one."

"That's actually very funny," the man said. He was no longer affecting an accent. He gestured with the barrel of his gun to the aft deck. "Outside."

Bailey put his hands up, even though the man hadn't asked him to do so. He walked out to the aft deck, sat down hard on the portside bench, braced his hands on his knees and shook his head.

"Diego, I delivered my end of the bargain. You don't have to do this. It's not the smart play."

"Actually, it is." The man kept the pistol aimed at Bailey's chest.

"I'm an accessory, before *and* after the fact—you know I won't talk."

"No, you won't."

"Killing me is only going to raise questions. I turn up dead, it'll only bring more heat. You're making a stupid move, here. Really stupid."

The man smiled. A cruel smile. "But you're not going to turn up dead. You're just making a move."

Bailey shook his head like he didn't understand, and leaned back with his hands planted on the bench behind him. "I don't understand. Where am I moving?"

"Grand Cayman. It's lovely there."

"They've got private banking in Cayman."

The man's smile broadened. "I know."

"Please, you really don't have to do this."

"No, I really do have to do this."

"I'm telling you. Don't be stupid."

The man pulled the trigger.

Click.

The man snorted derisively. "Clever," he said. He dropped the pistol on the deck and reached behind his back and came up with a throwing knife, as Bailey slid his hand under the bench cushion and came up with the pre-loaded spear gun he'd stashed there a couple hours earlier.

Both men froze.

"Mexican standoff," said the man who called himself Diego.

"Not really," said Bailey. "You may be good, but no arm can match the velocity of this thing. You'll lose." He locked eyes with the man, but instructed his peripheral vision to watch for any twitch in the man's knife hand, poised to throw.

"What do you propose?"

"I'll give you a choice. If you really think you can beat me, fire away. Or, you can take a swim."

"You're kidding."

"I don't think so."

"I'll never make it to shore."

"No, you won't. You'll tread water for a while, then you'll get tired and drown. You could get lucky, a boat may come along and pick you up. But that's unlikely. You have a choice to make. Either way, it's a calculated risk."

The man thought for a second, nodded to himself.

The knife hand moved forward. Bailey pulled the trigger. The knife clattered to the deck at Bailey's feet.

The man groped for the metal spear sticking out of his chest. He made a horrible gurgling sound, staggered backward. His arms flailed in the air as he toppled over the gunwale and into the Caribbean Sea.

Bailey crossed over to where the man who called himself Diego had stood, picked up the gun and tossed it overboard. He stuck his hand in his pocket, pulled out the bullets and dropped them into the sea.

Then he went inside and poured himself a long drink of rum.

Cayman. That's where he'd find the money. It would be waiting for him in a bank account in his own name. He plotted a course for Grand Cayman and sipped his drink.

A calculated risk. And it had paid off.

JAVIER SIERRA

Spanish writer Javier Sierra is known for seamlessly weaving history and science together in stories that not only entertain, but which attempt to solve some of the great mysteries of the past. His meticulous research has taken him across the globe, and his knowledge of faraway places and forgotten cultures is abundantly clear in "The Fifth World."

When murder and mysticism meet, Tess Mitchell is left with only a yellow butterfly found at the feet of her slain professor. The Mayan Calendar and its prophecies had always seemed academic to the young woman, but in Javier's chilling and believable style, they come alive in uncertain, frightening new ways.

THE FIFTH WORLD

"You've gotten yourself into a quite a mess, young lady."

Tess Mitchell's blue eyes flashed at the precinct commander as he entered the interrogation room where she had been placed in isolation. She had seen his face before on the local TV in Tucson.

"My name is Lincoln Lewis and I'm in charge of this precinct," he said with a sneer. His overall manner, however, was entirely professional. "I know you've spoken with some of our agents already, but it would be a real help if you could clear up a couple of things from your statement."

"Of course."

"For one thing, I need you to tell me what, exactly, you were doing at four o'clock this afternoon in Professor Jack Bennewitz's office."

"You mean, when I discovered...the body?"

The policeman nodded. Tess swallowed hard.

"Well, we had been working together on a project connected to his field of investigation. I was doing research for him and this morning I came across some data that I thought would interest him. Observational data. Technical things."

"I see. And what was it that Professor Bennewitz taught?"

"Theory of the solar system, sir."

"Did you have an appointment with him?"

A blush suddenly came over Tess's cheeks and, unable to conceal it, she cast her eyes downward at the steel-and-wood table.

"To be honest I didn't need one," she explained. "He let me come and see him whenever I had to, and since I knew that he had office hours for his students around then, I just decided to go by. That's all."

"And what did you find when you got there, Miss Mitchell?"

"I already told your colleagues—the first thing I noticed was how silent it was in Building B. Jack always spoke in such a loud voice. Whenever he yelled—which was often—you could practically hear him at the other end of campus. He was a very intense kind of person, you know? But I noticed something else, too—there was a very odd smell in the waiting room. It even drifted out into part of the hallway, a very strong, acidic odor, really awful." Tess made a face at the thought of it before continuing. "So I went in without knocking."

"And what did you find?"

Tess Mitchell closed her eyes, trying to conjure up the scene in her head. The image of her friend Jack Bennewitz lying back in his leather armchair, his face contorted and his eyes fixed on some indeterminate point between the plaster ceiling and the case filled with his chess trophies, flashed through her mind for a brief moment. Despite the fact that his jacket was fully buttoned, there was no way to miss the chocolate-colored stain that had soaked through the shirt underneath. There was no sign of a struggle. Books and papers were meticulously organized, and even the coffee that he must have poured himself shortly before ending up in that gruesome state remained in a mug on his desk, cold and untouched.

"Did you touch Professor Bennewitz's body? Did you make any attempt to revive him?" Officer Lewis insisted.

"Good God, no!" the young woman exclaimed. "Of course not! Jack was dead, dead! Don't you get it?"

"Didn't you notice anything at all out of the ordinary? Something that might have been missing from the office?"

Tess Mitchell pondered these questions a few seconds before shaking her head no. There was no way, she thought, that the wooden box containing a butterfly with giant yellow wings that she had found at Jack's feet could be of any use to the investigation. She had put it in her bag almost instinctively; she had no idea why a prominent theoretical physicist like Bennewitz would have been an insect collector, even though she herself was a real aficionado.

"May I tell you something, miss?" Officer Lewis said, in a conspiratorial tone of voice. "Jack Bennewitz's death is one of the strangest I've ever seen. And since you were the person who phoned it in, I'll have to ask you to remain in the precinct a while longer. You're our only witness."

"Is it absolutely necessary?"

"I'm afraid so, Miss Mitchell. You may not know this, but the majority of all crimes are solved using information gathered in the first few hours of the investigation."

No one would ever recommend the area around the Museo de América in Madrid as a place for a midnight stroll. Francisco Ruiz glanced at the dark pathway that stretched out from the Moncloa tower and checked his watch. Realizing that it was already past 11:00 p.m. he stepped up his pace, so that he could get across that part of the walkway as fast as possible. Neither the empty echo of the Christmas carols nor the distant Christmas lights that framed the entrance to the city could dispel the pervading sense of total solitude that surrounded him. Temperatures had dropped considerably and almost instinctively he pulled up his coat collar and began walking even faster.

"Where are you going in such a rush, Professor?"

Ruiz recognized the voice right away. Of the many places to be caught by surprise in Madrid, this was by far the most forbidding. The man speaking to him had the same Central American accent as that of the individual who had been making threatening phone calls to his house for the past two weeks.

"You...!" he said, in a distressed whisper. Despite his arrogant facade, Ruiz was a coward. "Are you going to tell me for once and for all what it is that you want from me?"

"Don't play tough with me, man. Not with me."

The shadow that had intercepted him took a few steps forward, and was now standing directly beneath the only streetlamp that shed any light at all on the area, and Ruiz was perplexed by the image that now stood before him. The man was far shorter than he had imagined, and his face was graced by the most perfect Mayan features: aquiline nose, sharp cheekbones, tanned skin and a braid of hair so black that it blended right into the wretched night. A row of exceedingly white teeth glinted in the middle of his dark eagle's face. He went on:

"I saw that you didn't listen to me, Professor. The article you were working on came out in the paper...."

"And why would you care about that?"

"Oh, I care a lot, Professor. More than you imagine. In fact, you know what? The reason I'm here now is to make sure that you don't publish the second part of that article you mentioned. You made the same mistake before, about nine years ago. You know, I'm amazed. In all this time you haven't learned anything, have you?"

"What the hell are you talking about?"

Francisco Ruiz clung tightly to the folder in his hands, which contained the documents he needed to finish the groundbreaking article he was writing on the Soho Project. In the past few days he had met with several experts in pre-Hispanic history in an effort to lend his piece, which was purely scientific in nature, a more startling angle. That was why he had gone all the way to the Museo de América… but now that he thought about it, the harassment had begun at the same time that he'd started meeting with these historians. This little Mayan man with the fierce gaze, barely five feet tall, had really managed to make him nervous. By now he was within inches of Ruiz's face, so close that if Ruiz took two steps forward, he would bang right into him. His hands, buried deep in the pockets of his polar fleece jacket, seemed only to confirm Ruiz's hunch that he was up to no good.

"You must be the worst journalism professor in the entire university," said the Mayan man. His accent was getting stronger and stronger, his voice becoming increasingly vehement. "Or have you already forgotten about Y2K, Don Francisco?"

A lightbulb suddenly went off in his head. So that was what this was all about? A reader who had been disappointed by an article of his? Ruiz had been one of Europe's fiercest proponents of the hypothesis that after midnight on December 31, 1999, computer systems the world over would simultaneously collapse because their internal calendars would be unable to make the leap from 1999 to 2000. Since the very earliest computers used two-digit date formats—1997 was 97, 1998 was 98, and so on—some people became convinced that at the dawn of the year 2000 operating systems would identify "00" as the year 1900 instead of 2000, which would, in turn, cause everything to go haywire. In his columns, Francisco Ruiz had envisioned a kind of cyber-apocalypse: airports and hospitals in total meltdown, bank accounts and transactions on the blink, pensions unpaid, power stations, nuclear plants, and gas and oil lines completely cut off by the dysfunctional computer system, to say nothing of world financial systems, satellites, nuclear weapons and streetlights, which would all become deprogrammed at the very same instant. Caught in the throes of his millennium fever, he had actually advised his readers to stockpile extra cash and provisions before New Year's Eve…just in case.

But of course, January 1, 2000, had come and gone, and none of the predicted calamities ever came to pass. Francisco had moved on to other topics in his columns, and quite soon the world forgot about the crisis that never was.

"Soho is different," he found himself saying. "It's quite a bit more serious."

"Yes, I know it's serious!" retorted the Mayan. "Everything that has to do with the sun is serious. That's why I'm here."

Soho, shorthand for the Solar and Heliospheric Observatory, was one of the technological playthings that had recently given NASA and the European Space Agency some of its most promising moments. From the day it was launched in 1995, Soho had sent the Goddard Space Flight

Center in Maryland literally billions of data regarding the sun, its magnetic storms, sunspots and coronal mass ejections. Soho had even found the time to identify no less than 1,500 comets that were not visible from Earth. The sinister-looking Mayan, however, did not seem the least bit interested in these achievements.

Before Francisco Ruiz could change direction and escape, his inconvenient interlocutor suddenly pounced upon him like a bulldog. The impact, which caught Ruiz totally by surprise, sent the two men rolling downhill. The Mayan's determination to immobilize him, along with his quickened breathing, now had Ruiz scared for his life. The next thing he felt was a hot sensation in his chest followed by a dreadful noise, like a drain gulping down the last mouthfuls of filth spilling out from a broken pipe. It took a few moments for Francisco to realize that the noise was, in fact, emanating from him. From his solar plexus. Then everything felt cold, as if someone had taken off his coat. A sharp pain followed. Cloudy vision. Darkness.

Then, everything went black.

The precinct commander at the Stone Avenue station in Tucson, Arizona, served himself another cup of coffee from the vending machine in the corridor without taking his eyes off of Tess Mitchell. The young woman with the blond braids and frightened eyes couldn't stop fidgeting in the uncomfortable metal chair.

"You sure you wouldn't like something to drink, young lady?"

She shook her head. Lincoln Lewis had just informed her that federal agents were going to take over the case of Jack Bennewitz's death. Apparently, on his computer, they had found some interesting links between her physics mentor and various university professors in Central America, the Middle East and Europe. One of them, Juan Martorell, from the University of Mexico, had been murdered not twenty-four hours earlier in Mexico City, his body thrown from the seventeenth floor of the Hotel Reforma. In the best interests of his investigation, the police chief withheld this last bit of information.

"You and Jack were close?" he asked.

Tess nodded. They had known each other for four years. Together they had visited the most important telescopes in the U.S., and had even made a few trips out of the country, to Arecibo, in Puerto Rico and Mexico City, just a month earlier. Together they had gone to the pyramids at Teotihuacán, "the oldest astronomical observatory in the Americas," as Bennewitz had admiringly called it.

"Did they tell you how Jack died?"

At this point, Tess had been in the police station for five hours, answering the same questions over and over again to a parade of different agents. It was clear that they had no leads. Just her. And she also knew, as the policeman she had seen on TV seemed to suggest, that they were prepared to put her through hell for as long as they could.

The young woman shook her head in response.

"A gunshot fired at him point-blank?" she guessed aloud.

"I'm afraid not, Tess. They tore his heart out, in one fell swoop. They did it with some kind of very sharp object, a blade or a prod that they sunk into him in a single motion, slicing directly through his arteries."

The young woman's eyes widened with fright. Now she understood that dark stain on Professor Bennewitz's shirt.

"We know it wasn't you," the police chief assured her. "You wouldn't have the strength for something like that. Plus, Jack Bennewitz died at least two hours before you got to him. In all likelihood the murder did not even occur in that office. We found no traces of blood whatsoever there, except for the stains on his clothing. They must have brought him there after they did it, sat him down and left him for someone else to find him."

"Really?"

The police chief nodded.

"Tell me, where were you at two o'clock this afternoon?"

Tess didn't hesitate. "I had just left the Kitt Peak observatory," she said, swallowing air as if muffling a sob. "I was there all morning, gathering information from the main telescope. When I found what I was looking for, I went to Jack's office to show him. From the observatory it takes about ninety minutes to get to Tucson, so I would have been on the road at around that time...."

"Right. Now, since you weren't on campus when the

crime occurred, I wonder if you could tell me if you or any of your friends saw anything unusual on campus today, either this morning or later this afternoon. Anything at all that struck you as unusual?"

Tess said nothing. She bowed her head, as if trying to extract a memory, any kind of recollection at all that might offer the police some kind of clue to aid their investigation. The matter of the butterfly seemed irrelevant and anyway, she was too embarrassed to admit that she had taken something from a crime scene, so she just put it out of her mind. In a matter of seconds she replayed her arrival at the university, the ham-and-cheese sandwich she'd eaten in the Building B cafeteria, her thoughts about the university lecture they would be attending that afternoon… "Of course!" she suddenly exclaimed. "The university lecture, that's it!" Suppressing an incipient smile, she searched the police officer's eyes.

"We-well," she stuttered. "I don't know if this means anything, but Jack Bennewitz was going to give a very important lecture this afternoon in the auditorium of the main building. His students were all very excited about it. He was going to announce a major discovery."

"Go on, please."

"Well, Professor Bennewitz was going to announce the results of his latest work—a theoretical model capable of predicting high-intensity solar storms and eruptions. X-class eruptions, and even higher-level ones. It was rumored that the scale might have to be raised to Z-class. He was especially concerned about a storm that could reach Z-class. He called it the Big One."

Lincoln Lewis's eyes opened wide. He had heard the techies in his department mention precisely those words, *Big One,* just minutes earlier. Several folders on the victim's computer were filled with references to it.

The Big One.

On the sixth floor of the United States Embassy in Madrid, Eileen Garrett and Bill Dafoe of the intelligence unit were having a heated discussion about those two words. The Spanish national police had just been asking them about it, after a journalism professor at the Complutense University had been found dead in the neighborhood of Moncloa with a briefcase full of Internet printouts about the Big One, as well as original documents that bore the letterhead of the Goddard Space Flight Center. The professor's folder was now sitting open on a conference room table at the embassy. Apparently, what the local police had found so unusual was the way the body had been mutilated: the aggressors had removed the man's heart and, while he was still alive, thrown his body down onto the entrance to the La Coruña road from the overpass between the Moncloa tower and the university rector's office.

"So, do you have any idea what the hell this Big One is, Bill?"

Eileen's eyes bore into the back of her colleague, who could scarcely tear his eyes away from the most recent science supplement of the Spanish newspaper *El País.*

"Well…it turns out that just yesterday this Ruiz character published an article explaining it," he said, smacking the paper with his index finger.

"Are you serious? Really?"

"Listen—'In 1989 a solar eruption sparked one of the most significant plasma expulsions documented by astrophysicists to date. They classified it as an X-class flare and discovered that it had sent a proton cloud into space that took several hours to reach Earth. When it finally did, a magnetic storm shifted the planet's field by eight degrees, short-circuited telephone and power lines in Canada and caused aurorae boreales in nonpolar zones. Sixteen years later, in January 2005, another X-class flare showered Earth with a proton storm—high-frequency transmissions in the U.S. and Canada collapsed, and this time the aurorae were visible in Arizona. Fortunately, none of these sudden flareups directly impacted the Earth—they only struck us laterally. The day we receive a frontal impact, the consequences of the Big One will be devastating.'"

"Wow! It sounds like an ad for a horror movie."

"Well, Ruiz took all of this very seriously. And get this— at the end of the article it says that tomorrow's paper will include part two of the article in which the author promises to give readers a probable date for the Big One… The news desk at the paper confirmed for me that they were expecting the article this afternoon."

"Excellent. Do you think this has something to do with his death?"

"It doesn't matter what I think, Eileen. Washington's already asked us to follow up. Until a few days ago, only a handful of people in the entire world had ever even heard of the Big One…and now, it looks like there's someone out there who wants to eliminate them, one by one."

As soon as Tess got back to her tiny apartment on Lester Street, she opened her laptop. She had received instructions not to leave the city without alerting Chief Lewis, but they hadn't said anything about suspending her professional activities. Nervously, she opened a search engine, typed in the words *Big One* and waited the fraction of a second it took for the first results to appear. She took a deep breath. Interestingly, the search engine produced only three news items related to the term. For the moment, it seemed, nobody knew about what she had discovered at Kitt Peak.

Not even the police had bothered to ask her about her work. The minute they sensed the hint of a technical explanation, they seemed to lose interest.

The articles Google produced were as follows:

NBA signs Roger Williams, Basketball's new Big One. She dismissed that one.

Madrid journalism professor murdered while researching article on solar storms.

The Legacy of Juan Martorell: A Life dedicated to the Maya.

Tess clicked on the second item and read through the article without blinking. It was a chronicle of events that briefly described the death of a Spanish professor whose heart had been ripped out and his body thrown from the top of an overpass. The police had no leads but were speculating that it was some kind of ritual murder. They said that the victim had achieved some notoriety in the hours before his death because of an article he had written in which he speculated that the imminent arrival of a magnetic storm from the sun might plunge civilization into a pre-digital era and cause severe damage to the cellular composition of a number of animal species. He had named this storm "the Big One."

When she read the professor's name, she suddenly became agitated. She had heard Jack talk about this Francisco Ruiz on several different occasions. In fact, Jack had been supplying Ruiz with information about the Soho satellite and its discoveries for several months before his death.

Distressed, Tess clicked on the third article. Although the Mayans were not a subject of particular interest to her, she wanted to make sure the article didn't contain any more surprises.

As it turned out, the details of this piece were even more astonishing than the last. Another professor—a historian this time—had also been murdered, after giving a seminar on the Mayan Calendar and the decline of the Mayan civilization. According to Martorell, the Mayan culture disappeared after a series of sudden natural disasters—droughts, hurricanes—swept through Mexico in the tenth century. According to the professor, the Mayan people foretold the advent of their own apocalypse through meticulous observation of the sun. They came to believe that every fifty-two years the sun experienced a rebirth, and that this mutation necessarily affected them, as well. According to their belief system, every fifty-two cycles of fifty-two years—in other words, every 2,704 years—the world disappeared completely, and gave way to an entirely new one. In fact, said the professor, this was the only possible explanation for the mysterious and abrupt manner in which the Mayan people abandoned their pyramids and cities, as documented by archeologists. According to this odd logic the final cycle, which would herald the arrival of the Fifth World, would come to an end at midnight on December 21, 2012.

"December 21, 2012," repeated Tess in a whisper.

Exactly nineteen hours away.

The facade of the Institute of Anatomical Forensics on the campus of Madrid's Complutense University flashed and twinkled beneath the glow of its Christmas lights. It was an odd sight to behold: a gray, somber-looking edifice so gaily illuminated at eight o'clock in the morning. But despite the early hour, the activity contained within its walls was at full pitch.

Eileen Garrett had found her way to the building in a sleepy haze, unaware of why she had been summoned with such urgency. Doctor Aguirre was waiting for her at the entrance to the building with a folder in his hands.

"I'm sorry for waking you in the middle of the night,

miss," he said. He seemed like a circumspect sort of man. "Last night the police asked us to phone the embassy as soon as we completed the autopsy on Ruiz."

"Yes?"

"Well…" The doctor's pause banished the last traces of slumber in Garrett's head. "To tell the truth, we don't know quite what to say."

"What do you mean?"

"The method used to remove the heart of this poor man. We believe it was done with an obsidian knife. Under the microscope we identified a few particles of the volcanic rock. What's so odd is that this is the kind of weapon used by primitive cultures, like the Mayans or the Aztecs. The skill with which it was used requires a tremendous degree of strength."

"Are you trying to tell me, Doctor, that this man was stabbed with an Aztec sacrificial knife?"

"I know it sounds bizarre, miss, but there's no doubt in my mind. And it was done by someone who knew exactly what he was doing."

Four people in the world knew all the details of the Big One. All four were connected to Jack Bennewitz—including Juan Martorell, according to the article Tess had found on the Internet—and three of them had been found dead, victims of some sort of ritual murder, in the last few hours. The only one left alive was Tess Mitchell, who spent a fitful, sleepless night thinking that before midnight on this new day of December 21, her name would be added to that macabre list. She had to do something to stop it from happening. Anything. Something that would keep her hidden from a bunch of murderers who, just like the ancient Aztec sun-worshippers, believed that the end of the day would mark the end of the world.

Could this really be happening? Or was she just going mad?

It was barely four in the morning when Tess quickly packed her laptop and notes in her car, along with the images she had obtained from the Kitt Peak observatory, and headed for Nogales. For a moment she thought if she could cross the Mexican border within an hour or so and then get herself to Mexico City, it would be very hard for anyone to locate her in a city of nineteen million. She did not warn the police, nor did she realize that what was behind the deaths of Jack, Juan and Francisco was about to crash onto her with all the weight of the laws of physics.

What Tess did know, however, was that at noon on December 20, 2012, a massive solar eruption or Coronal Mass Ejection—CME—had been recorded on Sunspot 1108 at approximately 60° west longitude, perfectly aligned with Earth. The resulting proton storm, picked up by the monitors of the National Astronomical Observatory, was heading toward Earth at that very moment, and would crash into the planet's surface in a short period of time. This was—what else could it be?—the first sign of the Big One that Professor Bennewitz had been talking about for years: an indeterminate sequence of solar eruptions with a subsequent magnetic emission that was heading straight for planet Earth. Tess had little trouble seeing that the sheer force of the event would be enough to plunge half the planet into total darkness, paralyze radioelectronic emissions in the hemisphere where it landed and destroy no less than eighty or ninety basic communications satellites in its path. But it was also possible that this occurrence might be the sign of something far worse: it still remained to be seen what, exactly, the relationship was between those proton storms and certain climate and chromosomal alterations. That was why she had gone to Jack's office that morning. That was why his death had left her so perplexed.

As she drove her gray Ford Mustang onto Interstate 19 and headed south for Mexico, she had no idea that she was being followed. The vehicle tailing her was a modern red Nissan Quest minivan with a Yucatán license plate. Tess drove for the remainder of the night, as did the red minivan. When the young physics student finally stopped to sit down to a hearty breakfast at a roadside restaurant near Ciudad Obregón in Sonora state, the men following kept an eye on her from afar. There was no way she could have known it, but the apathy with which she gazed at the cyber-café across the way from the restaurant saved her life. She was far more transfixed watching CNN on the television set there.

"To date, power outages have been reported in seven European countries, to greater and lesser degrees, for reasons that are still unknown," announced the voice of morning newscaster Terry White, jolting her out of her ruminations. "And in addition to what appears to be the most significant simultaneous blackout in the history of Europe, we are now receiving reports of problems with telecommunications, trains and air traffic. We are now advising anyone with plans to travel to the Mediterranean coast area…"

"Holy Mary mother of God!" exclaimed an old indigenous-looking woman, who crossed herself as she looked away from the television. Despite the early hour, she was already nursing a tall glass of tequila. "Did you see that, young lady? That's just the beginning!"

"The beginning?" Tess swallowed hard. She spoke very little Spanish, just enough to maintain a short conversation. "The beginning of what, ma'am?"

"Come on, honey! Are you the only person in the world who doesn't know about what's going to happen tonight?"

"What is supposed to happen?"

"The end of the world, honey! That's what the Mayan prophecies predict. And from the look of things," she said, pointing to the television, "it's already started in Europe. The land of our executioners."

Two sharp beeps emanating from her cell phone forced Tess to turn her attention to the liquid crystal display of its tiny screen. It was an RSS message from the Kitt Peak observatory.

"Sunspot 1108 has entered into eruption again. Colossal. The CME are increasing in number now."

The cell phone went dead.

★ ★ ★

"I've found something, Eileen. Luckily before this damn blackout cut off our access to the internal network."

Bill Dafoe's face was radiant. Despite the fact that electricity lines in Spain—and, along with them, those of Portugal, France, Italy, Belgium, Switzerland and Holland—were completely down, the embassy's emergency generators had given him a window of time to finish what he had been working on. He went on to explain to Eileen that he had been nosing around the archives of Madrid's Complutense University in search of information on Francisco Ruiz, when he hit upon the professor's e-mails, which included a number of messages to a certain Professor Bennewitz, who had been murdered in Tucson at almost the exact same time as Ruiz, and in the very same manner.

"So?"

"Bennewitz was working with a talented student by the name of Tess Mitchell. I've been trying to locate her but last night she disappeared from her apartment and her neighbors haven't seen her since. The Tucson police interrogated her a few hours earlier, but found no reasons to name her as a suspect in the murder. They're searching for her now, though."

"Do you think she left town?"

"Well…" Bill still had another piece of information in his possession. "According to border control in Nogales, a vehicle with her license plate left the U.S. and entered Mexico at around five-thirty this morning."

Eileen's face suddenly lit up.

"We have to find her, Bill. That girl knows something. I'll put out a search order for her right away."

The drive to Mexico City dragged on until well after 11:00 p.m. The vehicle's radio, oddly enough, was unable to tune in to a single radio station, just a lot of empty static. Tess's cell phone had lost reception as of Ciudad Obregón and none of the electronic signs on the road to Mexico City were working. Though these were clearly the symptoms of the fallout from the first proton storm, the physics student decided not to overestimate their importance.

As she approached the highway into the Mexican capital, Tess Mitchell decided that it would be more practical for her to find a hotel somewhere near the Teotihuacán archeological complex. There, at least, she could be sure of finding a room, and she knew the area relatively well. She had spent an entire week there, visiting the ruins with a research team from the university, and Jack Bennewitz had shown her some of the best and cheapest places to stay in the vicinity. As she turned off the ignition in front of the Albergue San Juan she was overcome by a torrent of mixed emotions: her evening strolls with Jack along the Avenida de los Muertos in the heart of the pyramid complex, gazing up at the Milky Way; his explanations of the relationship between each of those monuments and the planets known in pre-Hispanic times; even his remarks about how the people who built Teotihuacán believed that they were feeding the sun with every heart they pulled from someone's body. All these memories passed through her mind, more vivid than ever. How ironic that Jack would surrender his life to the sun, in the very same way that people did all the way back then, she thought.

"Are you Tess Mitchell?"

An indigenous-looking man nearing forty, with a thin beard and a face weathered by the sun, yanked her out of her thoughts as he stepped out of a red minivan that had just pulled up alongside her car. He wore a brightly colored poncho with geometric motifs that she could barely make out, because his headlights were still on.

"How…?"

"What? How do I know your name?" He smiled. "A good friend of yours told us. Professor Jack Bennewitz."

As he spoke, two other men stepped out of the minivan and walked over to her. She had a difficult time seeing them because, despite the clarity shed by the first-quarter moon, the hotel lights suddenly went out, and with them all the lights in the neighborhood. Tess jumped with a start.

"You don't have to be afraid anymore, miss," the indigenous man said.

"Anymore? What's that supposed to mean?"

"That time has reached its end and the cosmic clock has done its job. We have just crossed the threshold from the twenty-first to the twenty-second of December."

Then he added, "Welcome to the Fifth World, Miss Mitchell."

Tess shook her head.

"Please don't be afraid. Yesterday we paid a visit to your physics professor to convince him not to publish the information he had regarding the solar storm that the two of you detected. The same information that you are carrying right now in that laptop of yours."

"You…you were the ones who killed him?" Tess was incredulous. More than reproach, what echoed in her voice was fear.

"Oh, come on! We only sped up his passage, Miss Mitchell," the man said, without a trace of emotion. "We couldn't risk allowing Doctor Bennewitz to reveal his findings to the scientific community because, without realizing it, he would have prevented the sky from opening up as it just did."

"I don't know what you're talking about…."

"I'm sure you understand the scientific jargon better than I do, miss. But what just happened, though you and many other people may not realize it, is that the planet Earth has experienced a blast of cosmic energy so powerful that it produced a dimensional leap. Our position in the universe has shifted, and just as was foretold thousands of years ago, a new world has been born."

"That's ridiculous!" replied Tess. "Who are you people? Where did you come from?"

"We are the survivors of the Mayan people, miss. Descendants of those few people who remained on this plane of reality when our ancestors transcended dimensions at the end of the Third World. The world that just left us—forever, in fact—was the fourth."

"Well, I…I haven't noticed a thing!"

"Oh, really?"

The man's ironic smile, fixed on his face, made her wary.

"Have you tried to make a phone call? You won't be able to," he said, laughing as he watched Tess unsuccessfully dial the emergency number from her cell phone. "Have you heard anything at all on the radio in the past few hours? No. And from now on you won't, not ever again. Have you tried plugging anything into an outlet? You might as well say goodbye to all that forever. In the Fifth World none of that will work anymore. The sun has altered the electrical balance in the ionosphere and, as such, in the entire planet."

"Just like that?"

"Look!" One of the other men with them pointed upward. The night sky had transformed into something phantasmagoric, surreal. The silvery sky seemed to have morphed into a spongy substance that flowed as if dragged by the wind. It was a kind of aurora borealis, one that was nothing like anything any human had ever before seen on Earth.

"Now do you believe us?" the man asked. "Everything is mutating. Even you. You don't realize it, but your entire molecular structure and DNA are changing at this moment."

"Right…" she said, quivering. "So, what do you want from me?"

"We've come to deliver you a message—Professor Jack Bennewitz is waiting for you at the Teotihuacán ruins. He wants to explain everything."

"Jack…?" Tess was unable to finish her sentence.

For the umpteenth time, Bill Dafoe checked, but without luck. The conventional communications grid, including the high-resolution microwave signal, was down. The order to search for Tess Mitchell hadn't made it beyond the four walls of the embassy. Instinctively, he leaned out the window of his office on the sixth floor of the building. To his surprise, all the Christmas lights lining Serrano had gone dark. Not a single bus traveled down this street, one of Madrid's main arteries, and even the many Santa Clauses that just a few hours earlier had been clogging the sidewalks of this commercial zone, had disappeared into thin air. The city seemed deserted.

"I have to check something," he said to Eileen, and bounded down the stairs. The elevator, along with all the electricity in the building, had gone dead, as well.

When he arrived at the building's front gate, the Marine Corps guards and the National Police in charge of watching over the embassy precinct were in a state of distress. Everything had stopped working. Even—and this was the strangest thing of all—the diesel engines of the two assault tanks that the Spanish police used to guard the surrounding streets.

"Bill! Now that's funny!" shouted the officer responsible for allowing outsiders to gain access to the building. He knew Dafoe from their years as schoolmates back in Lexington, Kentucky. "With this damn blackout I had no way of calling up to let you know. You've got a visitor. In the waiting area."

"A visitor?"

"Yeah…let's see," he said, automatically glancing down at the embassy's entry and exit list. "His name is Francisco Ruiz, and he says that you and your partner have a folder of his that he'd like to pick up."

"Francisco Ruiz?"

A solemn atmosphere pervaded the ceremonial complex of Teotihuacán. The grayish silhouette of the massive pyramids and the hulking magnificence of Cerro Gordo on the horizon shone dramatically beneath the powerful glow of the moon. Next to the smallest pyramid, in a plaza adorned with reliefs of the Quetzal, a curious cross between bird and insect, Tess just barely made out the familiar image of a man dressed in white. It seemed as though he'd been standing there for a millennium, waiting for her.

"The best place in the world for us to find each other again, Tess!"

Jack Bennewitz's booming voice reverberated between the empty structures. Tess Mitchell didn't understand anything, and her face showed it. Right at that moment, she was tempted to think that everything she had been through in the past few hours had been nothing more than a bad practical joke.

"It's me—Jack!" he said, opening his arms wide. "I don't know what the boys told you, but this is real! At midnight the planet entered into a totally new vibrational phase. All matter, including dark matter, has begun to resonate at a frequency that was unknown up until now. Do you understand, Tess?"

"But…you're alive!" she exclaimed.

"Alive, dead…what does it matter? Those are states of being that belong to the old world. We're in a new dimension now."

The young woman's hands stroked the soft white cotton of Jack Bennewitz's suit. It had to be an illusion.

"Come on, Tess! Okay, maybe I didn't enter this dimension voluntarily, but the men who killed me knew that they were just speeding up my passage by a few hours. They even left you a sign so that you wouldn't worry…."

"They didn't leave me anything!" she protested, stepping away from him.

"Yes they did, Tess. They left you a Quetzal butterfly, like the ones on these reliefs. Don't you recognize it? For the people that built Teotihuacán, as well as the ancestors that established the Mayan calendar, the butterfly symbolized the passage of time. The shift from one dimension to another. I just stopped being a larva before you did. But now both of us are like them…."

The young woman touched her handbag, feeling around for the little box she had taken from Jack's office. Jack looked at her, content.

"And the rest of the world, Jack? What's happening to them? Are they all butterflies now, too?"

"The rest of the world, too, Tess. Little by little they'll all begin to realize it."

Jack Bennewitz put his arms around her shoulders before saying anything else. His touch was real. Physical. Just as it had always been.

"You know something?" he said. "It's funny that your instinct brought you here to this place tonight, a night of such transformation."

"Funny? What's so funny about it?"

"Well, Tess. You should know that Teotihuacán means 'the place where men become gods.' And now that you and I have died, that's precisely what we have become. How does it feel to be a god, Tess?"

GARY BRAVER

Before settling in a teaching position at Northeastern University, Gary Braver worked as a soda jerk, newspaper reporter, tech writer, foundry laborer and project physicist, a job that taught him lab work wasn't for him. But teaching and writing were, and his double-duty as both a teacher and student of the art of writing gave him exceptional insight that he uses to great effect in "Ghost Writer."

Some thrillers tap into that part of our subconscious where the worst mistakes from our past linger, waiting for an opportunity to come back into the light. Gary's compelling portrayal of a disillusioned author asks a question that we all must answer eventually. Are we the authors of our own destiny, or is our fate already written? Turn the page to find out.

GHOST WRITER

"I don't ghostwrite stories. I write my own books."

Geoffrey Dane uttered those words and felt as if he were chewing gravel. He hadn't sold a story in five years.

"Professor Dane, please don't be offended," the young woman said. "But it's really a terrific idea and I think you're the best person to do it."

"I'm not offended." But he was. Offended and bitter. Bitter that he wasn't what she had assumed—a still actively published bestselling author. Offended because if she were the fan she claimed, she'd know he was a has-been. "I just don't write other people's material."

They were in the English department lounge where he had been sitting, sunk in a couch, reading student stories. Since he was part-time, he had no office of his own, rather a room he shared with other adjuncts and TAs—a space so cramped and noisy he did his paperwork in the lounge, a comfortable space usually empty. That was where this Lauren Grant had found him—this student with the scrubbed good looks, the pricey clothes and a gold Movado watch with diamond baguettes.

As she continued to plead with him, resentment rose up like acid. Here he was a forty-nine-year-old former *New York Times* list resident now teaching workshops for a pittance and entertaining some rich woman half his age offering to pay him to ghost her novel.

"I thought it might be something you could do between your own writing projects."

Yeah, rewrite after rewrite that your agent can't place with a fucking vanity press, whispered a voice in his head. Either this woman had no idea about him or the publishing business, or she was patronizing him. "I'm sorry, but I'm really not interested."

"But it's really a terrific idea," she insisted. "Really. And I think you'd agree. The details we could work out in your favor. But, basically, I provide the idea and you write the book."

"With whose name on it?"

"Mine. I know I can't pay you enough, but I'm hoping you'd accept a reasonable fee."

No, she couldn't pay him enough. He had spent the last four years struggling unsuccessfully to write himself back into print and was barely making ends meet. It didn't help that Maggie, his ex-wife, kept squeezing him for alimony. Maggie. The very thought of her made his stomach grind.

"Of course, we'd work out the contractual matters with your agent."

His agent! He hadn't talked to his agent in over a year, when she had told him that another house had passed on his previous manuscript.

"It's really a terrific idea."

That was the third time she made that claim, and he could see how eager she was to share it. "I'm sure, so why don't you write it yourself?"

"Because I don't have the talent. I can't even come up with a decent ending."

"Maybe you should take a workshop."

"I tried to enroll in yours this semester, but it was full. Same in the spring."

"I'm scheduled to offer it again next fall."

And the following spring and the fall after that, he thought. In fact, that was how he regarded the remainder of his pathetic life—one continuous workshop until the day despair finally stopped his heart. Or, better, a bullet from his Smith & Wesson.

"I could take a hundred workshops and it wouldn't be good."

"You won't know if you don't try."

"I have tried, believe me, but I don't have the gene. I read your works and I'm in awe of how you create characters with depth and dialogue that sounds like real people talking. And the narrative thrust that keeps the pages turning—"

Blah, blah, blah, he thought as she prattled on.

"Frankly, it's too good an idea to be wasted on me or some hack writer. You can create the tension and sense of dread that it needs."

Only because I have a paranoid personality, lady. Only because deep down I'm a frightened little man who writes thrillers to get bigger than the things that scare me.

"Really, you have what it takes."

No, I used to, he thought. *Geoffrey Dane—"Boy Genius" they called him on his first novel. "Brings class to the thriller genre." Now: Adult wannabe. Can't write shit.*

"Plus you always have great surprises at the end. That's what I love best. Those twists we never see coming. Really, you're a modern O. Henry."

He could feel himself begin to soften to the conviction that lit up her eyes. But her flattery only made his heart slump even more. Everything she said was true—but in the past. And the thought of being a ghost writer made him want to vomit. He also didn't care to hear her idea because if it was good, he'd wish it were his own. Furthermore, he had no interest in entering complicated contractual arrangements with a perfect stranger. Plus she couldn't pay him enough. He glanced at his watch. "Thanks for thinking of me, but I really have to go."

"Oh, I'm sorry you have a class. But will you think it over?"

"Think what over? You haven't said what the idea is."

"If I can get a commitment, I'll be happy to tell you."

He packed the student stories into his briefcase and got up to leave.

"So, we can talk again?"

She was wearing a black shearling coat that probably cost more than the book value of the eleven-year-old BMW he drove. "I'll think about it."

Her face looked like a lacquered apple. "That's great," she chortled. "Thank you. Thank you."

As they walked out of the lounge and into the hall, she handed him a card. On it, embossed in gold script, was her name, cell-phone number and e-mail address. No mailing address, probably to be on the safe side, given the rise in identity thefts and sexual stalkings.

"I really appreciate this." Her eyes were sparking with expectation. "Okay to call you next week?"

"Yeah." Then he looked back at her. "By the way, what kind of story is it?"

"A ghost story."

A ghost story! He didn't write ghost stories. And he didn't ghostwrite ghost stories. Especially for students. What a bloody insult!

The weekend passed, and he had spent it at his place— a small cape at the end of a cul-de-sac in Carleton, ten miles west of Boston. From dawn to bedtime he tapped away on his keyboard, producing little more than a page of uninspired narrative. He was four chapters into another novel— the last two sitting in mailers on the shelf, cover letters from editors inside apologizing that the book was not right for their lists. The story was outlined, but he did not like the direction it was taking. And he could think of no decent alternatives. He had hit an impasse. He could, of course, just quit—blame the blockage on the imp of discouragement and take the self-fulfilling-prophecy route: haven't written anything saleable in years, can't do it again.

He really didn't believe in writer's block. That was nothing more than a phony excuse, a handy cop-out for laziness as if it were a legitimate pathology like viral pneumonia or hepatitis. But, Jesus, he was blocked! Nothing decent was coming—no plot-advancing ideas, no narrative thrust, no belly fire. All that kept coming were bills from Visa, Verizon, Allied Fuel, Carleton Mortgage Co. and e-mails from Maggie to pay up.

It was December and the houses on the street were decorated for Christmas. And through the woods behind his place was a path around Spy Pond. He liked its frozen bleakness, so he broke up the keyboard hours with long walks to open his mind to any inspiration that might wing by. Yet he returned with nothing but a chill.

He spent the next several days teaching his classes and reading student stories. On Thursday he received a voice message at his work number. "Hi, Professor, this is Lauren Grant. It's been nearly a week. I'm just wondering if you've thought over my proposal."

Proposal. The word jumped out at him. Talk about paranoid, she was probably afraid he'd steal the idea, so she had refused to reveal the story line until he signed a contract. Even if he wanted to, it was ridiculous strategy since you couldn't copyright ideas, only their execution. Instead of getting back to her, he stopped by the office of his chairman, Lloyd Harrington. "You know a student by the name of Lauren Grant?"

"Lauren Grant? Yeah. She's a part-timer, auditing courses here and there. What about her?"

"She came to me the other day asking if I'd ghost a story for her."

"Oh, yeah. She's been shopping that around for weeks, asking anyone in Greater Boston who's ever published a thriller to take her on."

Geoff felt his stomach leak acid. *The little bitch*. She had come on to him as if he were the one author in creation born to pen her tale.

"When she came in, I suggested you. I hope you don't mind."

"No, that's fine." But he did mind.

"Did she say what the idea was?"

"Not really. Something about a ghost."

"Whoopie," Lloyd said. "If it's something you're interest in pursuing, that's your business not the university's."

"Okay, thanks." Geoff started out the door.

"In case you're interested," Lloyd added, "I think she comes from money."

For the rest of the day, that phrase echoed and reechoed in Geoff's brain. That evening, while sitting at his desk at home, he sent her a brief e-mail to say he was interested and wanted to hear more. The curtness implied that out of politeness he'd suffer her another meeting before outright rejection. He suggested they meet in the student center, wondering just how much money she came from.

The food hall was a large open space filled with tables and chairs and flanked with several fast-food takeouts. Because it was midmorning, the place was half-empty. He bought them each a coffee, and they took a table in a quiet corner. "Okay, but before we get to the story, I think we should discuss the ugly stuff."

"Ugly stuff?"

"Writer's fee."

That caught her off guard. "Sure, of course." Then from her briefcase, she pulled out a manila envelope. "If you don't mind, I contacted a literary agent and had a contract drawn up."

"You're way ahead of the game."

"Because I want everything to be aboveboard."

"Then let's be straight—you've been to other writers with this, right?" He didn't want to betray Lloyd's confidence. "I mean, there are dozens of published thriller and horror writers in Greater Boston."

She studied his expression for a moment, and her eye did an involuntary twitch as she rummaged for a response. "I considered others, but decided that the quality and style of your writing best fits my story idea."

Bullshit! he thought. *She's saying that none of the others were interested, and she bottomed-out with you.* "Okay."

"If you agree, you will be paid a flat fee—twenty percent up front, the balance upon acceptance."

"Acceptance by whom?"

"By me."

"So, there's no stipulation that it has to be placed with a publisher first."

"No, just to write an acceptable synopsis and then an acceptable book."

"A synopsis?"

"Yes, I know from other students and your own Web site that you're big on writing a synopsis—that you don't start a novel until you've got a 'slam dunk' summary as you say. This way I'll see how everything fits into place and how it ends. When that's done to my liking, you'll be paid the advance."

He let that sink in, humiliating as it was.

"Okay, and if I write the book and it sells, what about royalties?"

"Well, actually, no royalties, just the flat fee, which I hope you'll accept."

"But your name on the book."

"Yes, and the copyright under my name."

He could hear the advice of her agent cutting through her nervousness. "And what if you don't like it?"

"I will because I will be reading it as you go along."

Jesus! This was like his workshops in reverse: he writes installments and submits them to a student for approval. "And what if you like it and your agent can't place it?"

She smiled self-consciously. "First, that won't happen since you're too talented for the book not to sell. Second, selling it is his problem. You will still be paid, no matter what."

He wondered about her agent. "You'd be putting a lot of trust in me."

"That's right." She nodded and smiled warmly.

He wished she'd stop that. The Geoffrey Dane she kept fawning over was all but dead. "How long a synopsis?"

"Ten pages."

What he suggested as maximum on his Web site. "And what exactly do you have in mind for a total fee?"

"One hundred thousand dollars."

Jesus! Where do I sign? he thought, trying to contain his astonishment. "That's a lot of money." The advance alone could get him out of hock with his creditors and Maggie for months. Ten pages! He couldn't write a decent novel anymore, but if her story line was viable, he could crank out a synopsis in a week.

"My grandparents were generous when I graduated from college." From the envelope she removed a multipage contract with his name on it and the breakdown of payment. There was a lot of legal jargon, but the important details were there: an advance of twenty thousand dollars, payable upon the completion of an acceptable synopsis. The balance to be paid upon acceptance by her of a completed manuscript.

His heart was pounding so hard he was sure it showed— like the throat of a bullfrog.

"Seem fair enough?"

The light in her eyes said that she was enjoying this, probably because she knew how destitute he was. It also crossed his mind that it might be interesting working with her. She was good-looking and clearly passionate. In a flash he saw her naked and in bed with him between chapters.

"Okay, so what's the story line?" He took a sip of his coffee and settled back.

"It's quite simple," she began. "It's the story of a vengeful ghost returned to kill her fiancé, who abandoned her." She paused for a moment as if to gauge his reaction.

It sounded corny, but he nodded her on. "Okay."

"What I'm imagining is a beautiful seventeen-year-old girl who's been dating this older boy for months. She's crazy about him and they talk of getting married someday. Then a few months before he's to go to college, she discovers she's pregnant. As the due date approaches, the boy abandons her—goes off to school hundreds of miles away and drops out of her life for good."

Again she glared at him with a strange expectancy. And a stir of discomfort registered in his gut. "Then what?"

"Well, she's very upset that he left her flat and wasn't there for the birth, not even moral support. Her parents are disgusted with her, but forbid her to have an abortion. Of course, her own plans for college are dashed.

"So she has the child. But a few days later, she dies from complications of childbirth. The daughter is raised by her grandparents. Meanwhile, the boy finishes college, never making contact with the girl's family, never learning what happened to the girl or his child. We jump ahead twenty-something years—the boy's a man, successful in his profession and happy with his life."

"And?"

"And the ghost of his dead girlfriend suddenly appears to take vengeance on him—a revenant."

"A what?"

"Revenant. A vengeful ghost."

His mouth was dry, and he swallowed some coffee.

"So what do you think?"

"Interesting, but execution is everything."

"Yes, it is."

"What will he be doing in the present? Is he married? Does he have a family? How does he spend his days? I've got to know what to have him do from chapter to chapter."

She nodded. "He's divorced with no kids," she said. Then like a half-glimpsed premonition she said, "He's a writer."

"A writer," he repeated, as if taking an oath.

"Yes, I like the irony of him being the supposed artistic sensitive type. Yet he's bad—if you pardon my French, a son of a bitch."

Geoff simply nodded.

"I've got some of their back stories in notes, which I can share with you—stuff that you can use to flesh things out. But it's the ending that I can't come up with. How the ghost shows up and gets back at him. That's where I'm stuck. And I want the best possible retribution."

"Uh-huh." He drained his cup and a prickly silence filled the moment.

"But I'm sure you can come up with the perfect justice."

"I take it you believe in ghosts."

"No, but I'm afraid of them." She smiled at the old joke. "What about you?"

"Nope."

"Well, I know you're supposed to write from what you know, but I'm sure your fertile imagination can flesh this out. So, what do you think?"

"Well, it's not really my kind of story. I write thrillers, not horror tales."

"But I've read your novels, and I think it *is* your kind of story. Just that the antagonist is a ghost, not the standard villain."

Maybe that was his problem: all his villains were standard.

He nodded and glanced around the food hall. Students were scattered at different tables, some of them reading, some working at their laptops. He didn't mind them, but he was tired of teaching kids how to write. Most had never written fiction before. And most made their first forays with dumb horror tales, hoping to be the next Stephen King. And most had zero talent. Like this woman. But she had money. Enough to buy his way out of here for a couple of years. And he was certain that if he didn't sign, she'd find someone else who would.

"I also think you'd enjoy working on it." She nudged the contract toward him.

Doubtful, he thought. And for a long moment he stared at it. Then he picked up the pen and signed.

And a small rat uncurled in his gut.

By six that evening, he was back home, thinking that this might turn out to be the toughest twenty thousand dollars he'd ever make. No, it wasn't the fact that he didn't write ghost stories. Nor was her story line too much of a challenge. As he sipped his second Scotch, he told himself: *Coincidence. Dumb, blind coincidence.*

Twenty-four years ago, while doing grad work in L.A., he had gotten a young undergraduate pregnant. They had dated less than a year while he finished his M.F.A. They had talked about marriage, but when a teaching post presented itself, he broke off the relationship and moved back to the East Coast. He gave Jessica some money to get an abortion, but she had refused. He left no forwarding address and never heard from her again, uncertain what had happened to her or her baby. Yes, he felt guilty. But he was also young, selfish and scared. And he couldn't turn down the job because it paid well and would allow him the time to write his first novel, which became an instant bestseller.

As he lay in bed staring into the black, it all came back to him. But did he really want to be shacked up for the next ten or twelve months slogging through that old muck?

But one hundred thousand dollars?

Two hours later he was still rolling around his mattress.

Maybe it was his inherent paranoia crossed with his writer's imagination, but suddenly he wondered if this Lauren Grant was really an innocent little rich kid who just wanted her name on a book.

He got out of bed and went to his laptop where he Googled *Lauren J. Grant*. A common enough name, but not a single hit came up. He tried other search engines and databases, and nothing. She had no Web site. No entry in Facebook, MySpace or any blog site. She had never registered a book or movie review anywhere under her name. Nothing. In the vast digital universe where most people had left evidence of their existence, she did not exist. It was as if she were a ghost.

The next day, feeling like roadkill from the lack of sleep, he went to the registrar's office and got a clerk to give him copies of Lauren J. Grant's application. While grades were confidential, their application forms were not. She was from Philadelphia. Her parents were Susan and John Grant—she was a real estate agent, he the owner of a trucking firm. Lauren was an only child. She had graduated from Prescott High School. All looked legitimate.

But that evening, back home at his laptop, anxiety was setting bats loose in his chest. The more he tried to work on the synopsis, the more distracted he became. What if she were some kind of writer stalker—a delusional nutcake, like the assistant who murdered that singer, Selena?

Or worse, the crazed groupie who shot John Lennon dead after getting his autograph?

Or worse still, his own Annie Wilkes, like in that story *Misery*?

It's your ol' fertile imagination getting the best of you, he told himself. Nonetheless, he went back online and found a Web site for Prescott High School. But probably because of the fear of pedophiles, students were not identified by name. However, using different search engines he located a site for the publisher of the school's yearbooks and ordered one for the year she had graduated. He then checked the online Yellow Pages and, with relief, he found an address for her parents that matched what she had written on the application. *Your imagination was always much richer than your real life,* he told himself and went to bed.

Over the next several days he threw himself into the synopsis. By the end of the next week, he had the story line filled out and an ending that satisfied him. So, he e-mailed Lauren a copy, humming for that twenty-grand advance.

Within the hour she called him. "Geoffrey, it's good but the ending is not there yet. You're letting him off too easily."

He didn't mind the presumptuous use of his first name as much as her sudden authority: this little twit wasn't satisfied with his synopsis. He resented that almost as much as he resented his need for her money. "Twentysomething years have passed," he said. "Do ghosts hold grudges that long?"

"In this story they do."

"Well, frankly, I think the ghost bit is silly. I told you I don't write ghost stories. I don't even read them. And I don't believe in them. They're cheesy gimmicks."

There was a long, uncomfortable silence filled only with the hush of the open phone line. "So what do you recommend?" she finally said.

"That it's the grown daughter who seeks him out."

"And then what?"

"There are some tense moments, but in the end they reconcile. He realizes how callous and irresponsible he had been, but he's a grown man now and has reformed and wants to bond with his long-lost daughter." He knew how trite that sounded, but it was the best he was willing to offer.

But she didn't approve. "I like the idea of the grown daughter replacing the ghost as an agent of justice," she said. "But it's got to be intense. I want his guilt and fear to be palpable. And I don't want forgiveness."

Suddenly she was all business and holding hostage his twenty thousand for an ending that was making him uncomfortable.

"And it has to be a surprise," she continued. "A surprise ending and a Grand Guignol."

"I'll see what I come up with."

"Okay," she said. "But I want blood."

The rat stirred in his gut again. "But why such harsh justice?"

"Because blood debts must be paid."

And the rat took a nip.

For another six days he worked on the synopsis, grabbing a few writing hours between classes. But that Friday classes were cancelled because of a freak snowstorm, producing lightning and thunder. Global warming, the radio said. So he took advantage of the day off and wrote without interruption. By early evening he had exhausted himself and downed a few glasses of Scotch to relax. He thought about going to bed early and getting up around four the next morning to continue working.

That's when the FedEx delivery man came by with a package. It was the Prescott High School yearbook. He tore through the portrait pages. Yes, there was a Lauren Grant, with a few school clubs and activities listed. But no portrait photo. Nor was she in group shots. Maybe she was sick and missed the photo sessions.

At the moment, he really didn't care. His head was soupy from exhaustion and alcohol, so he went to bed, satisfied that he had an ending that made sense—one that should satisfy her. She wanted the guy's death, so he gave him a weak heart. In the middle of the night he thinks he sees a ghost and dies of fright. Contrived, yes. And if she didn't like it, *fuck it!* It was the best he could come up with. So he e-mailed it to her and went to bed, thinking, *I don't have blood on my hands. Jessica could be alive and well today. I just didn't want to deal with her or the baby. I was just a kid. No way I should pay for that. Nor for cheating on Maggie.*

To rout the rabble in his head, he downed two sleeping pills and slipped into a dreamless oblivion.

It was a little after midnight when his phone rang. Through the furriness of his brain he heard the answering machine go on in the other room and a muffled female voice leave a message he couldn't make out. After several minutes of lying in the dark, he got up, went to the next room and hit the play button.

"Hi, Geoff, it's Lauren. I received your new ending and, frankly, it doesn't work. I'm really sorry, but it's still too weak. However, I think I've got the ending we've been looking for. Sorry about the hour, but I'm leaving first thing in the morning for the holidays and I want to share it with you in person. So, I'll be right over."

She clicked off, and when he tried to retrieve her number to call back, the message read Unavailable. She had called from an unlisted number. *Jesus!* It was past midnight. And why the hell didn't she just e-mail it?

Suddenly his mind was a fugue. What if she wasn't coming over simply to share her idea?

But another voice cut in: Get a grip, man. *You're letting your booze-and-Xanax-primed imagination get the best of you. That and the freak storm.*

But what if she was an imposter who knew about Jessica and was out to get him? *The best possible retribution.*

But to what end? Surely not blackmail. She was loaded, and he was broke.

Write about what you know.

Make the guilt and fear palpable.

Her words shot through his brain like an electric arc. She was his metaphorical revenant. And his penance was having to flesh out his own guilt. His own revenge. She didn't like it, and she was coming with the perfect payback.

No way! Impossible.

So is this freak thunder-and-lightning snowstorm.

No!

Maybe this was all Maggie's doing. In a drunken moment years ago he had told her about Jessica. What if all three of them were in collusion and they concocted this scheme, re-cruiting this Lauren Grant or whatever her name was—a hit woman to get back for Jessie, for his cheating on Maggie, for all his indiscretions against women?

Even more far-fetched, he told himself. Maggie was happily involved with another guy and didn't give a shit about him anymore. And Jessica could be dead for all he knew.

Outside the landscape lit up as if by strobe lights, and a moment later boulders rumbled across the sky. He stared through the window as lightning turn the stripped black trees behind the house into an X-rayed forest. As he watched and waited for the thunder, another thought cut across him mind like a shark fin. One that made all the sense in the world.

Because he was bad. Because he was selfish.

Because blood debts must be paid.

Suddenly he felt his gorge rise and he shot to the toilet where he flopped to his knees and threw up the contents of his stomach. As he hung over the bowl, gagging, the bathroom light began to flicker. The power lines. Every time Carleton experienced a heavy snow, sections of the town got hit with a brownout.

He wiped his mouth and flushed the toilet when he heard the doorbell ring. *Jesus!* He shot back into the bedroom. He was tearing through his bureau drawers, underwear and pullovers spilling to the floor, when he heard something from downstairs.

"Geoffrey."

She was inside. Had he forgotten to lock the door after the FedEx man left?

"Geoffrey, I'm here."

He did not respond.

"Geoffrey?"

Suddenly the lights flickered again. Then they blinked out. Black. The place was dead black. Not a stray photon in the room. Not even any light seepage from the outside. The whole neighborhood was out.

"Geoffrey, please come down."

He heard himself whimper, frozen in black, completely disoriented in his own bedroom, unable to move.

"I know you're there."

The next moment, the lights flickered back on.

"Come down and see what I've got."

He didn't answer. His brain still felt stunned.

"Geoffrey."

The lights were back on, and he took several deep breaths to compose himself.

"Shall I come up?"

"No."

"In the living room."

After a few moments, he felt centered again and crept his way out of the bedroom and down, the creaking of the stairs sounding like bones snapping. The only other sound was that of the furnace kicking on. At the bottom, the foyer overhead burned. The living room was still dark because the lamps had not been turned on. He inched his way to the entrance and braced himself against the frame.

She was in there, standing by the dead fireplace. Her long black shearling defining her form in negative. "Surprise."

His forehead was an aspic of fear. "I know what you want," he whispered.

"What?"

"I know what you're planning."

"You do?"

"Yes."

Her voice was barely audible. Over her shoulder hung her case. He could not see her hands. But in the foyer light he could see the white oval of her face. A weird grin distorted her features.

Satisfaction. Fulfillment. Retribution.

"I didn't think you'd guess." She removed the shoulder bag and began to open it.

"I know who you are," he said. His fingers were nearly bloodless with cold. "I know."

"Of course, but you can't imagine—"

But she never finished her sentence. Without thought, he pulled the gun from his back pocket and shot her three times. She collapsed to the floor without a sound.

He snapped on the lamp. The bullets had hit her face, reducing it to a bloodied mess.

He pulled the shoulder bag from under her and tore it open.

Inside was his copy of the fully executed contract and clipped to it a bank check for $20,000. Also hard-bound copies of his books that she had wanted him to autograph for her and her parents for Christmas next week. And a sheet with her ending: *He takes his own life.*

His neighbors must have heard gunshots, because sometime later he heard sirens wailing their approach.

As he sat there, looking down at the blasted red pulp of her face, he thought, *Well, we got our bloody surprise ending.*

Then he shot himself in the head.

KATHLEEN ANTRIM

With her speculative thriller *Capital Offense,* Kathleen Antrim leveraged an intimate knowledge of today's political landscape to send tremors through the Washington beltway and her readers. Unafraid of ruffling feathers attached to some very powerful government arms, Kathleen's work as an award-winning journalist gave her a firsthand look at the mechanisms of official power, and insight into where they might steer our future.

A dystopian tomorrow is under investigation in "Through a Veil Darkly," a timely story that taps into our secret fears and hidden biases. Kathleen shows us how a tense political climate can evolve into an environment where even murder can be justified and patriotic.

THROUGH A VEIL DARKLY

It's time to kill my husband. Izaan Bekkar. The forty-eighth president of the United States.

I suppose assassination is the correct term. No matter. It's my responsibility. Once done, I'll be a hero. Go figure. Only in America, where killing for religious reasons is deemed sacrilegious. Hypocrites, every damn one of them.

I'm alone now, sitting in my room. Outside, trees bare as brooms claw at my window, just as Izaan's deception scrapes at my raw conscience. A winter wind rattles the thick pane of glass. My only comfort comes from thoughts of retribution and the monotonous *drip…drip…drip* of a leaky faucet. I've listened to that torturous sound ever since Izaan locked me up. It's all I have for entertainment. I've noticed that its pitch is different at night—more baritone—than in the afternoon, when the water sings like a soprano.

Interesting what we notice when alone.

A digital clock reads 4:49 a.m.

Eleven minutes before the morning call to prayer. Five hours and eleven minutes before my meeting with Dr. Truman North. Fourteen hours and eleven minutes until lights out and another sleepless night.

There are people, like the self-righteous Dr. North, who want me to accept their version of my predicament. But I silently refuse, and play along. I'll do anything to guarantee my release from this hell.

The key is the burqa.

My life didn't start in a burqa.

But it may end in one.

I stood backstage, listening, wearing a navy St. John suit that Izaan bought for me.

"America is on the brink of destruction," Izaan boomed to a packed auditorium.

Network and cable news cameras focused on his keen blue eyes and crisp, angular features. "Global warming. Oil dependence. Nuclear war. America needs leadership she can believe in."

Izaan ran his life and his campaign on high-octane fear. Constituents guzzled his message. When he swerved for emphasis, they leaned into his turn. He'd brake for effect, and they'd relax. He'd race his cadence, their hearts seemed to pound.

"That's why, at your insistence, I'm announcing my candidacy for president of the United States."

The crowd roared their approval.

He beamed, pausing for effect, his ego swelling from their admiration. Like a snake charmer he wooed them, just as he'd wooed me years before.

After a few moments, the crowd calmed.

"It gives me great pleasure to introduce you to the love of my life. My wife. My partner. Sylvia Bekkar."

I dutifully walked onto the stage and gripped his hand. Strobes flashed. He raised our clasped fingers high in the air. My heart soared at his touch. Gentle and loving. Together we left the stage and greeted constituents at the rope line. Afterward, as I tumbled over the edge of false impressions into a cold reality, staffers swept me out of the way.

"You ooze charisma," the campaign manager told Izaan, patting him on the back.

I watched as Izaan pushed past him and headed for the campaign bus. And so it went, stop after stop, month after month. Izaan's poll numbers rose. My spirits fell. Slowly, Izaan's mask of confident composure shattered under the pressure. Nervous glances over his shoulder escalated once we were issued Secret Service.

"Get them away from me," he ordered, pointing at the agents posted outside the campaign bus. "I don't need government spies watching my every move."

"They're here for your protection," an advisor said.

Izaan leveled him with a glare. "I know their claims. I also know the truth."

The campaign manager pulled Izaan inside the bus. "Are you all right?"

Izaan held up a document. "You hand me sacrilege like this and call it a speech?" He tore it in two. "Then you ask if I'm all right? Leave, before I fire you."

Drunk on the prospect of riding their horse into the White House, the staff attributed Izaan's outbursts to exhaustion.

"I don't care what the hell you need to do, just get him through the election," I overheard the campaign manager say to a deputy. "We'll deal with him after November."

Fools.

A day later, we were back home for a night. I entered Izaan's bedroom to check on him, determined to show him that I cared, that I wanted to be a part of his life. Our life.

He emerged from his bathroom wearing only a towel. "What are you doing in here? Snooping around?"

"I—"

He grabbed a handful of my red hair. "Filthy American whore. Tempting me. Is this what you want?" He dropped his towel, revealing his naked muscular frame. "Is it?"

I said nothing.

He yanked my head back, his face inches from mine. "You want to know my secrets."

I fought against crying. "You're hurting me."

"What are you?" he asked in a voice as soft as a caress.

"Please. I love—"

He jerked my hair again.

I grabbed his arm. "I'm a—"

"Say it."

"Filthy whore." I spit the words at him. "I'm a filthy whore."

"This is what happens to whores."

He shoved me facedown on the bed. I scrambled for safety. He caught my foot, knocked me to the floor, then wrenched my nightgown up over my head, tangling my face and arms in the silk, pinning me down.

A knock on the door. "You all right, sir?"

Secret Service.

Izaan slammed his palm over my mouth.

I writhed for air.

"Leave me be," Izaan yelled.

Footsteps retreated.

He held me down, thrusting his hatred into me. For days afterward, my body ached and his words replayed in my mind like a stale song. I'd seen his anger before. Felt its wrath. But this was different, raw and exposed.

Drip…drip…drip.

I plotted to leave him. Later. After the campaign. He was under so much pressure. He didn't mean it. He loved me. Needed me. I couldn't leave. A continuous loop of rationalization circled around my mind coming back to the same awful conclusion. He was the force that held my world together, and without him, I'd spin out of control.

"'You may hate a thing although it is good for you, and love a thing although it is bad for you,'" Izaan would say.

I didn't know from where the quote originated, but it nagged at me, made me wonder.

November loomed.

★ ★ ★

Izaan won.

Nonstop news coverage of the most recent beheading in the Middle East wound my anxiety into a tangled knot. Forty-eight hours after the election, Izaan's staff showed up at our home. Izaan jerked me to my feet, his fingers digging into my arm. He turned me to face men I'd never seen before and insisted that I look them in the eye.

"'Men have status above women.'" Another of those quotes. "'Good women are obedient.'"

"What are you talking about?"

With forefinger and thumb, he wrenched my chin around to face his all-male staff. I dropped my gaze. He smiled. Then he ordered them to scour our home, to cleanse it of the world of the infidel. Nothing unclean would follow us to 1600 Pennsylvania Avenue.

Infidel? I'd never heard him utter this word before.

He smacked the side of my head. I reeled. Humiliation stained my cheeks. His men ripped the designer wardrobe from my closet. I suddenly realized that they were the costumes of a disposable prop: me. I fought Izaan as he dragged me to the cellar.

"You've learned so little."

He shoved me next to the old incinerator. Radiating heat singed the hair on my arm and snapped at my skin. They fed my wardrobe into the flames, reducing the clothing he'd taught me to wear to ashes. They incinerated the lifestyle he'd insisted I master in order to project the flawless image of a model American couple: the next president and first lady of the United States of America.

Photographs of our smiling faces at our wedding, political events and holidays were burned, along with books, bibles, magazines and artwork. Only pictures of Izaan—without my presence, or that of any other woman—were kept. Beyond tears, I stood speechless. I'd kept his secret. Helped him build a secular image that America would swallow.

"Do you see how it is now?" he asked. "Do you see what we worked so hard to achieve? Now this country will be led to Allah."

Then I knew.

The Quran.

His quotes were paraphrased from the Quran.

I met his gaze.

He would pay.

Only one bag accompanied me to Washington and the Hay Adams Hotel. Demoralized, I donned Izaan's latest demand—a burqa. The top of the burqa was shaped like a pillbox hat. From there, black fabric fell in a deliberately formless shape to the floor. The only other detail was the mesh veil that hid my face and eyes. Tears slashed mascara across my cheeks.

The burqa gripped me in a bone-crushing depression. It devoured my peripheral vision and my self-respect. The veil distorted my perception. Through it, even the brightly upholstered chairs and ornately carved bed of the hotel appeared worn and worthless.

Reality, terrifying and ugly as a cobra about to strike, snapped into focus. Thoughts flew at me from a thousand broken places. I wanted to scream. If I started, I wouldn't stop. I needed to think.

To act.

A high-pitched ringing grew in my ears, and buzzed through my brain like a menacing swarm of bees. I walked into my bathroom and retrieved the prescription Izaan demanded I take.

I stared at the bottle.

Until now, he controlled me, inside and out. His precious pills were supposed to help with the ringing, my depression and everything else. They didn't. When I took them, I felt submerged beneath the world, slogging upstream against a relentless current. Detached and passive.

I studied the label. What was really in the bottle?

I unscrewed the top and dumped the entire contents into the toilet.

Izaan would be furious.

I was delighted.

Water swirled around the bowl, sucking the venomous capsules into the vortex, siphoning them down the drain, just as I'd been sucked into the dizzying eddy of Izaan's deception.

Secret Service Agent Frank Harrigan knocked on my door. "It's time."

I fought to find a smile, but instead I found hate and clung to it.

I greeted Frank.

The burqa so impaired my vision that I caught my hip on the door handle as I exited my room.

Frank ignored my clumsiness.

I massaged the pain.

He escorted me through the halls to my husband's temporary headquarters at the Hay Adams, across from the White House. It was a suite, of course, for U.S. President-Elect Izaan Bekkar. Heat *built up beneath the burqa. My head itched. Perspiration clung to the back of my neck. Anxiety raced in my chest, seemingly appropriate for a warrior going into battle. A bead of sweat trickled over my temple.*

Frank ushered me into Izaan's temporary office. Arms crossed over his chest, Frank took up his post in the back of the room. I sat on the couch across from Izaan, who aimed that smile at me, the one that blinded everyone to the truth. Everyone that is, except me.

"You look nice in your burqa."

"Islamo-fascist bastard."

He shook his head in tight, controlled movements.

"They'll impeach you." I kept my words short. Chatter and questions agitated Izaan, provoked his paranoia.

"Impeach?" His gaze narrowed, hard and dark. He leaned toward me and glared with laserlike intensity. "The first amendment protects religious freedom."

"But it won't protect you from the people when they learn their president is a radical Islamist."

"You've got to let go of this, Sylvia. It will destroy you."

A small victory. He was angry.

"Do you understand me?"

I smiled.

He sucked a deep breath. "How are you?"

Interesting. A change of strategy. Act like you care. Try to keep the wife happy.

"It's important that you work with me, Sylvia."

A bitter laugh rose in my throat. I swallowed it and kept quiet.

"We're so close." He spoke softly, but I could hear the threat that weighted his words. "Do you understand how important this is?"

I kept silent.

After my appointment with Izaan, Frank took me back to my room.

I wrenched the burqa over my head and threw it into the corner. I stood naked before the mirror, my boney ribs angled to a concave stomach. A purplish knot bloomed on my hip like a shriveled rose. I leaned into the mirror. Dirty green eyes stared back at me. My cheeks were free of bruise or blemish. A disfigured face would have defeated Izaan Bekkar's political agenda. The face wasn't to be touched. But that rule was about to end. The veil of a burqa would see to that.

"You must do exactly as I say." Izaan's orders and instructions permeated my mind.

Drip…drip…drip.

Fanaticism indeed had a face. President-Elect Izaan Bekkar. America would be brought to Allah, or die on her knees. Could I face the destruction I'd enabled? Turning from the mirror, I opened my suitcase. How could I have spent years married to this man without even knowing him? The answer was easy. I didn't want to know the truth.

I worked a finger into the edge of the suitcase lining. The seam gave way, revealing the long-bladed knife that I'd sewn into the gap behind the fabric. I peered out through the window into the dusky darkness and the flickering lights of the White House. I laid the blade against my wrist. How easy it would be to run a hot bath, settle into the soothing water, and slice my skin. How long would it take before I fell into an unending sleep? A gentle press and beads of blood popped up along the edge of the knife.

Drip…drip…drip.

The handle, mahogany inlaid with mother of pearl, felt smooth and reassuring in my grasp.

Not a chance.

I tossed it back onto the bed.

The bloodstained blade left a swath of pink on the comforter.

There was another way. Something Izaan would never expect from me.

Courage.

Inauguration day arrived with a flurry of snow and vibrant activity. I needed to move quickly. Not an easy task on icy ground clad in a burqa.

We walked out to the waiting motorcade and were ushered into limousines. Unable to see my feet and the floor of the car, I stumbled.

My knee clipped the door.

Another bruise.

Izaan and I were seated in separate vehicles. Snow coated my burqa and melted into the fabric. Wet material clung to my body like a cold, soggy blanket. Images swirled before me, pulsing forward, retracting. The saturated cotton clung to my face, threatening to suffocate me. I fought the urge to gasp for air. I wanted to rip the fabric off my skin.

The knife.

Focus on the knife.

Under the folds of cloth, I stroked it with my fingertips. It anchored me. Steadied my breathing.

But could I do it?

We circled the Capitol and entered the building through a private hallway behind the podium. Marble pillars towered over us, sleek and smooth. People scurried everywhere. I'd learned that no matter the amount of money spent on coordination, planning and security, the Secret Service could never manage to completely control grand events, such as a presidential inauguration. The sheer number of bodies made that impossible.

If they only knew where the real threat lay.

I suppressed the urge to laugh at the irony.

An agent guarded me. The Secret Service thought they directed all my movements. Izaan thought he controlled me. As first lady, the agents acted as my protectors, my lifeline. But soon they'd have to kill me.

Through the veil of the chadri, I stared out at the crowd that scurried like ants in and around the seats. My gaze landed on a man wearing a dingy down parka.

"Now arriving…" an amplified voice boomed. "Take your seats…."

Down Parka stood next to a denim-clad teenager, who bent over to tie his shoe. A woman hurried past in a faux leopard-print coat and snow boots.

Why were they so poorly dressed?

I shivered.

A cluster of pain mounted behind my eyes. I stood in the wings, waiting for my cue. Savage fluorescent lights hung low over our heads. *I squinted against the glare. Pain as sharp as the tip of an ice pick scraped behind my eyes. Nausea clamped down on my stomach. I rubbed my temples through the fabric of my headdress.*

Too late to take a pill. The pills are gone, remember?

Music played. It didn't sound right. *Pain distorted everything. The bass thrummed in my head like a boom box. Where were the Secret Service agents? Why didn't they stop that racket?*

Nonsensical chatter filled my mind as I told myself to follow Izaan.

We walked onto the stage.

A collective gasp whooshed around me as the burqa caused a stir. People dashed around us, taking their positions.

"This way, doctor," someone said.

So much scurrying. So much rush, rush.

I expected to know everyone on the stage, but strangers filled the seats around us. Dignitaries. Izaan's friends. Supporters. My gaze snagged on a police officer trailing a German shepherd. The dog's nose led their progress through the crowd. Gazes darted in my direction. I tucked myself in close to Izaan.

He shot me a hard glance.

A vice of pain pinched my eyes. I closed them to fight the building misery. When I opened them, Chief Justice Deborah Steman stood to my left. The fine fabric of her black robe glimmered in the bright light. A large gold cross dangled at her throat. She looked like a nun.

Izaan nodded. I knew my role. His instructions were explicit. I took the Quran from Izaan's grasp, and handed it to the chief justice.

Another gasp sucked through the crowd.

The chief justice's eyebrows arched over her wide eyes. Her lips parted with a quick intake of breath. I bit the side of my mouth to quell my nervous energy. Trembling knees threatened to buckle.

Why did the chief justice's robes resemble a nun's habit?

Where was Frank? And the other agents? With my limited vision, I couldn't locate them.

I fingered the knife hidden in the folds of my dress. The enemy burqa suddenly became my confidant, hiding my secret. What was the double-talk they loved to spout in political circles? Ah, yes, the enemy of my enemy is my friend.

Izaan glared at Chief Justice Steman, then surveyed the crowd who'd come to celebrate. They'd voted for him but were now puzzled into silence.

The shadow of a new beard dusted his cheeks and chin. The audience's confusion morphed into outrage. Distorted, angry faces stared at us. Shouts echoed around me. I knew what I needed to do.

My gaze followed the justice's questioning glance as it darted over the faces of the other dignitaries. Many looked as stunned as the crowd. Others looked pleased. I focused on the knife, which sobered me.

"Raise your right hand," the chief justice said.

Izaan obeyed.

He'd raised that hand to me countless times. Every time he did so, my body absorbed another punishing blow. Now the country would take his beating. Unless—

He reverently rested his left hand on the Quran, presenting me a perfect target.

"Repeat after me," the chief justice said.

I flashed back to the countless times he'd repeated his message to woo the American people and me. The hypnotic song of the snake charmer.

"I do solemnly swear," the chief justice said.

I moved in a bit closer to Izaan as he repeated the words.

"That I will faithfully execute—"

Pain arched through my skull from the depths behind my eyes to the base of my neck. My legs quivered. Nausea rolled over me.

"—the office of president of the United States—"

The crowd pressed in.

Were they straining to hear Izaan's every word? Were they threatening the ceremony? Did they sense my intent?

I couldn't tell.

"—and will to the best of my ability—"

"—preserve—"

"—protect—"

"—and defend—"

"—the Constitution of the United States of America."

I withdrew the knife from the folds of the burqa. A slice of midday light glinted off the blade. I thrust it between Izaan's ribs, aiming deep, twisting hard. He arched toward me, mouth gaping. His fingers reached for the knife protruding from his side. Blood oozed into the fabric of his dark suit.

I braced myself for the impact of the Secret Service agents' bullets.

A woman screamed.

The body twisted. Knees buckled.

He crumpled to the floor.

A shoulder plowed into me. My chin cracked against the cold marble floor.

"Don't hurt her," a man gasped. "She's my patient."

Air whooshed from my lungs. Searing pain soared through my head. Shrill wails descended upon me. My hands were yanked behind my back and handcuffs snapped over my wrists.

The screaming continued.

"Got a stabbing at Union Station," I heard a man say. "Need an ambulance."

A radio squawked. "Man down in the main terminal. Ground level. I repeat. Man down."

"She's wearing a burlap sack over her head."

The uniformed officer removed the burqa from my head and shoulders.

I stared at the burlap sack in his hand. Bold print declared, Pioneer Brand, Idaho Potatoes, 100 lbs. "That's not a burqa," I said as confusion engulfed me.

I glanced around. Trains? Union Station?

A second cop walked over. "The victim was talking to that nun over there. Looks like this woman," he said, pointing at me, "knocked the nun down, then stabbed the guy."

"What's your name?" I was asked.

The first cop lifted me to my feet. "Do you know your name?"

I said nothing.

"Sylvia?" I heard a voice call out.

Frank shuffled toward us.

"She lives across the street with me at the homeless shelter." Frank tugged at his unwashed beard. A tattered herringbone overcoat snugged tight around his rotund middle. "She just got out of the nuthouse."

"Liar." I spun toward him. "Why are you saying that?"

Frank continued, "We were in the shelter, watching the inauguration on television. President Bekkar was taking the oath. Then Sylvia ran out."

"According to the victim's ID, he's Dr. Truman North," one of the cops said. "Psychiatrist."

My mind reeled. No, no, no—not Dr. North. President Bekkar. Couldn't they see?

"He's her doctor," Frank said. "I told him she stopped taking her medicine."

"North refuses to go to the hospital," the other policeman said, "without talking to his patient first."

I squinted at the officer. "Dr. North's here?"

He nodded and walked me over to a gurney. I stared down into North's blue eyes and said, "I'm a hero. I killed the Islamo-fascist president."

"No, Sylvia." North paused to catch his breath. "You didn't kill the president." Racking coughs overcame him. "You stabbed me."

"No, I—"

"We've got to go," a paramedic said.

"You stabbed *me*," North said again. His eyes rolled back in his head as his jaw went slack.

"No." I shook my head. "I would never do that. I—"

Paramedics rushed North's gurney toward the ambulance. Blood seeped through the blanket that covered him.

My God, what did I do?

Drip…drip…drip.

It's almost four years later now. Dr. North made me see that I didn't kill any president. Instead, delusional, I stabbed North. I understand what happened—my break with reality—and I'm all better.

Gray clouds coat the sky with a steady drizzle, and I listen to the relentless *drip…drip…drip* of rain off the nearby eaves.

Funny how some things never change.

I stand at the rope line waiting for President Izaan Bekkar to swing through his campaign stop in Fairfield, Virginia. Television vans line the street awaiting his arrival. A petite blond in a short skirt and matching jacket advances to the rope line and thrusts her microphone in front of the man next to me.

"After a controversial presidency, President Izaan Bekkar is determined to run for a second term. Sir, how did you feel four years ago when President Bekkar revealed he was a Muslim?"

"Being a Muslim didn't bother me," the man says. "Man has a right to his own religion, so long as it doesn't get forced on anybody."

"President Bekkar has said that if he wins, he'll be sworn in on the Quran. Does that bother you?"

"No. Why should it? He's been a damn good president."

I step away, fearing the reporter will approach me. Fools. Every one of them is too stupid to be afraid. They don't understand agendas. I understand. I see the truth.

I also know habit.

I've watched footage from all of Bekkar's campaign stops. He always starts on the left, shaking hands with his supporters as he moves right. I chose this spot well. He'll come directly to me. He'll like my burqa.

I wore it for him.

Beneath it, I grip the knife.

DAVID J. MONTGOMERY

David writes for several of the country's largest newspapers as a book critic, but we won't hold that against him. Recently he's begun producing fiction the rest of us can critique, discuss…and enjoy. Because he's good. One of the most prolific and respected reviewers of thrillers in the business, he not only has an eye for writing, "Bedtime for Mr. Li" demonstrates he has a pen for it as well.

Jason Ryder: a hit man you wouldn't mind having a beer with. Certainly, it would have to be a casual drink—you wouldn't want to get mixed up in *his* business—but it you could talk to such a man, wouldn't you? In a world of uncertain moral landscapes, an antihero like Ryder is an intriguing figure from beyond the pale, but not beyond redemption. Just don't say anything bad about the Lakers around him.

BEDTIME FOR MR. LI

Jason Ryder sat slumped behind the wheel of the rented Ford, watching the raindrops chase each other down the windshield. He'd been sitting there for over an hour already and his ass was starting to go numb. On the radio was a playoff game between the Los Angeles Lakers and the Portland Trailblazers, with the Lakers ahead by three in the fourth quarter. Listening to basketball on the radio was like watching a porno movie with the picture turned off, but he had to make do.

Ryder had been on the job for a week already, enough time to make him more than a little antsy. He was never one to hurry—he was nothing if not meticulous, an essential requirement for success in his line of work—but that didn't mean he wanted to waste time, either. There were places he'd rather be than the front seat of an '06 Taurus, and things he'd rather do than drink lukewarm McDonald's coffee while watching a middle-aged Chinese man negotiate with hookers.

Officially, Li Jinping held the position of Cultural Attaché in the Washington, D.C., embassy of the People's Republic of China. He spent his days overseeing the loan of endangered giant pandas to various zoos across the United States, as well as organizing tours of the Shanghai Acrobats and Beijing Opera.

Unofficially, Li was a colonel in the Second Department of the People's Liberation Army—PLA—and the head of all human intelligence gathering operations in the United States. In other words, he was China's top spy in North America.

Li wasn't a very good spy—he had only successfully re-cruited one American: a disgruntled line cook working in the White House mess—but that never dampened his en-thusiasm for the job. He fancied himself as the Chinese James Bond, despite his receding hairline and expanding waistline. He would likely have been fired for incompe-tence long ago, had he not gotten lucky during his previous posting in Beijing, a posting that had allowed him to gather some juicy intel on select Politburo members and high-ranking officials in the Party.

Li loved life in the U.S. He ate like a trencherman and drank like a sailor. He had not one but two mistresses—in addition, of course, to his doting wife back home in Beijing. He was the very picture of ill health, but he didn't care. He was master of his domain in Washington and would only leave when he dropped dead of the inevitable heart attack.

If only Li Jinping were a better spy. Or perhaps if he had been more modest in his appetites. Or, most of all, if he hadn't hired a room service waiter at the Beijing Hilton to secretly take pictures of the vice chairman of the National People's Congress while he was rendezvousing with his much younger boyfriend, a gymnastic star predicted to make a fine showing at the Olympics. But he had. And that was why he was going to die.

Jason Ryder didn't really care about the reasons. Li Jinping's misdeeds, outsize appetites and poor judgment were of no concern to him. He could have been screwing the giant pandas instead of renting them out to American zoos and Ryder still wouldn't have cared. He had only one reason to kill Li—and it came with five zeros after it.

Ryder had been hired, via a circuitous path involving two diplomats, one general and a transsexual Korean bartender, to eliminate Li, through whatever method proved most convenient. The vice chairman of the National People's Congress hadn't specified any requirements, other than that Li had to die, soon if possible, painfully if it happened to work out that way.

The vice chairman had also promised a bonus of an additional $50,000 if Li's elimination could be handled in a particularly embarrassing way, but Ryder hadn't quite figured out how to handle that one yet. He'd been giving it some consideration, however, and had purchased a size

XXL pair of frilly undergarments from a plus-size women's store at the mall. He didn't relish the prospect of undressing Li in order to paint him as a cross-dresser—but when the time came, he thought he'd be able to persuade himself with the hefty bonus. Even so, he was keeping an open mind to the possibilities, just in case a better opportunity presented itself.

Ryder didn't anticipate that Li's removal would be particularly difficult. For a man in the intelligence business, Li was surprisingly dumb, taking unnecessary risks seemingly at every turn. He failed to take even the basic precautions to guard his identity or his person. Ryder was surprised that he hadn't yet seen Li appear on CNN as a talking head, commenting on how it had grown increasingly difficult to conduct military espionage in a post-9/11 United States. The guy was that obvious.

Even so, the job had to be handled carefully. There was always significant risk involved in eliminating an official of a foreign government; a risk made even greater when the individual was a member of the clandestine community. Ryder was unaware of the identity of the client who had hired him, but even if he had known that he was a senior member of the Chinese Politburo, it wouldn't have changed the equation any. Just because one man in the PRC government wanted Li dead didn't mean they would turn a blind eye to his murder. All the more reason to make his death appear to be something it wasn't.

Ryder had been tracking Li's activities and movements

for over a week now. He'd had what turned out to be a golden opportunity to complete the job two days before, but he hadn't been ready to pull the trigger. Li had met his number-two mistress, an exotic dancer at a gentleman's club just over the D.C. border in Arlington, at a run-down hotel on Capitol Hill. Ryder had followed them into the lobby where he observed them having a heated disagreement of some sort. The girl had stormed away in anger, leaving Li to head for the elevators by himself. Ryder assumed that Li was going to make use of the room one way or another, a fact apparently confirmed when a busty blonde decked out in whore's garb arrived thirty-five minutes later and headed up to Li's floor.

Patience was something Ryder had amassed in abundance over the years, so he wasn't overly concerned about the missed chance. He was, however, starting to get a little annoyed that he was missing the Lakers in the playoffs. But he knew there would be another opportunity. Li just couldn't help himself. The man seemed to attract compromising circumstances like Lindsay Lohan attracts paparazzi.

The trail that evening had brought Ryder to the parking lot outside a Szechuan restaurant in northwest D.C. One of the area's frequent summer squalls had risen up awhile before, pelting the car with a torrent of rain. Ryder welcomed the weather, as it provided excellent cover for his activities. No one was likely to linger in the parking lot and wonder why the man in the dark sedan had been sitting there for the past hour.

Li had gone in alone, but Ryder's quick peek in the front door while studying the menu had revealed that he was not dining solo. He had a woman with him—yet another too-tall, too-obvious blonde who would surely tower over the diminutive Li like an NBA all-star. Clearly the man liked his women large and blond—and for sale.

After he spotted Li with the pro, Ryder wondered if being found dead with a hooker would be enough of an embarrassment to earn the bonus payment. Of course, that would require him to eliminate the woman, as well, something he wasn't willing to do. A working girl has a hard enough life without some random guy offing her because she signed on for a trick with the wrong john. Ryder was a man of flexible ethics, but even so there were lines that he drew, and that was one of them.

Still, the situation presented potential opportunities. If Li took the girl back to another anonymous hotel for a quick wham-bam-thank-you-ma'am, the circumstances would be ripe for action. All Ryder would have to do was wait for the pro to leave, then he could dispatch the target at his leisure. Two nights before, under similar circumstances, Li had stayed the rest of the night after his date left. Apparently he didn't mind staying in less-than-luxury accommodations, even though the mere thought of what the sheets were like made Ryder's skin crawl.

Ryder was in the middle of trying to decide if he needed to relieve himself bad enough to urinate in an empty coffee cup when the door to the restaurant opened and Li and the woman emerged. Ever the gentleman, Li opened an umbrella to shield himself and hurried ahead, leaving his companion to fend for herself. Li's Corvette was parked four cars away from Ryder, but the Chinese spy never even glanced in the direction of the Ford. Ryder shook his head. The man's tradecraft was appalling. It was surprising that nobody had eliminated him before. Li was so careless it seemed a miracle he hadn't been killed simply by accident.

Li climbed behind the wheel of the Corvette and was joined a few moments later by the blond prostitute, now dripping wet and complaining loudly. Ryder couldn't hear all of what she was saying, but it sounded like she was cursing Li for the lazy, inconsiderate bastard he was. Ryder doubted that Li's understanding of English was enough to appreciate the nuances of fine swearing, but even if he did, he seemed like the kind of guy who would probably find it a turn-on.

The Corvette pulled out of the parking lot and Ryder followed at a discreet distance. Even though there were only ninety seconds left in the basketball game, he turned the radio off. Now that he was actively working, Ryder wouldn't allow himself any distractions. He'd just have to rely on the Lakers to win it on their own.

Sure, Ryder could probably tailgate Li from one side of D.C. to the other and the spy would never even notice. But the hooker likely had some street savvy, so there was no reason to push it. At any rate, the trip ended up being a short one, as less than ten minutes later they pulled into the parking garage adjacent to a large, but shabby-looking hotel not far from the White House.

Li was no big spender, that was for sure. Apparently the PLA didn't give its spies an expense account. It was all good news for Ryder's purposes. Crummy hotel meant crummy security, high turnover of guests and no questions asked. Things were looking good. If all went as planned, he'd be able to complete the job and get out of Washington in time to watch some basketball.

The Corvette's doors opened and Li came spilling out. He stumbled as he walked across the parking garage, catching hold of the girl in order to stay upright. The alcohol he presumably drunk with dinner was catching up with him. Ryder half expected the girl to roll him right there and beat feet down the exit ramp. But apparently there was still honor among whores, if not thieves, and she instead led him to the elevator.

Ryder climbed out of his car, then leaned back inside to grab a small black duffel bag from the floorboards on the passenger side. The bag contained all the equipment he would need to complete the job—including the size XXL women's lingerie. Just thinking about it made Ryder shudder a little.

The elevator bell dinged loudly and the doors slowly slid open. There was no way Ryder could ride up in the elevator with them, so he waited at a reasonable distance while Li and his date stepped aboard and the doors closed behind them. He then hurried over to punch the button for the next car. He didn't have long to wait, and the second bay of elevator doors opened and he climbed aboard.

Stepping out onto the lobby level a minute later, Ryder scanned the large, poorly lit room, searching for Li. He spotted him weaving his way across the threadbare carpet to the registration desk. You know a hotel has open-minded standards when the desk clerk doesn't even bat his eyes when a guy shows up for what is clearly a sex-for-hire assignation. The clerk just took Li's credit card, typed for a couple minutes on his keyboard and handed over a room key.

The next part was going to be tricky. Ryder needed to learn what room Li was staying in, without connecting himself to Li in anybody's minds. That left out the obvious solutions, like walking up to registration and asking, "Say, which room did you just give that guy?" Fortunately, Ryder had an alternate plan.

Seeing that Li and the girl were heading for the bank of elevators just off the lobby, Ryder walked past them to the nearby stairs. After Li punched the up button and waited for the elevator to arrive, Ryder opened the door leading to the stairs and jogged up the first two flights. The hotel had eight floors, so if the clerk had assigned Li a room on the top level, Ryder was probably going to be in trouble. But assuming that the law of averages gave him a good shot for a lower floor, he had a decent chance of success.

Emerging onto the third-floor landing, Ryder sucked in air and tried to slow his breathing. Two flights shouldn't have winded him already, but clearly he hadn't been hitting the gym often enough. He watched the illuminated numbers above the bank of elevators. One of them was fixed on eight, so that couldn't be Li. There was no way he could have risen to the top floor already. The other was on four. As Ryder watched, it switched to five. A few seconds later, it was still frozen on the number five. That was it.

Ryder returned to the stairs and started jogging up again. He arrived at the door marked five and paused again to suck in air. He tried to calm his breathing as he opened the solid metal fire door as quietly as possible. He peeked out the door and looked to the left. Nothing. He looked to the right. Again, nothing. Could he have miscalculated? Another look to the left. Still nothing.

Then Ryder heard a loud, feminine giggle come from somewhere to his right. Emerging into the corridor from the stairwell, Ryder saw that the hallway made a sharp turn about fifty feet to his right, just out of sight from where he was standing a moment before. He hurried down the corridor and peered around the bend.

Li and his date were weaving down the hall, his hands all over her, groping at her ample breasts and full derriere. As Ryder watched, Li goosed her in the ass, causing another high-pitched squeal. Li was a pig, a fact for which Ryder gave thanks. This was going to work, he thought.

About halfway down the corridor, Li stopped at a door on the left. He fumbled with his room key for several seconds before the girl finally took it away from him and unlocked the door herself. Pushing it open, she shoved Li in ahead of her, allowing the door to slam shut behind them.

Ryder strode down the hallway and glanced at the door Li had just entered. Number 535. Ryder continued down the hall, then paused to look at the numbers on the doors around him. He pantomimed looking down at his hand, as if to confirm his room number. Shaking his head, he pivoted and headed back the way he'd come. It was unlikely that his act was being observed by anyone, but it was worth doing all the same. Ryder had found himself heading the wrong way down hotel corridors for real enough times to know that it was a very believable mistake.

After heading back down in the elevator, Ryder emerged into the lobby. He made his way to the bar, which was ahead of him approximately fifty yards, in a direct line of sight with the bank of elevators. For the next part of his plan to work, Li had to be alone. That meant Ryder had to wait for the pro to leave. He didn't anticipate it taking more than an hour at most. There was no way that a man like Li, who hadn't even been willing to pay for a decent hotel, had bought the girl for the entire night.

Ryder ordered a light beer at the bar—he didn't want his senses to be dulled by too much alcohol—and sat down at the table nearest the entrance. He was just another out-of-town businessman killing time and spending the night alone. There were a couple of other men in the bar likewise doing a little solitary drinking. He wondered what kind of companies they worked for, given the quality of the accommodations. Maybe they just didn't know what kind of hotel they were booking. Its address—on Pennsylvania Avenue—was decent enough to fool people. He doubted the hotel got much return business, however.

Ryder nursed his beer for the next half hour, but there was no sign of the girl. He had to admit to a little grudging respect for Li. He'd half assumed the man would have passed out by now. He decided he'd better order another beer, just to avoid making anyone curious.

As he stood at the bar waiting for his drink, SportsCenter came on the TV. The lead story was the Lakers victory in overtime just moments before, a victory that the anchorman called "one of the most exciting basketball games in recent memory." Ryder just shook his head. It was bad enough that he was stuck in this fleabag hotel, tracking a fat, washed-up spy. Now he'd missed the best game of the season. He was more determined than ever to kill Li and go home.

As Ryder was returning from the bar, beer in hand, he spotted the prostitute emerging from the elevator. She strolled across the lobby, headed in the direction of the registration desk. Ryder sat down at this table to watch her. He took a sip of beer as she stopped at the desk and spoke briefly with the clerk who had checked them in. She slipped him something—a payoff, presumably—and headed for the exit. Ryder glanced around the bar, confirmed that no one was watching him and poured half his beer into the base of a fake tree next to his table. He didn't want to leave a full beer behind, which might make someone curious as to where he'd gone. He put the bottle down on the table and left the bar.

Riding the elevator back up to the fifth floor, Ryder prepared himself for what he was going to do. Killing a man in cold blood was never an easy task, but he had long ago steeled himself against the emotions connected to the act. He had done it enough times before that, although not automatic, it was the next closest thing to it. Like Michael Corleone so famously said, it wasn't personal, it was just business. Ryder had a job to do and he planned to do it; quickly, efficiently and without hesitation.

Arriving at the fifth floor, Ryder walked down the corridor to Room 535. He had been in the hotel long enough and was anxious to finish the job and get the hell out of there.

Ryder unzipped the duffel bag, then knocked sharply on the door, two staccato beats. Ryder hoped the man hadn't sunk into postcoital oblivion. Apparently not, as he heard a fumbling with the door's safety catch. "Who there, please?" asked the voice on the other side of the door.

"Hotel security," Ryder answered. "Please open the door, sir."

The door opened to reveal Li Jinping standing there in his underwear, a dingy white T-shirt stretched tight over his ample belly. Li blinked at Ryder, bleary-eyed and obviously concerned. "What is a matter, please?"

"Please step back, sir. I need to check the room."

Li hesitated before taking a step backward, allowing Ryder to enter. He did so, and closed the door behind him.

"You're Mr. Li, right?"

"Yes, I am Li."

Ryder already knew who he was, but he figured it couldn't hurt to check. He reached his hand into the duffel bag and wrapped his fingers around the grip of the .22 semiautomatic pistol. He was about to whip it out of the bag when a soft knock sounded on the door at his back.

Ryder jerked his hand out of the bag with a start. Shit. Was it the real hotel security? Or the cops? Who else would be knocking on the door in the middle of the night? He doubted the hotel had room service. Ryder had to decide how he wanted to play it, and fast. So far he hadn't done anything too incriminating. But he also couldn't allow any official connection to be made between him and Li.

Another knock sounded on the door. Louder this time. Ryder put his hand back in the bag and felt for the pistol again. He was tired of pussyfooting around with this job. If drastic action needed to be taken, he was going to take it. One way or another, this was going to end tonight.

"Li, honey?" A muffled voice came from the hallway. "It's me, Candy. I forgot my phone."

Ryder cursed his luck. It was the prostitute, back just in time to screw up everything. There was no way he could let her see him with Li. Not unless he wanted to kill her, too. He would if he had to, but that would make what he had planned almost impossible to pull off. He had to think of some other way around it.

He turned to Li and locked eyes with him. "Listen to me carefully. We know you had a prostitute here in your room with you. Is that her at the door?"

Li nodded, his eyes wide. "Yes, I have girl. But I'm diplomat. You can no arrest—"

"Shut up and listen to me. I'm going to step into the bathroom. You're going to get rid of the whore as quickly as possible. Do you understand?" Li nodded. "We don't want to embarrass the hotel any more than has already happened. So just get rid of her and I'll handle everything else. Understand?" Another nod.

None of it made much sense, but Ryder wasn't giving him time to think. Li was scared and smashed and hardly thinking his best. Ryder was counting on that to make him compliant with his demands.

The knocking was louder now. "Li? Are you asleep, sweetie? I really need my phone."

"Where's her phone?" Ryder asked. Li just shrugged. Ryder walked over the bed and looked around. There was a bottle of Jim Beam and a glass on the nightstand. Li's clothes were tossed in a heap on the chair next to the bed. The phone could be anywhere.

With Li standing there uselessly, Ryder rushed past him into the bathroom and flipped on the light. There. A pink cell phone was sitting on the counter next to the dirty water glass and no-name shampoo. Ryder grabbed it and returned to Li.

"Give the girl her phone and get rid of her." Ryder handed it to him. "Do what I say and this will all be over soon."

Ryder returned to the bathroom and closed the door until it was open just a crack. He withdrew the pistol from his bag and peered through the gap.

Li opened the door to the corridor and Candy started to step in. Li didn't move, though, forcing her to stop abruptly. He held her phone out toward her. "Here your phone. I find it."

"Thanks, sweetie." Candy took the phone. "I was afraid you'd be asleep."

"Not yet, but I go bed now. Very tired."

"Are you sure you wouldn't like to—"

"No. Very tired. Thank you."

Li gently urged the girl out and closed the door. Ryder stepped out and slid the security bolt closed.

"Good job, Li."

"I do what you say. Now you go?"

"I'm afraid not."

It was then that Li looked down and saw that Ryder was pointing the pistol at him.

Ryder led Li at gunpoint over to the bed. Picking up the remote control from the bedside table, Ryder turned up the volume on the television—conveniently enough, it was already turned on, playing a porno movie—and told Li to lie down on the bed.

Li's face turned a bright shade of crimson and sweat

poured down his face as he started speaking in rapid-fire Chinese, his voice strained and high-pitched. Ryder didn't understand a word of it, but he assumed the man was pleading for his life. He'd heard it all before, in more languages than he could count.

"Save it," Ryder said, gesturing with the pistol. "Get over on the bed."

But Li's voice grew even more agonized. He was talking so fast he couldn't even catch his breath.

"Last chance," Ryder said. "Lie down on the bed or this is really going to get nasty."

It was then that Li started clutching at his chest. His face had turned nearly purple and he was no longer even looking at Ryder. His eyes were tightly closed, his face a mask of pain.

A few seconds later, he keeled over.

Ryder looked down at Li, lying on the floor next to a used condom wrapper, his movements slower now, his face a rictus of agony. He watched the Chinese man for a few minutes, but it was obvious that he was on his way out. A few moments later, his movements stopped completely. He was dead.

Sonuvabitch, Ryder muttered to himself. If that wasn't the easiest money he'd ever made, he didn't know what was. Smiling at his good fortune, he put the pistol back in his bag and started making a few alterations to the scene.

Acting quickly, before the lividity in Li's body could set, Ryder hauled the corpse up onto the bed, arranging him back against the pillows. He turned the volume down on the TV before wiping the remote clean of prints. He then placed the remote in Li's hand to get his fingerprints on it before dropping it to his side.

Looking down at the corpse, Ryder briefly considered whether he should try stripping the body and dressing him in the woman's underwear. He couldn't bring himself to do it, though. Too much risk—and too damn disgusting—even for fifty grand. He did grit his teeth long enough to pull down Li's boxer shorts. He also reached into the duffel bag and withdrew two hardcore gay porno magazines, not very politically correct in China. He put Li's prints on them, as well, and laid them on the bed next to the body. That would have to be good enough.

The stage set, Ryder glanced around the room, making sure he hadn't left any incriminating evidence behind. One of the advantages to doing a job in such a questionable environment was that it would be nearly impossible for the CSI geeks to find any usable DNA. The room probably held the fingerprints, hairs and assorted bodily secretions of enough people to fill RFK stadium.

Ryder exited the room, smearing the doorknobs and locks as he left. He didn't think anyone would look too closely at the case. Once they realized Li was a Chinese diplomat—and saw the circumstances under which he died—they'd chalk the death up as an obvious heart attack and leave it at that. If anyone on the outside got implicated, it was going to be Candy, not him. But he doubted it would come to that. If there was one thing the Chinese hated more than anything, it was embarrassment.

As he rode the elevator back down to the ground floor, Ryder wondered if his client would be satisfied enough to give him the bonus. It didn't really matter. One hundred grand was enough for the job, even without the extra money.

Now if he could just get home in time to watch the NBA finals, he'd be a happy man.

SIMON WOOD

Few authors in the thriller community are as borderline 007 as Simon Wood, former racecar driver, licensed airplane pilot, private investigator and world traveler—replete with adventures featuring Transylvanian wolves and Thai railroads. It seems Simon is a bit of an adrenaline junkie.

So it's no wonder that Nick, the stubbornly love-struck protagonist in "Protecting the Innocent" isn't adverse to a little risk, either. This story asks you to consider how far you'd go for love. Would you risk your own life? If you're anything like Nick—or Simon—you might go just a little too far.

PROTECTING THE INNOCENT

"See you later." Nick kissed Melanie goodbye and watched her walk away. The lunchtime throng on Market Street swallowed her up, but the crowd parted at different times to expose glimpses of an arm, a leg, a shoulder.

He couldn't get enough of her. The last couple of months had been a whirlwind. It was more than just an infatuation—he felt a connection with her on every level possible. For the first time in his life, he was thinking about marriage, although he didn't want to share that with her until he was sure she felt the same way. If things carried on the way they were going, he'd test the waters, maybe whisk her off to somewhere romantic and let the moment sweep both of them away.

A friendly sounding voice called his name. Instinctively, he turned.

The man looked familiar and at the same time didn't.

He was tall, blond and well-attired. His suit certainly hadn't come off the rack.

"Nick Forbes, yes?" The man put out a hand.

"Yes." Nick took it and shook. "Do I know you?"

"Sort of. I'm Melanie's brother, Jamie."

Now Nick saw the resemblance. Melanie had mentioned a brother, but they'd never met.

"If you're looking for Mel, she's just gone." He pointed in the direction of the Wells Fargo building.

"I came to see you, not Melanie."

"Me?"

"Yes, you. You and Melanie have become close."

"There's no become about it. We are close."

"Please let me finish."

People brushed by them, so eager to get on with their own lives that they paid scant regard to this encounter. It was if the two men had fallen off the world and no longer had any impact on society.

"Your relationship with my sister is a problem." The smile went out of Jamie's eyes. Coldness replaced the warmth.

Who did this son of bitch think he was? Nick thought. "A problem?"

"Yes, a problem. You have to stop seeing her."

"Look, I don't know who you think you're talking to, but you have no right to tell me or Melanie how to live our lives."

"Yes, I do." Jamie pressed his fingers into Nick's chest. "Stay away from her or there will be trouble."

Nick knocked Jamie's hand aside. "Is that a threat?"

"Just do as I tell you and you won't get hurt."

"Now that is a threat."

Jamie shrugged the response away like he'd heard it all before. "I'm not going to argue with you anymore. Just do as I say. It's not a threat. It's a warning. Break it off with Melanie before it's too late." Jamie walked by Nick and let the current of people sweep him away. "I'll be watching."

"What's that supposed to mean?" Nick called out to Jamie's retreating form.

Nick picked up Melanie at her condo the next night. He wanted to mention Jamie's reprehensible scene but couldn't do it. From what she'd mentioned about him, they were close. Very close. Telling her about what happened yesterday might force her to choose sides.

While he waited for Melanie to finish changing, Nick tried to make sense of what had happened. The guy was just trying to protect his sister. That was understandable. His outburst was almost admirable. Except it wasn't. It was excessive and totally uncalled for. There was no way Nick could tell Melanie about it. She took his arm and led him to the elevator.

Nick had reservations at her favorite restaurant in the city, a French place called The Fifth Floor. He had planned on taking her to a Greek place he liked on Battery, but he'd switched at the last minute. The reason—privacy. The Fifth Floor was secluded and somewhat exclusive. If Jamie wanted to create a scene, he'd have a hard job.

During the drive, Nick's animal instincts kicked in. He sensed a car was tailing him. This wasn't the first time he'd had this feeling. For the past couple of weeks, he would have sworn he'd seen the same car outside his home, at the gym and parked across from his job. If it wasn't a car, it was someone following him on foot. He'd put it down to paranoia, but after Jamie's warning, he wasn't so sure.

"You're quiet tonight," Melanie said.

He dragged his gaze away from his rearview mirror and the Acura that had been trailing him since he left the office. "Just a little distracted is all. Sorry."

She smiled at him. "Well, don't be. You're with me tonight. I demand attention."

He laughed. "Yes, my queen."

"That's more like it."

He looked back in his rearview. The Acura was gone.

The hostess showed them to a corner table. Nick took the seat that gave him the best view of the bar leading into the dining area. If Jamie planned any sort of confrontation, he'd see it coming.

They ordered. Melanie chatted and Nick struggled to concentrate on what she said. She called him on it a couple of times and he apologized, promising to do better. He expected Jamie to appear at any moment, but he didn't show. By the time the entrées were served, Nick felt this wasn't the night Jamie would make his scene. His tension lifted and clarity seeped in. A thought came to him.

He wondered if he'd really been accosted by Melanie's brother and not by some jealous ex-boyfriend. Melanie had mentioned she hadn't had much luck in the relationship department over the years. The men she bared her soul to always ran out on her. Was it possible these men might not have run out, but have been helped on their way?

"You've mentioned your brother, Jamie, but you've never told me much about him."

"He's a great guy. I'm sure you two would really like each other. He's older than me by a couple of years and of course that makes him my protector. He's always looking out for me. I don't know what he wouldn't do for me," she enthused.

This description matched the guy Nick had met yesterday, but that still didn't mean anything.

"Have you got a picture of him?"

"Of course. I'm surprised I haven't shown it to you before now."

Melanie fished in her purse and removed a photo from her pocketbook. Nick took the picture and examined it and his theory went up in smoke. The Jamie in the picture was the Jamie on Market Street. Nick squeezed out a polite smile and handed the picture back.

"He looks how I expected him to look."

"The three of us should go out together."

"I'd like that," Nick said, and meant it. It would be a

good opportunity to show this guy how happy he made his sister. If that didn't work, he doubted Jamie could keep a lid on his jealously and he'd expose himself for the person he really was. Either way, it'd be a win-win for Nick. "Jamie doesn't have to play third wheel. He should bring his girl-friend. Make it a double date. I haven't double-dated in years."

"Jamie doesn't have a girlfriend. I don't know why."

I do, Nick thought. "Maybe he doesn't put himself out there," he suggested.

They skipped dessert and hooked up with some friends at a club, but left early to go back to Melanie's condo. They fooled around and Melanie wanted him to spend the night, but he couldn't get Jamie off his mind.

He went home, his head full of Jamie. Goddamn the guy for thinking he could destroy his relationship with Melanie. Well, he wasn't going to stand for it. Jamie's threatening ways might have worked with Melanie's past boyfriends, but they wouldn't with him. His blood was up when he went to bed, but it turned icy cold when he picked up the newspaper off his stoop the following morning. The *Chronicle* had been turned to the third page. The headline read Man Killed in Senseless Mugging.

It took Nick a minute to realize the newspaper wasn't current, but six months old. The story detailed the botched mugging. A Wells Fargo employee—Miles Talbot, twenty-six—had been returning home after a night out in the city.

He'd been stabbed repeatedly on the Embarcadero and his wallet and valuables had been taken. His body had been dragged from the main thoroughfare and dumped under the archway of Pier 26. After Nick read the story, a vague recollection of the incident filtered through. The cops had never found the person responsible.

There were no prizes for guessing who'd left this piece of San Francisco history for him. It was a cheap and tactless attempt to intimidate him. It was also vague. Was Jamie saying that if he didn't stop seeing his sister, he'd end up in the same condition? Christ, it was as pathetic as it was infuriating. Nick went to toss the newspaper in the trash, but a second thought struck him. He'd taken the news story for a veiled threat. Maybe it wasn't. Maybe Talbot's murder was an example of what happened to Melanie's boyfriends who didn't take a hint. The strength went out of his legs and he flopped into a chair at his kitchen table.

Had Melanie's brother killed this guy? It seemed incredible that he would resort to that. Nick couldn't bring himself to believe it, but an itch at the back of his skull believed it was not only possible but true. There was only one way to find out.

He Googled Miles Talbot's murder. The hits revealed various incarnations of the story he'd read in the *Chronicle*. There were a few more column inches dedicated to announcing when the investigation went cold. None of the hits revealed the one fact Nick looked for—the name of a girlfriend. He called Wells Fargo and asked for Talbot's extension. He received the expected awkward silence before the switchboard operator said, "I'll transfer you. Hold one moment."

Nick was connected to Julia Chastain in the private clients department, who spoke in a hushed tone. "You wanted to speak to Miles Talbot?"

"Yes. Is he there?"

"No."

"Okay, I'll leave a message."

"You don't know, then."

"Know what?"

Julia gave him the Cliff's Notes version. He acted suitably shocked and tossed in the factoid that he'd been an old college buddy of Talbot's, which took him closer into her confidence.

"How did his girlfriend take it?"

"Melanie Lassen? I don't know. I imagine she took it hard. Do you know her?"

Nick sagged under the weight of the confirmation. It was as if his flesh couldn't support the immense weight of his bones. It was an effort to speak but he forced the words out. "Yeah, I know her."

Julia said something but he wasn't listening anymore. He thanked her and hung up.

The guys in his office wanted to hit Gordon Biersch for lunch. He possessed the desire to drink, but not the thirst. He hit the streets instead. He stood in line at a Subway, but walked away before his turn came. He was wandering along

Spear Street when a voice interrupted him from his thoughts.

"Looks like you've read some bad news," Jamie said.

He had a smug look plastered over his face. Nick would have loved to have wiped it off for him, but this wasn't the time or the place, so he bottled his disgust.

"Ha, ha, very funny."

Jamie fell in at Nick's side. "I take it you've worked out the meaning."

"Yes."

"Then you'll be getting out of Melanie's life."

"You can't control her like this. She's a woman, not a child." Nick failed to keep his anger in check. "And you're not her father."

"From that, I assume you're going to continue with the relationship."

Nick didn't have a choice. He couldn't abandon Melanie. He guessed this was the decision Miles Talbot had come to and he had paid the ultimate price. Still, Nick couldn't walk away.

"The murder of a man isn't enough of a deterrent for you?"

"No. Not even if it was a dozen."

Jamie shook his head in disbelief. "I can't make out if you're dumb or brave, but I'm leaning toward the former."

Nick grabbed Jamie by the throat and slammed him up against the smoked glass windows of a faceless building. Jamie made no effort to fight Nick off. "You can't break us up."

"It's looking that way," Jamie said with sincerity.

A handful of people streamed from the office building. A couple of guys puffed themselves up to look more foreboding than they were. "We've called the cops," one of the men said and held up a cell phone.

Nick released his hold on Jamie and wiped his hands on his pants. "Just leave Melanie and me alone."

Nick backed away from Jamie as Jamie's unwitting supporters closed in around him, asking him if he was okay.

Nick turned his back on them and walked away.

"Ask her about the others, Nick," Jamie called out after him. "Miles Talbot wasn't an isolated incident."

Nick lay in Melanie's bed. A sheen of sweat glistened on his chest. He'd made love to Melanie like it was the last time. It left them breathless, but for totally different reasons. He couldn't get Jamie's parting remark out of his head. What had he meant? He'd killed for Melanie before? How many times? Two? Five? A dozen? How did anyone get away with that many murders and how did Melanie cope? She'd have to think she was some sort of kiss of death with a trail of dead boyfriends left in her wake. That was if she even knew they were dead. Melanie said her boyfriends had run out on her, not died on her. Christ, he should go to the cops, but with what? He needed something concrete to give them. If he went to them half-cocked, he'd achieve nothing beyond alienating Melanie and blowing any kind of future with her.

"Wow, don't look too depressed." Melanie returned to

the bedroom with a glass of water in her hand. She slipped between the sheets and pressed her naked body up against his. She offered him the glass and he sat up and took it. "You can't be sad after all that."

"No." He sipped the water. "I was just thinking."

"About what?"

"Stuff."

She pinched his arm playfully. "Come on, spit it out. What's eating you?"

"I was wondering how important I was to you."

"Very."

"Really?"

She took the glass from his hand and placed it on the nightstand. She took his face in her hands and stared directly at him. Her eyes shone with a brightness that blinded him. "At this very moment in space and time, you are the most important person to me."

"At this very moment."

She smiled. "Yes. What's all this about? Are you feeling insecure?"

"I feel I know you and at the same time, I don't." This wasn't a line. He really did feel this way. He hadn't realized how much he felt this until Jamie came on the scene.

Concern clouded her expression, but the remark pushed her away from him. She retreated to her side of the bed. "What do you want to know?"

"Anything." He took her hand in his. "Everything."

A single tear leaked from her right eye. "What do you want to know?"

* ★ ★

They held each other for a time, not saying anything. Then she told him to get up. He showered and when he returned to the bedroom, she wasn't there. He found her in the living room surrounded by boxes.

"What's going on?"

"Get dressed and I'll tell you my life story."

The boxes contained photo albums dating back to her baby years. She introduced him to two-dimensional images of family and friends, past and present. It didn't matter which photos she showed him, Jamie was always there, lurking in the corners, glued to her heels like an unwanted shadow.

"Who's that?" Nick pointed to a good-looking boy no more than twelve dressed in a *Miami Vice* sport jacket over a pastel T-shirt and white pants. Melanie was at his side. The photo had captured some sort of school dance. It was the first picture that failed to feature Jamie.

Melanie flushed and turned the page.

"No secrets." Nick turned the page back. He tapped the boy's image with his index finger. "A first love, perhaps?"

"Yes," she conceded. "His name was Mikey Pryce. We went steady for six months." She slapped a hand over her face. "I can't believe I'm telling you this."

"So how did Mikey break your heart?"

She pulled back from him. The temperature in the room plunged. "He died."

Nick's stomach clenched as a sense of foreboding overcame him. He forced out a single word. "How?"

"Drowned during a family vacation."

Nick turned the pages. He pointed out something that lightened her mood, then steered her to a picture of another boyfriend. This sparked a long conversation about the boyfriends and girlfriends they'd both had. He pumped her for everything he could get—names, places, dates. His mind was on fire. He committed every detail to memory. Ask him to do this at any other time and he'd have never managed the feat, but tonight it was all about saving his life and every nugget of data was stored. There'd been seven great loves in Melanie's life, including Mikey Pryce and Miles Talbot. Each of these guys had skipped out on her. She didn't make it clear whether they'd all been killed, but they'd all broken things off abruptly.

"All my boyfriends have a habit of walking out on me one way or another." She turned the page on Miles Talbot.

Nick took the album from her. "I won't. You have my word on it."

Seven people. It didn't seem like a lot of people, but digging up seven life stories consumed time like Nick wouldn't have believed. He possessed a newfound respect for the police. It took hours just to come up with one single facet of someone's life. But Nick persevered. If he was going to serve Jamie up to the cops, this was how it would happen.

He used every spare moment researching Melanie's old boyfriends. This came at the expense of Melanie. He saw her twice a week if he was lucky. She complained, but he blamed a big project at work for his absence. On the plus side, Jamie stopped pestering him. If he was daring Nick to learn the truth, it looked as if he'd get his wish.

Nick's first break came with Mikey Pryce. He found a newspaper story detailing that the boy had drowned at a watering hole in Sacramento where the Sacto and American Rivers met. The competing currents had swept him away. Melanie had neglected to mention that she and Jamie were there, too. Jamie had provided the eyewitness account to the police. Was he just thirteen when he'd committed his first murder?

Looking for a pattern, Nick tracked down Melanie's high school boyfriend, Trent Barber. Unlike Mikey Pryce, Trent was alive and well. He hadn't strayed far from his Orange County roots. He was a sound engineer for the movies. Nick used the movie angle to get Trent to speak to him on the phone, but Nick soon found he was out of his depth when the movie talk got technical.

"I hear we have a mutual friend," Nick said.

"In this business you need friends. Who is it?"

"Melanie Lassen."

"Who are you?" The question came through gritted teeth.

Nick saw no point in lying. "Melanie's boyfriend."

"So what are you doing—checking up on her?"

"Yeah."

"If you want to know about STDs, ask for a blood test."

"I'm more interested in her brother, Jamie."

Nick got the feeling Trent was about to hang up but the mention of Jamie stopped him. Trent's tone changed from anger to concern.

"So, he's given you the speech."

"What speech?"

"Don't piss around. You wouldn't be tracking down her high school sweetheart unless he'd given you the no-one-is-good-enough-for-my-sister speech."

"And what did you do about it?"

"I blew the freak off. What do you think?"

"I think he convinced you to stop seeing his sister."

Trent went silent for a good minute before speaking again.

"I was a good tight end in school. Could have gotten a scholarship."

"Why didn't you?"

"Jamie broke my hand with a hammer. Happy? Now, would you mind doing me a favor and go to hell?"

Nick received similar accounts from Jonathon Tripp and Tommy Frist, both college boyfriends. Both took Jamie's hints before bodily harm was involved. Matthew Warner wasn't so lucky. He was an intern at a San Francisco architecture firm when he dated Melanie. They'd gotten real close, according to Warner's sister, Penny. He was found at the Marin Headlands across from the Golden Gate Bridge with his throat cut. The police theorized the murder was a product of a carjacking, since his car had been found abandoned and burnt out in San Rafael. The only odd factor to the case was that Matt was discovered stretched out on a picnic blanket. When Nick hung up on Penny, she was crying.

Mark Bale proved to be the exception to the boyfriend rule. He'd dated Melanie nine months before Miles Talbot did. He lived in the city and he agreed to meet Nick at a bar on the Embarcadero.

"Did you ever get a visit from her brother?"

Bale turned his nose up. "Not really. He called me once but that was about it. He tried some line with me but I didn't pay much attention."

"So, he didn't scare you off?"

"No."

"Then why'd you break up with her?"

"Why's this so important to you?"

"Indulge me," Nick said. "Call it a commitment thing."

Bale grinned. "She's done it to you, hasn't she?"

If he meant made him fall in love, then yes. Nick grinned back but shrugged.

"If you want the God's honest truth, the reason Mel and I didn't last was the plain fact that she got weird. I was ready to settle down, but then the vibe changed. I didn't like it, so I called it quits."

Nick's roommate yelled out, "Phone."

Nick answered it.

"Good, I'm glad you're in," Jamie said.

"What do you want?"

"Melanie decided we should have a night out. I've got reservations for three at One Market for Thursday at eight."

"Okay."

"I'd appreciate if it you didn't make it."

"I would hate to disappoint Melanie."

"It would be the kinder thing to do."

Nick ignored Jamie's request and met them at the restaurant. Melanie's face lit up when she saw him approach the table, but Jamie just scowled. Nick kissed Melanie and shook hands with Jamie. To Nick's surprise and relief, Jamie chose to keep the dinner cordial. He and Nick may have exchanged penetrating stares, but that was as far as it went. Melanie led the conversation, choosing to reminisce about her childhood. As Melanie told it, every day had been a Norman Rockwell painting. Mikey Pryce's drowning never even featured. Nick fought the urge to resurrect the ghosts. If Jamie was playing nice, so would he. Despite the circumstances, Nick was having an enjoyable time.

After they finished their entrées, Melanie excused herself and retreated to the restroom. The two men in her life watched her go.

"I told you not to come," Jamie said. "This would be a good time to leave. I'll provide excuses."

"You don't get it, do you? I'm here for the long haul."

"Haven't I shown you what'll happen to you?"

"Jamie, I have enough on you to go to the cops right now."

Jamie smirked.

"I know about the others. All the way from Mikey Pryce."

That sent Jamie's smirk running for the hills.

"I don't want to turn you in because Melanie means so much to me, so I'll give you a break. You leave now and I don't just mean the restaurant. I'm talking about the city, the state, the country, I don't care. Just go. Leave us in peace. I'll make excuses for you."

Jamie picked up his glass and polished off the rest of his wine. "I can't do that."

"Then this one is going to get messy."

"I think you're right."

Melanie rejoined them. "You two seem to be getting on like a house on fire."

"Truer words were never said," Jamie remarked. His eyes sparkled with the irony of Melanie's statement.

"We've got so much in common." Nick reached over and kissed Melanie. "Like you."

When the check came, a brief fight over who would pay for the bill ensued. Jamie won. Nick couldn't help but feel he'd been provided his last meal. While Jamie waited for the waiter to return with his credit card and receipt, Nick took his chance.

"I'll check in with the valets for our cars." He snatched up Jamie's ticket stub.

"That's okay."

"No, I insist. Join me, Mel?" He forced the issue by holding out her coat.

Jamie fumed as Nick walked Melanie out. The valet approached them on the street, but Nick waved him away.

"What's going on?" Melanie asked.

"Three's a crowd. We need some alone time." Nick smiled. "I have a surprise."

They crossed the street over to Nick's car. He'd gotten lucky and snagged a parking spot directly across the restaurant. He gunned the engine and was pulling away when Jamie came tearing out of the restaurant. Melanie waved goodbye to him.

"I feel so bad," Melanie said. "Where are we going?"

"Don't ask questions. You'll spoil the surprise."

He headed out of the city and across the Bay Bridge. When he reached Berkeley, he pointed the car in the direction of the marina. The place was deserted. The restaurants had closed for the night. If it hadn't been for the street lighting, the marina would have been in total darkness. He parked in the red zone fronting the pier.

"What are we doing here?" Melanie asked.

"You'll see. Come on."

He came around to her side of the car and opened the door for her. He took her hand and led her onto the pier, then guided her toward the streetlamp at the end of it.

"I know we haven't been dating long," Nick began, "but I feel I've known you all my life."

She squeezed his hand. "You're very sweet."

With every step they took, he cataloged his affection for her. His outpourings left her speechless. She never interrupted. She just listened and that was good. Her silence gave him the courage for what he had to do. When they reached the end of the pier, he released her hand and turned to face her. He looked into her eyes and his throat closed up.

"C'mon. Don't stop now," she encouraged. "What is it?"

Out in the bay, a buoy chimed. The water slapped against the pier.

He needed encouragement to finish this, to go all the way, and he got it. A racing engine and squealing tires cut through the calm. Jamie had caught up with him. Nick thought he'd spotted Jamie's Acura on the freeway. He'd hoped for a longer lead. It didn't matter. Jamie was too late.

"Melanie, I love you."

"I love you, too."

"That's why I wanted to give you this."

Nick reached inside his pocket. A distant voice cried out but he and Melanie ignored it. The moment was all that counted. He produced his gift, a small box containing a ring. He fell to one knee.

"Will you marry me?"

"Stop," Jamie cried out. His feet pounded on the wooden planking.

"Oh, Nick, you shouldn't have."

"Why?" Nick asked.

"I can't."

"You can. Forget Jamie. Forget everything he's done. Just think about us."

"I'm sorry, Nick." Melanie turned away from him.

Jamie cried out again.

Damn him, Nick thought. That son of a bitch wouldn't

win. He jumped to his feet and grabbed Melanie's arm to prevent her from leaving. She whirled on him. He didn't see the switchblade she'd removed from her purse until she plunged it into his stomach. Confusion dulled his pain. She jerked the blade free and his legs went out from under him.

"Why?" Nick asked, his words weak in his throat.

Jamie caught up a moment later. He fell to his knees at Nick's side to examine the wound. "Not again," he murmured.

"Not again?"

Nick looked straight at Melanie. Her gaze was glassy, absent, and a stiffness had overcome her. She was a million miles away from this.

"Nick, why didn't you listen to me?" Jamie said. "I tried to warn you. I did everything I could to protect you."

"You made me think it was you."

"It was easier that way. I didn't want you thinking it was her. She's not a bad person. She's just damaged."

"What are you talking about?" Nick tried to move, but the pain in his abdomen stopped him cold.

"Our father." Jamie tried to apply pressure to the wound, but blood oozed between his fingers and Nick groaned. "He loved her. Loved her too much. Loved her so much he ruined her. You must have noticed she never talks about him and has no pictures of him in the condo."

It started sinking in. "She killed Mikey Pryce."

"And all the others. Father was the first."

The pain in his heart matched the pain in his stomach. "I don't understand. What did I do wrong?"

"I can't explain it. It doesn't make sense to anyone except her. You crossed the line for her."

"I just wanted to love her."

"That's crossing the line. You can love her. You just can't love her all the way."

It made a twisted kind of sense. Nick pictured the day at the watering hole where Mikey Pryce had promised to love Melanie forever, even promising to marry her. Unwittingly, he'd triggered Melanie's murderous reflex, which she repeated with Matthew Warner, Miles Talbot and now him. They'd all promised their undying love only to see it die.

"God, you're bleeding bad." Jamie took his hands away. Blood pulsed from the wound and Nick felt his strength drain from him with every pulse. "There's nothing I can do. I'm sorry, Nick. Truly, I am."

Jamie rose to his feet and hugged his sister. "It's okay. You've done nothing wrong. I'll make this all go away."

"Call 911," Nick pleaded.

"I wish I could, but I can't let the police take her," Jamie said and turned to Melanie. "It's okay. You're safe. Now, go back to the car and I'll take care of this."

Seemingly under a hypnotic trance, Melanie followed Jamie's command and ambled back to the car. Nick screamed out to her, but she was lost to him.

"You can't keep protecting her, Jamie," Nick said as Jamie bent toward him.

"I know," Jamie said with genuine regret, "but I can this time."

It was the last thing Nick heard as Jamie lifted him over the pier railing and rolled him into the bay.

JOAN JOHNSTON

In the hands of Joan Johnston, the human heart becomes a catalyst for suspense. With more than forty novels and ten million copies of her books in print worldwide, she is a proven master of the craft who knows how to complicate the tensions behind everyday relationships. If there's a character's heart to be broken, Joan will snap it in two and decide later if it should be allowed to heal.

In "Watch Out for My Girl," Nash Benedict finds himself turning Benedict Arnold after promising to look after his brother's girl while he serves in Iraq. An accidental crush becomes an inappropriate affair of the heart. And *that* leads the characters headlong into a meeting with murder.

WATCH OUT FOR MY GIRL

"I had a helluva time getting your number, Benedict. I called because Morgan Hunter is missing."

Nash Benedict heard the irritation in the voice of Morgan's boss, Captain Hart, Commander of Fire Station 7 in Chevy Chase, Maryland. He made no apology. He was hard to reach for good reason. A picture of Morgan's anguished face the last time he'd seen her flashed across his mind. His voice was unexpectedly thick with emotion as he confirmed, "Morgan's missing?"

"She didn't show up this morning at seven for her twenty-four-hour shift and didn't call to say she wouldn't be showing up. She's never missed a day of work in five years. Never even been late. You can see why I'd be concerned."

Nash glanced at his watch. 6:00 p.m. "She's been missing since seven this morning and you're just now calling me?"

"I'd have called you sooner, but nobody knew how to reach you," the captain retorted.

Someday soon, Morgan Hunter would be his sister-in-law. She was dating his younger brother, Carter, who'd left six months ago for a one-year tour of duty in Iraq.

"Watch out for my girl, Nash. Don't let anything happen to her while I'm serving my country overseas."

Nash had known what Carter really meant was *Don't let some son of a bitch move in on Morgan while I'm serving my country overseas.* Carter had never imagined that something sinister might threaten his girl. Or that the something sinister might be his elder brother.

Nash felt the blood pound in his temples. Carter had asked only one favor. And Nash had failed to deliver. Completely.

He'd done his best over the past six months, while Carter was dismantling IEDs—improvised explosive devices—in Iraq, to keep an eye on Carter's girl. In between covert missions for the U.S. president, Nash had gone sailing with Morgan on Chesapeake Bay, laughed with her at a revival of *A Funny Thing Happened on the Way to the Forum* at the Kennedy Center and picked crabs with her at the Crab Shack in Baltimore.

Nash hadn't expected to fall in love with his brother's girl any more than he'd expected her to disappear.

But he was in love with Morgan Hunter. And no one had seen hide nor hair of the woman for the past eighteen hours.

Nash felt a wave of guilt wash over him. This was his

fault. Morgan had run from him. Because of what he'd done last night on her front doorstep.

He hadn't meant to kiss her. They'd been convulsed with laughter, leaning helplessly on each other. She'd turned her face up to his, sharing the hilarious moment. On impulse he'd lowered his head, and his mouth had found hers. For a moment, she'd responded. Hungrily.

Then she'd gasped and backed up a step. And stared at him in the harsh porch light with wide, wounded brown eyes. Asking him without words how he could betray his brother. How he could betray her trust.

Nash didn't want Morgan to be the victim of some accident, but he grasped at that possibility as something besides his behavior that might have caused her absence from work. "You've checked with the area hospitals?" he asked the commander.

"I called the hospitals, I checked with her father in Bethesda, I've left messages on her cell—which have gone straight to voice mail. I even sent another firefighter to her apartment in Avendale," Captain Hart said.

"The front door was unlocked, but the place was pristine, no signs of disturbance. Her purse was there with her wallet inside. But her keys and her cell phone and her Jeep were missing."

"Are you telling me no one has any idea where she might have gone?" Nash asked the station commander.

"I figured you would know, Benedict. You're the one

she's been spending all her free time with." Captain Hart made it an accusation.

"I don't have a clue where she is," Nash snapped. "She was fine when I left her about ten last night." Except, perhaps, for feeling as guilty then about what had happened between them as Nash did now.

"I can't believe you kissed me! What were you thinking? I'm going to marry your brother when he comes home. I love him." She'd swiped the back of her hand across her mouth as though to wipe away his kiss, staring at him above that erasing hand through wary, watery eyes.

"I miss Carter," she'd said quietly, using his brother's name to stab him in the heart. "I think it would be better if we don't see each other anymore," she'd added, twisting the knife.

Nash shuddered at the memory.

"One of my best firefighters has disappeared," the captain said. "If you know anything—"

"I don't!" Nash could hear the affection and agony in the commander's voice. He knew exactly how the man felt.

"I'll be calling the local precinct to file a missing persons report when enough time has passed. I don't like the looks of this, Benedict. I don't like it at all."

Nash closed his cell phone and slipped it back into the pocket of his cammies. He was scheduled to leave for El Salvador with his team on a covert presidential mission at midnight.

Which gave him just six hours to find his brother's girl.

And make amends. Assuming she would let him apologize. Assuming that the reason she'd disappeared was nothing more sinister than an unwanted kiss.

Nash felt the hairs rise on the back of his neck as he thought of what else might have happened to Morgan Hunter.

What if Juan Espinoza, the drug lord whose coca crop Nash had ruined the last time he was in Colombia, had figured out the identity of his nemesis, "The Ghost," and made good on his threat.

"I'll find you, El Fantasma. *Then I'll find what you love most. And I'll destroy it."*

Nash huffed out a breath. He hadn't feared the threat because he'd been sure his cover was unassailable. No one except his elite team knew that Nash Benedict, son of presidential advisor Foster Benedict, was the scourge of the South American drug trade. And of Montana militiamen. And Basque separatists. And Somalian war lords.

What if one of his many foes had found him out? And come seeking vengeance—through the woman he loved. Maybe his kiss had nothing to do with Morgan's disappearance.

Nash felt adrenaline spill into his veins. Felt his muscles cord with tension and his neck hairs hackle, a feral beast readying for battle.

But he was also a rational man, and his thoughts held him in place. If Morgan had been kidnapped, why hadn't he received a ransom note? Or a vindictive message telling him that what he loved most was lost forever?

Maybe the note is on the way.

That thought sent a chill rattling down his spine.

And maybe you're freaking out over nothing. Maybe Morgan took off for a while to think.

And missed work? Without calling her boss?

Morgan Hunter was the strongest, most confident, most "together" woman he knew, which was a great part of his attraction to her. She was a firefighter who often dealt with life-and-death emergencies. Would a woman with her self-confidence, her physical and emotional strength, fall apart from a single kiss, for which the perpetrator had been well-chastised on the spot?

He had to find Morgan and bring her home safe. That was the least he could do after kissing his brother's girl.

Morgan Hunter couldn't believe the predicament in which she found herself. She'd felt confused and upset when she'd grabbed her keys an hour after Nash Benedict had kissed her and gone for a drive to think.

She hadn't planned to be gone long. She'd left the radio off in her Jeep, because she didn't want to be distracted or soothed. She wanted to examine her feelings with brutal honesty. Because she had strong feelings for Nash Benedict that conflicted with her love for his brother.

She'd left home without thinking which direction she was going. When she finally noticed her surroundings an hour later, she was driving along a winding, deserted rock-and-gravel road. Almost at the same instant a deer appeared in her headlights.

The deer froze. And so did she.

At least, for that part of a second that would have allowed her to brake before she hit the animal. Or make a wiser choice than the one she made.

Morgan had seen enough accident victims as a fire-fighter to know that hitting anything head-on, even if she was only going forty-five, was a bad move. So she jerked the wheel to miss the deer, then jerked it again to miss the gnarled trunk of an ancient black walnut—and flipped her Jeep.

It rolled three times before it came to an abrupt and jarring halt right-side-up in the embrace of a copse of spruce. Sometime during one of those rolls, the driver's side air bag had deployed. It was already deflating, but Morgan smelled the acrid scent of the cartridge that had exploded to fill it with air, and watched wide-eyed as a stream of white smoke rose behind the steering wheel.

It had all happened so fast!

Morgan couldn't believe she was alive. And apparently unhurt. She gasped with relief and felt a sharp pain in her chest. Not entirely unhurt. She had either badly bruised or broken a rib. She reached down with a trembling hand to fumble at the seat belt release.

She felt tremendously relieved when she heard a click and the seat belt let go. With the constricting pressure gone from her chest, she took another deep breath.

"Ow," she croaked. Could that excruciating pain be the result of a rib that was simply bruised? She would have to be very careful. If she put a broken rib through her lung out here in the middle of nowhere, it was goodbye, so long, adios, baby.

She recognized the swelling along the back of her neck as a whiplash injury. Warm blood dripped from her chin, and she realized she must have bitten her cheek or her lip.

Morgan was afraid to move. Afraid to discover another injury. Most of the full moon's light was blocked by trees that had only half shed their autumn leaves. She reached around the deflated air bag, searching for the keys, which she found in the ignition. She tasted blood as she caught her lower lip in her teeth for luck—and turned the key.

The car was dead.

"Bad words. Bad words. Bad words," she muttered.

There was no sign of civilization from where she was sitting. Thank God she'd brought her cell phone with her. She'd almost left it at home, because she was afraid Nash would call, and she didn't want to speak to him until she'd sorted out what she was going to say. She certainly didn't want to talk to him now. Not after doing something so stupid. Better to call 911.

Morgan reached—carefully—into the shallow pocket of her black leather jacket.

And found it empty.

"Bad, bad words."

She reached up gingerly to turn on the interior light to search for where her phone might have landed. Which was when she realized the windows on the passenger's side of the car were shattered. Had her cell phone gone out one of those broken windows?

She felt a flash of panic and shoved it down. She'd recently heard a story about a woman who'd lost control of her car on Route 40 and hit a tree. She'd been found—ten days later—partially consumed by wild animals and riddled with insects.

"That's not me," she said out loud.

She tried to turn her head to look in the backseat, but it hurt too much. She shoved at the driver's side door and it screeched open. She eased herself sideways, groaning when she realized that one of her ankles was swollen the size of a grapefruit.

"Great. That's just great."

Her Jeep footwell was high enough off that ground that she would have a drop when she got out of the car. She braced herself with her hands, then scooted off the seat and landed on her uninjured foot.

Even that little bit of jarring hurt both her chest and her ankle. She hissed in a breath and held it as she put pressure on her injured foot.

"Ow," she said again. "Oh, ow."

She closed her eyes for a moment, relieved that her ankle was only sprained. Painful, but not impossible to walk on. The back passenger door was crushed and wouldn't budge. She limped to the hatch and opened it and crawled up inside on hands and knees, leaning over the backseat to search for her phone.

She was appalled at how weak she felt. Shock, she realized. Maybe she was even bleeding internally, if that rib was broken and tearing into her flesh.

She knew too much about internal bleeding. Too much about broken ribs stabbing into lungs. Too much about shock killing you as fast—or even faster—than your actual injuries.

She couldn't find her phone. She consoled herself with the thought that, even if she found it, there might not be any reception out here. If someone picked her up on the road, she wouldn't need her cell phone. And if no one picked her up tonight, she could always hobble back here and hunt for her phone in the daylight.

She suddenly realized how cold it was. Cold enough to see her breath. Cold enough to make her shiver in the light leather jacket she'd grabbed on her way out the door.

Morgan found a dogwood limb she could use for a make-shift cane and followed the trail of destruction caused by her Jeep back to the road. Her flourescent watch showed it was six minutes past midnight. What were the chances someone would be coming along this two-lane, rock-and-gravel road at this hour?

Morgan stood at the edge of the road and looked in both directions. She wasn't even sure which way led to the closet place where help could be found. She hadn't walked ten steps before—to her amazement and delight—she saw a pair of headlights in the distance.

Almost sagging with relief, she watched the car make its

slow, winding way toward her. To her surprise, the car stopped fifty yards downhill from her. She started to yell at the driver as he stepped out of the car into the bright moonlight. For some reason her breath caught in her throat and held her silent.

Why is he stopping there?

As she watched, he slid a small, slender body out of the backseat and hefted it over his shoulder. A very long striped, light-and-dark scarf was draped around his neck. The woman's long blond hair hung almost to his butt, nearly even with the length of his scarf.

Morgan instinctively stepped back into the shadows a moment before the stranger looked in her direction. Her heart was racketing in her chest, and she held her hands over her mouth to keep him from seeing her breath in the cold air.

She stared hard at the license plate of the car, so she could identify this probable killer to the police. But it was too far away to make out the numbers. She had no idea of the make or model. To her, it was simply a dark-colored, four-door car.

The man disappeared into the undergrowth at the side of the road. He came back empty-handed five minutes later, got into his car and drove away.

Morgan realized what a narrow escape she'd had. What if she'd shouted out to the man? What if she'd become his next victim? No one—not Nash, not Carter—would have known what had become of her. She chastised herself for naming Nash first.

You've been spending time with Nash. That's all. You miss Carter. You love Carter. In six months you will marry Carter.

If she survived the night.

When the car disappeared from sight, she struggled back onto the road and began hobbling in the opposite direction the killer had taken. Even with her makeshift cane, her ankle hurt. Her chest hurt. And she was very, very cold.

Morgan saw the headlights appear over her shoulder before she heard the car wheels on the stone-and-gravel road. She turned and saw a dark-colored car. For an instant, she was afraid it was the killer. She glanced at her watch. Ten minutes had passed.

Surely this was someone else. Just in case, she would stay closer to the forest than the road. If the driver was wearing that distinctive scarf, she'd fade into the forest and hide.

She cried out in agony when she raised her arm to flag down the dark-colored car. She saw it had four doors and felt a shiver run down her spine.

When the car stopped, the power window slid down on the passenger's side. Morgan held a hand to her aching chest as she leaned to peer inside. And nearly cried out with relief. The driver was a woman. There was no sign of a scarf, dark-and-light-striped or any other color.

"You need a ride?" the woman asked.

"Yes. Thank you," Morgan said as she opened the door and slid into the amazing warmth of the car. "I nearly hit a deer. I ended up driving off the road."

"You're bleeding."

Morgan touched her chin where the blood had dried. "I think I bit my lip when my car flipped."

"You're lucky to be alive."

"Don't I know it! I was starting to think I'd have to walk home. This road doesn't seem to get much traffic."

"No, it doesn't," the woman said.

As Morgan pulled the door closed and reached carefully for the seat beat, she saw the fringe of a navy-and-white-striped scarf on the floor of the backseat. And hissed in a tortured, terrified breath.

"I didn't see your car," the woman said as she put her car in gear and continued in the direction she'd been driving.

Morgan hesitated, then said, "It's back a ways, off in the bushes."

"My husband just got home from work," the woman said. "I asked him to pick me up some cigarettes on his way home, but he forgot—lucky for you."

Morgan was very much afraid that she was riding in a murderer's car—with his wife. Did the woman know what her husband had done? Was she an accomplice? Morgan realized she might have made a mistake getting into the car. "Do you have a cell phone I could use?"

"Sorry," the woman said, shaking her head. "There's a pay phone at the convenience store where we're headed."

The woman's cell phone rang.

Morgan's neck hurt when she jerked it toward the woman, who reached into the pocket of her fur-trimmed coat and retrieved a cell phone, flipped it open and said,

"You were right. There was someone on the road. Yeah, she's in the car with me now."

Morgan didn't think, she simply grabbed the wheel and yanked it hard. And found herself headed for another large tree trunk.

"Let go of the wheel!" the woman cried.

Morgan heard the shriek of tearing metal. And a woman's scream.

The police would eventually have checked out the GPS on Morgan's cell phone, but Nash was able to access the information immediately. Thank God she'd left it on. If she was still in possession of her phone, she was about an hour north of Chevy Chase, somewhere along Route 40 northwest of Frederick, Maryland.

Nash made good time on I-270 north and merged onto US-40. The coordinates he'd put into his GPS sent him to Hamburg Road. The sun had disappeared behind the mountains and the sudden chill had created patches of fog, making visibility iffy.

He stopped at a convenience store before he headed up the mountain and showed a picture of Morgan and described her vehicle to the clerk.

The man shook his head. "I'd have remembered a woman like that."

He showed the picture to another man in the store and said, "Have you seen this woman?"

The man shook his head.

There would be no moonlight for hours, and even then, Nash wondered if it would penetrate the thick undergrowth on the sides of the road. The pavement ended and he found himself driving on a rough rock-and-gravel road. Except where humans had carved hiking trails, the mountain terrain seemed impenetrable.

What the hell had she been doing up here? It seemed impossible he could find a lone woman in this vast wilderness. Except he had precise GPS coordinates that told him where to find her cell phone.

Nash stopped when his headlights picked out the torn-up grass where Morgan's Jeep had apparently left the road. His heart was in his throat as he grabbed a flashlight and headed off into the undergrowth.

The trail of destruction left a clear path to follow. He found Morgan's cell phone near a crushed elderberry tree. He hurried forward, but when he reached her car, it was empty.

"Morgan!" he shouted, feeling frantic. "Morgan! Are you out here?"

He was greeted by an eerie silence.

He turned in a circle and saw a light down the hill in the distance, on the opposite side of the road, moving through the underbrush. That must be her! He ran back to his SUV and raced down the winding road, despite the fog that had gathered in the hollows, afraid the moving light wouldn't be visible when he got to where he'd seen it from above.

When he reached the bottom of the hill, he found a

rusted-out Chevy pickup parked where he'd seen the light. But the light he'd seen from above had disappeared.

He heard the engine ticking on the pickup, so he knew it hadn't been there long. He shined his flashlight in the front seat of the truck. When he tried the doors, they were locked. Then he checked the truck bed and saw blood. Dried blood. Had Morgan been lying in the bed of that truck sometime during the past eighteen hours?

Nash swore in frustration as he tried to find a way through the thick undergrowth on the side of the road. There was a lot of blood in the bed of that truck. Was he too late?

"Is anybody out there?" he shouted. There was no sound, not even a breath of wind to rustle the trees. He fought back his fear and shouted again, "Morgan! It's Nash. Are you out there?"

He heard branches crackling as though someone was moving through the underbrush. He shined his flashlight toward the sound but couldn't see much beyond the first colorful layer of bushes. As he was lowering the light, he caught sight of a broken branch. More than a few broken branches. And realized the swath of destruction was wide enough to have been made by a vehicle.

Another accident? He was confused for a moment, but he knew from the light he'd seen—and the truck on the side of the road—that someone was here. He followed the trail, shouting as he ran, "Morgan, I'm coming. Hold on, baby, I'm coming!"

If he'd been in another line of work, Nash would have died a moment later. Some instinct caused him to duck as he felt a rush of air near his ear, and the thick branch that would have brained him made contact with his right shoulder instead, causing him to drop his flashlight. He grunted in pain and turned to confront his attacker.

The man was swinging the branch in the opposite direction when Nash stepped under it and hit him in the solar plexus, doubling him over. Nash followed with an uppercut that rocked the man's head back. Arms flailing, his attacker fell over backward. Nash followed him, grabbing two handfuls of the man's corduroy jacket and dragging him upright to hit him again.

The heavyset man put his hands up and cried, "Stop! Stop!"

Nash frisked him one-handed, then dropped him on the ground and retrieved his flashlight. He shined it on the man's face and realized he'd seen him before. At the convenience store.

"What are you doing out here?" he asked.

"My wife is missing. She went out last night to get some cigarettes and never came back. We had an argument, so I thought maybe she spent the night with her mother. When she never showed up this morning, I thought maybe she had an accident. I've been looking for her along this road most of the day."

"Why did you attack me?"

"I was afraid. People are always dumping stuff up here

at night. That's illegal, you know. So I thought maybe…" His voice trailed off and he shrugged sheepishly.

"There's dried blood in the back of your pickup."

"Oh. That's nothing."

"Nothing?" Nash shot back.

"I found a deer on the side of the road—hit by a car, I guess. I put it in my truck, figuring I'd butcher it. But it wasn't dead and it woke up and jumped out."

Animal blood. Nash shook his head in disgust. He turned and followed the trail of broken branches and car wreckage to a dark-colored Toyota. It had run head-on into a sycamore.

His heart began thudding hard when he spied the blood-stained windshield on the driver's side. His flashlight reflected something on the passenger's window. A bloody handprint.

Then he saw the long-legged female body lying on the leaf-strewn ground. The head and shoulders were covered with a black leather jacket. He recognized the distinctive silver buttons.

The jacket belonged to Morgan.

He gave a cry of anguish as he ran forward and dropped to his knees beside the body. He gently eased the jacket away, even though the woman was apparently dead. And swallowed the sob that erupted as he realized…*it isn't Morgan!*

This must be his attacker's wife. But who had covered her dead face with Morgan's jacket? And where was Morgan?

"Nash."

His name came as a whisper on the wind. He felt his heart surge with joy as he called into the darkness, "Morgan! Where are you!"

Equally quiet, a ghostly warning, "Look out!"

Nash whirled and rose in one motion and found himself facing a Colt .45 automatic.

"Where the hell is she?" the stranger said in a harsh voice. "That bitch killed my wife!"

"What's your connection to the woman who owns that leather jacket?" Nash asked.

The stranger sneered. "She saw me dump a body. Couldn't leave her out here after that. Sent my wife to pick her up. And that bitch crashed my car."

Nash glanced at the car and realized how desperate Morgan must have been. And how brave. And how precious she was to him.

"She killed my wife!" the stranger ranted.

Nash glanced at the dead body. He knew Morgan must have done everything in her power to save the woman. It was what she did.

"When I'm done with you, I'll find her, and she'll pay." The stranger was distracted by a crash in the underbrush.

The instant he turned his head, Nash leapt. He was nearly deafened by the gunshot, but the bullet shot past his ear into the night. He made short work of disarming the stranger. This time he used the man's own weapon to knock him out.

When the short life-and-death struggle was over, Nash shoved himself onto his feet and said in a calm, quiet voice, "Where are you, Morgan?"

A faint voice said, "I'm here."

He followed Morgan's voice to a spot in the bushes behind the sycamore tree. She was sitting up with her back braced against a red maple. He kept his flashlight lowered, so it wouldn't hit her in the eyes. But he couldn't help noticing her blood-soaked shirt. And her bloody, lacerated face.

His knees surprised him by buckling, and he dropped onto the leaves beside her. "What kind of shape are you in?" He was afraid to touch her. She was covered in blood.

"Cracked rib, I think. Sprained—maybe fractured—ankle. Whiplash. Multiple cuts on my face and arms. Broken finger."

"That's all?"

"That's enough!" she said with asperity. "You took long enough getting here."

"I was waiting for your call."

She avoided his gaze and said matter-of-factly, "I lost my phone. And the dead woman's phone got broken in a million little bits in the crash. I was afraid to go out on the road, because I knew that killer would come hunting his wife. So I've been hiding." She paused, met his gaze and said, "Waiting for you to find me."

Nash brushed the knuckles of his hand across her blood-crusted cheek. "When I saw that body, I thought you were dead."

"When I saw that tree coming at me—"

"I'm sorry, Morgan."

"I know. So am I."

"I'm leaving the country in a few hours. If you need me—for anything—leave a message on my phone and—"

She moaned as she lifted her arm to brush her scraped knuckles across his cheek. Her eyes brimmed with tears as she said, "Goodbye, Nash."

He didn't pretend to misunderstand what she was saying. He couldn't fight for her. Not when she loved his brother. He had to let her go.

"So, do I call an ambulance?" he said at last. "Or can I just pick you up and drive you to the nearest hospital?"

She managed a tenuous smile. "Call the cops to come get that murdering son of a bitch. Then take me to the nearest hospital."

JON LAND

"Killing Time" has all the earmarks of international best-selling author Jon Land. A tense situation in which time is your enemy. Impossible odds. And a villain you're not likely to ever forget, even if he happens to be on your side.

The main character in "Killing Time," Fallon, is a sociopath. He's a professional killer who—after a kill goes horribly wrong—hides out by murdering and impersonating an English teacher at Hampton Lake Middle School. Jon got the idea for this story after the tragic events that happened in Chechnya when terrorists seized a school—killing and wounding hundreds of students. It fascinated him to think about what would have happened if the terrorists had come across someone as demented and violent as they were. "Killing Time" is the answer to that question. And it's not pretty.

KILLING TIME

"We're glad to have you aboard, Mr. Beechum," said Roger Meeks, principal of Hampton Lake Middle School, rising from behind his desk. "I think you're going to be most happy here."

Fallon thought about how he'd killed the last man he shook hands with and released the principal's flaccid grip quickly. That man's name was Beechum and he'd had the misfortune to pick up a sodden, weary Fallon hitchhiking on the side of a lonely interstate. Poor Beechum also had the misfortune of being in the process of relocating to a new state to take a new job and for having a passing resemblance to Fallon. Passing in that they both had dark hair and features, close enough to allow Fallon to effortlessly fool principal Meeks with only minor modifications to his own appearance.

"Your résumé is quite impressive," Meeks continued,

retaking his seat and looking up from the pages before him. Their eyes met and for just a moment Fallon thought the principal was studying him, perhaps noticing the anomalies with the face of the now-dead teacher clipped to the top sheet. But then he smiled. "I think you're going to be very happy at Hampton Lake Middle School. Let's show you the building."

The "tour," as Meeks called it, was important to Fallon. Though he smiled through its course, careful to ask all the right questions, he was actually cataloguing various routes of escape and hiding. That his former employers were after him was not in doubt at all, any more than the fact they would eventually be successful. Because Fallon had failed them. Worse, Fallon had misbehaved by executing those sent to make him pay for his failure.

His former employers would have been wise to let him go and be done with it. But they couldn't take the chance Fallon would come after them. Here he became a victim of his own well-deserved reputation. His background in Special Forces had taught him to not just accept killing, but embrace it as a skill to be mastered like any other: with practice. The means—knife, gun, bare hand, explosives—mattered not at all, only the result. And with Fallon the result was always the same.

Except once. And now because of that he was on the run. Killing time in the guise of a middle-school English teacher. Or Language Arts, as they called it these days.

Meeks continued the tour of Hampton Lake Middle School in perfunctory fashion, Fallon nodding and smiling at all the appropriate times. The building was T-shaped with two long hallways separated by an enclosed courtyard adjoining a perpendicular two-story wing at the building's front end located farthest from the road. A gym and presentation room were located in the back end, the cafeteria in the front. Fallon noted a drop ceiling heavy enough to support a man's weight, accessing a crawl space that ran the length of the building on both sides. The location of the subbasement, containing the electrical and heating elements, was more difficult to pin down at this point.

Normally, Fallon would look for places to stash weapons, as well. Here he didn't consider that to be a factor. If he was found, escape would be the thing, not confrontation.

"Now," Meeks said, the cursory tour over, "let's show you your classroom."

Eighth-grade honors English, Language Arts, was just finishing an abridged, heavily censored version of a book called *Catch-22*. Fallon rented the movie that night and didn't really get most of it, except the title concept of a wartime pilot in search of a loophole to be deemed too crazy to fly. Fallon thought parts were supposed to be funny, but didn't laugh and was glad when it was time for the class to move on to *Frankenstein*. Fallon hadn't read the book, either, but he'd seen the movie, the old one with Boris Karloff, and figured that was close enough.

His classroom overlooked the front of the building, including an oval-shaped drive that enclosed a parking lot used by teachers, as well as visitors. Fallon couldn't see the main entrance but had a clear view of any vehicle approaching it, which was the next best thing.

"So who do we think is the villain in the story?" Fallon asked his class.

His remark was greeted by shrugs and quick glances cast amidst his young charges. Having no real concept of how to teach exactly, he'd constructed his classes around discussion. Fortunately, he'd come at a time of the semester devoted to literature and didn't expect to still be around for the next unit. More than a month in any one setting would be tempting fate indeed.

"The villain?" Fallon prompted, leaning back so he was halfway sitting on the lip of his desk.

"Frankenstein," a boy named Trent said from the rear. Trent had floppy hair and the first signs of acne.

Fallon liked him because he recognized a worn patch in the rear pocket of his jeans as the outline of a switchblade. Fallon looked into Trent's eyes and saw emotionless, stone-cold resignation. A boy after his own heart.

"Not the monster," Trent continued, without further prompt. "The doctor."

"Why?" Fallon asked him.

"'Cause he fucked with nature."

The moment froze, everyone staring at Fallon in shock. Trent resumed again, saving him the bother of coming up with an appropriate response.

"So the monster kills all these people, terrorizes the village, scares the crap out of people. But it's not his fault, not really."

"So he's not responsible for his own actions?" Fallon challenged.

"Poor bastard doesn't even know what he's doing. Blame Frankenstein for bringing him to life."

"Like parents," a frizzy-haired girl named Chelsea chimed in between crackling chomps on a wad of gum, sending a brief laugh rippling through the classroom.

"Maybe that's Shelley's point," someone else said.

"So the monster's not evil," Fallon raised.

"No," came the multiple response.

"But he's not good, either."

"No."

"So what is he?"

"The same as everybody else," Trent said, booted feet propped up on the desk before him.

Five weeks earlier Fallon had received his next job through the usual means. A text message sent to his cell phone dispatched him to a public e-mail Web site. He logged in at the nearest FedEx-Kinkos and entered the coded details into his PDA. Fallon never knew the reason for his targets' selection. He only needed to know who and where; sometimes how and when. His log-on automatically triggered the deposit of half his fee into a previously designated offshore bank account.

Setting up a kill could take considerable time, up to several weeks, a period during which Fallon became intimately acquainted with the habits of his targets without immersing himself into the minutia of their lives. The last job was different because it specified the target's entire family be included. Someone out to set an example, obviously, make a point.

Discussion here was not an option. Even if Fallon had wanted, he couldn't have asked for confirmation and clarification. And if the fact that the target's family consisted of a wife and three young children bothered Fallon, there was no way to contact his employer to change his mind. The URL from which his assignment had been sent was a dummy site automatically deactivated as soon as Fallon logged off. Declining a job was never an option, once the mechanical triggering apparatus made Fallon an even richer man. Catch-23.

Wiring the target's house with explosives was easy enough, doing it in a way that would make it look like a tragic accident only slightly harder. The only drawback: he'd have to trigger the blast manually himself. Not an attractive prospect, considering he much preferred being somewhere else far away when the explosion ripped lumber and concrete, flesh and blood, apart.

Fallon was not a man prone to question or marred by

pangs of conscience. And the early stages of the job progressed without being terribly struck by either. A man like Fallon could not view human beings with any higher regard than, say, crash-test dummies or department-store mannequins. They were his means to an end, though with ample funds for a secure retirement in place he was hard-pressed to say exactly what those ends were. Except he couldn't retire; he enjoyed his work too much. Catch-24.

And his latest assignment should've have gone down like all the others, all in place and on schedule. Fallon following his instructions to the letter to make sure all family members were inside before triggering the blast.

Detonators were a thing of the past mostly, cell phones the thing these days. Simple matter of wiring the trigger chip with a number and then dialing it at the appropriate time. There'd be a brief delay, several seconds or more, but that wasn't a problem in this case.

Fallon took his throwaway cell phone from his pocket and dialed. Let it ring once and then settled back to wait from his car parked safely down the street, counting the seconds out in his head.

One…two…three…

By *five,* Fallon began to feel edgy, and at *ten* he redialed, let it ring twice this time. Counted the seconds again.

Same result. Nothing.

Setbacks were nothing new to Fallon; failure something else again. There was no time to consider what had gone wrong. Better to focus on damage control, what to do from here. Fallon had weapons, a bounty of them. But murdering an entire family in the suburbs with guns and knives without a clear plan of access and approach would be a desperate move not befitting a professional of his level. Worse, he'd be acting rashly with the eventual outcome dictated by fortune instead of forethought. Better to come back, rethink the next step tomorrow.

Except tomorrow turned out worse.

The next book on the honors English list was called *Johnny Got His Gun*. Fallon couldn't find a movie version, but the book was short and supposedly about war, so he decided to read it.

The book *was* short. And Fallon understood nary a word, much less what the book was supposed to be about. Antiwar, that much was clear, if nothing else. So he decided to focus the class's discussion on war itself, something he knew plenty about.

But Mr. Beechum, of course, didn't, which meant Fallon couldn't appear to, either. He listened to the surprisingly intelligent, unsettling comments made by his students. Unsettling because it made him realize how much he missed that part of his life for its simplicity and clarity. The ability to kill for a cause with impunity. Of course, the cause meant little to Fallon; it was the impunity he embraced with a fervor and passion unknown in any previous segment of his life.

An unpleasant end to his military career was as expected

as it was inevitable. Fortunately, there were plenty of private firms willing to pay far more while letting him practice his same skills. That, too, ended badly, in an embarrassing scandal for the company and yet another inglorious dismissal for Fallon. But there was no shortage of work for a man with Fallon's skills, and he'd been stateside barely a week when a similarly ex-member of the same private firm came calling with an offer to join a network of professionals whose work was appreciated instead of vilified. Fallon didn't bother himself with delusions of morality, of right and wrong. He did what he did, and he liked it. Simple as that.

The class agreed with the book's antiwar stance. Fallon wished he'd been able to tell them the true side of things. About the various pleasures a man could derive from watching a face explode to a bullet or the guttural gasps a victim makes when a knife digs deep and tears. He wished he could explain that violence was something to neither be shunned nor embraced. It simply was.

Just like him.

To make his point, Fallon decided to stray from the lesson plan and introduce the only story he actually remembered reading as a boy. Read so much the pages actually disintegrated, the words disappearing until there were no sentences left and Fallon reluctantly discarded the handout. He hadn't thought of that story in a very long time until now, glad to find a copy ripe for photocopying in the school library.

"'The Most Dangerous Game,'" the librarian said, reading over Fallon's shoulder as collated copies spit out from the machine's feeder. "A true classic. But a bit violent, don't you think?"

When Fallon returned the following morning, the target family was gone, whisked away in the dawn hours by shadowy men in black SUVs, if the neighbors were to be believed. FBI or federal marshals, no doubt, extricating Fallon's targets into witness protection

Fallon had never failed before, but there were percentages involved in everything and here the odds had finally caught up with him. He found himself obsessing over every move he had made to retrace where he'd gone wrong. The wiring, perhaps. Maybe a bad chip. A reception or transmission problem, even.

That was why Fallon was awake in his motel room when they came. Four of them, all well-armed and well-skilled enough to know not to drive their car too close to his room in the motor court. But they'd left their headlights on a second too long, enough to alert Fallon that someone was coming.

He gauged the distance suggested by the strength of the headlights and counted the seconds again.

One...two...three...

The door blew inward at *six,* Fallon unleashing a fusillade that was every bit the equal of his four would-be killers. So much passed through his mind as the bullets chewed up the walls around him and the smell of blood mixed with sulfur and cordite. The roar from the three guns he managed to reach drowned out the screams mostly, and Fallon was screeching away from the scene before another light snapped on in any of the nearby rooms.

The reality of the moment struck him, and fast. The fact that his employers wouldn't stop with these four men, especially since Fallon had so effortlessly executed them, was no less a reality than the fact that his time as a contractor was effectively over. There was no redemption or second chances. He had gone from the very best at what he did to irrelevant in the seconds it had taken him to gun down four men.

Catch-25.

Fallon had effectively prepared for this moment, while never really considering it a possibility. Money would not be a problem; he had plenty of it stashed away. The issue was getting to it safely, making the necessary arrangements with according precautions, and such things took time. That meant disappearing without the use of any of his various identifies, all of which could be compromised now. His employers and conduits knew too much about him, his habits and patterns. Disappearing meant relying on none of them, becoming someone else entirely while laying the groundwork for his permanent departure from parts known.

There were plenty of Third World countries into which he could vanish, only to resurface as a man with a different identity boasting the kind of skills that were always in need. Fallon couldn't imagine himself wallowing away the time on a beach, no matter how beautiful or plentiful the women. His life had been defined by killing for too long to either risk or want change.

For now going off the grid meant avoiding all forms of security cameras and public transportation, including buses, trains and airplanes. Rental cars were out, as well, and stealing too many cars could leave the kind of pattern he needed to avoid.

That left hitchhiking. Mr. Beechum's was the fifth car in a week to chance picking him up. Fallon didn't kill the others and hadn't expected to kill Beechum until the ditzy man kept speaking enthusiastically of the new job he was headed for. That's when the plan unfolded for Fallon, and the best he was able to do for Beechum in return was kill him in quick, painless fashion.

"I love kids" was the last thing the teacher said. "Making a difference in their lives and all."

In that moment Fallon couldn't have known the kind of difference he'd end up making.

Fallon saw the two vans creep toward the school's entrance when he was in the third day of discussing "The Most Dangerous Game." They were noteworthy first for the fact they drove onto the grounds down the wrong side of the U-shaped drive fronting the building and second because the vans wore the markings of a professional cleaning service.

Such markings always allowed for unquestioned access to buildings, public and otherwise, but why would a middle school with a full janitorial staff need a professional cleaning service?

Fallon's heart began to beat faster as the vans drifted out of his line of sight. Two vans meant a dozen men or more, certainly overkill on the part of his former employers. And if they had ascertained his presence here at Hampton Lake, they'd be much better off laying an ambush instead of storming the building in full awareness of his conceivable escape.

That reality should have made him feel better.

But it didn't.

Instincts had saved his life often enough for Fallon to learn to trust them, and right now they were scratching at his spine like scalpels peeling back the flesh.

"Rainsford's my kind of guy," Trent was saying from his customary perch in the back of the room.

"Why?" Fallon managed to ask, not really paying attention. His eyes strayed out the window again, but the vans did not reappear. He moved closer to the glass, hoping to better his angle.

"Because he kicks General Zaroff's ass. And it was Zaroff's own fucking fault."

"Why?" Fallon asked, intrigued in spite of the nagging feeling that wouldn't go away.

"Because he'd been playing the game too long. Hunting men, who knows how many of them."

"So why stop?"

"Because he should've known he'd meet his match. Sooner or later. It's like, you know, inevitable."

Fallon moved away from the window, suddenly intrigued. "So why'd he keep doing it? Come on, people, put yourself in Zaroff's shoes."

"'Cause it's all he had," said a girl in the front row. "All he knew."

"What else?"

"He was good at it," someone else answered. "When you're that good, you don't think anybody'll ever beat you."

"Was Rainsford better at the game than the general?" Fallon asked his class.

"No," said Trent. "Zaroff lost 'cause he got lazy. When you get lazy, you get beat every time. But Rainsford, he was a hero."

"Why?"

"He saved lives. Of Zaroff's future victims. Not all heroes mean to be heroes, if you get my drift."

"May I have your attention please?"

The voice of Principal Meeks boomed over the school's PA system.

"All students and teachers, please report to the gymnasium immediately. That's all students and teachers, please report to the—"

The principal's voice cut off in midsentence, as if he'd accidentally hit the wrong switch. Fallon watched his students begin to rise from their desks, replaying Meeks's words in his head—not for content so much as cadence. Something all wrong about the tone and import. Fallon knew the sound of a man under duress, because he'd put countless men in just that position.

When you get lazy, you get beat every time....

"No," Fallon said before the student closest to the door could open it. "Back to your seats."

"But—"

"Back to your seats."

The edge in Fallon's voice had his students returning to their desks without further question. The hallway beyond filled with students spilling out of nearby classrooms, the heavy trampling of feet signaling the approach of those emerging from the two-story wing at the building's head.

"Mr. Beechum?"

Fallon swung toward the windows again. They only opened inward at the very top, enough to provide ventilation but not escape.

"Mr. Beechum?"

Fallon didn't answer. Mr. Beechum was gone.

"Trent," Fallon said, the persona shed, cold eyes boring down on the boy who'd been his favorite, "give me your switchblade."

"My wh—"

"Now, Trent."

The voice not raised, just measured and certain.

"It's a butterfly knife."

Trent fished the butterfly knife out of his backpack,

brought it up to Fallon and extended it toward him in a trembling hand. Fallon wished he could smile at him reassuringly, the way Mr. Beechum would.

Except Mr. Beechum was gone.

"Okay," Fallon said, "everyone line up starting on this wall and wrapping around to the back of the room. Shoulder to shoulder. Very close. Out of sight from the door."

"Why?" a girl asked, moving to obey.

Fallon didn't answer. Beyond his classroom, the thick flow of students and their teacher escorts continued down the corridor, oblivious to whatever might be transpiring. Fallon hoped he was wrong, but knew he wasn't. He had spent his life as Zaroff, the odds stacked heavily in his favor. But now suddenly he found himself as Rainsford.

When you're that good, you don't think anybody'll ever beat you.

Well, whoever had come in those vans was in for a big surprise, weren't they?

The moments passed in silence broken only by the loud breathing of his students. Or maybe it wasn't loud. Maybe Fallon just heard it that way.

The hallway emptied, a few stragglers passing the windowed door and then no one. A pause, then fresh footsteps crackling atop tile alone followed by the creaking echo of doors being thrust open, each growing louder.

Fallon snapped the butterfly knife's blade into position.

A boy whimpered. Two girls began to sob, then a third.

Fallon pressed a single finger against his lips, signaling them to be quiet, ducked back so he was out of sight from the doorway.

The heavy footsteps drew closer. The knob rattled, door easing inward.

A student gasped.

A man lurched past Fallon, never seeing him. Fallon noted the high-end submachine gun he was steadying with a second hand in the last moment before he pounced. Arm wrapped around the man's neck to silence him as he drew Trent's butterfly knife on a sharp upward angle required to slice through bone and gristle, digging into the lungs and shredding them.

The man gurgled and rasped, fighting against Fallon as bloody froth poured from his mouth. Fallon snapped his neck for good measure, studying his face as he dragged him across the room before the horrified stares of his students.

The man was Arab; Fallon could tell that from sight, as well as smell. Smells were important to him. You spend enough time all over the world, in the various cesspits of humanity, and you begin to know men by their smells as much as anything. An Arab, all right, and in that moment Fallon realized everything he had been dispatched to Iraq to prevent had finally come to pass. The foreign stink come home.

Fallon was free to escape now. Two vans meant a dozen men at least, the other eleven likely scattered throughout the building. He could flee the building without so much as killing another, or, perhaps, just one. Maybe use one of their vans as his escape vehicle and leave them to whatever debacle they intended to perpetrate on the school and the world. It wasn't his world anyway, not anymore.

Or was it?

He glanced at his students, bunched tighter together now, hugging each other as they stared at him in terror the way they would a monster, like the one Frankenstein had created. Or maybe General Zaroff, mad for the hunt.

Johnny got his gun, all right.

Flee and these students, *his* students, would inevitably end up in the gym with the others. Perhaps to be made an example of for disobeying. Terrorists like these were not very original, and that awareness sparked a memory in Fallon's head of Chechnyan terrorists taking a school over in that particular godforsaken hostage situation. The students brought to the gymnasium, just like here. And then the gym was blown up while the whole world watched.

No, not very original, but effective all the same.

Fallon tried to imagine how he'd do it, how many men in the gym versus how many patrolling and securing the building. He settled on four in the gym, eight for the building.

Seven now.

Fallon stooped and began working the dead man's jacket free.

"I need you all to stay here," Fallon told his students. "Don't make a sound and wait for me to come back for you."

They looked at him as the stranger he had become even before he'd donned the terrorist's jacket and bandana, squeezed his feet into the dead man's work boots and slung his submachine gun from his shoulder. Enough to pass for the dead man from a reasonable distance, which was the best he could hope for. The 9/11 hijackers had never all met each other, but this kind of operation was different, requiring practice and synchronization. They would know the building as well as he did; every crawl space, every nook, every cranny. The difference, of course, was he knew the terrorists were here while they had no idea he was.

Wait for me to come back for you....

Why had he said that? Fallon wondered, once he was in the hallway, careful to leave the door open as all the others on the hallway were. It would be so easy for him to flee the building now before the inevitable appearance of the authorities on the scene. That was no longer an option for him, the challenge, the game, before him much too great to consider walking away from.

But was he Zaroff or was he Rainsford?

The building was eerily quiet, save for the din coming from the gymnasium area, where nearly 700 students were being crammed in even now. Fallon tried to remember all the details of the Chechnyan school seizing. Those terrorists had waited for the authorities to arrive, waited for them to mount their ill-fated raid, before triggering the explosives and killing hundreds. It would be the same way here, the strategy aimed at drawing the most attention possible.

Round-the-clock coverage on the networks for days before the entire country paid witness to a mass murder in prime time.

Fallon made sure to conceal the considerable bulk of his shoulders within the terrorist's shapeless, now bloodstained, jacket. He tied the dead man's bandana low over his forehead, hoping it would conceal the differences in their faces and hair from the distance he required. He made sure the walkie-talkie, simple Radio Shack variety, was secured to his belt and started back up the corridor the way the dead terrorist would if he were retracing his steps.

At the head of the hallway, the office directly on his left and the science wing just down the hall to his right, Fallon glimpsed another of the terrorists rushing away from the main entrance with extra chains clanking. By now, all such doors would have been secured and wired with explosives, to detour both escape from within and attack from the outside. Fallon had a clear shot at the man but opted not to take it until he was sure no others were in the vicinity. Instead he made his footsteps just loud enough to be heard. Then swung about, gun leading, back to the stairwell up which number two had rushed.

"Hey," the man called to him in Arabic, *"shoo hada?"*

Fallon's response to the man asking him "What is this?" was to swing and fire. A single headshot that dropped the terrorist where he stood. He crumpled to the steps and slid halfway back down the stairs. Not Fallon's intention, but by this point instinct had taken over.

Two down.

Fallon heard footsteps converging on the stairwell from opposite directions on the second floor. He crouched over the body and angled low, submachine gun angled at the main entry doors as if to suggest that's where the deadly fire had originated. He could see the plastic explosives layered into place over the glass. Not the way he would've done it exactly, but still effective.

The footsteps grew louder, voices in Arabic shouted his way. Fallon swung when the two men were close enough to take in a single sweep. Two shots, both to the head again to be sure.

Four down.

This time his shots coincided with the rattling echo of machine-gun fire coming from the other end of the building. Screams and cries answered the barrage, greeted by a second longer one that drove the students and teachers to silence. Four to six of the remaining terrorists would be down there. Doors chained from the inside, denying him both access and the element of surprise. Without either, never mind both, the game would be over.

Fallon's Radio Shack walkie-talkie crackled. He snapped it from his belt, listened.

"Shoofi mafi? What's the matter?"

"Mafi Mushkil," Fallon replied, hoping he had chosen the right word in Arabic. "No problem."

"Dilwaati. Hurry."

Fallon clasped the walkie-talkie back on his belt and

headed down the stairs, banking left toward the school's science wing as the blare of sirens descended on Hampton Lake Middle School.

The students of his eighth-grade honors Language Arts class were arranged two-by-two, fourteen deep, with Fallon bringing up the rear. After rousing them from the classroom against the tearful protestations of many, he placed Trent at the head of the group to lead the way toward the gym.

He'd encountered another terrorist in the science wing who approached him in the half-light, noticing the ruse too late and making the mistake of trying to right his submachine gun. Fallon was close enough to use Trent's butterfly knife this time, a single swipe across the man's throat for silence and surety.

He spent just over a minute gathering up two vials of clear liquid in one of the science labs and ran into another of the terrorists, literally, at the head of the corridor. Their eyes had met; the terrorist's gaping, Fallon's steeling as his hands came up, thumbs pressing into the man's eyes to mash brain tissue and send him spasming toward death.

Six down.

Then back fast to his classroom to affect the final phase of his plan, the students suitably scared and confused. He marched them down the hall toward the gymnasium, pretending to prod with the submachine gun while concealing a capped glass vial in either hand.

A hundred feet away, a pair of terrorists guarding that

booby-trapped entry to the building spotted him coming and twisted his way, keeping tight to the wall while shouting instructions Fallon ignored. They approached on either side of his marching phalanx and as soon as they were close enough to realize something was very wrong, Fallon popped the caps off his vials and tossed the acid compound at their faces. Not directly on line, but enough splashing home to send their hands upward to comfort their ravaged eyes.

Fallon took each down with a single, quick burst, then pushed his shocked charges on faster. Through the glass doors and half-wall he glimpsed a nonstop onslaught of police vehicles and media vans, continuing with his charges toward the chained entrance to the gym.

He moved to the front of the apparent stragglers he had rounded up, pounding on the door and then swinging away with gun leading.

"Open up! Hurry!" he screamed in Arabic, desperation forced into his voice. "They're in the building!"

The chains rattled, locks and explosives being thrust aside. The double door entrance jerked open by a sweaty man who bled garlic through his pores.

Fallon started shooting, willing to sacrifice a few innocents to get the last of the job done. He felled the three terrorists converging on the door, before turning his attention on the one who had yanked it open, because his hands were too full to go fast for a weapon. That man had barely hit the floor when Fallon whirled sideways, scanning the room for motion.

He fired at whatever moved, like a cheap arcade game now, hoping no bystanders got caught in the fire but knowing he couldn't let that concern stop him. He fired his last spray upward into the sprinkler apparatus, activating a spray of water, which almost instantly doused the cavernous room and drenched its occupants.

His submachine gun clicked empty. Fallon was twisting to retrieve the sidearm of a dead terrorist when a bearded rail of a man came at him, showcasing a detonator as he blithered away in Arabic.

"Maashallah! Maashallah!"

Fallon palmed Trent's butterfly knife, locked the blade into place.

"Maashallah! Maashallah!" The man's wild hair a soaked tangle that swept over his face, seeming to merge it with his beard.

"Maashallah!"

Fallon snapped his hand outward, sending the knife whizzing through the air. It took the final terrorist in the eye, buried to the hilt in his brain. He fell to the floor. The detonator rattled across the floor.

Fourteen down, Fallon thought, realizing his initial estimate had been off as he looked up and let the cascading water wash over his face. *And not a single bystander with them.*

Fallon emerged from the boys' locker room, wearing the uniform and visor of a SWAT officer who'd gone in there to secure the site. Confusion was his ally now, confusion and chaos as the police stormed the building to find bodies everywhere and had to sort through the tales of the mysterious teacher who had killed them. They'd never believe it at first and before they did, Fallon would be gone.

In the foyer beyond the gym, he passed his eighth-grade honors Language Arts class being questioned by an expanding bevy of officers. Fallon kept his head turned low and to the side, cocking his gaze back just once when he was almost to the door, to meet Trent's.

"So if he wasn't Beechum, any of you have an idea who he was?" an official in plain clothes was asking his students.

"Rainsford," Trent said as his eyes locked and held with Fallon's through the SWAT visor. "His name was Rainsford."

RIDLEY PEARSON

Not only is bestselling author Ridley Pearson a master of forensic detail but he also plays in a rock band with other bestselling writers like Amy Tan, Mitch Albom and Stephen King. "We play music as well as Metallica writes novels," he said, so it's good news that Ridley agreed to contribute a story to this collection rather than an original song.

"Boldt's Broken Angel" opens with one of the most haunting and powerful scenes you'll ever read. The reader follows detective Lou Boldt on the trail of a serial killer who is as twisted as Ridley's brilliant plot. Fight the urge to skip ahead, because you won't want to miss a single word. This is a model thriller by a modern master, the perfect story to complete the collection.

BOLDT'S BROKEN ANGEL

Erastus Malster—they called him Rastus—hooked both feet beneath the large gray cleat on the bow of the fishing trawler *Sea Spirits* and, holding himself fast, lifted his arms straight out at his sides like Leonardo DiCaprio in *Titanic*. The salt spray peppered his wide-mouthed grin, stung his eyes and seasoned his fourteen-year-old tongue.

It was his uncle's boat, his uncle's idea to wave to his mother in the jet as it took off from SEATAC. They had no real way to track the flight, bound for Israel where she was set to join up with a two-star cruise ship tour of Israel ports and Egyptian treasures, so Rastus waved at all the planes, while his uncle drank beer and laughed from the wheelhouse. His uncle loved to laugh.

His uncle had also judged wrong. They were far too distant from the airport to catch any of the planes taking off. In fact, they could barely seen any metal in the sky. A flicker or a flash as the aluminum skin caught the retreating sun.

Rastus saw one blaze in particular as he rode the bow: a brilliant white-and-orange glint that held the intensity of a camera's flash. He pointed up to it and gasped.

"Uncle! Uncle!" he called out.

His uncle only laughed and hoisted the beer.

At first, he thought they were salmon, or seals or even Orca whales surfacing—an exciting splash a hundred yards to his left. *Port,* as his uncle called it. Why they couldn't just call it *left* Rastus wasn't sure.

The moment that first splash occurred, his uncle cranked the wheel in that direction, so severely that the cleat was not enough to hold Rastus, and he fell to his right, barely catching hold of the wire rail at the last possible second. He regained his balance, righted himself and looked back at his uncle in the wheelhouse.

The man's face had contorted into a full flood of surprise and excitement.

Rastus turned to see why: three more giant splashes. Had to be whales, the way the water shot up.

His uncle was running the boat right into the same area, having goosed the mighty engine and thrown something of a duck tail into their now violent wake. The man hoisted a pair of binoculars and surveyed the distant splashes—for now there were three more. Then five. And suddenly the water was boiling all around them—ten, twenty, fifty.

His uncle dropped the glasses, let go of the wheel and ran to the railing. He hurled vomit into the water—a man who had never been seasick in his life.

Rastus looked down into the water as a white fish, dead and floating, passed incredibly close. The boat struck the next.

It wasn't a fish at all: it was a naked woman. Big, and flabby and disgusting. Her skin around her chest and pelvis as white as bone; a patch of wet black hair where her legs met. And there, not twenty yards away, a man. Also naked. Faceup. Arms at his sides.

The sky was raining dead bodies.

A dozen a second now. Two dozen.

Rastus heard a tremendous explosion. He looked to where his uncle had been at the rail. There was nothing but a splash of red there now and a deep dent in the metal decking.

"Uncle!" Rastus screamed. "Uncle?"

Six more bodies streamed by the boat, now running out of control.

All naked. Every face locked—*or were they frozen?*—in an unforgiving expression of pure terror.

The fifth that passed by was unmistakable.

It was his mother.

As he'd never seen her.

Nine years later

The Joke's on U was a comedy club in Seattle's university district, on Friday and Saturday nights, a haunt for college kids, but during the week an escape for aging software wizards, Green-party candidates, some white-haired hippies wearing bifocals and, on this evening, an oversize man at the beat-up piano on stage, a long-in-the-tooth police lieutenant—or former police lieutenant, he wasn't sure—plugging through a killer rendition of an Oscar Peterson arrangement.

The establishment had moved around town, mostly along 45th Avenue, occasionally changing or at least modifying its name, trying to retain its former clientele while simultaneously skating on some existing debt. It's owner, Bear Berenson, was a fiftysomething hempie, round in the middle and pallid in the face, a man with a contagious laugh, an agreeable disposition, and a bad left hip. He'd fallen off a bicycle two years earlier, riding at night, without any light, while royally stoned and busy trying to do some math in his head. "The hip has never been right since," he liked to say, counting how long it took whoever would listen to realize it was a pun. Those who missed the pun altogether were people that didn't interest Bear. The man at the piano had not only gotten the joke the first time he'd heard it—of many—but had been quick enough to finish the sentence, and therefore the joke, for him. It was just this kind of person that interested Bear—fiercely intelligent, yet humble; nimbly facile, but reserved. Able to leap small buildings—with a ladder and rope.

Lou Boldt kept the song going with his right hand while he sipped some very cold milk, using his left. It was a good happy-hour crowd, all things considered. Some pretty coeds had wandered in, no doubt expecting stand-up, but had stayed the better part of an hour, were presently on the back end of several rounds of margaritas and, without knowing it—or maybe they did—were providing eye candy for the true jazz aficionados who populated the lounge.

Boldt brought the bass line back into the improvisation, but didn't have time to wipe his mouth so he wore a Who's Got Milk mustache for as long as it took him to lean into his own shoulder and drag his lips across the white button-down oxford. If you looked closely, you could see the JCPenney fabric tag escaping the starched collar for it was half-torn off and trying to act as a small flag beneath the buzz cut, graying stubble of head hair that held the texture of a kitchen scrub brush. Boldt smiled and grimaced when he played, his face a marvel to watch as it reacted to the shapes of the sound and the story his fingers told, as if surprised himself by what he heard. Enigmatic in conversation and generally not known for talking much at all, here at the piano, Lord of the Eighty-Eight Keys, Lou Boldt shined. For ninety minutes, once a week—sometimes twice—he revealed things about himself that only his closest friends understood. Bear Berenson was one of those friends. So was Phil Shoswitz, a former lieutenant himself, then a captain, now a deputy commissioner. He wasn't a regular to these happy-hour performances, but he was no stranger, either. His presence at the moment, however, signaled something else to Boldt. Boldt had been blackballed by anyone of equal or higher rank within the department during his suspension, a leave of absence now in it's third month. Only his homicide detectives treated him humanly. The inquiry had seen to that. Internal Investigations. Unsubstantiated charges of criminal misconduct meted out in a brutally partisan moment of city politics—as far as Boldt was concerned. I.I. looked at it a little differently—they believed they had proven that Boldt had sneaked nearly ten thousand dollars in cash back into the property room in an attempt to save a former homicide detective's "past, pension and future," who'd been stupid enough to "borrow" it in the first place.

For the past forty-three minutes—but who was counting?—Boldt had been assuming that Shoswitz had been sent here to dole out his sentence, to deliver the ruling, to answer the one question that had been hanging over Boldt's head for the past eighty-seven days.

Did he, or did he not have a job?

For him it wasn't about guilt or innocence, because he knew the truth. It was about how far I.I. could wear that stick up their ass and still sit down at the table. It was about ignoring fact for fiction, the exact way so many young detectives chose to do when first on the job—on Boldt's homicide squad. People like Barbara "Bobbie" Gaynes, who was also in the crowd, but back in a dark corner staying away from Shoswitz as if the man were an AIDS carrier. The two had gotten along once—Gaynes and Shoswitz—back when Boldt had promoted her into the ranks of homicide detective, breaking a glass ceiling that still had shards on the floor.

You learned to tiptoe on the job. Gaynes was as good, or maybe better, at it than most. Than most of the most. A clear thinker and possessing single-minded determination, she fit the qualifications that Boldt sought for any and all of his teams. His staff. His bloodhounds. Her being here didn't surprise him: she loved jazz piano, or claimed to. But she kept her eyes on Shoswitz the same way that Boldt tried not to. She knew. He knew.

But what did Shoswitz know? And when the hell was he just going to march up to the slightly raised platform and "Deliver us from evil," as Boldt thought of it.

It was either a pardon or a pattern. Boldt was resolved to it being either. But the waiting. God...the ninety-minute set had never—not ever—dragged on for this long.

This was pain.

The call that came into the Seattle Police Department's Broadway substation set off a controlled series of events that echoed through the halls of the sound-dampened Public Safety building, bouncing from one department to another over a series of three days that would later be put onto the official books as a period lasting precisely forty-nine hours. It wasn't often the clocks were adjusted inside SPD, and it would take weeks for the adjustment to be made, but by then "the damage had been done," as Lou Boldt put it to the press. Boldt, who had nothing to do with making three days look like two, could only reflect on what might have been had his department been informed of the missing person some twenty hours earlier. Perhaps nothing, he mused. But then again, maybe several lives would have been saved.

"What are you doing here at this hour?" the woman asked from the open doorway to his lieutenant's office, one of two such offices in Crimes Against Persons. It was day three since the call had come in—the exact hour that the report had first appeared on Boldt's desk. "I thought you were playing happy hour."

"Was. Yes."

"But you headed back downtown."

"I did."

Daphne Matthews had a radiance about her. His compass pointed to her true north; always had, always would. He'd sensed her before she'd spoken, the way a bird knows to signal dawn before the night sky lightens a single lumen. Some of this he could put off to her unusual, though plain, beauty—a combination of girl-next-door and smoking hot babe that she could ignite with a look or a stance or a new texture to her sultry voice. But only some. Most of the attraction came at a level that neither of them understood well enough to voice, something subcutaneous, like an agreeable infection.

"Is it going to be twenty questions?" she asked.

"The lieu was there," he said, referring to Shoswitz by his former rank; Boldt had never fully adjusted to his own role of lieutenant, nor to Shoswitz having moved upstairs.

"I'm sensing anxiety. Hostility. You're closed off from me."

"Once a psychologist…" he said.

"Too close to home?"

"Don't leave."

She had turned to go.

"Please," he added.

"You sure?"

"It's not directed at you. None of it is meant for you."

"For Phil?"

"I'm to take Reamer's place," he told her.

"Reamer," she said. Her eyes rolled as she scanned her mental Rolodex. "Your Reamer?" She had a look like she'd been punched.

He felt that same thing in his belly.

"My Reamer."

"Kansas City?" she asked.

"St. Louis," he answered. "Which leaves his desk open beginning next week."

"Reamer's a sergeant," she said.

"Now you're catching on."

"No way," she said more boldly, now stepping inside.

"I'm told it's never happened at my pay scale," he said. "I think that was intended to make me feel better, but it didn't work."

"You're moving *back* to the sergeant's desk?"

"If I want to stay on, I am. I could have taken my twenty nearly a decade ago. We both know that. *They* know that. They obviously want me to take it now."

"And you?"

"I don't golf. I have two kids in elementary school who will go to college someday. If I sit around at home, I'll eat my service revolver. So what do you think?"

"Jesus, Lou."

"Yeah."

"Are you seriously going to take it? You could get a rep to—"

"No. This is their ruling. No more hearings. No more of this."

"But they're false charges. We all know that. There's no way they ruled *against* you in this."

"They just did. Of course they'll say they ruled in my favor. Phil…he can't say what he's thinking, but he all but did. They want me out. While respecting the record, they don't want the baggage."

"It's because so much of the force looks up to you. Hell, you're a living legend. That must scare the pee out of them."

"You know I hate that. Why do you do that? You, of all people?"

"You are what you are. You can swim in de Nile, or you can make for shore and climb out. But don't lay it on me. I don't mean 'legend' in the sense of superhero. I mean, the rank and file looks up to you in a way few, if any around here—I would say none—are looked up to. That's your burden, and that's a threat to everyone above you. Everyone but Phil because he gets it."

"I'm not saying I'm buying that."

"I'm not selling," she said. "And as to that, you've *never* bought in to it, but that's because you can be as blind, deaf and stubborn as a mule at times. Brilliant at others. Right now you're sitting on the pity pot, and it's your pot to sit on, but dammit, Lou, when people around here fear you, you're doing something right. Carpe diem."

"I was never comfortable looking out the window."

"You invented ways to get yourself onto investigations. The brass knows that about you. They're doing you a favor. Long-term, this is a favor. You just can't see it yet."

"Nearly a thirty percent pay cut."

"That hurts. That's supposed to keep you from accepting it."

"Shorter vacation. Back to a pool car."

"Ditto and ditto." She stepped even closer to him. It felt dangerous and warmer at the same time. "Did Phil give any opinion? Did he steer you one way or the other?"

"He said he wished they'd let him take my desk. That the only real police work is on the streets. Always has been. Says it's more like a corporation upstairs every day."

"That's a nice compliment, don't you think?"

"LaMoia and I the same rank," he said. A loaded statement because she'd been living with LaMoia for nearly a year now. The world's oddest couple, and yet they were still together. A rocky year, he thought, looking on from a distance. They'd struggled with Social Services to maintain guardianship of a young girl. There was no way it was going to happen. They weren't married. They weren't in the system for adoption. But LaMoia knew enough judges and had enough friends to keep pushing back the decision a week here, a month there. It was all thumbs and toes in the dike at this point. They were about go get washed downstream and he had a feeling the whole thing would go if the child led the way.

"He won't treat it that way. You know that. You walk on water for him."

"Anything but."

"It'll be your squad. Both teams. I pity the lieu who comes in above you."

"You make it sound as if my decision's been made."

"Hasn't it?"

There were times, like right now, that he wanted to take her by the hips and pull her close to him. He wanted to experience her. Not so much sexual as just a physical contact to bridge all the words that flowed between them. Liz, his wife, would never understand. LaMoia would never understand. But he felt they would—he and Daphne. They would get it. They wouldn't abuse it, or misuse it or push it. But it wasn't to be. Not today. He'd learned to contain it, like locking up the neighborhood dog. He muzzled its bark. He tried not to feed it, hoping it would just roll over and die. But it never did.

Not ever.

"Yeah," he said. "I suppose it has."

"Can I help you move your things across the room?"

"I'd like that," he said.

"Do you need to call Liz?"

"Do you need to call John?"

They were maybe a foot apart. Her chest rose and fell more quickly than only a minute earlier. There was mirth in her eyes—he could swear there was—and invitation on her lips, and God, he didn't dare look below her waist. He'd been there once, a long, long time ago, but he remembered it like they were still tasting the other's skin. How could time stand still like that, while the world rushed by?

The phone at the sergeant's desk rang.

His desk.

It rang and rang, and Lou Boldt marched toward it with both reluctance and hunger, the same way he would have marched toward her—just this once—if she had dared to ask.

"Get used to it," Boldt said. He was standing outside an office high-rise at the northern end of Third Avenue where no local had ever foreseen a high-rise taking root. He addressed John LaMoia, who wore his trademark deer-skin jacket, so soft and supple it looked like a chamois, and the pressed jeans above the exotic cowboy boots. He couldn't see Daphne pressing the jeans as other girlfriends had done for him over the years; it meant he had to send them out, had to actually *pay* to have them that way, and the thought of that amused Boldt to no end.

"I'm good," LaMoia said. "Welcome back, Sarge."

Technically, the graveyard was Boldt's shift—another disincentive Shoswitz had thrown at him. LaMoia would be the day sergeant for CAP for the next month. But apparently Daphne had said something, and a phone call had followed, and just as Boldt had been about to tap one of his team to join him, LaMoia had volunteered "for old time's sake."

"So?" LaMoia said.

"Call's been on the books over two days," Boldt said. "How that happened has to be looked into, but the fact is, a woman's gone missing and we're now officially past the first forty-eight—"

"So we're screwed."

"We're challenged," Boldt said.

"And we're here because this is where she was last seen?"

"We don't know if she was seen. We're here to check the surveillance cameras because work was all the boyfriend gave me."

"You brought him in?"

"Phone call." Boldt answered LaMoia's questioning look. "I wanted to expedite things. The extra day and all."

"All that time behind a desk," LaMoia said, "can't help a person's game."

"One phone call," Boldt said. "It saved us something like two, three hours."

"I'm not arguing," LaMoia said. But he clearly disapproved of Boldt's cutting a corner, and Boldt marveled how quickly his world had turned upside down: LaMoia—the rogue of all time—questioning *his* practices!

"I'd like to find her alive."

"Would the boyfriend?" LaMoia asked, knowing that statistics put the crime squarely on the man.

"Who knows? He sounded genuine enough, but maybe he's taking Internet acting classes."

Boldt called into the high-rise over his mobile and they were approached moments later by a uniformed guard. As the man worked to open the doors, LaMoia spoke.

"How can we gain access to security tape at this hour?"

"Frankie Malone's the top guy."

"No way."

"I called him at home. He gave us the keys to the store."

"When it works, it works," LaMoia said.

They were ushered in and taken to the security department and shown an hour of tapes. They had the missing woman arriving two days earlier. Had her going out to lunch with friends. Back in the hallways and elevators upon her return. Couldn't find her leaving the building. Boldt asked the tapes be set aside and that half-inch copies be sent over to Public Safety by noon the same day.

Boldt and LaMoia walked the hallways. Rode the elevator. Repeated what they'd seen.

"I doubt it was here," Boldt said.

"I'm with you."

"But then how'd she disappear?"

"That's quite a crush at the end of the day."

"True enough."

"We might have missed her."

"You think?"

"No."

"Me, neither."

"So it was here?" LaMoia ventured.

"Don't see how. But, yeah, maybe."

"Locked in a closet somewhere? Down in parking in a trunk?"

"Dogs?" Boldt asked.

"Expensive."

"We're past the forty-eight," Boldt said. "We've cut the probability of finding her alive by—"

"Fi'ty, sixty percent. I know the stats, Sarge."

"If we did miss her in the crowd, then it was between here and home."

"And the boyfriend gets a much closer look either way," LaMoia said. "Did you search for similars?"

"With the number of missing persons reports we get? I didn't have all night."

"We do now," LaMoia said.

"Don't you have to get home to the baby?"

"Let's not go there, okay?"

The men were outside the building now, the background whine of rubber on I-5. A jet just behind the Space Needle, on final approach to SEATAC. A motorboat was cutting across Lake Union. Some rowdy voices echoed from a half block away. The city stayed up later and later. It was in its adolescence. Boldt felt as if he'd known it from birth.

"Two-thirds…hell, more like ninety-five percent, are

going to be underage, or just overage girls," LaMoia said. "We toss them, the database is manageable."

"You know me and computers."

"I got it, Sarge," LaMoia said. "We can crunch this data in minutes. Trust me."

He would never fully trust LaMoia again. With Daphne he'd made his peace, but LaMoia's going after her would never sit right. He let it pass. For now.

An hour later they were sitting alongside one another, staring at a flat-screen display. It was nearing midnight.

"Should we run it again?" Boldt asked.

"That's the third time, Sarge. It ain't lying to us."

"How could this have slipped through? They put me on leave and no one mans the shop?"

"It was DeFalgo. You know how he is. He's waiting out his twenty-two. It's all done with mirrors with him anyway. Always has been."

"Buddy DeFalgo couldn't figure out a scratch-and-win lotto card," Boldt said. "What are they doing putting him in my chair?"

"It's more like a corporation upstairs," LaMoia said. "That's what I hear."

Boldt wanted to smack him. Had Daphne told him that as she'd gotten home?

On the screen was a woman's face. Attractive. Early to middle thirties. A driver's-license photo, but one that Boldt assumed would be on every morning news show in town by 6:00 a.m.

It was on.

They weren't trying to find a missing woman.

They were trying to find two.

The facts of the reports were far too similar to put it off to chance: last seen at work. Never made it home.

"Maybe not the boyfriend," Boldt whispered, his throat dry, his chest painful.

"Yeah, " LaMoia said. "I was just thinking the same thing."

Rastus Malster applied the finishing touches. This was no dab-on-some-blush exercise. The fact that he had to accomplish it inside a restroom stall only added to the thrill. He heard the unique, whistling stream of a female peeing from the adjacent stall and looked low to see a wide, black leather toe-end of a shoe pointing toward him to where he swore if he'd bent over he could have seen his face in its polish. But he kept his eyes, if not his mind, on the work before him—the small mirror hanging from a wire thrown over the coat hook on the back of the door. Every line was carefully applied. If he didn't like his work, he used a moist towelette to clear the slate, and tried again. A great deal of admiration went into his work; he took time to study and appreciate his expertise. Transformation took time; Rome wasn't built in a day. The soiled, white leather work shoes helped him—in case Miss Hissy Thighs next door was looking at his footwear the way he was looking at hers. But no: she was in and done, up and gone before the automatic flusher had a chance to catch up with her. Besides, even if she had glanced his way, he'd Naired both legs the night before to baby-bottom-smooth; he might look a little thick at the ankle, but not everyone fit into a size two.

The trick now was to time his exit well. He'd entered when there was no one in here; he hoped to leave the same. Long on patience—for he would never have taken on any of this without his mother's patience—he found himself in no hurry. He waited for the last click of a heel, the last spray of a toilet flushing or the electronic peal of the automatic paper dispenser. Then he gave it an extra thirty seconds. *Twenty-eight…twenty-nine…*

And, having collected his small mirror and his bag of goodies, he swung open the stall door to behold true artistry at work.

He slipped out the printout of the *Intelligencer*'s Web page from his pocket, took one last look at it, memorizing both the face and the name, and crumpled it up. He disposed of it immediately in front of him. She had a royal, almost equestrian look about her—a high princess, a lady-in-waiting. He looked like a corn-fed Midwesterner with a graying buzz cut.

If they wanted to make comments about him to the press, then they deserved the opportunity to meet him. They'd earned it.

When a uniformed woman entered the restroom, Rastus startled, his heart racing.

"Hello," she said.

Reconsidering his location, he heaved a sigh of relief as

the woman slipped into a stall and immediately was heard unzipping her pants—all without waiting for any kind of reply from him.

Rastus moved along the sinks, pleased as punch she'd never given him a second glance.

The piece of paper he'd tossed into the trash uncurled slightly, like the dancers at the beginning of Swan Lake. Not enough to catch the face again. Only part of the two names:

oldt and Lieutenant D. Matthews, seen here at a DARE fund-raiser in 2006.

The first body surfaced at sunrise, bobbing up out of murky depths of Bowman's Bay like a decomposing mermaid. Phen Shiffman was who spotted her as he motored out for his morning work of checking the hatchery. He'd been enjoying a smoke and a fresh cup of strong coffee when her breasts arched out of the water, followed by the dark trim between her legs. It was like one of those synchronized swimming moves he'd seen on the Olympics—"only she was naked as a jaybird, not wearing any kind of bathing suit or undies or nothing," as he would later tell Mike Rickert, the prosecuting attorney whose desk the case landed on. Though he hadn't seen it, he supposed her head had surfaced first, led by her arms, maybe. Whatever the case, she'd continued in a graceful, back arch, like a dancer: head, shoulders, chest, groin, knees, feet, and she was under again. If he'd been drinking the night before, or he'd been smoking some rope on the way out, as he sometimes did, he might have considered saying nothing about her because once she was gone she was gone. But on the other hand, he knew this was serious—she was as dead as a salmon, bruised and fed-on some, as pale as the silver flash of a trout. This, he had to call in.

Boldt read about it on a briefing page that arrived on one's computer screen at the start of every shift. The victim's toenails had been elaborately painted in a way that suggested city life, not Skagit County. Rickert, for his part, had done his homework; he knew of the missing Seattle women. He posted the information and made a few calls suggesting SPD might want to visit the county morgue, or might want some dental records sent down—the crabs had gotten half her face. By midafternoon, Boldt and Daphne had made the ninety-minute drive north together, arriving at the county hospital. Dental records had confirmed the deceased's identity: the second of the two women who'd gone missing.

Dressed in surgical kits, and wearing paper masks over their faces, having smeared Mentholatum liberally beneath their noses—because *floaters* were the worst of the worst— they studied the rotting corpse. At one point Boldt looked over at Daphne and wondered if the stains on the mask beneath her eyes were tears of emotion or from the Mentholatum vapors getting in her eyes.

They worked with a young pathologist who seemed to know his stuff. Boldt longed for his longtime friend, Dr.

Ray, but the man had retired and would likely never stand under the lights again.

"Her spine is broken," the pathologist explained in a toneless voice. "Cracked clean in half, which might explain the dance the fisherman saw in the water when she surfaced. There are severe ligature marks, here and here. Two more on both shoulders. Her vaginal and rectal area are torn, though from the same ligature, I'm suggesting."

"She was trussed," Boldt said.

This won a sharp snap of Daphne's neck as she looked up at Boldt.

"Couldn't have said it better," the pathologist said. "Bound and trussed...and...well, maybe not."

"Please," Boldt said.

Daphne's eyes said, "Please don't."

"It's just...if I had to guess...and this is only wild speculation with only a small amount of science to support it... Nah...I shouldn't."

Boldt encouraged him yet again.

"Conjecture is all. There is at least some circumstantial evidence to suggest the binding was a flexible material. In several weight-bearing places it appears to have pinched the skin."

"Weight-bearing," Boldt repeated, for the term caught his ear.

"Yes. That's the conjecture part," the man answered. "If I had to guess I would say she was trussed facedown. The ligature was jerked or tugged severely, and was improperly arranged so that maximum stress came here—" he pointed to her shoulders "—and here." He pointed to her crotch. "It was excessive force, enough to shatter L7 and L8 and to sever the cord."

"Could she have been dropped?" Daphne asked.

"Dropped? Yes, I suppose that would account for it, but it would have had to have been from a very great height."

"The elastic cord," Boldt said. "Could it have been bungee cord?" He leaned in for a close look at the rope burns on her side.

"Indeed," the doctor said. "Are you telling me she was bungee jumping? The clothes came off during her time in the water?"

"Is it possible?" Boldt asked.

"She was naked," Daphne said with authority. "He threw her off...I don't know...a bridge?"

"Threw her?" the doctor asked, "or was it accidental? Too much alcohol, a stupid idea gone wrong."

"Was alcohol found in her system?" Boldt asked.

"Blood workup will be a day or two, minimum."

"He threw her," Daphne repeated, her voice softer. "We're going to find that the position is important to him. The angel pose. Flying like that. He's Roman Catholic, or was raised Roman Catholic. Single. Lives or lived with a single parent. He's under thirty, over eighteen. Uses mass transit, but has a driver's license. Probably cross-dresses, though not in public."

"We're going to need every hair and fiber, every X-ray, every detail of this corpse before it degrades any further."

"Threw her?" The doctor could barely get out the words. "You're sure?" This, meant for Daphne.

"He wanted the angel to fly," she said, having not taken her eyes off the dead woman for the past few minutes. "But he got it wrong, tied it wrong, from what you tell us, and he broke her back instead. Who knows how long he might have kept her alive if she'd have only flown for him?"

The doctor stepped back, as if a few feet might separate him from the truth.

"And the first one?" Boldt asked, also staring at the cadaver.

"I imagine that one went wrong, as well, or he wouldn't have failed so miserably with her. Poor her," she whispered. "If she'd only known how to fly."

The drive back began in silence. Traumatic death had a way of making anything else seem inconsequential and of no importance, even if the discussion was to be the solution of that death. A black hood pulled down over all existence. The road ran before them, people racing to pass, to maintain a position, and to both of them it seemed so insignificant, though neither spoke of it directly. Life's uglies revealed themselves at such times, man's clambering for space and position.

"Maybe you should have quit," she said.

"Then I wouldn't be in a car with you."

"Don't start."

"Way too late for that," he said.

"What is it with us?"

He grinned. Didn't mean to, but it was irrepressible.

"Do you think we'll ever—"

"No!" he said, cutting her off. "I try to not think about it."

"—catch him," she said, finishing her thought. "But thank you for sharing."

The grin was vanquished. "Oh," he said.

"And as to that other thing, I couldn't disagree more. I, too, try not to think about it, but I find I'm not very good at it."

"We'll get this guy," Boldt said.

"But the window of time…"

"Has closed. Yes. We're way behind the eight ball. No question about it. But it's you and it's me. What chance has he got?"

"You sound like John," she quipped.

"Him, too," Boldt said. "I've got a guy at the U-dub. Dr. Brian Rutledge. Oceanography. He's going to make a careful study of this and tell us—" the car rounded a bend and faced a long bridge with a dramatic drop, so Boldt slowed the vehicle "—that she was tossed off this bridge. Deception Pass. He's going to tell us what day, and at what time she went off, because it's what he does. We're going to back up and use traffic cams to spot every car that left the highway for this road at the appropriate time. We're going to box this guy in."

He pulled to a stop and the two wandered out on to the

bridge. Again, they were gripped in silence—in part because of the majesty of the view, gray water and green island shrouded in a descending mist, in part because of what had happened here. They both could visualize it: the body coming out of the trunk, already roped up. He ties a knot; he throws her over.

"Early, early, morning," Daphne said.

"Because?"

"First light. No traffic—he's got to hope for no traffic. But there's no way this guy is tossing her in the dark. He wants to see her fly. This is about satisfying some need in him. His sister jumped off the barn roof and died when he was a kid. His mother fell from a ladder, broke her back. There's a payoff here that's fundamental to the crime."

"Okay," he said.

"More than you wanted?"

"From you? Get a clue." He walked farther, into the very middle of the bridge. He squatted, examining the thick metal rail from a variety of angles.

"I doubt bungee jumping is anything new to this bridge," he said.

"No."

"So he can take his time tying it. Rigging it. Getting it just right. It's pulling her out of the trunk, that's the trick."

"A public appeal?" she said.

"That's what I'm thinking, yes. Someone saw his car. Him. Thought nothing of it. Maybe we jog a memory." He surveyed the surrounding area: rocks and water and nothing but beauty. He found it difficult to think in terms of crime. "Did he use this same bridge for the first one?"

"Yes, I believe he did," she said. "It wasn't the location, it was his rigging that failed. Probably failed a lot worse the first time."

"So we check the waters."

"Your oceanographer may be able to help you, from what you've said."

"Yes. Odds?"

"That he sent the first one off this bridge? High. You want a number?"

He spit a laugh. "No. I see your point."

"With two failures, he may now blame the bridge. If you elect to involve the press, then he'll certainly abandon the area."

"So we look for other, isolated locations with significant drops."

"Maybe with some distance parameters. He's got a woman alive in his trunk. He doesn't want to test that, to push that. It's a means to an end—the trunk. It worries him having her back there, and not just out of fear of being caught. He has more respect for the victim than we'd understand. It's the sister, the mother, the girlfriend. This isn't a hate crime. Quite the opposite—it's reverential, a form of worship for him. He wants to bless her with flight. He wants to give her a chance at resurrection."

"I can look at dead bodies all day long. But I talk to you for five minutes and I've got chills."

She laid a hand on his shoulder. "Glad to hear it, buddy."

A flight of gulls cawed overhead as they played in the wind. Boldt followed behind Daphne back to the car, watching that machine of hers drive her forward.

Could have walked all day.

With the lab work expedited, Boldt had the building blocks for a possible modus by midday the following day, a Wednesday. He was supposed to be working the graveyard, but had already used up several favors to get someone to sub for him—this, in his first week of duty as CAP sergeant. He and LaMoia, who technically was the shift sergeant, rode in LaMoia's mid-size pool car, a replacement for a series of Trans-Ams and Cameros he'd owned and driven proudly through the years.

"You gonna explain it?" LaMoia asked.

"Several strands of human hair that weren't hers. All Asian, but consisting of two different DNAs."

"Two other women."

"And one of the hairs was carrying traces of a polymer adhesive. Maybe more than one."

"A piece. A wig."

"Yes. And we've got a smudge of lipstick in the vic's hair along with traces of blood. Not her blood, but it is female and it is rich in stem cells."

"Stem cells?"

"Menstrual blood."

"On her head?" LaMoia said. "Are you just being gross,

Sarge, or is this going somewhere. Is this some stab at me and—"

"No," Boldt said, cutting him off. "We have hair evidence. We have contradictory evidence of menstrual blood in her head hair. We have two women that simply vanished from their office buildings. Is any of this clicking yet?"

"Two Asians. The polymer. A wig?"

"Well done."

"But the blood?"

"Where would such bl—"

"A bathroom. A women's room."

"And how could a woman possibly get it on her head?" LaMoia drove through three more sets of lights, dodging angry traffic. He was just pulling up in front of the office tower with the lake view as he barked out his answer. "A trash bin in a woman's restroom."

"Our boy goes in drag," Boldt said. "It has to be damn convincing. He's wearing an Asian wig—hair from several women. He's cleaning sinks, mopping floors, waiting for that moment it's just him and a woman that looks right to him—has to be a certain look."

"He thumps her," LaMoia said, "dumps her into one of those waste bins, those giant things on the rollers."

"Covers her with waste product," Boldt said. "Including, in this case, some used feminine products. She's unconscious in there and can't be seen from the outside."

"And he wheels her right out past everyone. Down to

an alley or a parking garage, someplace innocuous but convenient. And lays her out in the trunk. Changes back to a man in the car—"

"And is gone," Boldt completed.

"Jesus H.! The way your mind works."

"Fine line," Boldt said, making a point of meeting eyes with LaMoia.

"We're here," LaMoia said, "to look at security tape."

"We weren't looking for housecleaners the first time," Boldt said.

"We go back and review parking-garage tape."

"I think we'd have caught it. Has to be the alley. No cameras in the alley—at least from this building."

"You think a neighboring building?" LaMoia asked.

"Or maybe a CCTV. You check that out while I put up with these security guys."

LaMoia was twenty yards away when he called back enthusiastically. "We're close, Sarge."

Boldt held up his hand to his ear indicating he wanted LaMoia to call him.

Security guys could really drag things out.

Cynthia Storm had been working Health and Human Services for Public Safety for two years. It was a long way up from Social Services, where she'd had to deal with teenage miscreants of every variety. Since the publication of a series of teenage vampire books, and a movie, Seattle had played host to a flood of teenage runaways. A city that typically saw far more than its fair share of vagrant minors, the number had nearly doubled in the past eighteen months, and as far as anyone could tell the only common denominator was that the vampire series had been set in the Pacific Northwest. Portland had seen a large increase, as well. Cynthia was more than happy not to have that on her watch; give her the meter maids and the men in uniform any day. But she hadn't been promoted to the badges yet. She still mostly dealt with the service staff—all of whom had to be vetted to work Public Safety, and their absences had to be accounted for.

Today, she was chasing down Jasmina Vladavich, a Bosnian housecleaner who'd failed to show to work for two days, had not answered her phone and, as it turned out, had not been seen by her cousin, the woman she'd listed as her emergency contact. Jasmina had a good track record with the department, but was rumored by the cousin to be in the early stages of pregnancy. She was unmarried and dis- traught about it. Cynthia and her supervisor had decided Jasmina worthy of a house call, to make sure that the baby had not led to prenatal depression or illness.

She rang the bell. It was an apartment complex twenty minutes south of the city, near SEATAC, a neighborhood known for strip joints, drugs and borderline import/export businesses. Laundry hung from wires on half balconies at- tempting to dry in a climate that dictated otherwise. The sound of televisions competed. Jasmina didn't answer the bell—no surprise there—but Cynthia used her credentials to talk the super into having a look. The elevator had not worked for three years, she was told. She trudged up five flights, down a hall marked with graffiti and was let into 514.

"Jasmina?" she called out. The super waited at the door. "Hello?"

She heard the groan. It came faintly from the back, barely heard over an episode of *In Living Color* playing next door. "Stay there!" she told the super, who looked ready to bolt.

"Hello?" She followed the soft groans into a back bedroom where a woman was hog-tied and lying on her belly. She'd soiled herself, and her face was streaked with tears and mucus. A nylon knee sock had been used to gag her. She was wearing only underwear and a bra, and there were raw bruise marks— she'd been rocking on her legs, rolling around the room.

"Call 911!" she hollered. "We need an ambulance *right now!*"

She approached the woman cautiously. Jasmina looked a little wild around the eyes. "I'm going to help you, okay?"

Jasmina nodded.

"I'm going to remove the gag and the ropes. Jasmina? Do you hear me?"

But the woman had lapsed into unconsciousness.

Cynthia got the gag off and Jasmina sucked for air and came back awake.

"Baby…" the woman moaned.

"We'll get you the hospital! Who did this to you, Jasmina? The father of the baby?"

"No. Was my card," the woman moaned. "My card."

"It's all right. It's all right." She was talking nonsense, Cynthia realized.

"Man…took my card. My ID card." With her hand free now, she touched the plastic ID card that Cynthia had fastened to her own belt. "Public Safety card."

Cynthia didn't care about any work card. Her concerns were dehydration, malnutrition and the condition of the baby inside this woman. "We've called an ambulance," she reminded.

"Why this for stupid card?" Jasmina groaned. She shook as she began to cry.

Why indeed? Cynthia now thought as she focused more on what she was being told. She reached out, somewhat reluctantly because of the filth, and cradled the crying woman in her arms.

Why indeed?

Daphne had been briefed over the phone by an energetic Lou Boldt she had not known for the past three years. When he locked onto a case he not only possessed, but emitted a contagious energy, a force field of curiosity, optimism and bizarre self-confidence that she found utterly intoxicating and physically stimulating. She responded to his passion bodily, so privately that were her condition ever known to others it would have proved embarrassing. Her skin prickling, she stepped around the yellow Wet Floor cone and entered the women's washroom to relieve her bladder and check her makeup. She feared her chest was likely flushed, along with her face.

A cleaner was doing the sinks. She had a large brown trash canister behind her and appeared to be emptying the trash containers of used hand towels.

Bothered by an earring that hadn't sat right all day, she unhooked it from her ear.

"Okay if I…?" she asked the cleaner, motioning to the stall.

"Mmm." The woman nodded back at her.

Daphne took two steps and felt a shock of electricity so powerful she could neither scream nor move. Her mind flashed unconscious, but only for a split second.

"Shit! Shit! Shit!" she coughed out softly, the pain so intense, so immobilizing and overpowering. She wanted desperately to blink; her eyes stung. But instead her eyelids fluttered, partially open, as if the juice were still flowing through her. She gasped for air.

The woman picked her up then, and Daphne understood from the strength and the way the person cradled her, that this wasn't a woman after all. It was a man in drag.

It was the man Boldt had just described to her.

She was his captive.

He folded her into the trash can and then began stuffing newsprint and damp paper towels on top of her. The next blast from the stun stick connected with her neck. Again she passed out. When she came awake, the trash canister was moving—rolling across a hard floor. A stone floor.

Public Safety.

The guy—it had to be a guy—was taking her out of the building.

She tried to raise her voice, to say something—anything. Tried to call out but either her lungs or vocal cords were in full disconnect. Her brain told them to shout. They did nothing. Her body had disowned her.

An elevator grunted and jerked—it could only be a service elevator by how poorly it was operating.

Her heart beat so strongly in her chest she feared it might stop beating altogether. Surely no heart could take such abuse. It was as if all the adrenaline summoned by the thousands of volts of electricity had concentrated into the center of her chest and was now looking for a way out.

She moved her mouth to say the word *help* but nothing came out.

A dark purple cloud loomed at the crown of her head, a massive headache like an avalanche awaiting release. It shifted like Jell-O, an amorphous orb of unconsciousness. Now a black goo as thick as tar pitch.

It flowed down toward her ears, as well as into the vacant space behind her forehead where her sinuses should have been. But nothing was right. It was only this oozing purplish black wave of silence that descended.

Then, it owned her, and she was no more.

"Where's Matthews?" LaMoia asked Bobbie Gaynes, a detective who'd worked his squad for the past few years.

"She was supposed to pull together the squad and get the Command Center ready for us."

"No clue," answered Gaynes, returning to what she considered a stupid report. She was a terrible typist, and her own limitations frustrated her. Seeing Boldt in the office, she rolled her chair away from her terminal and leapt out of the chair, and just stopped herself short of hugging the lieutenant-turned-sergeant. "Welcome back...Sarge!"

"She said she would pull the Command Center together for me," Boldt said.

"Little girls room, I think," Gaynes said. "I saw her in the hallway heading that direction."

"Go check, would you? We need her, you, and everyone we've got in the building who's a detective. Command Center. Five minutes."

"Yes, sir."

Boldt raised his voice and made an announcement. Bodies started moving immediately.

The coach was back. The game was on. And everyone in the room knew it.

The players assembled in the Command Center briefing room. Designed like a college lecture hall, it could seat fifty, all with Internet access, all facing a lectern and PowerPoint projection screen, five 42-inch LCD HD monitors suspended from the ceiling and two large white boards. There were eleven detectives facing Boldt and LaMoia, who quickly brought the others up to speed. Most had read their daily briefings, as charged, and needed nothing more than to be caught up on the discovery of the bridge and the connection to the killer's use of disguise as a women's restroom attendant.

Teams were created to chase down specifics: other area bridges to consider; the traffic cams that might reveal a vehicle going out to Deception Pass bridge; area retail stores that sold Asian wigs; costume shops or tailors that might have provided the coveralls specific to the office buildings where he/she had preyed on his victims. They were smart cops and barely needed instruction to get started. Within minutes, the Command Center hummed with conversation. Some teams stayed. Some broke off to other parts of the building. But a machine had been started with Boldt and LaMoia sharing the driver's seat, and that machine was intent to narrow down various aspects of the case and begin to focus on suspects.

When Bobbie Gaynes stepped into the center and shrugged across the room at Boldt, Boldt felt his hackles raise. He pulled out his cell phone and speed-dialed Daphne. It went immediately to voice mail, indicating the phone was turned off.

"Why would Daffy have her phone off?" he asked LaMoia, her lover.

"She wouldn't."

"She does."

LaMoia pulled out his mobile and gave it a try. "No," he said, disconnecting. "Must have forgotten to charge it or something. Her office?" He raised his voice across to Gaynes. "Her office?"

"Not there." Gaynes looked worried. "And her car's downstairs. I checked."

LaMoia dialed another number, presumably his loft apartment where Daphne now lived with him. He disconnected, his skin a shade grayer.

"I'd like to say that there's a reason for this, but we both know her too well," he said.

"This is not like her," Boldt said.

"No."

"So?"

LaMoia stepped to a landline. "Let me check my office voice mail." He did so. No message.

Gaynes had joined them. "I'm sure she was headed to the bathroom. Earlier. When I last saw her."

Photographs of the two women victims: one deceased, one still missing, played on the center LCD TV overhead. It was here that LaMoia looked. "Oh, shit," he said.

Boldt looked up, as well.

"Hair color. Eyes. You and Daphne said—"

"She said. Not me. Yes," Boldt interrupted. "A similarity between his victims."

"You see the resemblance?"

"I do. It's unmistakable."

"But it's just not possible," LaMoia said. "Not with our level of security."

"If I may?" Gaynes asked somewhat timidly.

"Go ahead," Boldt said.

"You're suggesting that Lieutenant Matthews shares a certain look with the two prior victims?"

"We are. Yes."

"And that…well…" She stepped up to the computer that ran the various overhead displays. She called up the daily alerts that opened with one filed by Cynthia Storm of HHS.

Boldt and LaMoia spun around to read the alerts on the overhead screen.

"My eyes suck," Boldt said anxiously. "What the hell does it say?"

LaMoia's voice broke as he read aloud, summarizing. "One of our staff…a housecleaner…Jasmina Something-avich…was found tied up in her apartment. This is like, three hours ago. She'd been there, left that way for nearly…forty-eight hours. Thirty-nine hours," he corrected himself. "She said the doer…it wasn't burglary or sexual assault. He wanted…he confiscated her photo ID. Her Public Safety ID."

The three moved as a unit, a team, as they first walked and then ran from the Command Center, down the hall with such intensity that everyone moved out of their way; others jumped up from their desks and peered into the hallway to see what was going on. Gaynes knocked, but LaMoia didn't wait for an answer. He pushed through the door.

"Men inside," he announced.

A woman cursed and complained from inside a stall. A toilet flushed.

Boldt went to the janitor's closet. "It's locked! I want this unlocked!"

Gaynes hurried from the bathroom, shouting for a key.

LaMoia dropped to a knee, stood and started opening stalls. He banged on the locked stall from where the woman had cursed. "Open it! Now."

"I'm a little busy here."

"Open the fucking door!" LaMoia ordered.

The woman leaned forward and threw open the lock and covered her legs as LaMoia swung the door open.

He stared at the tile floor.

His voice rasped as he said, "Finish with your business. Stick to this panel as you stand. You go out to my right. You understand?"

"You have no right—"

"Shut up and do as I say."

The woman came off the toilet, pulled up her underwear and pants and was holding them as she nudged by LaMoia and then Boldt, who was by now looking over LaMoia's shoulder.

The toilet flushed automatically.

"It's just not possible," Boldt whispered gravely.

"You and Matthews," said her lover, "your photos were in the paper two days ago. She brought it home to show me. Her photo. He saw her photo. He knew she was looking for him. He's a sick fuck. That much we know already."

"Are you sure it's hers?"

The two men had not stopped staring at the tile floor where a wire hoop earring lay.

"I bought it for her," LaMoia said. "The six-month anniversary of her moving in. It was the last really good night we had," he said.

Boldt didn't want to hear such things.

Gaynes returned with the closet key in hand, out of breath.

"S.I.D.," Boldt said to her. *Scientific Identification Division*. "Get them up here."

"What is it?" Gaynes said desperately.

"Get them up here," Boldt repeated, his head beginning to spin.

Boldt had been through this once before, back when the fires had been hotter between them, back when he'd been younger and less experienced with the overlap of personal and professional. He had that behind him now, had that to build upon, but still felt his knees weak with terror and his mind a runaway train careening down memory and emotion toward an unknown abyss.

He couldn't think about her. That was the point. He had to make the disconnect to give her the best chance of being found alive. Regulations called for LaMoia to step aside. Boldt wouldn't force the issue, but John knew enough to keep his mouth shut and his ideas to himself. He could share them with Boldt in private, but to actively push his own agenda would only drive himself out of the wheelhouse. He was an observer now, not even that if he misstepped.

There was no time to pull the threads together. Boldt had done the best he could: he turned up the heat on the team trying to identify area bridges; he doubled the man power reviewing traffic cams and assigned two other detectives to review Public Safety surveillance video to locate the imposter housecleaner and follow him to wherever he'd gone. He worked Shoswitz to provide the department's helicopter, either to race him and a small team to possible sites, or for use as air surveillance if they got a bead on what vehicle the man was driving.

Boldt fought to remain focused, to forget about who was riding in a trunk or the back of a van, to forget about the cadaver he'd seen so recently he could still smell the room, about the victim being stripped naked and trussed and thrown off a bridge.

Not this life. Not her. Not on his watch.

The worst moment came as the Control Center lulled into a library silence, as the initial adrenaline subsided, giving way to police work—the often monotonous, repetitive process of attempting to move from wide angle to telephoto.

LaMoia spoke up for the first time in ten minutes. "It's been on the skids for months. I told you that, right?"

Boldt didn't answer.

"I don't know if it was…you know…the little one, or just a mismatch or what, but we've both known it was over for way too long. Funny how you hold on to things you know are broken. Right? Like you're going to find the glue. You're going to find out how to fix it? And we both did that. She did it, too. And the thing is, we never said a thing about it. It was all done with looks and silences and fake smiles and forced sex—"

"That's enough," Boldt said.

"I'm just saying…shit, I don't know what I'm saying."

Boldt heard him sniff.

"We've got video!" Taggart shouted from across the room. "Screen two."

Everyone in the room watched a housecleaner pushing a garage bin down the hall. It looked heavy and difficult to control. The person stopped in front of the service elevator. It took Taggart another five minutes to call up the elevator's interior in the correct time frame. But there was the house-cleaner looking calm and easy, the trash can beside her. She wheeled it off the elevator.

Another five minutes to pick up the parking garage.

"He found himself a dark enough corner," Boldt said. The video showed nothing of his transferring Daphne to the car. They couldn't be sure that a transfer had ever happened.

"Get S.I.D. down there," Boldt called out.

"Done!" Taggart answered.

The car pulled out. Taggart and his team did a phenomenal job of freezing the picture at just the right moment where the camera afforded the best clarity. It was an older model Ford Taurus. They had a partial plate: 43 2. The photo suggested a number preceded the four, but no one could be certain. Not knowing the position of the plate numbers increased the database exponentially.

The machine of the Seattle Police Department continued to roll forward. The description of the vehicle went out along with the partial. The same information was transmitted to King County Sheriff's Department and other regional law enforcement. Police cruisers across five jurisdictions were mobilized to inspect and station themselves on all area bridges. In the Control Center the deployment of personnel was kept track of on screen 4. Bridge by bridge, they accounted for those now under the observation of law enforcement.

Boldt watched all this as a disconnected observer. As, one by one, the area bridges were accounted for, a feeling welled up in him that he couldn't shake, and he'd been here too many times before to ignore such feelings.

"It's Deception Pass," Boldt said aloud, speaking to no one. Then he turned to LaMoia to press his point. "This guy isn't creative enough to reinvent the wheel. He showed us that today and we've not paid any attention. He went about this in the exact same way as he did before. The same MO. Daphne called this—she said he'd throw them at sunrise before traffic of any sort developed. She said he might change his location if we made our knowledge of the bridge public, but we never did that. We made our knowledge of the killing public, yes, but we left the bridge out."

"He's keeping her overnight?"

"Yes, he is. Either in the vehicle or at a home or apartment or trailer. Keeping her. Daphne said how this is some kind of ritual for him. The preparation. The trying to make her fly. It's reverential. That's why he didn't assault them, didn't harm them. Bottom line, John—we have *time*. The one thing we didn't have with the other two. We have that here. She has time. We can keep people on the bridges but move them to where they can't be seen so easily. We can lay some traps. He's giving us the time we need to be in position."

"But where?"

"Daniels!" Boldt called out.

"Sarge?"

"I need a name attached to that partial plate registration."

"Working on it."

"I'll take ten names. I'll take twenty. But zero isn't going to cut it."

"We've got more like seventeen hundred at the moment. We're working to narrow it down."

"Run it through Skagit," Boldt said.

"How's that?"

Calling across the room had raised some heads. Boldt was making a nuisance of himself.

"Skagit County—a Taurus with that same partial. You want to narrow it down? Narrow it down."

Some in the room laughed. Not Daniels. He sank back into his chair and picked up his telephone receiver.

"Because of the bridge? Deception Pass?" LaMoia asked.

"She said he wouldn't want to move them far. It's a long way from here—nearly two hours when the traffic's bad. That doesn't fit with what she told us."

"You're telling me she's running this thing from wherever she is?" LaMoia sounded skeptical.

"Who are you going to trust more?"

It hit LaMoia in the chest. He sat down, looking wounded.

Five minutes passed feeling like twenty. Twenty, like forty.

"James Erwin Malster," Daniels said from behind Boldt.

He placed a photocopy of a driver's license in front of the sergeant.

"Fifty-one years old. Caucasian. Male. Registered with the pipe fitting union. Member of the United Association—"

"Pipe fitters. Plumbers," Boldt said.

"Exactly. Retired in good standing nine years ago, following the death of his wife. Health complications."

"This is who the car is registered to?"

"Correct."

"But it's not correct," Boldt said. "She gave me a profile. Twenties. Thirties at the oldest. Is this the father?"

"It's his car."

"It's not him."

"A pipe fitter," LaMoia said. "So he knows how to rig things."

"It's *not* him," Boldt said.

"She could have had the profile wrong," LaMoia said. "Guy loses his wife, spends years grieving...comes apart at the seams."

"There's a son," Boldt said to Daniels. "Find the son."

"I'm not showing—"

"Find the son," Boldt repeated.

"Yes, sir."

"You have the location of residence?"

"Oak Harbor."

"Christ," LaMoia said.

"I say something wrong?" Daniels asked.

"Oak Harbor's only a few miles from Deception Pass," Boldt said. He turned to LaMoia. "She called that one right."

"She also said he'd change bridges once we publicized the death, and we publicized the death."

"Which is what got us in trouble. Is that what you're saying, John? Are you laying this onto me, because I can take it. But it isn't going to do a damn thing in terms of bringing her back."

"She said he'd switch bridges."

"She was wrong about that," Boldt said.

"Because? Which is it, Sarge? Was she right or wrong, because I don't think you can have it both ways."

Boldt had been having it both ways for years: part of his heart left behind while the rest of him loved and stayed with his family. He'd built a Great Wall between his true emotions and the Presentable Parent to where no one could see the other side, not even him most of the time. But LaMoia had loosened the lid with that last comment. *Contents may explode under pressure.*

Boldt said, "He's going to throw her off Deception Pass bridge. His angel is going to fly this time. He's screwed this up twice. If it is the pipe fitter, he's not a give-up guy."

"You're not the psychologist, she is," LaMoia said, his arms crossed, his voice hoarse.

"Father or son? Pipe fitter, or who knows what? You're all over the map, Sarge."

"I'll disregard that," Boldt said.

"LaMoia," Daniels said in a cautionary tone.

"You think she was wrong, John?" Boldt asked. "Then what if she was wrong about his doing this at sunrise. What if sunset works just as well for him?" He eyed LaMoia up and down. "You want to sit here, or you want to take a ride in the chopper?"

Daniels squirmed, caught in the crosshairs. "Sarge?" he said.

"Call a prosecuting attorney named Rickert up there. Mount Vernon. Tell him to rally the best guys his sheriff's office can muster and to have them put eyes on the residence. We want an open channel with our dispatch. Real time updates. You getting all this?"

"I got it."

"I can be up there in twenty, twenty-five minutes." Boldt looked over at LaMoia. All the bravado was gone, the luster, the very sense of who John LaMoia was. Someone, something, now inhabited his body.

"You coming?"

LaMoia looked up through fixed eyes. "I hate helicopters," he said.

"That's been…the mistake," Daphne told him. It took all of her courage, and more than a little part of what energy she could summon. He had her tied to a narrow wooden-slat table, a scratchy rope across her bare chest, her hands connected by a rope beneath the table, another rope at her knees and yet another holding her ankles apart, also connecting under the table. She was naked, her legs spread, at once both horribly embarrassing and making her feel incredibly vulnerable. He could do whatever he wanted to her; there would be no stopping him.

She was in a dreary, dimly lit room. The windows were small and high on the wall and covered in soiled, decaying curtains. The pungent oily, stale-salt smell told her water was close.

She was not blindfolded; he had no fear of her seeing his face, her being able to identify him. This increased her panic.

He hovered over her, paying her nakedness no mind, preparing to administer a pill and what smelled like cough syrup. He was intending to drug her. He would then either leave her here to sleep it off, or walk her to his car while she was numb and transport her.

He was a soft-looking man, with piggish, squinting eyes

smudged with a horrid blue eye shadow, and a pallor to his facial skin.

Her comment stopped him. She seized upon his hesitation.

"You broke her back. She…was too relaxed. The drugs…whatever it is you're about to give me…it's what killed her… what will kill me. If you…take away my strength to resist the force of the fall…you'll break my back."

He stared at her expressionless. He seemed to be thinking: *How could she read my mind like this? How could she possibly know…?*

"You want them to fly…want me to fly, don't you?" she said, gaining some strength to her voice, though not much. The lingering effect of the stun stick was a massive migraine, a dry throat and pain radiating throughout her body. On top of that she was absurdly cold, chilled to the bone, a kind of chill that might be chemical, or a response to shock, but was unlike anything she knew.

"I can't fly if you drug me. The harness…must distribute the force of the fall better. Shoulders to hips. Bigger harness… maybe."

He held up a series of nylon straps and buckles. It look liked he'd made it himself—there were nuts and bolts where a harness might have had stitching or grommets.

"You don't need…to drug me…to put that on," she said. "I won't fight. I want…to help you…be the first to fly."

She watched his eyes mist. She'd triggered something painful in him. She clawed through the purple and black orbs that threatened on the sides of her vision, that warmth flowing down from her skull, trying to overtake her.

He looked her over, head to toe, his eyes lingering where a woman always felt men looking. She thought perhaps she didn't fit the look—the look that he sought. The victim they'd seen had been slightly heavier, wider in the hips. Maybe he was considering rejecting her. Maybe she'd spoken too much. But speaking was her living. Her life…depended on it.

"To make this work," she said, "we must be a team. The two of us." She thought that more than anything he missed whatever angel he was trying to recreate, that to include him, to embrace him, to let him in was the secret to unlocking him.

"What do you know about the two of us?" He appeared bewildered and confused.

She understood she had caused this. Had her mind been clearer, she could have had more tools at her disposal, but her education took a backseat to instinct—it came down to getting him to loosen the ropes; everything depended on his loosening the ropes.

"We should…try on the harness. You think?"

"You didn't know her."

"I'd like to have."

"Shut up."

"She meant a great deal to you."

"*I said shut up!*"

He lashed out with the harness, whipping her bare skin across her middle and raising welts.

She shut up. She looked away, her arms beginning to shake from the fear. She hated herself for giving this away, for feeding him this. She must not, at all costs, give him a connection between him beating her and her fear. She fought herself, her desire to hide, to retreat. To stay silent was to ask him to strike her again; to speak was most likely the same invitation; but she could control her speech whereas he controlled her silence and this was a very big difference to her.

"You didn't mean to do that," she said. "I forgive you."

His gaze locked onto her.

"I forgive you for all of this. I can see it stems from your pain. I will fly for you. I will help you. But if you drug me, you'll break my back. You'll kill me. Now…what about the harness? Shouldn't we get the harness on?"

She had him. She fought through the goo, the descending veil of approaching unconsciousness long enough to understand she'd gotten through to him. As a psychologist, she'd learned to spot these moments. To seize upon them.

His arm moved toward the knot that tied one ankle to the other, but it was a motion filled with suspicion and distrust.

Come on! she silently pleaded.

The man untied the first knot.

Five khaki-clad sheriff deputies stormed the Malster residence with a precision Boldt had not expected. He and LaMoia, wearing flak jackets, followed closely behind.

"Dead body," Boldt said, knowing that smell.

The deputies quickly swarmed through the rooms, shouting, "Clear!" within seconds of one another.

"Got something!" a voice called out.

LaMoia and Boldt slipped down a narrow hallway to one of the home's two bedrooms. It was a small room, crowded with a double bed and a low dresser. Atop the dresser were several photographs of a younger woman wearing clothes and a haircut from a decade earlier.

"Burrito," LaMoia said.

A human burrito. A wrap of thick plastic tarp secured with a half roll or more of duct tape. Whoever had done the job had tried to seal the body inside, but the putrid smell overcame the room.

"Weeks," Boldt said, his gloved hand pressing the plastic closer to where the face should have been. The corpse was in a high degree of decay, squirming larvae smeared the plastic from inside.

"Oh…crap," LaMoia said. "This guy is sick."

"This guy is trying to hold on to the one parent he had left," Boldt said. "Daphne said the doer would be living with a single parent."

"So where is she?"

"He's not living here," Boldt said, back in the hall now, looking around. The place had been cleaned up. The kitchen was immaculate but a wire strainer had left a rust ring in the sink, suggesting the passage of a good deal of time. "This is his mausoleum." He indicated the small living room where two of the deputies stood awaiting instruction.

There were no fewer than twenty framed photographs of the same woman spread around the room.

"We gotta find him," LaMoia insisted, stating the obvious. "How're we going to do that, Sarge?" He sounded on the edge of tears.

"We're good," Boldt said. "Basement?" he called to the deputies.

"Clear," a deputy answered.

Boldt stepped into the living room, studying the various photographs more closely. Answers weren't handed you; you had to extract them.

"It's here somewhere," he told LaMoia. "Start looking."

LaMoia joined him. They worked the house: drawers, closets, cabinets.

Boldt made a phone call and announced himself to his Skagit Sheriff's Office counterpart with whom he'd been dealing for the past hour and a half. "We need to check tax records for other properties, a trailer or mobile home. A boat? Someplace he could have taken her... Yes. Okay. As soon as possible."

He called out for LaMoia to bring him the photos from the bedroom. Even with the front and back doors open it reeked inside the small house, but Boldt wasn't going anywhere.

Together the two lined up and rearranged the nearly three dozen framed photographs. Then they reshuffled them several times.

"These five," Boldt said, rearranging them yet again. All

were taken in bright sunlight. In three of the five, water could be seen behind the woman's head. One was clearly taken on a boat, but not a pleasure craft.

LaMoia turned to say something but Boldt's phone rang. It was his contact at the Sheriff's Office.

"We struck out on the tax records, at least for this guy, but we did pick up tax records for a commercial trawler, registered to Norman Malster. It's in arrears, but until about a year ago it had been paid up regularly for nearly twenty years."

"A brother?"

"Not a common name," the sheriff's deputy said.

"Do we know where—?"

"I got my guys making some calls. Everyone knows everyone here. It shouldn't be—"

"Orange metal," Boldt said, pulling one of the photos closer. "One piece is curved down, the other straight."

"That's not Oak Harbor. Hang on a second…" The deputy went off the line. When he returned he said, "La Conner. That's the bridge in La Conner."

Boldt and LaMoia were out the door to the shouts of deputies. Across the street to a vacant lot where the helicopter waited.

"Have you there in three minutes!" shouted the pilot.

The door was slid shut, the helicopter already lifting into a graying sky.

Daphne contained her impatience. With the first knot untied, both ankles were free. But her upper legs remained bound, and her captor, perhaps sensing her intentions, pulled the harness up her calves, restricting her movement before loosening the rope that bound her legs.

She needed a split second. Her legs were painful and weary from the stun stick. But she couldn't allow him to slip the harness past her knees where it would immobilize her once again—clearly his plan.

"It was your mother, wasn't it?" she said.

Her captor froze, his stunned expression exactly what she'd hoped for.

She pulled her knees toward her chest, leaned to the right and kicked out like she was on a rowing machine. Her captor flew back and into the wall.

She rocked and fell off the table, turning sideways, her hands and arms still bound, her left shoulder twisting toward dislocation. She kicked him again. And again.

The third blow did damage: his head struck the wall.

Metal, she knew from the sound of it. *A boat!*

The loop of rope binding her wrists slipped off the head end of the table. Her wrists were connected by three feet of loose rope. She pulled the rope to her mouth and sank her teeth into the knot.

Her captor leaned forward.

Daphne kicked him again, this time in the groin, and he buckled forward.

But his hand came up holding a fish knife, and he lashed out at her, catching her forearm.

"Your mother is dead!" she shouted, assuming that to be

the case and knowing this was the message that would unnerve him.

She whipped the rope in front of her, catching him in the side of the face. He slashed with the knife, catching her knee.

She screamed and kicked out, and in her effort to push him away the rope caught around his head and she had him by the neck now, his back to her, her knee on his spine and she pulled back with all her strength.

Something came at her from the side—a gas canister. It caught her in the temple and she went down hard. She rolled beneath the table and the rope, still caught around his neck pulled him with her. She couldn't get away from him now—they were tied by the rope around his neck.

He punched the knife toward her. She dodged it and, in the process, looped another length of rope around his neck.

He swung the knife upward. The rope cut.

Her hands were free.

She scurried under the table and rose to her feet while he unwrapped the rope and gasped for breath. He turned to face her.

"My angel," he said.

"Not going to happen," Daphne said.

She reached out for anything—the nearest thing she could grab.

She blasted an air horn that was so loud in the enclosed space they both went deaf.

Then she saw it: the stun stick. He had it in his hand as

he came around the table toward her. He'd made the right choice, driving her toward the bow and away from the only steps she saw.

She fired off the air horn again: three short, three long, three short. *SOS.*

"She's dead," Daphne repeated, hoping to incite his rage, to drive him to emotion and toward making mistakes as a result.

"Did she jump to her death?" she said, guessing. "Did she leave you unfairly?"

"You don't deserve to be like her," he said, brandishing the stun stick as he moved ever closer. "What are we going to do with you?"

An explosion behind him, turned him around. It was not an explosion after all, but the door to the cabin disintegrating behind LaMoia's efforts to kick it in. LaMoia took one step and fell into the cabin, and her captor lunged forward and hit him with the stun stick. LaMoia's body spasmed and then fell limp—unconcious.

But a stun stick took time to recycle its charge. Daphne rushed him and struck the back of his head with the air horn canister.

Boldt slid down the stairs, landing on LaMoia, knocked the stun stick from the captor's hand, took the man under the arms and threw him—threw him like he was a matter of a few pounds—across the narrow hold and into the metal hull. He followed around and pulled the man to him and struck the man in the face, blow after blow.

"Lou!" she shouted, the man's blood coming off Boldt's knotted fist. Again she shouted his name.

Boldt stopped and looked back at her, still holding the captor by his shirt.

He averted his eyes.

"You'll kill him," she said, her voice nothing but a faint whisper. She pulled a mackinaw around her. She staggered back and sat down.

"SOS," he said. "That was a nice touch."

"His mother," she mumbled.

Boldt let the man go. He hit the floor with a thud. Boldt came around toward her, but she recoiled and he raised his hands.

"We'll get you help," he said.

She nodded, a look of defiance in her eyes, her right hand still gripping the air horn.

Boldt sat down on a folding patio chair next to her, a small drink table between them. Daphne wore extra makeup to cover a bruise on her face, a long sleeve T-shirt and blue jeans. The little girl for whom Daphne served as guardian played inside a childproofed area of the balcony. Boldt couldn't see LaMoia setting up something like this; it had probably been Daphne.

"Are you coming back?" he asked, within seconds of sitting down.

"Two weeks paid leave," she said. "More if I ask. I'm not an idiot."

She'd asked him over. He hadn't been to LaMoia's loft since Daphne had moved in. He wasn't sure why that was, but he wasn't sure he wanted to figure it out, either.

She made him tea, with no offer of coffee. Milk and sugar. She drank chai, the cloves and cinnamon heavy in the air.

"But that's a yes," he said.

"It is," she confirmed. "Are you kidding me? You think I'd quit?"

"Not likely," he said.

"Thank you."

"But no one would blame you—"

"Stuff it," she said. "Don't say another word."

"You invited me," he reminded.

"Not to discuss the case. His mother was on that Pacific West flight ten years ago. He was out there on the Sound when the bodies started to fall. I don't pretend to know… There's no fixing everyone. There's no blame. The human mind…well, it's why I want to get back to work."

"We come from such different places," he said. "I blame them all the time. I have no means, no way to fix any of them. I just want them put away. I suppose I'm the dog catcher and you're the person, the volunteer at the shelter. Something like that."

"Are you getting enough sleep?"

"Maybe not." He watched the girl playing. Then he realized how relaxed Daphne was with the child. He'd pictured her the stressed and worrying type—he should have known. She couldn't have been more at ease. "This suits you."

"It does. Though it may not last. We've pretty much exhausted all the various channels. If we get to keep her it will be a miracle."

"Miracles happen," Boldt said. "Liz tells me that all the time."

"How is she?"

He didn't feel right talking about his wife, his family with this woman. He thought he understood why, but marveled that that kind of discussion still made him feel restless.

Daphne said, "We're going to give it another chance. John and me."

Here then, was the reason she'd called. He wondered why she'd made such a deal out of it. Then he didn't wonder at all.

"Not a quitter," he said.

"I wanted to tell you. Like this. Here. You and me. Don't ask me why."

But he wanted to ask her why. "Okay," he said.

"Is this awkward?"

"With you?"

"Okay. Thanks for that."

"You don't owe me this," he said.

"Sure I do."

"Liz is good," he said. "The kids are great. Seriously."

She smiled over at a building. Smiled for herself. Nodded. Gripped the arms of the folding chair a little tightly.

"Listen," he said. "Listen closely because I don't know if I can get this out right even once."

She nodded, biting her lips so that they folded into her mouth.

"Whatever this is, it has never gone away… I'm talking for me. Okay? Just for me. It runs like one of those tantric chords they talk about, this hum that operates out of the spectrum of human hearing—"

"Always the musician. I love that about you—your music."

"What I'm talking about, it's not music, exactly. It pulsates. Quavers. But it never stops. Never ceases. It's just there. Now, then, just there." He swallowed dryly. "For a long time I let it, let you, haunt me. Own me. Then I realized it was more a tone than a handcuff. So I harmonize with it. I vamp off it. I've learned…to *love* it—" she went tight with that word "—without actually ever hearing it. It's just…there. Like air. Water. Elemental. I don't allow it to get in my way, to stop my life. I just let it hum down there, wherever it is. Hum and resonate and sing to me."

She squinted her eyes tightly. He felt he should leave without another word.

"Are you okay?" he finally asked.

"Trying to lock that in. To memorize it. Store it, so that I can recall it whenever I want. Whenever I need, which is more often than it should be."

"I ramble when I'm nervous."

"But you're never nervous," she said, opening her eyes again. "I wish you'd be nervous more often."

"I'm glad for you and John," he said.

"Shut up, Lou. Shut up and let me hear it, too."

They sat there in silence for another fifteen minutes. The girl made squeaks, asked her mommy for some juice. Daphne got up to fetch it, and Boldt stood with her.

He made for the door. Turned back. She had the box of juice out of the refrigerator. Was punching a straw through the top.

She wore a smile of satisfaction as she headed back to the balcony.

Boldt turned the handle, and let himself out.

Humming as he went.

AUTHOR BIOGRAPHIES

Kathleen Antrim is a columnist for the *San Francisco Examiner* newspaper, author of the political thriller *Capital Offense*, a correspondent for *NewsMax* magazine and a political commentator appearing on radio and television in the US. She has won numerous awards for her writing, including the prestigious Rupert Hughes Award. Her short story "Torn" was included in *Pronto! Writings from Rome*, an anthology of work by such authors as Dorothy Allison, John Saul, Elizabeth Engstrom and Terry Brooks. She divides her time between working in California and on Capitol Hill in Washington, D.C. Her website is www.kathleenantrim.com.

Gary Braver is the bestselling author of seven critically acclaimed thrillers including *Elixir, Gray Matter* and *Flashback*, which *Publishers Weekly* called "an exceptional medical thriller." An award-winning professor of English at Northeastern University, he has taught fiction-writing workshops across the United States and Europe for over twenty years and authored five popular non-fiction books on writing. His seventh novel, *Skin Deep*, a medical thriller centred on cosmetic surgery, was published in the US in July 2008 to rave reviews. He lives with his family in Arlington, MA. Visit his website at www.garybraver.com.

Formerly a private investigator in Chicago and New Orleans, **Sean Chercover** has written for film, television and print. He's held a motley assortment of other jobs over the years, including video editor, scuba diver, nightclub magician, encyclopaedia salesman, waiter, car-jockey and truck driver. His debut *Big City, Bad Blood* was one of the most acclaimed novels of the year, appearing on numerous top-ten lists. Sean, his wife and their son live with a clever dog and an unusual cat. They reside in Chicago and Toronto and several undisclosed locations. You can learn more at www.chercover.com.

Blake Crouch is the author of *Desert Places* and *Locked Doors*. He currently lives in Durango, Colorado. Blake has additional short fiction forthcoming in 2009 from *Ellery Queen Mystery Magazine* and *Uncaged*, an anthology of crime fiction from Bleak House Books. His next novel, *Abandon*, which takes place in a ghost town high in the mountains of Colorado, will be published by St. Martin's Press, also in 2009 in the US. For more information, please visit his website at www.blakecrouch.com.

A former journalist, folksinger and attorney, **Jeffery Deaver** has appeared on bestseller lists around the world. His books are sold in one hundred and fifty countries and translated into twenty-five languages. The author of twenty-three novels and two collections of short stories, he's been awarded the Steel Dagger and Short Story Dagger from the Crime Writers' Association, is a three-time recipient of the Ellery Queen Reader's Award for Best Short Story of the Year and is a winner of the WH Smith Thumping Good Read Award. He's been nominated for six Edgar Awards from the Mystery Writers of America, an Anthony Award and a Gumshoe Award. Deaver is presently alternating his series featuring Kathryn Dance, who will make her appearance in odd-number years, and Lincoln Rhyme, who will appear in even years. To learn more go to www.jefferydeaver.com.

Robert Ferrigno burst onto the crime scene in 1990 with *The Horse Latitudes*, which *Time Magazine* called "The most memorable fiction debut of the season." Almost two decades later, Ferrigno still makes critics gush and readers lose sleep. His breakthrough thriller *Prayers for the Assassin* began a trilogy of international bestsellers that took current events from the war on terror and twisted them into an alternative reality that was provocative, compelling and unnervingly plausible. Contemporaries such as Robert Crais, Michael Connelly and Carl Hiaasen are among his many fans. His website is www.robertferrigno.com.

Joe Hartlaub has been an entertainment attorney specialising in the areas of musical and literary intellectual property rights, a book and music reviewer and critic and most recently an author and actor. Joe will make his acting debut in the film *LA-308*, to be released in 2009. He lives with his wife, Lisa, and four children in central Ohio.

Award-winning journalist and former columnist for *The Times*, **David Hewson** is the author of more than thirteen novels. His series set in Rome featuring detective Nic Costa have made Hewson an international bestseller. Hewson's novels have been translated into a wide range of languages, from Italian to Japanese, and his debut work, *Semana Santa*, set in Holy Week Spain, was filmed with Mira Sorvino. *Dante's Numbers* is his thirteenth published novel. David lives close to Wye, Kent. His website is www.davidhewson.com.

Harry Hunsicker claims to have been raised by wolves in the rain forests of central Dallas, near the headwaters of Turtle Creek. He is an active member of the International Thriller Writers, the Mystery Writers of America, the Private Eye Writers of America and the Writers League of Texas. *Still River*, his debut novel featuring investigator Lee Henry Oswald, was nominated for a Shamus Award for Best First Novel. The series about the Dallas P.I. continues with *The Next Time You Die* and *Crosshairs*. For more information visit www.harryhunsicker.com.

One of the most prolific and admired writers working today, **Lisa Jackson** writes contemporary romantic suspense novels and medieval romantic suspense novels that regularly place high on the *New York Times, USA TODAY* and *Publishers Weekly* bestseller lists, with her recent novel, *Fatal Burn*, climbing to number one on the *New York Times* list. Born and raised in Oregon, Lisa calls the Northwest home and continues her love affair with the coast and the Columbia River region. Surrounded by family, including sister and writer Nancy Bush, she spends most of her time writing, babysitting dogs of various and sundry breeds and walking through the surf. Her books *Wicked Game,* written with Nancy Bush, *Malice* and *Chosen To Die* will all be published in 2009. Lisa may be reached via www.lisajackson.com.

Joan Johnston's books have appeared on the *New York Times, USA TODAY* and *Publishers Weekly* bestseller lists. The award-winning author of forty-six novels, she was formerly an attorney in Virginia and Florida. She also worked as a newspaper editor and drama critic in San Antonio, Texas, as a director of theatre in Southwest Texas and as a college professor, most recently at the University of Miami. Joan loves to travel and visited England and Scotland to do research for her Captive Hearts series and toured the legendary King Ranch in South Texas for her Bitter Creek series. Joan is a member of the Authors Guild, Novelists, Inc., Romance Writers of America and Florida Romance Writers. She divides her time between homes in Colorado and Florida. She has over ten million books in print worldwide. Her website is www.joanjohnston.com.

Recently hailed as "the greatest thriller writer alive today" by *Bookviews*, screenwriter and novelist **Jon Land** is the author of twenty-six books, fifteen of which have been US bestsellers. Jon is published in over fifty countries and six different languages, including German and Japanese. There are currently almost seven million copies of his books in print. Jon's book *The Last Prophecy* appeared on over thirty national, local and regional bestseller lists. His novel *The Seven Sins* is the first in a new series. Visit Jon at www.geocities.com/Athens/Acropolis/7015.

Lawrence Light, a finance editor at the *Wall Street Journal* and previously the Wall Street editor of *Forbes* magazine, is the author of the Karen Glick mystery series. He is a member of the Mystery Writers of America and of the Thriller Writers of America. In 1993 he published a humour book with his talented and beautiful wife, Meredith Anthony, called *101 Reasons Why We're Doomed*. He and his wife live on the Upper East Side of Manhattan, where they give great parties. He has no children, dogs or cats, although the occasional rabbit is welcome in his home. His website is www.lawrencelight.com.

Tim Maleeny is the award-winning author of *Stealing the Dragon*, a novel about San Francisco's Chinatown that began a series featuring private investigator Cape Weathers and his deadly companion, Sally. "Maleeny smoothly mixes wry humour with a serious plot without sacrificing either," according to *Publishers Weekly*. His short fiction has won the prestigious Macavity Award and appears in *Alfred Hitchcock's Mystery Magazine, Ellery Queen Mystery Magazine, Crimespree Magazine* and several anthologies, including *Death Do Us Part* and *Uncaged*. A stand-alone novel, *Jump*, was recently published in the US. Visit his website at www.timmaleeny.com.

A former teacher in the Bronx, a Peace Corps volunteer in Liberia and a criminal defence attorney for many years, **Phillip Margolin** has brought a lifetime of studying human nature to his storytelling. Perhaps that's why every one of his novels has been a *New York Times* bestseller. His books have been nominated for the Edgar Award, made into films and published in more than twenty-five languages and his short fiction has appeared in the annual anthology *The Best American Mystery Stories*. His new book *Fugitive* was recently published in the US. Visit his website at www.phillipmargolin.com.

David J. Montgomery writes about authors and books for several of the country's largest newspapers, including the *Chicago Sun-Times, Philadelphia Inquirer, Boston Globe* and *South Florida Sun-Sentinel*. In the past, he has contributed to such publications as *USA TODAY,* the *Washington Post, Kansas City Star, Milwaukee Journal-Sentinel* and *National Review Online*. He recently completed his first novel, a thriller called *Counterstrike*. He lives in the Washington, D.C. suburbs with his wife and daughter. His website is www.davidjmontgomery.com.

A regular *New York Times* bestseller, **Carla Negge**rs has written more than fifty novels including *Cut and Run, Abandon, Breakwater, Dark Sky* and *The Widow*. She has earned raves from critics and readers alike for her unique blend of fast-paced action, suspense and romance. Her stories are modern adventure tales eagerly anticipated by millions of readers around the globe. She lives with her family in Vermont, not far from picturesque Quechee Gorge. You can visit her at www.carlaneggers.com.

With more than twenty novels to his credit, including *Killer Weekend* and the Lou Boldt crime series, *New York Times* best-selling author **Ridley Pearson** has earned a reputation for stories that grip the imagination and emphasise high-tech crime and dazzling forensic detail. He has written for television and film and is the co-author with Dave Barry of the bestselling young adult series based on the adventures of Peter Pan. Pearson lives with his wife and two daughters, dividing their time between Missouri and Idaho. Visit his website at www.ridley pearson.com.

Ten years working in advertising and marketing gave **Marcus Sakey** the perfect experience to write about thieves and killers. His first novel, *The Blade Itself*, was featured on *CBS Sunday Morning* and chosen both as *New York Times* Editor's Pick and one of *Esquire* magazine's "Top 5 Reads of 2007." It also won the 2007 Strand Magazine Critics Award for best first mystery novel. Ben Affleck and Matt Damon's production company bought the film rights for Miramax. The *Chicago Tribune* called Sakey's second novel, *At the City's Edge*, "nothing short of brilliant" and it is available now. His website is www.marcussakey.com.

An icon of the Spanish literary scene, **Javier Sierra** is the best-selling author of both non-fiction and fiction concerning historical and scientific enigmas, including *The Secret Supper* and *The Lady In Blue*. His meticulous research and gripping prose have made him an international sensation. His books are read in more than twenty-five countries. Learn more about Javier at www.javiersierra.com.

Mariah Stewart is the *New York Times* bestselling author of twenty-four novels and three novellas. A former teacher and insurance company V.P., she has no regrets over having left her day job to work at home, alone, in her office overlooking a wooded hill and a horse farm. She lives amidst the rolling hills of Chester County, Pennsylvania, with her husband, the occasional daughter, two golden retrievers and a Jack Russell Terrorizer. Sometimes a puggle joins the pack to make life just a little more interesting. Visit her at www.mariahstewart.com.

R. L. Stine is one of the best selling children's authors in history. His *Goosebumps* series, along with such series as *Fear Street, The Nightmare Room* and *Mostly Ghostly* have sold nearly four hundred million books in the US alone. And they are translated into thirty-two languages. His most recent books for adults are *The Sitter* and *Eye Candy*. He lives in New York City with his wife, Jane, and King Charles spaniel, Minnie. His son, Matthew, is a sound designer and music producer. His website is www.rlstine.com.

Simon Wood is a California transplant originally from England. He's an ex-racecar driver, a licensed pilot and works part-time as a P.I. He shares his world with his American wife, Julie, and their lives are dominated by a long-haired dachshund and five cats. He's had over one hundred and fifty stories and articles published. His stories have been included in "Best of " anthologies and he's a frequent contributor to *Writer's Digest*. He's the Anthony Award-winning author of *Working Stiffs, Accidents Waiting to Happen, Paying the Piper* and *We All Fall Down*. Visit his website at www.simonwood.net.